THE HEIR

THE HEIR

PAUL ROBERSTON

BETHANY HOUSE PUBLISHERS
Minneapolis, Minnesota

The Heir
Copyright © 2007
Paul Robertson

Cover design by Paul Higdon
Cover art by Carmelo Bongiomo/Getty Images

Published by Bethany House Publishers
11400 Hampshire Avenue South
Bloomington, Minnesota 55438

Bethany House Publishers is a division of
Baker Publishing Group, Grand Rapids, Michigan.

Printed in the United States of America

ISBN-13:   978-0-7642-0324-4
ISBN-10:   0-7642-0324-X

Library of Congress Cataloging-in-Publication Data

Robertson, Paul J., 1957–
    The heir / Paul Robertson.
        p.   cm.
    ISBN-13:   978-0-7642-0324-4 (hardcover : alk. paper)
    ISBN-10:   0-7642-0324-X (hardcover : alk. paper)
    1. Inheritance and succession—Fiction. 2. Corporations—Corrupt practices—
Fiction. I. Title.
    PS3618.O3173H45   2007
    813'.6—dc22

                                                                        2006037952

✦ ACKNOWLEDGMENTS

It may be that only a man who has struggled toward a goal for many years and finally reached it can know how much I thank my wife, Lisa, for her love and faith.

Thank you to my parents, Ken and Nancy, and of course to the excellent Ellen, Greg, and Jeff.

To my friends who prayed for and encouraged me and commented on the manuscript, to Steve Laube, and to the superlative staff at Bethany, thanks to you all.

And my gratitude to Mill Mountain Coffee and Tea in Blacksburg, Virginia—what a great place to write.

. . . I say unto you,

It is easier for a camel to go through

the eye of a needle, than for a rich man to

enter into the kingdom of God. . . .

I couldn't take my eyes off the casket. It was expensive, and it glowed, resting among the candles and the heaps of flowers. It so perfectly expressed the man inside.

The dignitaries droned, and I didn't hear them. We knew it all. We knew what he had done with his life. If a man knows his purpose, then everyone else will know it, too.

They'd been told what to say and to keep it short, and they obeyed. They'd all gotten where they were by doing what they were told.

It was tribute by catalog listing: achievements, philanthropy, and Senate career. The real man was never mentioned—the companies he inherited, the rivals he crushed, the cold blood behind the politics—but everyone knew. Was anyone else listening? It's easy to eulogize a man who knew why he lived his life.

I just stared at that gleaming box and wondered why I was living mine.

We sang a hymn, and that brought me back—words obscure enough to drive any clear thoughts from a man's brain. A voice behind me sang off-key.

I watched the man's wife instead. Her name was Angela, and she was sitting between my brother, Eric, and me. I might have given her a hug, but she had always objected to my familiarity. It was nothing personal; she objected to anyone. Her brother and sister were not at the service.

She was his second wife. The other one died young of cancer, which had been worth a lot of sympathy in his first election. If he had grieved for her, I wouldn't know.

I looked back. The off-key voice behind me was another senator, a man I'd never liked. He had no speaking part. It was probably a snub.

For a moment it seemed a pity the whole thing was going by so fast. The church was flawless, and the funeral was such a good use for it. Now I even knew the true purpose of candles: to reflect off that casket. They were going to look tacky anywhere else. And there I was staring at it again.

Candles knew their purpose, but I didn't have a clue about mine.

The governor said his few words about what he had felt when he heard about the accident—the shock and sadness, the great man cut down in his prime, what a loss to the state. He shook his head at the whole sad mystery of life and death and checked his watch.

"Jason?"

I pushed past Katie and got up to the pulpit. Now the box was right in front of me, shining like a waxed floor. I needed something else to look at.

The back wall of the place had a row of statues in it, saints or angels, and one had his hand up waving at me. I never had written anything to say.

"Why am I here?" The little saint seemed friendly, so I figured I'd just talk to him. "I wish I knew." Maybe it was a her, not a him. They all wear robes.

"I think he could have told me. He knew why he was here, what he was doing. He never doubted anything he did." Somehow, I was staring at the casket again. I found my friend on the wall. "Maybe he is now."

They were all watching me, but I watched the back of the church. "The one thing I ever really knew for sure in my life was that he was there. I only saw him a few times a year and I won't miss him for that. It's more like a mountain is gone—one you'd see off in the distance."

Katie wanted me to be impressive for the assembled personages. She knew they'd be measuring and calculating, putting me in their equations. After three years of marriage, she also knew me enough to know I didn't care. I did hope she wasn't embarrassed. Her mother was sitting behind her and she'd be embarrassed enough for all of us.

I wouldn't inherit anything anyway. It was all going to his foundation. Eric and I would just get our monthly checks, as we always had.

The saint's stone hand was palm up, as if it had been holding something that had just flown away. "Anyway, he's gone and we're still here, so we'll get by without him." I finally got myself to look at the people. What a well-dressed crowd. "And everything he knew about life is gone with him, so I'll get by without that, too."

I didn't have anything else to say. I smiled at Angela, and then I nodded at Eric on her other side.

I waited at the end of the pew as Eric got out, and he patted me on the back. Katie gave me a tight smile as I sat. She was annoyed, but not mad.

Eric was tall, dark, and clueless behind the heavy wood pulpit. We look alike, especially with him wearing one of my suits. For all the money he has, he'd never figured out how to buy clothes. It was loose on him, and maybe that was why he looked so young. Or maybe it was because he *was* so young. There were no questions about life beneath that spiky black hair.

But he kept his eyes on the audience the whole time and told them what a loving father the man had been. He did a good job. I appreciated him because he did the right thing, what I should have done, and maybe he thought what he said was true.

Then the priest said whatever he had to, and it was over. When I got out into the light of day, I was so glad it had lasted no longer than it did.

The rest of the festivities went about the same. In the limo, Katie chattered and Angela sighed about how nice the service had been. Eric was watching boats in the bay.

I watched them, too. I prefer water to land because land is unmoving; the water is never still and has nothing fixed. Long Island Sound, Nantucket Sound, Block Island Sound—we were surrounded by silent waters named for the lands that confined them.

Eric turned to me. "What did you mean, you wouldn't miss him?"

"That's not what I said."

"And what were you looking at?"

"Nothing."

He turned back to the boats and I did, too. I would rather have been out there. Anyone whose ancestors lived on these coasts would feel the same pull.

Across from me, Katie was glaring, so maybe she was mad after all. She had her hair down straight, over her shoulders. Her simple, dark blue dress with the string of pearls was as perfect as the church. She had me done up just right, too, with the black suit she'd picked out a year ago for weddings and funerals. She had a tailor come every six months to keep all the suits fitted. That's why it hung so loose around Eric's shoulders.

Change the subject. "He really was a great man," I said to Angela.

She smiled, and it was genuine. The funeral had penetrated the pink plastic armor. She wasn't even fifty. Her husband had been fifteen years older, but she'd still expected a lot more years with him. They'd been married for nineteen.

Katie smiled at me, and I was out of trouble. I pushed my luck. "What do you think he would have been most proud of?"

"Most proud?" Angela always spoke so quietly, like a kitten. I'd wondered if it was an act, but it was no asset to a political wife, being so fluffy. She wasn't striking or brilliant. Why did he marry her? He must have actually loved something about her. I wouldn't even recognize her without the platinum hair and bubblegum lipstick. "He did so much. He didn't enjoy Washington, but he accomplished so much there. He was happier here at home. And he was proud of his foundation. I think that's what he was most proud of."

Not of his sons. Not of his oldest son, anyway. "I hope it will keep going," I said.

"Mr. Kern will run it. He's always done such a good job there. And now he'll have charge of all of Melvin's companies."

Melvin. The name of the deceased hovered in the air for a moment like cigarette smoke, and Nathan Kern's name was the smell of stale beer that went with it so well. I was not a patron of that saloon. I'd get my little allowance, and the big wad would go to the foundation. Melvin had made it very clear that Eric and I should have no expectations beyond simply living in the style to which we had become accustomed.

We were born to be idle rich, Eric and I, and we'd never risen above it. I wondered what our new allowance would be. Katie was feeling constrained by our thirty thousand a month.

Ahead of us, the hearse turned onto the gravel road into the cemetery. We parked beside it. As we waited for the other cars to park, I walked to the open grave. What a view he'd have, of the cliffs and the waves breaking. I was about fifty feet from the edge of the grass, and it was twenty feet straight down from there into the violent water. In a thousand years the whole place would be gone, worn down by the surf. Usually he planned better than that, but while it lasted, it would definitely be a view to die for.

There were six pallbearers. Nathan Kern and the governor took the middle on each side, for show. The casket was heavy, though, and it needed at least four strong men out of the six. So Eric and I were in front, and two gardeners from the estate were in back. We walked the short distance slowly. The sun was bright, between clouds; the better to dramatize the moment. The mourners added darker colors to the brilliant blue and greens, and the brown of the earth piled by the grave.

Five minutes after we set the box down, we were done with the words and the gardeners were lowering it into the ground. I took the shovel they handed me and dropped some ceremonial dirt down on top of the box, and then a couple more good heavy loads just for the exercise. I was just kicking into gear, and I would have filled the whole pit, but then I had to stop. I felt lightheaded and my vision blurred and my breath stuck in my throat, and that was when I knew he was gone. I dropped the shovel and walked over to the cliff, and I didn't know if the pounding I heard was the waves or my own blood filling my ears.

Then Katie was beside me. "Jason? Are you all right, dear?"

I nodded. Wherever we all end up going, he was there now—where he knew the answers to all my questions and where I couldn't ask them of him. I looked around again at the strength and ferocity of that place with its hard stone and unrelenting breakers. It was everything hard, without mercy or forgiveness. I hoped he'd enjoy it.

"Come on, let's go back." Katie sounded nervous. She knew me well enough to want me away from the cliff.

"Don't worry." The moment was over. I took her hand and we strolled back to the others.

We stood for the right number of minutes in the rolling clouds and sun, nodding to the mourners, saying the proper words. The cloud shadows were chill, a reminder that the New England summer would soon have its own abrupt end.

"I'm getting cold, dear."

I hadn't noticed Francine next to us. The last I'd seen her, she'd been talking to the senator.

"You should go home, Mother," Katie said. "I'll call tonight." We watched her skitter across the grass, like a little crab.

"I'm getting cold, too," I said.

"No, you aren't."

"Let's go home anyway."

My own car was waiting for us. I was about to open the door for Katie when Melvin's lawyer waddled over to us.

Fred Spellman was a nice man. He must have been very smart to have been Privy Counsellor, but I'd never seen him in action. To us, he had always been Uncle Fred, and I had better childhood memories of him than of Melvin.

He gave me a paternal pat on the back and kissed Katie's hand, and I might have thought he'd been crying. But he took a deep breath and pulled himself together.

"Well, well." Then he paused and took another breath and tried again. "Well. We have some things to discuss, Jason, my boy. I need to have you and Eric come see me."

"Right. The reading of the will."

Melvin's secretary, Pamela, was next to us. She really had been crying, and she still was. She hugged Katie, patted my shoulder, and walked on, all without words. I watched her.

"It won't take long," Fred was saying. "Would tomorrow morning be too soon? Or do you need time to . . . adjust? I don't want to hurry you, but there are some things that will need attention, sooner rather than later."

"That's fine. The body's still warm, but at least it's underground." I looked away from Pamela to my watch. "We could do it right now, sitting on his grave. That would be poetic. I'll call Eric."

"He's not serious," Katie said. "What time tomorrow?"

Maybe I had gone too far with him. He stared at me in a way I hadn't seen. "Nine o'clock?" he suggested. "Eric is available."

"What about Angela?" I said. "The grieving widow, you know. The scene wouldn't be complete."

"She will have her own meeting."

"Whatever." I opened the door and Katie slipped in. "May I bring my wife?"

"That will be at your discretion." He smiled, the old teddy bear smile. "I think you should. It helps to face these things together."

I shrugged. "It's really not a big deal, Fred. Not to me. We'll just putter along like always. Nathan Kern will have the headaches."

That look again. I couldn't read it, and it was not from the kindly family friend I'd always known. But then we both turned to watch Eric *vroom vroom* out of the cemetery on his Yamaha. Nice touch, or it would have been if the thought had occurred to him. I would have done the motorcycle-at-the-funeral thing to make some kind of statement. He did it because he was oblivious.

Or maybe the bike was the most presentable thing he had. None of his five cars was very solemn. The leather jacket was going to mangle the borrowed suit.

"Tomorrow morning, nine o'clock."

"I'll be there, Fred."

I got in the car, but not fast enough. Nathan Kern floated elegantly up to the window.

"Jason! I don't know what to say." Not that that had ever stopped him from saying it. "It just doesn't seem possible." If Fred was the king's chamberlain, Nathan was the archbishop.

"Apparently it was," I said. I was the court jester.

"We will need to talk. I know the foundation will be as important for you as for your father." Selfless nobility, thy name is Nathan Kern.

"I don't plan to have much part in it."

He was surprised at that, and he shouldn't have been. He knew me better. "But it was always Melvin's foremost concern." His elegant fingers were trembling. I thought the diamonds would fall out of his cuff links.

"He left his estate to it. I feel sorry for you, Mr. Kern. You have some big responsibilities now." I was getting tired of the day or I might have been a little nicer. I could feel Katie preparing the lecture. "Give me a week, and I'll be glad to come see you." By then I might even build up some curiosity about him and his world. There had to be something beneath the sanctimony.

"Yes, yes, of course," he said.

I took that as a good-bye and closed my window.

We finally got out onto the road. "You could have acted like an adult," Katie said.

"That's not my way."

We'd come up behind a truck, and there was no place to pass. The coast road went on a few more miles like this, two winding lanes. "Everyone there was looking to you to take your father's place."

"I'd rather die."

"Jason."

I punched the accelerator and passed blind on a curve. The road ahead was clear so I kept the speed up. Katie held on to her shoulder belt.

"You don't have to kill me, too."

I slowed down. "All right, I won't. But the only reason I'm not taking this car off a cliff is because I don't want to die the same way Melvin did."

"Thank you." She would have bitten through the guardrail, her jaw was clenched so tight. I needed to make a gesture.

There was a gas station after a few minutes, and I stopped beside some landscaping and pulled up two flowers.

"Here."

She relented. "I accept your apology." We got back out on the road and she held them, treating them with far more respect than they deserved. "Why did I marry you, anyway?"

"For my money," I said.

"Then I made a big mistake." She said it with a smile, though, for which I was very grateful. "I don't know if your money is worth putting up with you. If you worked with those people—Nathan Kern and all the rest of them—you could be rich."

"I am rich."

"Not as rich as you could be." The edges of the smile hardened a little. "He'd put you on the board of the foundation, and you could get control of everything your father had." She looked out the window. "It should have been yours anyway."

"Look, all I did was get born into this family," I said. "It wasn't my choice. As long as they send my check each month, nobody gets hurt. If they want anything else I'll inflict damage." I waited until she looked back at me. The two daisies in her hand were a little damaged. "You like your flowers?"

"Yes."

The road was bending through hills, away from the ocean. I stopped again, just off the edge, where the guardrail actually was bitten through. Out of the car, I stood and looked down the hillside at the scraped dirt and torn bushes and the broken tree at the bottom. They'd cleaned away the wreckage, every piece of it.

Katie got out with me.

"Why am I here?" I said. "What is the point?"

She pulled a knot of wildflowers from the ground, much nicer than the daisies, and handed it to me.

"Here."

"You don't need to apologize for anything," I said.

"I just want to give you some flowers."

I stood for a moment. Then I tossed them down the steep hill and the wind caught them and they landed just where his car had. I'd seen it there, with yellow police tape and spotlights, and the trucks pulling it up the embankment.

"He's gone, Jason," she said. "It might really be different now."

Fred was stacked behind a desk as big as he was in his thirtieth-floor corner office. I didn't know if he had any other clients. I avoided the big armchair in front of the desk and settled with Katie into a sofa at the side.

"Good morning," he said as he took out a pile of thick folders, a formal greeting for the official occasion. "These are copies for you and Eric to take. We will not be reading the whole thing today."

"I guess I just want to get it over with," I said. "Is there anything we don't already know? Tell me the bottom line."

Pause. "We will just wait for Eric." It was making me uncomfortable, the way he was staring at me. The whole office made me uncomfortable, the way it was a little dim, a little worn, just a little disorganized. But it was still just Uncle Fred.

And then Eric blew in, his helmet under his arm. He dropped it and his leather jacket on the floor next to the armchair. "Sorry. Construction." He was dressed like a peasant, in khakis and a lime polo.

"My suit better still be in three pieces," I said.

"Yeah, it's okay."

He wasn't looking good. His eyes were red and his face was pale, and the green shirt made it look worse.

"Are you okay?"

He blinked. "I guess so. I was out late." He had no extra fat on his body, but now he even seemed gaunt. The shirt was loose.

"It shows."

"I couldn't sleep."

"Come over this afternoon," I said. "We'll feed you."

"I'll call Rosita," Katie said. "She'll have lunch."

"Thanks." He yawned and then straightened up in the armchair. "All right, Uncle Fred. I'm ready."

"Yes," I said. "Go ahead."

Fred went. "The first step is just a little legal exercise to make everything official." Fred looked at me. "You are Jason Rove Boyer, the son of Melvin Howard Boyer and his first wife, Ann Rove Boyer, deceased?"

"That's what they always said. I wouldn't remember."

I hadn't meant it to be funny, but he laughed, just like a family lawyer was supposed to, relieving the tension. He should have been in movies. "You are twenty-eight years old, you have been married once, to your present wife, Katherine Sevildray Boyer, and you have no children. That's all correct?"

"Unless there's something I don't know. We only got married once, didn't we?" I said to Katie. That was supposed to be funny.

"Just once."

I would do it again, though, and she would, too. The first time she really did do it for my money. But we'd come to know each other, even in just three years. I'm not much of a companion, and she has other friends for talking and spending time. It was deeper than that, something between two complex people. I hadn't known how much I needed someone like her.

Fred chuckled again, breaking my thoughts. Sometimes I wondered what he was thinking. "I need to know if someone is going to come out of the woodwork." Just a tiny edge on his voice. "No children?"

"Not a one," I said.

"And you are Eric Melvin Boyer, also the son of Melvin Howard Boyer and Ann Rove Boyer, deceased?"

"Yes, sir. They're both deceased now." This was bothering him more than the funeral. Or else he just wasn't feeling well.

"Yes, of course." Fred shifted into deep sympathy mode. "It will be fine, Eric. Now. You are twenty-five years old, you have never been married, and you have no children. That's correct?"

"No children, no wife."

"If there was a wife, or child, that I did not know about, it would be . . . well, a difficulty." Fred paused and gave us both a few seconds to have any sudden memories. "And to the best of your knowledge, you are Melvin's only children?"

"I'm probably not the one to ask," I said.

"But to the best of your knowledge?"

"We're the progeny."

"Well, then, we'll get to the main part. Jason, Eric, your father was very wealthy, as you know. Your father had discussed with you what he planned to do with his assets?"

"He was leaving them to his foundation," Eric said. "Jason and I would get enough to live on."

"Yes, that had been his original plan."

Original? What was the man saying? Katie stirred beside me.

"Eric, you will be getting a sizable income. I suggest you get advice on investing it. You are a young man, and you will have the opportunity to build up substantial wealth if you don't waste it."

Every kid needs an Uncle Fred. And maybe Fred knew how much Eric needed advice about money.

"What is 'sizable'?" I asked.

"Fifty thousand dollars per month, from a trust created for the purpose." He'd been living on twenty. No, he'd been getting twenty, but he'd been spending about twenty-five. BMWs were so expensive these days. Fifty would come in very handy for him, and his Jaguar dealer wouldn't complain, either. If he remembered what he'd borrowed from me, he might even start paying me back. I wouldn't remind him.

"And it will increase when you get married." Fred turned to me. "Yesterday, you asked about Angela. She will also have an income." Okay, good for Angela. I was sure it would be more than fifty thousand a month. "Then there are numerous other bequests to relatives, friends, and employees, which amount to less than two million dollars. As his executor, I will take care of those." He tapped the stack of papers. "You each have a list, although it is not complete. There were some bequests your father chose to not be made public."

All of that had been his original plan. What was no longer part of the plan? It was my name that had not yet been uttered. I was already thinking it through. Four years at Yale, I must have gotten a degree. Business, yeah, that was it. I could get a job with that. Or maybe I could drive trucks.

"Jason, you were to have received a similar monthly income. That has been changed."

I decided on the trucks. Maybe Katie could ride with me.

She was frozen beside me, and I felt two red hot lasers drilling into my shoulder. Maybe I'd be riding alone.

Maybe I could freeload off Eric. I could wash his cars. We'd make sure Rosita fixed him a real nice lunch today.

I didn't have enough time to build up real confusion. Fred's mouth was still moving.

"Your father had originally planned to leave the bulk of his estate to the Boyer Foundation, and Mr. Kern and the board of directors would have been trustees. However, except for the other distributions I've mentioned, you are now the sole heir of the estate."

"No."

There was pounding in my brain and a wave of heat shooting up through my chest and head, like a ring crushing me. It was a primal reaction, before I even really understood the words. Sole heir? It was rage, absolute fury. And it showed.

"Jason?" The lasers beside me had suddenly malfunctioned. The way she said my name, she sounded as if she were about to lose power completely.

I was so angry I didn't care. How could he mess it up so completely? When he'd been leaving it to someone else instead of me, I was annoyed by the rejection. But this was total idiocy. He hadn't even told me! I would have killed him if he hadn't already been dead.

Fred decided to keep going. "The estate is primarily stock in the companies your father owned and controlled, but also includes his properties, art and valuables, and," he was faltering, seeing my anger, "some other investments."

"Why?"

Fred took a deep breath. "I'm sorry, Jason. I know this wasn't what you expected."

"I won't take it."

I'd hit Fred's button. "Just a moment." He said it angrily and with exasperation. I hadn't seen him like this. "You have no idea what you are saying."

"But I don't want it. I refuse."

"Then I'll take it," Eric said, his eyes wide. "Give it to me. What's the problem?"

"At least listen to him." Katie had rebooted.

"Just tell me why he changed it," I said.

Fred was calm again. He shook his head. "I don't know why. When he instructed me to revise his will, I asked him why, but he chose not to confide in me."

"He could at least have told me," I said.

"I think he would have. But there was no opportunity."

"When did he come up with this brilliant strategy?"

"We first discussed it several months ago. He signed the will at my house Saturday evening last week and died on his way home."

On his way home. That was past stupidity, deep into farce. I couldn't even think, only feel, and all I felt was anger. Why couldn't he have said something to me? When did we even last talk? Two months ago? Three? What did it mean? Why am I here?

It was all too much. Minutes passed and I just sat, and the others knew better than to break my silence.

At least Fred and Katie knew better. "Deal with it, man. If someone gives you fifty million dollars, you just say yes. This is not hard to figure out."

It was too plain to put into words, but I tried. "I just want something to live on and to get rid of the rest."

"You can live on whatever you want."

"I don't want to be Melvin."

That shut him up. He didn't even know what it meant.

Katie knew nothing she could say would persuade me, so as desperately as she wanted to try, she wasn't talking. The harder you push a mule, the more obstinate it gets. She left it to the expert.

"It will take time to adjust." Fred shuffled the papers. "But you will. And it will take a short time for probate and transfer of titles." He risked a small smile. "You can't get rid of anything until it's actually yours."

"What do you mean, about not wanting to be him?" Eric said. "I still don't understand."

"Everything he was. His deals, his influence, his manipulations. Sitting in his mansion, being the big man. Being the king." Was that it? "Being so sure of who he was." I turned to Fred. "No. I won't do this. If I have to sign something to refuse it, then make it quick."

"You do not understand." Soft, round Fred had again lost patience and was finally, suddenly, very hard. "And the stakes are too high for childish behavior." He paused while he got my attention. Now I was seeing the Fred who counseled ruthless men.

"Listen to me, Jason. Your father had great power in this state, and his wealth was only part of it. He had thousands of employees and held immense sway over government. He could make or break anyone he wanted. He had no rivals because he had defeated them. You know who he was."

I had his attention. "I know who he was, Fred. Everyone knew exactly who he was."

"That is the point. Now his death has left a vacuum, and that is very dangerous." He was speaking deliberately, as if I were a child. "I had thought to wait before I had this discussion with you, but I see I need to do it now. You have no choice, Jason. You must take your father's position."

"I don't want it. You know me. I'd hate it." I looked away from him. "It wouldn't work, anyway. Let someone else be king."

"That is not an option. I said that a vacuum is dangerous." He was measuring me; I could see it in his eyes. "Your rivals have already taken the first steps to fill it."

"My rivals? I said I don't want it. If they do, let them have it."

"You don't know what you are saying. There will be war."

"You mean that literally?" I shook my head. "War? People getting killed?"

"Perhaps, yes, but I'm referring to a larger conflict. Political influence and union violence will be part of it. Organized crime would take sides. There are many ways battles would be fought."

"And this was how Melvin got to the top, I suppose?"

Fred shook his head. "I will not discuss that with you. But the Boyer companies could even be forced out of business, and your own wealth eliminated. If you do not choose to fight the war, you will lose it."

"But all I have to say is 'Yes,' and I'm king, and everything's fine."

"Not that easily. You will have to fight, and it will take some time to consolidate your position. But I will be helping you, and you will have other allies, and you will have your father's wealth and his name."

"What would have happened if he hadn't changed his will? Nathan Kern wasn't going to be fighting wars."

"Perhaps that was why your father changed his will."

Every time I started to get the boat upright, he shoved another wave in and swamped it.

"Does Kern know about this?"

"I'm not sure. I will meet with him this afternoon. You might wish to speak with him yourself soon. He is leaving the country next week on business."

Leaving the country sounded like a good idea. "Does anyone else know?" I asked.

"Not yet, but they soon will. You will start getting calls. It would be better if you signaled your intentions and initiated the calls yourself."

I was getting better at recovering. The more Fred talked, the easier it was getting to turn him down. I hadn't thought through the consequences, though. "So who would I call?"

"Governor Bright and Senator Forrester. They represent the two main political factions. The governor's chief of staff, Clinton Grainger, will approach you very soon, I expect. That will be critical. As

I said, he has already made some moves. Forrester is more cautious but more dangerous.

"Next, your father controlled his corporations through three boards of directors, and those gentlemen and ladies will be awaiting your instructions. The businesses themselves are all capably run. There is no day-to-day management involved, just strategic decisions.

"I will arrange for you to be offered your father's positions on nonprofit boards, particularly the opera. Those boards have a great deal of influence."

He was talking fast, to get it all in before I had a chance to stop him. "Your father also had a large minority share of First Media, which owns the newspaper and Channel Six. Stanley Morton is the chief executive and he will be very anxious to meet you."

"I know him. I dated his daughter at Yale."

Katie squeezed my hand. What was she thinking? That it was a done deal? We were talking specifics, the course of action. Katie could relate to this. Or maybe she just wanted me to remember that she'd won her own war against Natalie Morton.

Fred was still listing names, but I held up my hand. "That's enough. I understand. I'll think about it for a while."

"Of course, of course." It was jarring, how he suddenly turned back into Uncle Fred.

"I don't think I'll change my mind."

"I know it's difficult. I know it's not what you had expected. I am sorry, Jason. I truly am. But we do not always control our own destiny."

And I'd always hated the one who controlled mine. "I was never close to him," I said. "But I thought he knew me better."

"I think he knew you quite well. Better than you know yourself."

I've never really wanted to. My question has always been Why? not Who?

"It'll be tough," Eric said. "But you can do it, Jason. You can, really."

Big brother can do anything. "So what's in it for you?"

He beamed. "Everything I'd ever want. Right?"

"And what if I refuse it all?"

Eric laughed. "I'd kill you." He looked at Fred. "Would I get the money then?"

"I would," Katie said.

3

I didn't want Eric riding his motorcycle on this planet while his mind was on another one, so we stuffed him into our car and got home for lunch. I'd told Fred I'd think about it, so I did. I was over the emotional reaction, just down to annoyance and bewilderment and being tired of it all.

Fifty million. I knew at least enough about Melvin's business to know that Eric was wrong about that. My guess was five or six times as much, maybe. It didn't make any difference, except the more it was, the less I wanted it.

I was curious—that was all. But ask any cat about curiosity.

With what we had now, we still managed to pay the mortgage each month. As we pulled up to the house of that mortgage, I wondered what Katie would do with real money. Our little French Provincial cottage with six bedrooms, two formal and three casual living rooms, a dining room that could seat twenty—plus the few informal areas that I actually liked—all on two acres, would only be practice.

We chose the sunny dining nook overlooking the gardens for our lunch. Rosita did a great job.

Eric revived fine, or even too much, until he was excited and babbling, overpowered by too many massive issues in too short a time. I finally kicked him out of the room so Katie could get a few words in.

"Go ahead," I said.

"Stop being foolish." She'd been worn raw by the tension of the morning and by the funeral yesterday, and now by her own hopes. "Stop acting this way."

"I'm not being foolish. I don't want the money."

"I do."

"Then you're being foolish," I said.

"It's right there, right in your hand. Just think!"

"I am!" I said. "Don't you understand?"

"I do understand. You're so twisted by how you hated him that you can't see anything else."

"I didn't hate him." We both knew I hated him.

"Then what do you call it?"

Why were we talking about him? "It's not hate," I said. It was being overshadowed by a mountain.

Katie backed down. "I'm sorry. It's too much to deal with."

"That's what I'm saying."

"It's just that I want it," she said. It was almost a sigh. "I want the life we'd have together."

"We wouldn't be together. I wouldn't be here. Angela didn't have Melvin, just his houses and money."

"We'd make time for each other. It just wouldn't be as much."

"And it wouldn't be me, anyway. I'd be some other person." Maybe she wouldn't mind that too much.

"You'll always wonder what it would have been like," she said.

It was true. How did she know that? I hadn't realized it yet. What a marksman she was to find that chink. "I think I know."

"You haven't had time to think."

"I told Fred I'd think, so I'll think."

"What will you say to everyone?"

"Just that it'll take a couple days. It's a lot to deal with."

And that was enough to revive her hope. She hugged me, and I knew we were still in it together.

I found Eric in my office, playing a Grand Prix game on the

Ferrari Web site. I'd have to remember to lock the door when he was in the house.

"Have you already ordered a new car," I said, "or are you going to at least take a day to pick a color?"

"Red, of course."

"What number are we up to?"

"About eighty," he said.

"Rule number 80. Don't buy anything for one month after your father dies."

He grinned. "I was just looking."

Katie and I had one full-time employee, our cook and maid, Rosita. Eric had one part-time employee, his mechanic. That person was part time and Rosita was full time because Eric did a lot more of his own repairs than Katie cooked or cleaned. We also had a landscaping company to keep our grounds nice, and he has maid service, but the real priorities were clear—cars for him, food for us.

"Fred was right. Now that you've got money, you need to act like you've got a brain."

"I know." He closed the game. "But we've got millions now."

"Pretend like you don't."

"But we do." He stared at me. "Would you really turn it down?"

"I really would."

He looked straight at me. "I have never figured you out, Jason."

"You won't, either." Eric knew me better than anyone in the world, even than Katie, but it did him no good because he had no brain. Acting like he had one would be hard work.

"I'd like to. You're all I've got."

That's why I had always felt so sorry for him. "Then grow up. You won't understand an adult until you are one."

"Give me one clue, at least."

"Money is not everything."

"What else is there?"

"I don't know," I said. "I'm hoping there's something."

"You always make it so hard." He leaned back in my chair. "I figured it out a long time ago. Just maximize pleasure and minimize pain."

"It's the minimize pain part. Melvin's cash comes with a high pain factor."

"I still don't see it."

"Maybe you will. Now get out of here. I need to make some calls."

He closed the door behind him, and I was alone. I don't like other people in my office. It's the only room in the house that Katie didn't furnish, and she could have done a better job than I did, but then it wouldn't have been what it was for me. It's mostly bookshelves filled with books I've read and walls filled with pictures I like looking at. They're prints of old sailing boats and the men on them fighting the weather and sea. I soaked in their struggles for a moment and then picked up my phone.

I only had one call to make, to Pamela, the late Melvin's never-late secretary.

"Jason, sweetie, how nice to hear your voice. I didn't get to talk to you yesterday morning. How are you doing?"

"Sort of struggling," I said. "I could use your help."

"Of course, dear. What do you need?"

She hadn't been at family gatherings like Fred had, but she was the one who'd always called to tell us when to come. She was the one we'd called to make an appointment if we had to see him. When we were young, she was the one we called when we had a problem or, once in a while, just for some advice.

"Pamela, I just spent the morning with Fred. He tells me the foundation is not getting the estate. I am."

The pause was only a microsecond. "I see." It was a different voice, disconcerting to me—first the real Fred, and now the real Pamela.

"I may want you to set up some meetings," I said. "Could you do that for me?"

"Give me the list, dear, and your schedule, when you're ready."

And that was that. The only person in my life who'd ever call me "sweetie."

That was Thursday. I decided to let the world wonder for three more days. Fred started executing that afternoon, filing papers and transferring stock ownership, and the world saw, and it did wonder. It picked up its telephone and called me.

Sometimes I answer the phone, but once was enough that day. The first time it rang was about three o'clock, and I didn't recognize the name or number. It was a woman's voice, hard and polished as a marble floor.

"I'm calling for Jason Boyer, please. Mr. Grainger of the governor's staff would like to speak with him."

Number one on Fred's list. My survival instinct took over. "I'm sorry," I said in some kind of deep British accent. "Mr. Boyer is not available. May I take a message?"

"When will he be available?"

It was apparently unacceptable to be unavailable. I had a sudden image of my third-grade teacher at the boarding school, glaring at my homework page with monumental disapproval. I couldn't do annoyance and British together, so I dropped the British.

"He hasn't decided yet. Maybe you could try again Monday."

"I will give you a number if he could call before then."

She did, and I wrote it down.

I thought about turning the phone off, but instead I told Rosita to take messages. She did for a while, and then Katie took over while Rosita fixed spaghetti.

There were three places set when I sat down to eat, so I figured Eric must still be around. He came into the dining room after we started, and flicked on the television.

"Check it out."

It was the local news, Channel Five, the one I didn't own. I don't like television when I'm eating, and I don't like news any time.

A head was talking. ". . . our special report on the family of Melvin Boyer. Freda?"

"Turn it off," I said.

"No," Eric said. "I want to see it."

Freda appeared, and I could only imagine what her salon bills must be. "Thanks, Hugh. We have an update in our coverage of the death of former senator Melvin Boyer. In a surprise development, Channel Five has learned, the anticipated transfer of the wealthy industrialist's estate to the Boyer Foundation will not occur." She articulated every syllable so carefully, it was painful to watch her speak. "Melvin Boyer died last Saturday in an automobile accident. According to interviews with Channel Five, those associated with his many business and political interests had long understood that he planned to leave his estate to his Melvin H. Boyer Charitable Foundation, bringing an end to family control of his business empire. However, according to documents filed today with the Securities and Exchange Commission, his son Jason Boyer has been given complete control . . ."

"Turn it off now," I said.

"It's you, man."

"Really? I thought maybe he was talking about somebody else. Turn it off so I can eat."

He ignored me, and so did Freda. She just kept enunciating. ". . . twenty-eight-year-old son as the state's, and one of the nation's, wealthiest men." Freda had disappeared, and another face, handsome, with straight dark hair, green eyes and perfect teeth— the same face I see every morning in the mirror—peered at us. Freda got her looks from two hours a day with an army of professionals, but there was nothing fake about this face.

It stared out of the screen, and the eyes were a mirror of that soul. I could see the driving thought behind them.

Why am I here?

"It's you! It's from our wedding!" Katie said, swamped with joy. "You're famous now, Jason."

I was out of my chair and halfway to the box to turn it off.

"And sorry, ladies, he's married," Freda joked in the same monotone. She would have smiled, but her face was too brittle. All she could do was show more teeth, and she had plenty.

I'll admit my teeth are also the product of an army of professionals, but that was so long ago even the emotional scars have healed. And nothing else is fake. I lunged for the power button.

"But his younger brother, Eric, is still unattached." I hit the button, but the damage had been done.

Eric dropped into his chair, his eyes vacant and as wide open as his mouth. "Yes." He breathed out slowly. "I'm young, I'm beautiful, I'm unattached. I'm incredibly rich! Come get me!"

This was the wrong day for him to say that. It was time to get his attention, and I wasn't in the mood for quiet, brother-to-brother conversation. I took his plate of spaghetti and pushed it hard enough into his face that he and his chair crashed back onto the floor.

I had his attention.

"What was that for?" He was pretty stunned.

"What do you think?" I said, sitting back down. Katie just watched.

He picked himself up. The sauce looked wretched on his bright yellow-green shirt. "Okay." His disposition was also no longer bright. "But you could just *say* something, you don't have to knock me over."

"You want another shirt? I can get you one upstairs."

"I'll get it." He was mad, but it was more that he was hurt. I'd underestimated how much of a little kid he really was.

"You can return it with my suit," I said. "And I'll be glad to throw that shirt away for you." I stood up to look him straight on. "I'm sorry, Eric."

"Next time, just tell me if you're mad."

"You're acting stupid, and that always makes me mad." We stared at each other. "I'm trying to keep you out of trouble."

He was cooled off, and Katie started eating again. "Don't throw my shirt away. I like it."

"It's putrid. Let Katie take you shopping sometime."

"Then I'll look like you!" That was almost worth another plate of spaghetti.

"I'd be glad to," Katie said, calming the turbulent waters. "It would be fun. We could try something different."

The prospect of some attention and nurturing appealed to him. "Okay. I could try it."

"I'll pay for it," I said. "And it'll give Katie something to do."

We took the phone off the hook, and I called the phone

company to change our number. No one had found my cell number yet.

Friday morning I went running. When I got back, Katie had gone out with friends, and I settled in my office and read. *Bleak House,* by Charles Dickens. It's about a rich man's death and what happens to his money.

I sailed that weekend. I spent Friday night on the boat in the marina, and Katie came down Saturday, and we went out into Long Island Sound. There was plenty of wind but the waves were short and choppy, and I faced into them to keep the boat from rocking. We read while the sky was clear, and talked about her friends and a little about maybe taking a trip to Europe later in the fall. She tried to stay away from anything to do with money, which limited the subjects.

I merely enjoyed the breeze and motion and hearing her voice and watching the waves. There are so many colors in the water.

When the weather shifted and clouds started piling up in the southwest, I abandoned my torpor and tacked south across the wind toward Block Island. We watched the rain from across the water.

I could have as easily gone north toward home. "Let's find somewhere to stay tonight," I said.

Everywhere, sails were scattering, fat sheep in a blue field escaping a pack of hungry squalls. The boat picked up speed, and the storm had no chance of catching us.

When it finally reached us we were ashore, behind a huge window, eating shellfish and drinking wine, with the marina churning below us. Then we went back on the water, just a little way out, for the sunset and the stars, and finally we slept in the boat rocking quietly beside the pier.

Sunday morning I cleared the harbor, heading for home, and there was no way to delay it. The breeze was directly behind us.

Katie had been breathtakingly patient, but now she finally inhaled. "Rosita said there have been twenty more calls since yesterday."

"I thought we were leaving the phone off the hook."

"I told her to start taking messages again."

The weekend had been filled with all the happiness money could buy, which was the kind I liked best. Avoiding Monday was something money couldn't buy.

"I told the phone company to change our number."

"It takes three days. You can run, Jason, but you can't hide."

"They're not after me. They're after my wallet."

"Do you know what you're going to do when we get home?"

"Yes. I'll take a shower, have lunch, and call Fred."

"What will you tell him?"

"I don't have that part figured out yet."

"Let me know when you do." Fred was inescapable, and she wasn't worried. It was another gorgeous day, and if I'd taken the boat on another tangent somewhere, she wouldn't have minded. Instead I cut a straight gash through the waves.

I knew a third of the names on Rosita's list, I knew of another third, and from the messages the last third left, I knew their type.

"I want to meet Melvin's board members," I said to Fred on the phone after lunch. "The officers, or whatever. Pick five names to give to Pamela, and she'll arrange it."

"My secretary can arrange the meeting."

I wanted to stay in control. "No, give Pamela the list. But you should be there. And I'm not committing to anything, Fred."

"I understand."

"I still plan to be rid of it." Every time I said it, it meant less. "But I want to do it responsibly." That would be a new way for me to do anything.

"Of course, Jason. But keep your mind open."

"It's so open you could drive a truck through it. It even feels like someone has. I guess I need someone to give me a list of what I own."

"That would be George Elias. And by the way, has Clinton Grainger called from the governor's office?"

"You know he has. Lots of people have, but his secretary was first."

"Yes, I called him immediately after you left on Thursday. We need to discuss your meeting with him, and soon. We should do that tomorrow morning."

"Did you hear anything I just said?"

"That you are keeping an open mind."

Dinner was a standoff with Katie. She knew that time was on her side. I was meeting with Fred and with the board members. She just wanted to hear that we were really going to Disney World.

"It won't be that hard," she said. "You can hire people to do everything for you."

We usually eat in the formal dining room. It had been annoying to me at first until I got used to sitting at the head, Katie at my left, the other ten places stretching off into the distance. We never entertained. Katie liked the room, though. Royal blue walls and rococo ornamental plaster, tile floor, Windsor chairs. It made up with elegance what it lacked in geniality. It made a person feel like a king.

"It's the being, not the doing."

Philosophy was not the ground she wanted to fight on. "I talked to Angela this afternoon," she said.

"How is she?"

"She feels very alone."

"You need friends to not be alone, and she doesn't want friends. Or she'd at least have to be willing to talk to people," I said. "Maybe you should have lunch with her."

"We are tomorrow. I suggested it. Does she get to stay in the house?"

She meant the question to sound innocent, but did she have her eye on the Big House? It was only a matter of time. "All the properties are part of the estate. But Angela has exclusive use of the main house as long as she wants, and she can use any of the other houses."

"Good. I'd hate to think she'd have to move." Angela would be a good distraction for Katie.

I excused myself and went looking for my book. I don't always read so much. I was just in greater need of escape.

But I couldn't read. After a while I was back in my office. Pamela had me all fixed up with Fred at nine o'clock, with George Elias for lunch, and with the board members at three. Clinton Grainger was open Monday night.

"How did you know that?" I asked the sweet voice on the telephone.

"I talked with his secretary," she said. "Fred suggested it. I told her you were still very busy with your own people and it would take a couple days for you to be ready for outside meetings."

I thought about telling Pamela she worked for me and not Fred, but she was just trying to be helpful.

"Okay. I'll call you after I see Fred tomorrow. Thanks, Pamela."

"Glad to help, dear."

5

Riding an elevator thirty floors normally takes a while, but on Monday morning it took forever. At the seventh floor I'd chosen the path of self-preservation and a clockwork fifty thousand a month—that had always been the plan. At the tenth, I decided on an even million a year. It was my own decision, so why not be generous? At the fourteenth, I was wavering. Where was the line? If I could accept a million a year, then I could accept two million. I could accept it all.

Where was the line? It was somewhere around the twenty-third floor, and I crossed it. It really wasn't a decision. I was only deciding to not decide yet.

Fred saw through me when I dropped, defeated, into the grand armchair throne and put my elbows on his desk and my head in my hands.

I stared down at the floor so I wouldn't have to see him smirk, and when I finally looked up, he was trying real hard not to.

"Okay," I said. "Start with Clinton Grainger."

"Yes, a very good place to start."

Wasn't that where Julie Andrews started singing in *The Sound of Music*? I was having severe concentration problems.

"Governor Bright will be your biggest challenge, and you need to deal with him decisively at the very beginning. He might be too ambitious to be controlled. He is a reckless man."

"From what I've seen on television, the governor doesn't come across as very bright."

"Grainger is the brains. The problems come when he can't control his boss."

The irony of this statement, spoken to me by Fred Spellman, was not lost on either of us.

"Did you ever have that problem?" I said.

He laughed. "I never controlled your father; he was no one's fool. I doubt you are, either."

"I feel like a fool right now." I did, too. Fred's office was power, real power. The furniture was a bit worn—not from age or even use, but from weight. Heavy decisions were made there. Important words were spoken. It was serious, the real thing. I was just a little bubble waiting to be popped. "What do I say to Clinton Grainger? I guess I should meet him tonight."

"Yes, certainly. He will be making his own judgment, whether he thinks you or the governor will likely be stronger."

"I could just tell him. It'll be obvious anyway."

"You may change your mind as the days go by. For now, be direct. Tell him you expect the same working relationship with the governor that your father had."

"Which was?" I hadn't played poker since college, and bluffing wasn't my strong suit.

"You supply him with ample contributions, positive press coverage and union organization during elections, and he keeps the legislature friendly to your business interests and ensures that you receive the major share of state contracts. He also keeps law enforcement agencies from causing you inconvenience."

So simple, so obvious. What had the citizens done to deserve such a well-run state? And I certainly didn't want inconvenience.

"Why might the law enforcement agencies be inconvenient?"

Fred sighed, which he could do very deeply. "Your father's business dealings with the state did not operate within a normal legal framework."

"So he just built his own."

"Yes, and therefore any involvement by the state police would be inappropriate."

What a pile of words. "I've inherited this framework?"

"You should be thankful that it is already in place."

It was all in place, everything. I just needed to take my place inside it. No—I should stand up right now and spit in his eye and tell him I will not defile myself in this swamp. This is what I hated so much about being Melvin, this slimy stew of corruption and power. I will put an end to it!

"Okay, that's about what I thought," I said.

"Grainger knows the details intimately. You don't need to at the beginning, just understand the working relationship."

I'll find the details later. I can clean it up then.

"I should avoid saying anything blatantly illegal?" I said.

"Um, yes. He could be recording the meeting."

"Right." I don't want to play this game. Decide. Quit now. "Where should we meet?"

"You select a restaurant, near the capitol."

Here was another problem: lunch with the accountant, dinner with the chief of staff, and Pamela would have donuts at the board meeting. "I'm going to get fat."

"Then have fun doing it," said the three-hundred-pound mound in front of me, and he could just as well have been talking about all the other corruptions he was inducting me into. "Life is short, Jason."

Life is short. "Who was king before Melvin?" I said.

"King? No one. There were dukes and earls, or whatever. Your grandfather was a minor baron. No, your father created the position of sole ruler."

"But you say there has to be a king."

"You can't go back. The world had changed; your father changed it."

The metaphor seemed backward. "Once the people have had a king, they'll always want one?"

"The people have nothing to do with it." He was amused at the thought, or at my innocence, and it was fascinating to listen to him. I was a rat being hypnotized by a snake. "They are only necessary as an object for power to be wielded over."

What would a government do without a population to be governed? I repeated the question. "So who needs there to be a king?"

"The men who are strong enough to grasp power. Before your father consolidated his position, no one had been able to accomplish it. Now they know it can be done, and how. There are a million people in this state, and if just one of them, only one, has a desire for power, he will rule the rest. There are many more than one who have the desire."

"I still don't think I do, Fred."

"Then you may be the better man to wield power."

He didn't believe that. He knew what it took to wield power. It took determination and purpose, and purpose was what I lacked.

What am I doing here?

I was hoping for a return to sanity as I descended back through the twenty-third floor, but it didn't come. The line was gone. I looked for it in the lobby, but there was still no sign of it.

I walked the few blocks to the steak place George Elias had suggested, and cleared my head with the exercise. Maybe this would be more fun.

George wasn't an accountant. He was a major-league investment manager and banker, and it had been his job to shovel Melvin's cash between vaults whenever one got too full. If the restaurant was expensive, that would mean he managed other people's investments because he liked being around money. If the place was cheap, that meant he managed other people's money because they wanted him to.

It was respectable and an excellent value. I decided to give George a raise.

I was ten minutes early, and my guess was he would be five minutes early. When he came in at that, on the dot, I was ready to give him another raise. He was thin, or else everybody seemed to me to be thin after two hours with Fred, and he was friendly but very professional.

"If I'd known beforehand I was going to inherit the estate, I would have made sure I knew more about it," I said after we'd ordered. Actually, if I'd known beforehand that I was going to inherit, I would have made sure I didn't. But I was being open-minded. "As it is, I'm pretty much in the dark."

"I have some papers," he said. "Do I remember that your degree from Yale is in business administration?"

"Don't take that too seriously."

"But you know how to read a balance sheet, and you understand profit and loss, and cash flow statements."

"I think I can figure them out."

"Then let's start with the businesses you own."

It was not hard to figure out, even for a Yale business major. Through the fog of corporate identities was majority ownership of eleven factories, three construction companies, a trucking company, two distributors—all with over ten thousand direct employees.

"Now, these are your other major investments."

Lots of stock in the newspaper and Channel Six, in retail chains, hotels, banks, and a little more in anything else there was. And it was all local, everything based inside the state. Through four different real estate holding companies, I owned half the skyline. I owned the building Fred's office was in, I owned the company that had built it, I owned the company that had paved the road from there to this restaurant, I owned the trucks that delivered the tables we were sitting at, the distributor the tables came from, the contractor who'd installed the air conditioning.

The very air we breathed was mine. Well, more or less.

The balance sheets dealt with some real big numbers, and they weren't in the debit column. The cash flows looked like Niagara Falls. These were companies that did not keep their market share by cutting costs and competing on price. These were companies that didn't bother with competing at all. But of course, these businesses did not operate in a normal framework. It would be very important to keep a close working relationship with the governor.

George handed me the next sheets. "You may be familiar with the personal real estate you own."

There was the big house and the townhouse in Washington. He hadn't used the other houses much, except as knickknack shelves to set Angela in when he wanted to pretend they were vacationing.

She'd jet off for a few weeks, and he'd drop in for a couple weekends.

"And here are a few other assets."

The cars, the library, the art.

"I own a Matisse?"

George laughed. "Not a significant one. I believe it's in the Washington townhouse. Most of the art is impressionist and later, but nothing very modern. There are three that are very valuable— a Monet, a Cezanne, and a Picasso. They're in the main house."

I probably had seen them. "I never thought of him as a collector."

"Most of these he bought years ago, when he was in the Senate. And all of the jewelry went to Mrs. Boyer."

I still hadn't heard a bottom line, and I wasn't sure I wanted to. "So I guess you don't just keep all the cash in a checking account. Where is it all?"

"No, not in a checking account. Most of the wealth is in the assets, the stocks and real estate. But as you see, there is a substantial revenue stream. All the businesses are profitable and generate excess cash, which appears as stock dividends. Most of that cash has been reinvested in the other assets—for instance, the real estate and media properties, which have started generating their own profits in the last few years. And he kept a large reserve that he could get to easily."

"Could I get to that right now?" I just wondered.

"The probate will take a few days. He had the trusts designed to make the process easy. However, I have the authority to use my judgment in putting certain accounts at your service. You would just need to sign these papers."

I accepted the service of the accounts. "And what about the foundation?"

George shook his head. "That is outside of my responsibilities. You would have to speak with Mr. Kern."

"Then we'll stay inside your responsibilities." It was time to find out how far off Eric's guess had been. "What is it all worth?"

"This spreadsheet gives a good snapshot of that." He handed me one final paper with a summary list of everything and a total at the bottom in a little box. I was amazed, and I didn't pretend not to be.

I stopped at my bank—which it literally was—and opened a new account to put my new money into. Then I followed Pamela's directions out to the west edge of the city and found the particular factory I owned.

The board meeting that afternoon was short and sweet. The room looked out over a factory floor on one side and properly grimy smokestacks and brick buildings on the other side. Light refreshments costing more than a worker's weekly paycheck kept us happy as Fred and Pamela introduced me to a few of my company presidents. I'd had just enough time after lunch to look through George Elias's papers and learn the company names and what they made. I acted responsible and caring and interested. We decided to keep up the good work, and I would get more involved as I was able. I also met with a couple union leaders so I could be stern and tough. They were so heavily bribed, though, that they would have groveled if I'd been Shirley Temple.

I guessed that most of those people had seen right through my big cheese act, even though Fred told me I'd been very impressive. They were all twice my age and there was no rational reason that I should be their boss. No one asked me bluntly, What right did I have to be here? No one but me.

Driving back into town against the rush hour traffic, I started thinking about the governor and his chief of staff. Clinton Grainger would not pretend to be impressed.

And I thought about what I'd seen. The empire was vast but concentrated. It was all in one state, mainly in heavy industry, and dependent on government largesse and lack of strong competition. It was obvious why Melvin had kept such tight control on the governor's mansion. It was obvious why I needed to.

Clinton Grainger did not impress me. He was nondescript, flabby, a poor dresser, and he had bad hair. Even his eyes were blank where I'd expected some flash of brilliance to sneak out, and his voice was whiny. No wonder he was the brains behind, since he'd never make it as the politician out front.

"I'm so glad to meet you," he said, and it sounded like he had a clothespin on his nose.

"And likewise," I said. "I'm sorry it's taken so long."

"Yes." There was no sign of intelligence. Of course, Fred Spellman had fooled me for years.

"There's a lot of ground to cover." We established ourselves on opposite sides of the white tablecloth.

"You went sailing over the weekend," he said. What did that mean?

"I often do," I said.

He peered at me. "Are you serious about running your father's businesses, Mr. Boyer? Or are you just going to spend his money?" Fred had said, Be direct. Grainger was being very direct. I was being sacked before I even knew the game had started.

"I was taking a few days to decide."

"That's a lot of time to make a decision."

I was in way over my head, and there were sharks in the water. I had to think of what to say next, and I could see Grainger counting each second against me.

But why was I here, anyway? To impress this slob? The old Jason wouldn't have cared what Clinton Grainger thought about anything, so why was the rich and powerful Jason worrying?

I didn't want to play this game. I stood up. "To tell the truth," I said, "it's been a long day and I'm not very hungry."

He was surprised, and he stared up at me. "You're leaving?"

"Yes. I'm done with this conversation." I dropped a fifty on the table and started walking. He was up and after me.

I waited at the curb a moment until he caught up.

"Mr. Boyer . . ."

"And please give Mr. Bright my regards," I said. "I still hope we can work together, as partners."

Clinton Grainger stared at the darkening night, then turned to me with his blank eyes and bulbous nose. Then he shook his head. "He doesn't like partners." He shrugged; he was giving up, too. "Good night, Mr. Boyer."

I called Fred to report, and he was not impressed by my actions.

"We'll just have to wait for his response."

"I guess that will be soon?"

"Yes, and unmistakable."

It wasn't late when I got home, and Katie met me in the hall.

"I don't like this," I said.

"What happened? How did everything go?"

"Terrible. I nearly died."

"What?" She stepped back and looked me over for blood. "What happened?"

"I met with my financial adviser to find out how filthy rich I am and then I had a board meeting to hear how much more filthy rich I'm going to be and then I had dinner with the most powerful man in the state government to show off my filthy riches."

"Were you in an accident? What did you mean about dying?"

"What I said. Jason is just about dead. He barely survived, right at the end."

Her eyes narrowed. "Forget the melodrama. You're doing what you need to be doing." Then she smiled. "And you still look like Jason."

"The big bad wolf has eaten granny, and now he's wearing her clothes."

"You talk like Jason."

"That would be harder to fake."

"Now tell me what happened. What did George Elias say?"

I shrugged. "Let me sit down." I led the way to the study and called for Rosita to bring me some milk and a sandwich. I don't mind lying, but I'd told a real whopper to Grainger. I was plenty hungry.

I took my time. When I was done, and Katie had been very patient, I took my new checkbook and wrote her a check for a million dollars.

"Don't spend it all in one place."

Her mouth dropped open when I handed it to her. "What is this for?"

"You need me to tell you? Just take it. Celebrate a little. Have a party. Buy a new dress."

"But . . ."

"That's nothing, Katie. You want to know what I'm worth now? Guess."

"I can't."

"Yeah, I bet you couldn't. Remember Eric said fifty million?" I shook my head. "Wrong. Way wrong." I was being mean, but I couldn't help it. I was feeling a lot of pain from the day, and I wanted to share it.

"That seemed like a lot."

"It is a lot. Way too much for one person. That's why the truth hurts even more." I looked her in the eye. "A billion dollars."

"Jason!"

"Yeah. Who'd have thought? He acted rich, but not that rich."

It took her a few seconds to get her breath back. "A billion dollars?"

"That's right. That's not an M, it's a B. You have hit the jackpot, cupcake. Call your momma and tell her she was wrong. No, I think I'll call the little rapscallion myself."

"It's all ours?"

"To the last brass farthing. If you invested a billion dollars in the bank, do you know what the interest would be? Two hundred thousand. Per day. You could even have hard feelings against the old man for being stingy, with the paltry thirty grand a month he was giving us."

"What are we going to do?"

"If we keep on a budget and don't spend too much, we'll manage somehow. A billion dollars isn't what it used to be, you know."

She took a deep breath and we both calmed down. "That's not what I meant. Oh, never mind. Are you all right?"

I wasn't. A billion dollars weighs a lot, and right then I was feeling it all. "I want to get to bed."

"Come this way." Mama Katie took command.

Tuesday morning I went running. I do it for exercise and I don't push myself, but that morning I set a world record in the four mile Run Away From Your Problems event. Katie was still asleep when I left, and was just coming down to breakfast by the time I came back in.

"That was fast."

"Paparazzi. You have to sprint to keep ahead of them."

"Really?"

"No."

She was waiting when I came back down from my shower, and we ate together. We always eat breakfast looking out over the garden.

"What are you doing today?"

"I don't know," I said. "I want to meet more of the people who worked for Melvin. And I want to catch Nathan Kern before he goes to Africa tomorrow, to talk about the foundation. That'll be dinner out again tonight."

"Could we have him over here?"

Our house could use the blessing of his presence. "Yeah. I'll have Pamela set it up. It'll be friendlier, in case he has hard feelings about not getting Melvin's wad for the foundation."

I finished breakfast, and Katie was still there watching me. "Did you see Angela yesterday?"

"We had lunch downtown," she said. "It was very nice."

"Does she know what she's doing with her life?"

"No."

"She has no money worries."

"She's very lonely. And she's afraid to make friends."

"She should be. She's a rich, single, lonely sitting duck." Besides, she didn't know how to make a friend. She never had.

"I told her we'd take care of her."

"I guess we have to."

"She had a husband. Now she's by herself, and she never has been before."

A little kitten in the deep woods. I'd never get the adoration from Katie that Melvin did from Angela, and I'd hate it anyway. Maybe when I was older. Maybe for my second wife I'd pick an Angela.

"We'll take care of her," I said. "We'll assign you to watch her, and I'll keep Eric under control." Who needs kids? "Maybe we could set her up with Nathan."

Katie's eyes lit up. "What an idea, Jason. I'm going to think about it."

"Katie, I was joking."

"But still . . ."

"And they could adopt Eric. They could be the parents he's always wanted."

"Now, that's being silly. When are you seeing Eric again?"

"I'll call him today."

I didn't. It was a long day and I was being very conscientious regarding my many responsibilities, which involved mainly sitting upstairs in my little office and talking on the phone to people whose names were on lists that Fred Spellman and George Elias had given to me.

I left the house to meet with Stan Morton of the newspaper and television empire. We talked about his daughter Natalie, whom I hadn't seen since Yale, except at my wedding and then at hers.

She was married to one of Stan's vice presidents, but I was sure that this morning, she was thinking about the fish that got away. It wasn't her husband's fault that he wasn't the richest man in the state. She'd just make him feel like it was.

But Natalie did not inherit her claws from her father. Stan was a reasonable man, pleasant and to the point, and with the kind of beard grown by people who don't want to shave every morning. He was independent and not about to take orders from anyone about what his paper and television station were going to say. But he also knew where his bread was buttered. I had three of his nine board members in my pocket, and I was his biggest stockholder. We cordially reached an understanding that we would discuss anything of mutual interest and parted on friendly terms.

I met with Fred for a few minutes and then with two more of my corporate presidents, and then Pamela called with the disaster of the day.

"Nathan Kern will be at your house at eight." That was not the disaster. "And, Jason, do you know Felicity Nottingham Cavalieri Gildanov?" That was the disaster.

"This is a person, isn't it?"

"Oh yes, it certainly is."

I thought so. I'd heard of her in the news—kind of like I'd heard of the *Titanic*—but didn't know the exact details.

"She would like to meet with you," Pamela said.

"Well, put her on the list, and I'll get to her if I want to."

"That might be difficult."

"Isn't she with the opera?"

"That's right. She has a tour arranged for you at two o'clock."

"I'm not going to tour the opera."

"Dear, I've told presidents of the United States that your father was unavailable, but this is one lady I'm leaving to you."

At two o'clock sharp I arrived at the gilded portal of that great and so very important and beneficial institute, our state's own Warwick Opera House—home of that beacon of enlightenment and uplifting purpose, that instrument of civilizing culture, that bedrock of society, the State Opera. For over two hours I was honored, even privileged, to be in the company of the dignified, gracious chair-woman of that splendid temple of worthiness. She was all that a person of such exalted position should be, and much, much more. Much, much, much more. The sights I saw that precious day will stay with me always. But even that magnificent stage, the glistening lobby—itself a showcase of the first order—paled compared to the words I heard, the many, many descriptions, enlightening lectures, entire college courses on the sophisticated genius, the ancient history, the crucial importance of the most devastatingly wonderful achievement in the entire accomplishment of all mankind, the opera. It was with the greatest regret, and difficulty, that I cut short my visit to that hallowed place due to other pressing business, and I could only hope that my donation, on the spot, of one hundred thousand dollars would somehow mitigate my praiseworthy and admirable hostess' sublime sorrow that I could not stay for the second half of her tour.

"You got off easy," Fred said when I called.

"Melvin put up with that battleship?"

"He called her Stalin. You're going to be on her board of directors."

"No."

"Yes you are, Jason."

"I said no."

"It doesn't matter what you say to me. You'll have to deal with her."

"Fred, after this afternoon, I could do it. I could say no to her."

"Don't. Kindly say that you would be honored. Every person who could realistically be a rival to you is on that board, including Harry Bright and Bob Forrester. She has forced them all onto it, and you need to be there."

I was not in a good mood when I got home. Katie steered clear, and I had to sit still in my office for a few minutes before I could trust myself with the telephone.

"Yes, Jason?" said Pamela's voice. She sounded ready to be yelled at.

"It's okay. I won't blame you. This is something else. I need an office. Did Melvin just work out of his house?"

"Mostly. And he had offices at two of his plants, but he didn't use them much."

"Who's on the top floor of Fred's building?"

"Oh, let's see. I don't know, but I think it's bank executive offices."

My building, my bank. "I want some rooms up there."

"An office and a conference room?"

"Put in an office for you, and I don't need a conference room. And I want a secure room for storage."

"I'll find a contractor who can do it quickly."

From my bedroom window, I could see the downtown skyline ten miles away. For a while I watched the building I'd just confiscated. What was happening? In two days I'd become what I thought I would never be. I stared at the mirror, and the Why Am I Here? wasn't there. There was someone else looking back at me out of my eyes—the Big Bad Wolf looking out from under Granny's nightcap.

It was Melvin.

Why had he done this to me? What was he thinking, when he sat there in Fred's parlor and signed that new will? And then tried out the aerodynamic properties of a Mercedes sedan. If that merging of car and tree had happened two hours earlier, Nathan Kern would be jousting with Clinton Grainger and the governor. And I would not be on Felicity's board. I was having hard feelings toward Nathan.

I looked back out at the skyline, black against the late afternoon. I could almost touch it. Instead, the phone rang, and it touched me.

There was an interesting new note in Fred's voice, of anger and annoyance and maybe worry.

"Come here, right away."

Billionaires are not talked to in this manner, and Fred knew it. "What's wrong?" I said.

"The governor has made his move."

I gave Katie instructions to keep Nathan entertained if I was late.

I was there in twenty-five minutes, and someone was in my chair.

"Jason, this is Detective Wilcox, of the state police." Fred was exasperated.

"Thank you for coming," the man said, and my first impression was of the nastiest little mustache I had ever seen in my life. We completed the formalities.

Detective Wilcox was very good. His political instinct was sharp as a knife. He apparently had long had the wealthy-industrialist-and-high-powered-lawyer beat, and he was respectful, confident, circumspect, authoritative, well-dressed, trustworthy, loyal, clean, and reverent. His only flaw was the little pencil mustache. What was he thinking?

"Now, Detective Wilcox, let's get down to business." Fred leaned forward imperiously. "I'm sure I don't have to tell you how busy a man Mr. Boyer is." A man of Wilcox's experience would understand that this had better be very important.

He was not intimidated. He turned to me. "I'm afraid we have some disturbing information for you, Mr. Boyer, concerning your father's death."

"What?"

"His car had been tampered with."

It was suddenly the same feeling I'd had when Fred had read the will—ring of iron around my chest.

"We completed our laboratory analysis last week, and there is no doubt," Wilcox was saying. "The brake lines had been drained."

"I see."

I could see. That rotten, wretched old man, that idiot! An accident maybe can't be prevented, but getting murdered was pure malicious carelessness, specifically to spite me and ruin my life.

"This is a serious statement, Mr. Wilcox." Fred was in high dudgeon himself. "Do you realize the implications?"

"Very much. We have examined the evidence in every way, and we are completely sure."

I could feel a new wave of rage building, and this one was a tsunami. I stuffed it down to save for later, when I could really let it rip. "You had better be sure," I said.

Fred switched from indignant to menacing. "Very sure."

The mustache was not impressed. "We are. May I ask you some questions, Mr. Boyer?"

"Not yet." Fred leaned back in his chair. "Is Mr. Boyer under any suspicion?"

"We do not have any specific suspects."

"That is not a specific answer."

Wilcox frowned. "Everyone associated with Melvin Boyer has to be regarded with suspicion at this stage of the investigation."

Fred turned to me. "Do you understand, Jason? Be very careful in what you say."

I was not in any careful state of mind. "Why did you wait a week to tell me?"

"We were verifying the evidence."

Verifying the evidence. The first word that came to my mind was *fabricating*. Fred had said that the governor's response would be unmistakable, and I was not mistaking it. I was so angry at Melvin for leaving this mess.

"Right," I said. "I'll make a statement. I have no idea who might have killed Melvin, if anyone really did. He was a wealthy and powerful man, and there would be lots of people who were enemies or benefited from his death. You know all that. I don't know anything else."

"Could you list these enemies?" Wilcox's mustache quivered. I was supposed to start fingering people?

"You find them. I'm not going to do your job."

"Who benefited from his death?"

"Mr. Spellman will provide you with a copy of his will. Other than that, if you want to go fishing, you'll have to find a different pond."

Wilcox could see his fishing license was about to expire. "Mr. Boyer, don't you want us to find your father's murderer?" Was he surprised, or was this an attempt at intimidation? I was just too mad to put up with it.

"He's dead, and the rest doesn't matter. And if anyone is trying to use this, or has manufactured this, to cause me trouble, then he isn't very bright."

Wilcox blinked. "Let me assure you we will use discretion. We're only investigating a crime. We have no other purposes."

Fred snorted. "I understand your purpose."

Wilcox had left. I was in a hurry, but the situation required discussion. "Is this the governor asserting his independence?"

"Certainly." Fred scowled. "He wants to show us we are not above the law, and he can yank our chain whenever he wants. The police will question your family and associates, and embarrassing information will be leaked."

I was thinking about our special legal framework. "That could hurt Bright as badly as us."

"He controls the police. They'll uncover whatever he wants and nothing else. But the investigation could spread anywhere. The Boyer name will be demeaned."

There was a lot of static in my brain. "Do you think Melvin was murdered?"

"It was my first assumption when I heard about the accident, but I didn't think it was appropriate to discuss. There were other things more important. And for the governor's purposes it would certainly be convenient . . . but not necessary." Then he paused. "I'm sorry, Jason. I didn't mean to trivialize your father's death. We should take some time to think this through before we plan our next step."

"It does matter whether he was killed. That would mean there was a murderer somewhere."

"Yes . . . Are you suggesting we actually cooperate with the police?"

"I don't know." There were thoughts under the static. "They're going to need a suspect. What if there isn't one, or there is one but they can't find him?"

"Or if he, or she, isn't appropriate for their purposes. Exactly. And you would be an obvious choice. This is a substantial attack, and I have no doubt it will be used for political purposes."

I was sorting out my anger. There was the anger at Melvin for leaving me his money, without telling me first. Then there was the anger at him for leaving me his Special Framework. Now I had a third layer of anger at him for getting murdered, or at least appearing to, which was ammunition in the hands of a belligerent governor.

But there was anger beyond that, and it was pointed at that governor, and I did not feel like giving in to his attack. Maybe I was still planning to get rid of Melvin's money, but at the moment I started having other plans.

"What should we do?" I asked.

Fred was grim, but he'd calmed down. "For the moment, wait. He is just setting out a negotiating position. Next, he'll let us know what he wants."

"This doesn't look like negotiations."

"Oh, it is. That's all it is. This is how the world operates, Jason."

"But Bright, or Grainger, or whoever this is, could get anyone they want convicted. Would they do that?"

"If the stakes are high enough." And Fred smiled. Maybe he liked high stakes. "Eric. Angela. Katie. And, of course, especially you."

I don't like high stakes, and I was using a lot of energy keeping my lid on. "You're the last person who saw him alive, Fred."

Traffic was thin, and twenty minutes was just enough time to be home by eight. I thought for a moment about indulging my fury, but there were too many other things to think through.

Had he really been murdered? Sure. Why not? It was way more likely than an accident. So who did it?

Maybe somebody he'd crushed, or was currently crushing, or about to crush. I had a better idea after the last few days of all the crushees, but that was for the police. There were other names rattling about.

Brake tampering meant someone who worked on cars. Benefiting from his death meant someone who needed money. Two plus two equals . . .

I got out my cell phone and dialed.

"Pamela, I have another job for you."

"Yes, dear?"

"Get a credit report on Eric. He has no idea how much he's been spending for the last few years, and I'd like to make sure he's not in too much trouble on his credit cards."

"I'll e-mail it to you tonight."

"Thank you."

Or maybe Fred had been thinking I would be easier to control than Melvin had been. Maybe he and Clinton Grainger got together for lunch every week and commiserated about puppets who didn't do as they were told.

Or was Angela the kitten really a tiger? Who knew what went on in that relationship.

This was not going to be pretty. I'd already convicted three people who I should have been trusting.

Katie was a lot better off with Melvin dead than with him alive. I missed my exit over that one.

But neither Katie nor Eric knew the will had been changed.

Maybe it was the governor going for a double dip, getting rid of Melvin with the option of pinning it on the old man's heir. That was better, if not very real.

What else? The most obvious motive of all. He died the night he changed his will. Were the brakes meant to fail on the way *to* Fred's house? If it had been two hours earlier, Bishop Kern would have been pope.

"Katie."

"Where are you, Jason?"

"I'm on the way. Is Nathan there?"

"I think he's just pulling up."

"I'll be about ten minutes."

Money gave lots of people a reason to kill Melvin. Now the money was mine. What am I doing here? Why am I here? Is this what money and power are all about? I was actually just sitting at the curb down the block, but I needed a little more time. Nathan Kern might know about why Melvin changed the will. I'd cool off and give Katie time to soften him up.

Katie had been shopping.

The table was set with elegant heirloom china and silver and crystal that had been in the family for generations—just not our family; I'd never seen the stuff before. Rosita was setting out a floral centerpiece, and she had a new uniform on, very professional, with her head held high.

I found the merchants' darling in the parlor entertaining our guest. She had spent on herself no less than on anything else, but still exquisitely. The dress was dark green, the scarf was the life work of a thousand silkworms educated in every nuance of impressionism, and the emerald pin holding it on her shoulder made an even greater impression. She hadn't taken risks with her hair, which was still long and loose, as I liked it.

That's why I'd given her the check, to celebrate. She hadn't spent it all in one place, but she might well have spent it all.

Nathan was her equal in conspicuous taste. Medium gray Italian suit, with the diamond cuff links option, silk handkerchief the same vibrant yellow as his tie, distinguished graying hair, and what he could teach that detective about mustaches would fill a book.

And I? I could hold my own with these perfect people. No doubt. I hoped the last two hours didn't show in my striking features or jaunty demeanor, and the suit that draped my muscular frame cost at least as much as Nathan's. I promised myself a nice, refreshing temper tantrum sometime very soon, and smiled.

No more *Mr. Kern*. I was the man now. "Nathan, thank you for coming."

"It's so good to see you again, Jason," said Suspect Number One, and I shook his hand.

"It seems like forever since last Wednesday," I said.

"Yes, I understand you've had a busy few days." The pleasantries persisted for a few moments, and then Katie ushered us into the dining room.

Through the excellent meal we let him talk. He knew how to both speak and listen, but we encouraged him to speak, and he was very interesting. Tomorrow he would leave for a week in some African basket case to review the water and education and health projects that the foundation had funded. I pictured him wafting through villages of grass huts. Would he wear his gray suit? Brown might work better. Or he might try to fit in with the locals with khakis and a pith helmet.

In front of us was enough silverware for a Third World village to eat with proper manners for a week. Perhaps we should use plastic once a month to show solidarity with the Third World. I would discuss that with Katie.

Then the conversation turned to the more local projects the foundation funded. The African stuff was new; these were what the foundation had originally been created for. There were After-School Programs and Reading Programs and Food Pantries and Free Clinics, to the point that there were real advantages to being disadvantaged. Grants to be programmed, programs to be granted; projects to be funded, funds to be projected; boards to meet . . . I was getting bored.

My imagination wandered in other directions. Nathan vs. Felicity, super-heavyweight board meeting smackdown. Felicity might have the Vegas odds, but the smart money would be on Nathan.

Then we returned to the parlor, and Nathan asked permission and lit one of his little cigarettes, and we bandied over our brandy. The foundation was more than a word to me now, which was the official purpose of the evening. I did appreciate it. There was no question about continuing its funding. I had even gained some respect for its director.

And I was done with that conversation. Now it was time for the real business. Katie had left us and I made my move.

"Nathan, it's very interesting to learn more about the foundation. Tell me about how Melvin was involved. Was he active in it? Did he make decisions?"

He smiled sadly. "He attended board meetings. He suggested board members. He suggested quite a few things, but he never demanded them. And he could have. He had the right to remove any member he wished. That was how the foundation was set up."

The parlor was our nicest room, where Katie had smeared the largest slice of the decorating budget. It's hard, sometimes, to find a comfortable chair that's also expensive. "Did he have any differences with the board?"

"Oh, a few, but none major. Obviously, the membership was made of individuals he respected and who had a similar vision for the foundation. He had a hands-off attitude."

"Did you get along with him?"

He laughed, and it was pleasant. "Oh yes. By his choice we did."

Somehow the contrast of the dark patterns of the carpet, the walnut end tables, and the ebony fireplace against the pale green wallpaper imposed an atmosphere of calm. Katie and I usually tried to have our arguments in this room.

"By *his* choice?"

Nathan Kern put a graceful finger to his aquiline nose, propelled smoke past it, and considered. "Should I be frank? He can't defend himself here, can he? But you are his son, and certainly you knew him. Please understand me as I say this, that I dislike speaking anything besides good of a man who is not present."

He meant it, too. "I knew him well enough," I said. "And I've learned a lot more in the last few days."

"I'm certain you have. Your father had many sides to his affairs, and I only dealt with the altruistic ones. By common agreement, we did not discuss any others. He knew I was aware of them.

"And I suppose that was why I was working with him, so some good would come of his wealth. A few pluses on the ledger to balance the minuses. That was why he had created the foundation. And I don't mean that the foundation was his only positive effort, of course."

I nodded. "I understand. As I've said, I'm only beginning to discover all his efforts."

He blew smoke thoughtfully into the atmosphere. It clashed slightly with the room's colors. "Had your father spoken to you about the changes he made to the will?"

How helpful to bring that up. "No. It was quite a shock."

"I'm sure he meant to discuss it, probably very soon."

"He was driving home from Fred Spellman's house when he had the accident. He had signed the new will only an hour before he died."

I was watching very closely. Nathan's eyes showed his surprise.

"That very night?"

"Yes. It was a close thing, apparently, between whether you or I ended up here in the hot seat."

Nathan was still and silent, staring into the air. Despite his best efforts, it was still transparent. Finally he focused back onto me.

"Remarkable."

Well, yes. No doubt about that.

"I had no idea," he added. "I can see how great a shock this has been. You really had no idea you would be the principal heir?"

"Not at all," I said. "I didn't know until Fred told me last Thursday morning, after the funeral. When did you find out the foundation wasn't the heir?"

"When?" He was still bemused. "Well, officially when I met with Fred last Friday afternoon. But I knew, of course. Your father and I had discussed the reasons in detail."

It was a good thing I had just swallowed a mouthful of brandy, or I would have choked on it. I set the glass on the table beside me, trying to act calm, trying to be calm.

"So . . . do you know why he changed his will, Nathan?"

I was feeling something like panic. Since leaving Fred's office, all I'd been thinking about was brake lines and motives. Now I was back to how much I really wanted to know this, how it was so important.

"Yes, I do. As I said, we discussed it at length." His words came forth with the majesty and calmness of deep wisdom. Or maybe it was cigarette smoke. "I asked him to."

"This is your fault?" It was pure reaction.

"Well, now, not precisely," he said sympathetically and a little defensively. "I only requested that the foundation not be the principal recipient. I would hardly have been so bold as to suggest who should be."

"There weren't many other choices." So I was in the line of fire because he had ducked. "Why *not* the foundation? It was what he had always planned." I wasn't used to controlling my anger. I had it under control, but the boiler was going to explode soon.

And I knew the answer. It was obvious. Nathan was no Melvin Boyer. He might manipulate and bully if he had to, but he was a decent man. I might have done poorly with Clinton Grainger, but Nathan would have been laughable. So I laughed. Nathan smiled with me, uncertainly.

"I'm sorry," I said. "Too much pressure, I guess."

"Of course." He waited, maybe to make sure I wasn't going to have hysterics. "To answer your question . . ."

"No, I understand now. It would be impossible for the foundation to manage this empire. It takes someone like Melvin." Someone nasty, mean, hard, and efficient. Fred thought I'd done a reasonable job my first couple days. The more I thought about it, the more I wondered: Why had Melvin ever even considered having the Foundation manage his estate?

"I don't know that you understand," Nathan said.

But I did. The layers were peeling away like an onion under Rosita's knife. If Melvin wanted his empire to survive, Nathan was not the man. I was. I was the man. The Boyer blood was in my veins, as much as I hated it. The doom hadn't fallen that night when he had signed the will and died in a ditch. It had fallen on me the day I was born.

Nathan Kern was still talking. "It isn't a matter of who is most appropriate to manage the Boyer businesses, and their influence."

Yes it was. That was the matter, the crucial matter.

"It is more a matter of whether anyone should." He leaned back and blew more smoke, and I breathed it in. "Fred Spellman has been tutoring you in the use of power, which he understands as few others. But I don't mean that I, and the foundation, was the wrong one to wield this power. My opinion is that no one should."

What was he saying?

"Someone has to," I said. I was disoriented. Wasn't that Fred's line?

He shook his head and continued to blow smoke and sanctimony all over Katie's furniture. We'd have to have the room fumigated. "I think not. Hypothetically, what would happen if you just gave it up?"

That was my line. Just last week, that's what I'd told everyone I was going to do. I agreed with him, right?

"I disagree, Nathan. That's not practical."

"Is practicality important?"

This was suddenly very strange. "Yes. At this level it is. And it isn't practicality. It's necessity. It's too important to treat like a game."

"What is important? Why is it important? Perhaps those are the questions to answer first." He meant them literally, not rhetorically. He thought he knew the answers.

"Right now," I said, "it's important to me to figure out what I'm doing. I'll get to the why later."

He backed off, properly. "I'm not in your shoes." They wouldn't go with his suit, for one thing. He sighed, wearily. "And this last week has been very difficult for you. This isn't the time to philosophize. But I wish you would consider that there is an alternative to where you are right now." He smiled. "I have an early flight tomorrow. Perhaps we should continue this discussion some other time."

What? Was the lackey dismissing the billionaire? He would stay and discuss this until I was finished.

I was finished.

"Then have a good trip, Nathan."

It was time to explode now. Kern was safely away in his Volvo, and with massive self-control, I closed the front door and turned calmly to Katie.

"I've got a couple things to do in my office."

"We need to talk about the house."

Melvin was murdered. Or maybe not. All I knew was that Governor Bright had thrown a rock right through my front window, and I had to figure out how to put it back through his teeth. And if there was a real murderer, that was a problem, too, because it was probably somebody I knew. I was surrounded by people who were a lot better off with Melvin dead.

"Don't you think we need something bigger?" she asked.

And now that I was just barely settling down into being king, Nathan Kern had to poke his cigarette holder into the gears and jam them up. I was holding on by my fingernails. It was hard enough trying to kill all those questions I was asking myself without him blowing them at me. The foundation could maybe use a new director, somebody who knew when to shut up.

"I know it's only been a few days," Katie said. Angela would know when to shut up. On his second marriage, maybe Melvin had learned from experience.

"We'll talk about it soon," I said. "I'd rather not right now."

"Are you all right?"

"No, I am not, and this is not a good time to talk. About any-thing. I'll be in my office."

I turned away from her and forced my feet to move, one at a time, toward my office door. I opened and closed it with only nec-essary force, and sat in my chair. I took a deep breath and stared straight ahead.

Straight ahead was my computer screen, and the first thing I saw was a six-digit number. Then I saw that it was an e-mail from Pamela. Then I saw it was Eric's credit card balances. And then I didn't see anything for a few moments.

"Jason?"

Katie was standing in the doorway, staring at me, and at the shattered monitor in pieces on the floor, and at the splintered pan-eling where it had slammed against the wall. I stared back at her.

She saw that I was unharmed, and the alarm in her eyes faded. "I think we should talk."

I was standing. I wilted into my desk chair, and she sat on the couch.

"I can't do this," I said.

"Why not?"

"Being the king is too hard."

"You don't know how to be a king? You can learn."

"I don't know *why* to be a king."

"There's no answer to that, Jason." She was speaking very gen-tly, holding in her own frustration. "You were born into your family. Your father made his decision and wrote his will. That's why."

"It isn't. It's no reason I have to accept it."

"I was hoping we were past that."

I held out my hand to her, and she took it. "We are," I said. "Somehow it happened."

"I will always be with you," she said.

"But I need a reason to live this life that's been dropped on me. It won't work unless I know why I'm doing it."

"What would a reason look like? What reason did you have before?"

"I've never had one. I just can't ignore it anymore."

"What reason did your father have?"

It was time. "Melvin was murdered."

Her mouth dropped. "By who?"

"I don't know." I couldn't stop myself from wondering if an innocent person's first thought would be about the victim or the killer.

But she was shaking. It was all too much. I had my arms around her, and one of us was sobbing, or maybe both of us. I wanted so much to get out of it, to go back, but I couldn't.

Instead I was compelled to fight back. And through the night, I slowly realized how strong that compulsion was.

Wednesday morning at nine o'clock I sat in Fred Spellman's smoke-free office planning the destruction of the governor. Not everyone in the room was in agreement.

"Jason. There is no cause for reckless behavior." Fred's glare was withering. Too bad he was a minority of one.

"He started this war."

"He did not . . . this is not a war. I told you this is simply a negotiation."

I was a majority of one. "I'm not interested in negotiating. I want to take him down."

He leaned back in his chair, and I could feel the whole building lean with him. He shifted the glare from *wither* to *pierce*. "All right, then. First. Do you even have any idea how to overthrow a powerful politician entrenched in office?"

"No."

"Second. Have you thought through the consequences? Who do you expect to take his place? What if a prolonged fight shuts down your state contracts? What about Senator Forrester?" He leaned forward a little. "And what if you lose?" Then back again. "Those are just a few questions, and I could list more. You'll be letting a bull loose in a china shop. An angry bull."

"We'll deal with whatever happens."

"We will?" He moved forward, his wide, angry face jutting toward me. "We will? You have no idea what forces would be unleashed."

"Then I'll find out."

His eyes went cold. "Third. Why? This is not necessary. We can make a deal. That's what he wants."

"I said I'm not interested."

"You should be."

"I don't want a deal."

"You've only been in this position less than a week. You are not ready to make a decision like this."

I stood up from the armchair and looked down on him. There was some point over his desk where our glares met, and it must have been pretty hot there.

"First," I said. "I'm not going to be weak. He started it. Let everyone see what happens if they cross me, and no one else will. Second. He's messing with me and my family."

"This is politics, Jason," Fred snapped. "If you're going to get your poor little feelings hurt, you have no right to attempt anything this serious."

"I've got five rights, Fred—B, O, Y, E, and R. And a billion more, too. You're the one who told me I had no choice, that I had to take Melvin's place. Well, I am, my own way. Bright might think that threatening me with a murder investigation is just a friendly game, but I don't take it that way."

"I'm sure he would settle for a deal. A different division of construction profits, your pledge to continue to support him. Clinton Grainger would know exactly what he would accept."

"That would be a surrender."

"It would be a deal."

"Until he tries the next thing. If a man has a gun and he's trying to kill you, and you're locked in a room with him, you can either dodge bullets forever or kill him first."

"No. You can deal. There is always a deal."

"I don't trust him."

Fred rolled his eyes. "What do you care about trust? Do you

expect to meet anyone at this level you can trust? No, we make the deal but tighten the screws everywhere else. We arrange a nice public meeting between you and Senator Forrester. The next time the state awards a major contract to a competitor, we make sure they have enough labor problems to be an embarrassment. That's how your father operated."

"And he was murdered."

"Perhaps. I don't think you are contributing to your own longevity. More likely the opposite."

Was that a threat? "Here's my third reason," I said, sitting back into the deep chair. "I want the investigation stopped."

"Why? Do you know who killed him?"

"No." Second time in less than twelve hours I'd been asked that.

"If you struck a deal, the investigators would be instructed to leave you alone." He shook his head. "Just days ago you wanted nothing to do with any of this. You were going to be rid of the money and power. Now you can't wield it fast enough."

"I'm still going to be rid of it. But I'm going to take care of this first."

We were both somewhat exhausted, and we took a short break to breathe and think. Fred studied me. "Do you want to know who killed your father?"

"He's dead. It doesn't matter how." I couldn't imagine knowing. I didn't want to know. "If he really was murdered."

"Do you think he wasn't?" Fred asked.

"Of course he was. An accident would have been too trite."

He nodded. "All right. Let me think about all of this."

"I'll be back this evening," I said. "I have a lot to do today, and I don't want to waste time."

And now it was time for the hard part. I pointed the car toward home and dialed a number.

Eric answered right away.

"Jason! What's up?" I could hardly hear him, there was so much noise. The phone in his helmet was pretty poor considering how much it had cost him.

"Where are you?" I asked.

"Uh . . . I don't know. I'll see a sign in a minute."

"Come to my house—we need to talk."

"Now?"

"Yes."

"No problem. See you in a while."

In contrast, I did have problems. I drove past a police car parked beside the road, clocking the traffic. By reflex I checked my speed, the universal guilty reaction of any driver. Could that radar pick up other crimes? Corruption, bribery, extortion? Blackmail? Breaking my own resolve to not be Melvin? I slowed down because I was cautious, not because I was law abiding.

I had lunch with Katie in the back garden. She hadn't been down for breakfast, and it was the first I'd seen her. She had questions about Melvin and the police, but I put her off.

"Let's wait for Eric."

He must have been far away, because two hours later he had still not appeared. I was in my office reading papers Pamela had sent me, educating myself about my possessions. The new monitor had a bigger screen than the old one and there was no sign of the gouge in the wall. I'd have to give Katie a raise. It must have been hard getting people here that quickly.

It was three thirty, and I was on the phone with Stanley Morton discussing how to manage general publicity concerning my family concerns, when the little brother part of my family finally showed up. There was a roar in the driveway and two minutes later he was standing in the office doorway, head to toe in motorcycle leather, his helmet under his arm.

"Did you have lunch?" I asked.

Tough question. He wrinkled his forehead, thinking. "No. I came straight here when you called."

"You want something, or just wait for supper?"

"I'll eat."

I found Katie and Rosita and put in an order. Then I led everyone in the world I was related to by blood out to the garden.

It was warm, the tricky heat of October. Eric shed his leather.

Underneath he was dressed half decent for once, in jeans and a dark blue turtleneck.

For a while we just sat on a bench, surrounded by chrysanthemums. Most of the annuals were failing, massacred by an early frost. We were surrounded by casual death. I thought about the past spring, when the flowers had been planted, and now most of them were gone. The first color was showing in the leaves.

Eric was the image of blissful ignorance. I was tired of wearing suits and formality and maturity and what was happening to me.

"Have you been looking at your mail lately?" I asked.

"What do you mean?"

"Those letters with little windows in front that you see your name through."

"Huh? . . . Oh. Jason, it's no problem. I'll get everything paid off now."

"Do you even know how much you owe?"

Talk about a sheepish look. "Not that much." Baa, baa. It was good for him there was no spaghetti close by.

"Does a hundred eighty thousand sound familiar?"

He was alarmed. "No way. No."

"What have you been spending it on?" He didn't live that richly. His apartment was expensive, but it was just that and his cars. Certainly not clothes.

"I don't know." He looked at the heap beside him. "The leathers were three thousand, I think."

"And that doesn't include any sharks that don't report to credit agencies."

"None of those, Jason. I did a couple times back in college. Now I've got credit cards."

"Rule number 83—don't take money from anybody who doesn't own a building in Manhattan. Rule number 84—until you've got the cash under control, don't buy anything with a price more than three digits. Rule 85—don't be stupid, Eric."

He grinned. "The first one's easy, the second one maybe. Eighty-five would really cramp my lifestyle."

"So would breaking it. Things are different now."

"I don't get it. I mean, the difference is we've got a lot more money."

"You don't know how big a difference that is."

"You're getting way too tense, Jason." He was sitting next to me. He put his arm around my shoulder and squeezed, just being a friend, a brother. "Come on. It's okay."

For five seconds I almost broke open. I had always taken care of him, through school and life, and now I needed someone to take care of me. I wanted to tell him what my life had become, and what I hated about it. I wanted to tell one person about how I didn't know what I was doing and I was afraid, and I wanted someone to tell me why I was here. Just tell me why.

The man who could have told me wasn't there. We'd buried him a week ago.

There was sound from the path behind us. I turned, and maybe I was even expecting it was him. It was Katie.

She was also in jeans, and I felt even more out of place in that comfortable, informal place; she sat at my left and Eric at my right. I have very few moments that are intimate, where I know I am in love; and I loved both of them then, my wife and my brother. If only money could have kept the rest of the world away from us. But instead, it drew the world in.

"Have you told him?" she asked me.

I couldn't. I wouldn't have been able to tell Katie, except in anger. I regretted that I'd told her abruptly the way I had. And I couldn't get angry enough at Eric to hurt him that way. I'd rather drown a puppy than tell this puppy his daddy had been murdered. It didn't make any difference to me that it could have been either of them who did it.

"What?" Eric said.

I took a deep breath. "Last night I talked with a man from the police. He said that Melvin's accident . . . wasn't."

"Wasn't an accident?"

"That's what they think."

He stared right at me for a long time. "Someone killed him?"

"That's what they think," I said again.

"Do they know who?"

I tried to remember: what had I first said when Wilcox told me?

"I don't think they do."

"Who would want to?"

Did he really mean that? Was he that innocent?

"That's what the police will try to find out." I couldn't tell if it was worse for Eric that Melvin had been killed, or just that there might have been someone who would have wanted to kill him. He really didn't grasp what kind of man Melvin had been.

"How would they have done it?"

"The policeman said it was the brakes."

"The hydraulics or the pads?"

This was a puppy with a degree in mechanical engineering. "He said the lines had been drained."

He frowned. "How could they tell?"

"I guess they were empty."

He shook his head. "But I saw the car. The front axle was so smashed that the hydraulic lines were torn off. There's no way to tell if they'd been empty before the crash. And he would have known right away that something was wrong. Do they think it happened at Mr. Spellman's house? It couldn't have been low on brake fluid for very long."

"I don't know. Maybe we'll find out soon."

He put his chin on his hand and stared. "I . . . I wonder who would kill him." Then he was quiet. At least that was done.

It wasn't, though. Katie had a question. "What about Angela?"

"She could have killed him." No, I didn't say that, but only barely. Instead I said, "One of us needs to tell her."

"We should go over together."

Yes, we should. It was an hour to the big house, an hour to tell her, an hour back. I could get to Fred's office by eight. I had one more word for Eric.

"This is not public yet," I said. "Don't talk about it, okay?"

"Who would I talk to?" The kid must have some friends.

"If someone calls. A reporter maybe. Just hang up and call me."

"Okay."

"That's Rule 86—don't talk to anyone about it."

I left Eric to the hamburger Rosita had fixed for him and went back to my office, and dialed.

"Yes, honey?"

"Pamela," I said. "Would you please pay Eric's bills for me?"

"I'll do it this afternoon. Do I still have access to the personal expenses account?"

"I think so. Thank you very much."

Twenty minutes later Katie had changed into a somber dress and her pearls, and we were waving good-bye as Motorcycle Man shattered the peace of our neighbors. Then we were on the roads I knew so well, away from the city and down the coast. It wasn't that I had driven them with such frequency, but rather with such portent. It had been the Road to Melvin. What was this the road to now?

My card still worked at the gate, of course. We circled around the front lawn and into the courtyard, the endless brick walls surrounding us. The wings on either side were two stories, and the monolithic mass in front was three. Forty-eight windows looked down on us as we stepped out of the car. I used to count them every time I came home from boarding school.

Angela was expecting us. We were shown in to a feathery front parlor that Melvin had never used. It had always been hers. The rest of the house hadn't changed, but it had the feeling of a corpse at a viewing—the soul was gone. Angela had some of that feeling about her, too.

She watched me with her wide eyes, her fluffy lashes flittering about them. We smiled and exchanged just a few pleasantries, but she knew there had to be something unpleasant lurking. And Katie was looking at me.

"Angela," I said. "I'm sorry, but I have some bad news."

"I was afraid it must be," she whispered.

"The police believe that Melvin's death wasn't an accident."

Little tears glistened under the lashes, but not surprise. "Oh dear. I was so hoping it would just be over." She sighed. "When you called, I knew what you were going to say."

Well, it wasn't the same thing everyone else had said. "You suspected?"

She smiled, so sadly. "He had always been afraid that this might happen."

"He said that?" I had never before spoken abruptly to Angela, for fear of something breaking.

"No. But Emmanuel, the gardener, was really a bodyguard. Melvin never told anyone, but I knew."

Emmanuel had been there for years. "Did you have any idea who he was worried about?"

"No. And I wouldn't have asked, of course."

Of course. Poor Angela. Mr. Wilcox of the morbid mustache was going to give her a hard time. But she could defend herself.

She was not interested in brake fluid or other details, so I asked if I could look around a little. I left her and Katie to talk while I went on a nostalgia trip.

To me, the house had been an official place, for the formal occasions and staged events that made up our family relations. I found it uninteresting. I stood in the echoing foyer with the stairs on either wall. I wandered the halls, looked into the vast ballroom that he had never once used. Then I came to his office—a room of wood paneling and deep carpet, shelves lined with books he had never read. The walls were hung with original paintings, lesser known works by American luminists—cragged mountains by Kensett, storm-swept seas by Lane. A huge antique globe on a stand and his massive antique desk and wooden armchair sat before a wide window.

Later, Katie and Angela found me sitting at the desk, looking through drawers. It was a little awkward, but I apologized.

"I should have asked," I said.

"No, no," Angela mewed. "It's right for you to be here. This is your place now."

"I'll need to come back and go through his papers," I said. I'd found a few of the details that Fred had mentioned concerning Melvin's contract business with the state—the 'other legal framework' that I should be thankful was already in place for me. It was going to take a while to go through these drawers, and I didn't know where else he might have papers stashed.

But it had been something else I was looking for. There was a beautiful picture of Angela on the desk, but I'd wanted to see what he had of his first wife, and I'd found nothing, and nothing of his sons. I guess I hadn't really expected any, so I didn't know why it hurt. Maybe I felt he owed me something for what I was going through.

We left the house in a different confusion than we'd come.

"A penny for your thoughts." Stately Boyer Manor was fading into the distance behind us.

"I don't want more money," I said.

"What should I offer you?" Katie said.

"No. I mean that's my thoughts. You owe me a penny."

"That doesn't make sense." Some stretches of the road were tawdry with old gas stations, run-down diners, and tacky souvenir shops. These were in contrast with the stretches that were tawdry with new gas stations, plastic fast-food restaurants, and bland strip shopping centers. "I'll think of something else to give you."

"I don't want anything."

"Are you being surly?"

"Half."

She took note of the clenched jaw and pursed lips. "What's the other half?"

"That bothered me, Katie."

"Being at the house?"

"It made me feel like I was Melvin."

"What does that mean, anyway?"

"It means doing things that I never thought I'd do. I'm violating something inside myself."

"What have you done?"

"I'm having a feud with the governor."

"I've never liked him." We were passing through farms and villages now—much more scenic than the coast.

"I'm starting to dislike him a lot more," I said. "And when you're

Melvin, you don't just dislike a governor. You do something about it."

"What do you do?"

"That's what the world is wondering."

9

"So. Have you come up with some type of plan?" Fred was set very far back in his chair, at as great a distance from me and my reck-lessness as he could get.

"Yes, some type of one."

"What type?"

I laughed at the richness of his disdain. "And you still want to negotiate with the terrorists?"

"He is a governor, not a terrorist."

"Explain the difference."

He shook his head. "Tell me what you've thought of."

"The governor is corrupt. I'll expose him."

Fred blinked. "A good deal of his corruption has been as your partner."

"Not my partner."

"With the Boyer businesses. You know what I mean."

"But not with me."

His eyes narrowed. "What do you mean?"

"I was in Melvin's office this afternoon. I have enough evidence to sink Bright and half his administration with him."

Fred's mouth was open, but it took a while for words to come out.

"Of course you do." He could have added "you idiot," but it was there without being spoken. "You can't use any of it."

"I can."

"You'll destroy your own businesses."

"No. Somebody on my side will take the fall—whoever deserves it. I've been looking through Melvin's papers and I'm starting to figure out who that is. But of the two biggest crooks, one is in the governor's mansion, and the other is in his heavenly mansion."

Fred Spellman was reeling. "This would destroy your father's reputation."

"Where he is, he doesn't need it."

I had managed to disgust Fred, although there was also admiration in his look. "Where did you get this idea?"

Where, indeed. There were two answers to that one. The first was that it was obvious. Only a twisted, corrupt mind could have failed to see a plan so straightforward and honest.

But the second answer was corrupt, and much more twisted, and it was the real answer. The idea was a witch's brew: eye of newt, wart of toad, smoke of Nathan Kern, essence of Oedipus, hot blood of Boyer.

The main ingredient was the opportunity to get back at Melvin for every wrong against me. For ignoring me for twenty-eight years, for building an evil empire and then getting murdered and leaving me as his chosen replacement emperor. But add a pinch of Nathan's sanctimony concerning power and corruption for thickening and body, a dash of the prospect of Governor Bright's demolition for flavor, and a splash of hydraulic brake fluid as a little extra spice, and it was a potent concoction. Heat it over a hot temper and it was irresistible.

"I don't know," I answered.

"This is a bull in a . . . a . . ." Analogies were failing him. "In a dynamite factory. A herd of bulls."

"Calm down, Fred. Let's just talk about it a little."

"Then say something reasonable." He wasn't buying it. But he had to listen to me.

"I've taken over from Melvin and I've found out what he was doing. Now I want to make it right."

"You're much too young and inexperienced to try something like this."

"That's why I'm doing it. I'm young and idealistic."

That brought a fairly violent snort. "You are nothing of the sort."

"I might be."

"Your businesses are implicated. Melvin was not the only one involved. Bright will name names. He'll try to take everything you have down with him."

I shrugged. "Then they'll go down. They'll only be getting what they deserve."

"These are your highest officers and managers."

"Not the highest. One rank down. I'll pay fines. I'll help them as much as they deserve. The businesses will survive."

"Maybe." Fred had had enough. "Maybe they will. You wouldn't know. That is your greatest risk. Yes, you might cause significant damage to the governor without damaging yourself. But you would be removing the shelter your businesses currently enjoy. I am no businessman, but even I can guess what might happen."

"I can guess, too. They'll have to adjust."

"And with your immense business experience, you will lead them through this adjustment. Or will you have rid yourself of them first?"

"I won't answer that."

"You have no answer. You are proposing a reckless, foolish, lunatic plan."

"Yours is no better."

"Yes it is. Of course it is! It's realistic and prudent. It's what Bright is expecting, and he'll come to an agreement. What gives you the right to dictate to the governor?"

"Apparently someone has to. It's my job as king, isn't it? The man is a criminal."

"Don't be ridiculous."

We were stuck. I didn't want to just walk out, but I wasn't going to argue.

"Okay, Fred. We'll send out a warning. I've started looking through Melvin's papers, and I have some concerns to discuss with the governor. Or Clinton Grainger. Or that police detective, Wilcox. You tell me how to do it. That's about the same level of threat he's thrown at us."

Fred was scowling. "It's still leading into very dangerous territory."

"We're already there."

"I'll consider it. But I'm not advising you to do this."

"You've made that very clear, Fred. Remember what I said before. As far as I'm concerned, I'm still in the locked room and the man is still shooting at me."

"In your analogy, do you also have a gun?"

"In this case, yes."

Three days in my life had now passed since I had taken the throne. It took God six days to make the world, and then he needed a day off. I figured I was on the same pace. Another three days like these, and I would have about demolished everything he had done. Wait . . . not what God had made, just what Melvin had. God, Melvin—it was easy to get them mixed up.

What was the point of being rich if you still drove home from work every night just like any working peasant? I was stuck in traffic, and it wasn't helping my attitude.

Katie was right. We needed a better place to live. I didn't care what our guests and admirers thought, but to me the house felt vulnerable. Anybody could walk in the front door: a reporter, a murderer, whoever. I was surprised we hadn't had one of them knock on the door yet.

A reporter. Not a murderer.

So—a new house. Somewhere more secure. That would keep Katie busy for a while.

Oh yeah, murderer, right. Where were we on that one? I still had my list. Nathan Kern, too pious. Eric, too ingenuous. Katie, too unimaginative, or at least too mechanically challenged. Fred, too . . . actually, Fred seemed pretty likely.

It was just the list of people I knew, not the list of business rivals and politicians and mobsters the police would have come up with. But if it was someone I didn't know, I wouldn't care. Hopefully it would turn out to be a hit man that Governor Bright had hired—not that the police would ever press that charge.

The traffic moved a hundred yards and stopped.

I needed a break. I'd go somewhere for the weekend.

Katie had suggested Europe, but I wouldn't do that without her, and I wanted to be alone. Then I remembered the townhouse in Washington.

The cars were moving again, and I stuffed the whole murder suitcase into the trunk. I'd get to it later. I had more important things to work out at the moment.

"I have a job for you," I said to Katie over chicken Marsala. It's one of Rosita's best meals.

"What?" Her eyes sparkled. I don't know how she makes them do that.

"Buy us a new house."

"A what?" I was glad I could still surprise her.

"You're right. We need to move." I didn't want to make it sound scary. "I want someplace less accessible."

What she heard was, somewhere exclusive. Which was what I wanted her to hear.

But then she frowned. "By myself?"

"I'm getting real busy."

"But, Jason . . . I wanted to look together, with you. It'll be for both of us."

"Francine can help."

"Mother's leaving for Florida in two weeks."

"I bet it won't take that long. When you get it narrowed down, I'll go."

That was okay. She smiled. "What should I look for?"

"I don't think I want it as huge as Angela's place, or as far from town."

"All right. How soon would we move?"

"Right away," I said. This was her dream come true—even if she'd be flying solo. I didn't want her to faint, so I gave her a few more seconds to recover her equilibrium. Then I said, "And it really doesn't matter how much it costs."

Thursday dawned bright and clear and I saw it happen. When I got back to the house, huffing and puffing, Katie was up and dressed for lots of walking.

"It's too late to change your mind," she said.

"I won't. Who was the lady we used to get this house?"

"Harriet Postagini. I'm meeting her at noon."

Noon? "Why wait that long?"

"I told Eric I'd take him shopping this morning."

"Right. Be real sweet to him. And like I said, we're paying."

I was in a better mood that morning. I sat in my office for twenty minutes just being calm. Then it was time for not being calm.

"I'm not happy about this." It was true: Fred's voice in the phone was very unhappy.

"I agree," I said. "But it's not my fault. Bright started it. Do you have a suggestion for the best way to poke him, or should I think of something?"

"There is no best way."

"Okay. Is there some way that's less terrible?"

"Remember, I'm not advising that you follow this plan."

"I understand."

"You should be indirect to keep them confused, and to keep your own options open. Don't talk to Grainger or Bright directly in any way that they can ask you questions, unless you're willing to deal."

"I'm not."

"You should be."

"I'm not, yet."

"That's slightly better. Talk to Stanley Morton. Don't tell him any more than you need to, but get him to set a reporter on Clinton Grainger. Grainger needs to be asked if he's worried that Jason Boyer might uncover anything questionable about Melvin Boyer's dealings with the governor. You understand what I mean."

"Yes. They shouldn't ask the governor directly?"

"By asking Grainger, you will be indicating that this is a warning, not yet an actual attack. And who knows what the governor might answer. Also, go through your father's papers, quickly. You'll need to be ready for the governor's response."

"I'm getting them from his office this afternoon."

"Good. You should get them into a more secure place, as well."

"I'm planning to."

We said our good-byes, and I noticed the time. It had been exactly one week ago that Fred had read us Melvin's will, and the world had turned upside down.

I took Stan Morton to lunch. Not too direct, not too elusive.

"I've got an issue with Governor Bright."

We were high above the ground, in a very expensive French restaurant, at a table in the corner of two long windowed walls. Stan leaned forward, the better to hear my newsworthy words.

"Oh, do you?"

"I'm not sure the dealings between him and my companies have always been completely legitimate."

Stan blinked, once, then swallowed. "Of course they haven't been." I was really getting to like him.

"I wouldn't have known. I was never involved."

His eyes narrowed. "Are you telling me you're surprised?"

"Shocked. It's amazing how innocent I've been."

"I see." He leaned back. "So what's your issue with the governor?"

"What I just said, that I'm worried about what might happen to my businesses if anything became public. And I'd be especially worried for him. It might hurt me, but it could really hurt him."

"Is he worried?"

"I don't know. I think you should have someone ask him. Or it would be even better to ask Clinton Grainger. Maybe this afternoon, if you could manage it. I could write out the questions for you."

"My reporters know how to ask their own questions."

"Sure. It could be something like, 'Are you worried that Jason Boyer might go public with details of Melvin Boyer's deals with Governor Bright? The governor would have much more to lose than the Boyers.'"

"I understand. So what's your real issue with the governor?"

"No comment."

He smiled. "If you're trying to send a message, we've got a classified section."

"I'm not sure the governor reads the classifieds. I could call him, but politicians always pay extra attention to reporters."

"Yeah, I get it. I should charge you for a full page ad."

"No problem. What does that cost?"

"In this case . . ." He paused. "I'll put it on your account and bill you later."

"Then I want account credit for all the extra newspapers you sell," I said.

I was again shown into Angela's parlor. Without Katie, the greeting was much more formal, but I was as respectful as I could be.

"I need to go through Melvin's office," I said.

She nodded. "I understand. Will you take anything?"

"Yes. All his papers."

"I suppose they really are yours," she said. We were back to the way we'd always been—uncomfortable and softly hostile.

"I'm sorry to disturb you."

"It's no matter."

I could see her getting colder by the moment.

"Is the man you mentioned, Emmanuel, still here?"

"No. He hasn't been back since the accident."

I was in the office for two hours, packing and searching. Melvin had never chosen to own a computer, so I didn't have to deal with that. I wasn't reading everything, just organizing it in my boxes, but I could already tell the future was dim for Harry Bright.

I took only the state government file; I left the files on the foundation. That would be another day's job. And I was getting the creeps, too. The room was so much his, I felt like he'd walk in. Then I'd sure be in trouble. But after the last few days, I was mad enough to stand up to him.

I carried the boxes out to my car and looked in to Angela's parlor to say good-bye, but she was not there. I didn't look for her. It was only as I was accelerating down the driveway that I saw a brief flash of pink and platinum in a second-floor window.

I stopped at my bank and got a big safe-deposit box.

Katie's mother joined us for the evening. Francine had helped look at houses. She was in her usual crusty mood, torn between the pleasure of her daughter's good fortune and the pain of that fortune being through me. Behind every successful man stands a supportive wife and a very suspicious mother-in-law.

"Did you enjoy your afternoon?" I said to her. I wanted to see what she'd have to complain about.

She glared at me over her glasses. "Those big houses are so exhausting to look through."

It's almost a game. "I'll tell Katie to look at smaller places."

"If the big ones are too expensive, just say so, Jason."

"That's not what he meant, Mother," Katie said.

"She has a point, dear," I said. "You should let her pick some houses to look at, ones she thinks I deserve." I smiled sweetly at the dear little lady. "Maybe some one-room shacks."

She smirked back at me. "When I see what you move into, I'll know the truth about this so-called billion dollars. Have you seen an actual bank statement, Katie?"

"You two deserve each other," Katie said. It might be true. Sometimes I'm not sure but that I actually like Francine.

But our banter was cut short. Eric, scrubbed and shiny, was being presented.

Whatever-random-item-was-on-the-first-rack-at-Macy's Eric was gone. But instead of the feared Jason-Boyer-clone casual, tailored, and wealthy look, Katie had started from scratch and invented a whole new Eric—Eric the Untamed and Adorable.

"We started with play clothes today," Katie said. "We're just experimenting."

He changed twice in order to show the whole line, he was enjoying himself so much. Denim, leather, burnt oranges and dark blues—Katie was a master and he was a blank canvas.

Katie had not neglected herself. In the spirit of the morning, she'd snagged herself a leather jacket. It would be for those moments when she wanted to walk on the wild side, like maybe if we went to a restaurant where we had to park our own car and walk all the way from the lot.

And the little tykes had even remembered Daddy. I received a new windbreaker, which I liked, to keep on the boat, and I wondered how such a nautical preppy item could have been found within twenty miles of the establishments they had been patronizing.

And that had been only half of the exciting day!

Katie and Francine had viewed five houses and considered two as barely possible. Much more touring was planned.

Could they show me anything? I asked.

Of course! There were glossy photographs of stately estates and massive manors. I timed myself to look through them for at least three minutes and forty-five seconds.

"Harriet said it's a wonderful time to be looking. There's quite a bit on the market."

So Katie would have plenty to do. I thanked her for her hard work and encouraged her to keep it up. She needed very little encouraging.

"And you can keep going with her," I said to Francine, "if you'll be civil. You could use the exercise."

"I'm always civil, to her," Francine said.

"Is she?" I asked Katie.

"Of course. You might try it yourself."

But we were really all happy. Katie was buying a new house, Francine was having some excitement, Eric was feeling loved, and I had something of my own to look forward to.

"I'm going out of town this weekend," I said. "Down to Washington, on business. Just by myself."

11

I hadn't heard from Fred by Friday morning.
If Stan's lackey had not yet penetrated to
Clinton Grainger, he surely would before the
sun set.

I kissed Katie as she rushed out the door, made three business-
related calls, and packed and carried my suitcase out to my car.

But the drive to the airport was interrupted. I pulled off the
road as my phone rang, as it would be a distracting call.

"Come into town at once," Fred ordered. Stan's lackey had
been successful. If only I could get my own lackey to be as sub-
servient.

"I'm on my way out of town."

"Grainger is sitting in front of me." In my chair, probably. Now
what to do? This was more of a reaction than we'd expected.

Fred had said it himself—don't talk with the man unless I was
ready to deal. Well, I might as well talk to him.

"Okay, Fred. It'll take me a half hour. Keep him happy."

"Neither of us is happy."

That Fred, such a clown. As I turned the car and headed back,
I thought about the jovial Uncle Fred of my youth. One week had

erased that fraud quite thoroughly. I called the charter office at the airport and told them I'd be late.

Thirty-seven minutes later I stepped out of the elevator onto the thirtieth floor. Fred's office door was at the end of the hall. I decided they hadn't waited long enough.

If I hadn't been in a hurry to get on with my trip, I would have waited longer than five minutes. But finally their impatience was rewarded and I made my entrance into their gloomy den.

No pleasantries were exchanged.

"Mr. Grainger has been asking me about a newspaper reporter," Fred announced, pretending ignorance. Grainger just turned to stare at me.

I sat on the sofa. "What's your question?" I asked the watery eyes.

"Are you threatening the governor?" they asked back.

"It seemed the governor was threatening me."

Pause. Hard thinking. "This is dangerous," Grainger answered.

"I didn't start it."

"Your father did."

"Not this round."

Pause again. More hard thinking, this time with wrinkled brow. "Are you serious?"

It was time for sentences with more than five words. "It's been two weeks since Melvin died. I've only been on this job for five days. I think the governor needs to back off until I've had time to make some rational plans. Otherwise I'll do something irrational. A friend told me I was a bull in a china shop, and I'd consider the governor a big Ming vase right in the middle of the aisle."

"I can't call off a murder investigation," Grainger said.

Good, we were communicating. "Do you have any real evidence that Melvin was murdered? Or have you fabricated it all?"

"Do you have any evidence that the governor is corrupt?"

"Boxes of it."

Spit it out, Clinton. Was the old man really murdered?

"I believe the evidence was not conclusive," he said.

"Give me a straight answer."

"I don't know." A little frustration, perhaps? "A routine investigation had already been started. Detective Wilcox was directed to make sure something was found. I don't know whether the evidence was fabricated or not."

"Then un-fabricate it."

"I can't interfere with the state police."

"Then I'll give my boxes to the FBI, and I know you can't interfere with them."

"I'll discuss this with the governor."

I'd been in the room less than four minutes before he left. I like efficient people.

Fred glared at the door as it closed behind his guest. Then he glared at me. But not as angrily.

"You told me you wouldn't negotiate."

"I'm not. I'm dictating."

"It seems to come to you quite naturally."

"It's in my blood."

He shrugged. "The risk of real conflict is now very high, and it is your fault. You handled the conversation reasonably well, though."

"Thank you, I guess."

He nodded. "Yes. You are hotheaded and impatient, but I can see the same instincts your father had."

"I take back the thank-you."

He only smiled. "You are leaving town?"

"I'll call you Sunday night, when I get back."

"Where are you going?"

"Washington. I'm taking a vacation."

Fred was suspicious. "What is in Washington?"

"There are museums."

He didn't buy it. "Why are you going to Washington?" He was asking a lot of questions.

"Melvin lived there twelve years. I want to see the townhouse. It was a second home when I was in college."

He was still not satisfied. "I don't believe you are going for sentimental reasons."

"I don't care what you believe."

"Are you meeting with anyone?"

I was choosing to not be annoyed by the interrogation. "I'm not planning to. I just want to get away. I haven't had time to think this week."

Fred's gears were cranking. "Meet with Forrester."

Yuck. "Senator Forrester? I don't want to."

"You need to. It's time." He picked up his phone. "Get me Bob Forrester."

I chose to be annoyed. "Wait a minute."

"He can help you against the governor."

A powwow with Senator Forrester was not something I'd really been anxious to schedule. All us rich and powerful types, even marginal ones such as I had once used to be, had passed beneath the shadow of his loftiness. Not that most of us would ever be accepted socially.

"If I want help, I'll ask."

"Governor Bright may ask him first."

My growing impression was that Bright headed the sleaze faction of state politics and Forrester headed the snob faction. "Would they work together?"

"They never have. Your father prevented it."

Melvin had been able to move back and forth between the two factions so easily.

The phone buzzed. "Yes?" Fred said to it. Then, "I'll hold."

"I have a question," I said. "I met Big Bob at Melvin's townhouse in Washington about ten years ago. He wouldn't shake my hand. He obviously despised me, and Melvin, and everything to do with us. Was it personal or was it just general contempt?"

"Both." Fred chortled a bit. "He doesn't care much for anyone beneath him, which would be everyone. Newly rich upstart industrialists are especially painful to him."

"That doesn't sound like a good personality trait for a political career."

"Yes, most patricians don't dirty their hands with politics."

I could see the vague outline of something. "So Bob Forrester is ambitious?"

"Extremely. There is a driving force in certain people." Fred was philosophizing. It was soothing to him, after the seismic tremors I was causing to his world, to contemplate the unalterable nature of humans. "And anyone who is driven can be manipulated."

Yes, the outline was becoming clearer. It was Melvin's hand. "So there was a deal."

Fred smiled. His pupil was learning quickly. "Of course there was."

"Melvin sold him the Senate seat. What was the price?"

"It was more a rental than a sale. The rules are that the Boyer machine will get him elected, and he is not to build his own organization. He is to do as he is told. Outside of that he is free to preen and strut as he wishes."

"That sounds like Melvin might have wanted the seat back."

"Possibly." Fred stretched out the last syllable like a piece of taffy. "Mainly, it was to keep Forrester from becoming too powerful. But he may have wanted to keep the seat under his control for other reasons."

"He would have gone back to Washington?"

"No. He wouldn't have. But he could have been saving the seat for someone else."

As if it were a bus seat instead of a seat in the United States Senate. Why was Fred looking at me that way?

"You don't think . . ."

"I have no idea. But you will be thirty before the next election." A light was going on in his head. "Your father might have changed his will in your favor as part of a larger plan."

My head was going dark. "No. He changed his will because Nathan Kern asked him to."

"Your father never did anything at someone else's request. Perhaps Nathan did request the change. But Melvin wouldn't have made you his principal heir unless he chose to himself."

"Fred. The man hadn't spoken to me in three months. First he leaves me a billion dollars. Now you're adding a seat in the Senate. Don't you think he would have clued me in?" What am I doing here? Melvin's scorn for me was one of the great constants in my life, something I could always count on. Fred must be on drugs.

"Calm down, Jason."

"I am calm. You're the one who's raving."

"He would have discussed it with you. He did things in his own time."

"Except when he didn't, like getting himself killed."

"A rare exception."

"Right. And I bet he won't let it happen again. I don't think we're talking about the same person."

"I knew him much better than you."

"Yes. Exactly. Exactly. He and I didn't know each other at all. He had no plans for me."

"Then I won't argue. But why does it upset you?"

"I am not upset." Why was I so upset?

"Then when you are, it must be quite a sight."

"It is, believe me."

Fred's attention shifted to the phone. "Yes, this is Fred Spellman. I'm still here." Pause. Then the final connection. "Bob. Thank you for taking my call."

And here was another Fred. Yes, it was still the same large object, no mistaking it, but the voice was respectful, deferential, submissive. In other words, completely fake.

"Yes, I'm here with Jason Boyer. . . . That's right. He'll be in Washington this afternoon and tomorrow, and he asked me to schedule a short meeting, if there is a convenient time. . . . Yes, just to introduce himself to the important people in state politics, the people his father knew. . . . All right, yes, that would be fine. I'll tell him. I appreciate it very much, Bob. Thank you. . . . Thank you. Yes."

He set the phone down and stared at it with pursed lips.

"Disagreeable." He looked up at me. "You may have your secretary call his to arrange a time."

I had taken a deep breath. I was no longer upset, not that I had been anyway. "Is he seeing me because I'm rich and powerful or does he want to renew the deal?"

"The former. If you mention the deal, he will be offended and say he never heard of such a thing. But he knows he has to meet you, and he is wondering what you will do. He may feel that, at this point, the seat is his by right of his social position and tenure, and that you have no choice but to support him. I expect he will treat you as an important constituent and nothing more."

"But I can toss him."

"You could choose to not support him, which would make it very difficult for him to run again."

"Whatever. Do the voters get a say in any of this?"

"No. They are only allowed to choose between the party nominees, and the nomination processes are completely controlled."

"There are two parties."

"Each party has been allowed one Senate seat, and the candidates were approved by your father. He also chose every governor and representative in the last twenty years. No election has been close."

"I guess it's what I expected. Just like the state contract deals. Does it matter that it's rotten?"

"It is at least consistent. And it has been completely legal. The nominating process is straightforward: the biggest organization wins."

"I believe it stinks."

"I don't care what you believe. Look at the fools who get elected when no one is in charge."

I shrugged. "Okay. Never mind. What should I say to Forrester?"

He took his deep breath. "He can be as irrational as Harry Bright, but he is much smarter. He will be receiving information from his allies in the state senate, and he likely has indications about what is happening between you and the governor. You should talk about foreign affairs, talk about the economy, talk about the weather, and not use this as an opportunity to discuss political deals. But include one sentence about Harry Bright using the word *ineffective*, and he will know why you came. At this point, your main interest is to discourage any alliance between them. After your conversation, Senator Forrester will understand that he would be doing so against your wishes."

"Will he follow my wishes?"

"In this case, you both realize no precedent is being set. If you were giving him specific instructions, you would be much more forthright."

"Does he have anyone else to turn to?" I asked.

"He has lots of rich friends."

"Friends?"

"Acquaintances. He's the chairman of the board of the opera."

"The poor man."

"On the contrary, I believe he enjoys it."

Who needs a political machine when they have Felicity Nottingham Cavalieri Gildanov?

I called Pamela.

"I thought you were leaving town," she said.

"Almost. But I have a task for you. Call Senator Forrester's office to schedule a meeting between himself and myself. Your call is expected."

"When will you be available?"

"I'll get to Washington in a few hours and be there until Sunday afternoon."

"All right. . . . How much time do you want?"

"I don't know. It's all Fred's idea, not mine. Twenty minutes would be enough for me."

"Now, don't whine, Jason. It's part of the job."

"Don't you get on me, too," I whined.

It was late enough that I had lunch at the airport. I called Katie to check on her.

She was sounding worn out. "Angela called. She wanted to have lunch, but I just can't. I said you were gone, and I could do dinner tonight."

"You could try to make her not hate me," I said.

"I'll get it down to strong dislike. But it isn't personal, you know."

"No. She'd feel the same way toward anyone who was her husband's son."

I made one more call before I climbed into the airplane. Well, a couple, to get the right number. Then I waited ten minutes on hold, but finally I heard his voice.

"This is Wilcox."

"Detective Wilcox. This is Jason Boyer."

"Mr. Boyer. Yes, sir." The connection on my cell phone was tenuous, but I could still hear the tone in his words that I wanted to hear. "How can I help you?"

"I was just wondering how your investigation was going. It's been several days now."

"Well, Mr. Boyer, actually we've just had a meeting about it. We're giving the investigation a lower priority."

"Oh. Why is that?"

"We've had some questions about the evidence. The forensics lab is trying to be very careful, and they're not sure there's really enough to go on."

"I see. What does it mean to have a lower priority?"

"We'll keep the file open, but we won't commit any resources to it unless something new comes up."

"Well," I said, "I just wanted to know. Thank you."

"Yes, Mr. Boyer. Glad to help."

I could picture his mustache quivering as I took to the wind.

I have a fake driver's license and a credit card with the same name. Melvin had them created for me so that I could travel without being a Boyer. I might be ashamed of my real name, but I'd seldom used the fake.

For this trip, though, I decided Jeff Benson of Worcester, Massachusetts, would rent cars and manage any other transactions. I was becoming shy of publicity.

I let myself in to the Boyer Embassy in Georgetown. It was two side-by-side three-story townhouses, small by Boyer standards but large enough to entertain in intimate senatorial style.

I'd been there a dozen times during the twelve-year Washington residency. As a younger child, I'd not been welcome. I only visited Melvin and Angela when they were back home. In high school and college, when there was less chance of my breaking something valuable, I came for weekends two or three times a year. It had been empty, except for short visits, for the eight years that he'd loaned his Senate seat to Forrester.

This habitation was even more hostile in my memory than the big house, and now it was mine. I would stay in it and do as I wished. Maybe I'd shatter a Limoges plate on the Dutch-tile floor.

After I let myself in, though, I tiptoed up the stairs and set my suitcase quietly on the guestroom bed. But then, standing on the balcony over the living room, I got hold of myself and spoke to the ghosts.

"You're dead, Melvin."

There were even echoes.

"It's my house now."

And that was all I needed.

I walked through every floor, sweeping the memories away like cobwebs. Not that there were cobwebs. The place was still cleaned weekly and kept ready in wistful hope of being used.

There was no pink in the house anywhere. Angela had taken her things when they moved out, and she didn't travel with him when he came for business. Nothing there looked like she had touched it, or like anyone had touched it. Even the bedrooms were professionally furnished and barren of soul.

I found the Matisse. It didn't look very significant.

I read for a while that evening, but I soon found my eyes straying from the pages. I finally started walking the house again, looking through the rooms more carefully than I had before.

Yes, Melvin had been a senator. I was eight when he was first elected, three years after my mother died, and Eric and I had already been banished to the boarding schools that were our childhood. He'd married Angela a year later, here in Washington. She was twenty-eight, he was forty-three. We did not attend the wedding; at our young age, we could not be trusted to act with the proper decorum.

Our teachers and classmates all knew that Melvin was a senator. Of course, everyone at the school was cut from our same cloth, but even among the wealthy families and social elites, a senator would stand out. And if Eric and I had no real father, a senator would do.

Eventually the schools had rendered me presentable enough to be shown. I don't know whose hands I shook. There may have been cabinet secretaries and ambassadors. I know there were other senators. Those were the years the questions had started, the first Why am I here? It might have been from meeting so many important people and wondering what my value was.

The monthly checks started when I was in college. There was to be no making a living or working to put food on the table for me. No job to take my mind off the questions.

And now what? This was where Melvin had lived for twelve years. Maybe I'd find something here for myself.

12

I was up early Saturday to explore the neighborhood. The meeting was at ten.

No wonder Melvin had been drawn here.
This was a place for the powerful. It was writ-
ten in every storefront and every discreet, elegant facade. He'd had
equals here who weren't natural enemies, as well as many other
powerful people who had been less than equal. Only a handful had
been higher.

I walked to Capitol Hill. Melvin often had. Five blocks to the
head of Pennsylvania Avenue, then four miles to the Capitol. The
only thing that kept it from being a straight shot was the White
House smack dab in the way, and what thoughts that must have
put in his head. But he was a realist; he only owned one state, not
the whole country. Ultimately he'd come back home, where his
reign was unquestioned. Caesar or nothing.

And one of the few men who could question his position back
home was Bob Forrester. So Melvin had lured him away, to where
Bob could build his castle and Melvin owned the sand it was built
on.

I came to the senate office buildings and was expected. Then I
was accepted into the outer office of the senator. The greatest man
is still only a man, so his wealth and power have to be visible in

other ways. Big Bob was only a man—but through the window was the Capitol, and beyond it the Mall and the monuments and the departments and the great city. A man in that office would know he was very powerful.

The man stood as I entered his inner temple. "Jason Boyer," he said, standing taller than me. "I remember meeting you before, at your father's house." He stood very still, like a monument himself. It made him seem unmovable.

"I remember it, too," I said, choking back the *sir*. "It was after the election, at the end of his last term."

"Long ago." He turned to the window to make sure I had noticed the spectacle. "I want to offer you my sympathy concerning him. I didn't have an opportunity at his funeral." I was trying to remember. He hadn't been at the cemetery, only at the church. He'd sung the hymns off-key.

"Thank you." There are many shades of gray. Nathan Kern's hair, for example, was the discreet color of rain clouds. Bob Forrester's was light, marbled with darker veins. Each strand either black or white.

"I've entered a resolution in the Senate honoring his memory. There are still people here who remember him."

"Thank you again," I said. Since the first greeting he hadn't faced me. "Senator, I don't need to take much of your time. I wanted to meet you because your association with Melvin goes back a long time and was important to him."

He turned just his head toward me for a moment, and then away. "Yes. Although I'm afraid I didn't know him well personally."

Then he sat, and did not ask me to.

That made me angry. This was rudeness without reason unless there was a reason. My agenda was only to introduce myself and attempt to toss in the governor's name. The senator had his own agenda.

"I didn't mean socially. I've inherited his estate and his responsibilities."

"Indeed." It was a dismissal! He'd accepted the meeting for the purpose of snubbing me.

I did not accept it. It was a measure of the five days since my meeting with Clinton Grainger that I was not feeling at all intimidated in this conversation. As long as I was standing and he was sitting, I was taller. "You understand what I mean, Senator." If he would look at me at all, he'd have to look up.

He did look up and saw that I was still there. "Then take responsibility for your father's embarrassment in the governor's mansion. So far you haven't been able to." He had taken up his reading glasses. "And now, if you could excuse me. It has been a pleasure."

"I doubt that," I said. I walked out, but this time it was not a retreat, just a strategic move into camp, where I could begin my siege.

I sauntered back toward Georgetown, and it was an irate saunter. Melvin's kingdom was not passing to his heir easily.

I was back well before noon. I ate at an Indian restaurant, the hottest meal on the menu, and then I took a cold shower. Afterward I was still angry.

More walking finally helped, and I was civil enough later in the afternoon to call for a progress report from Katie, of which there was little, and to give a progress report to Fred, of whom there was much.

"Did you discuss the governor?"

"The senator brought the subject up."

"Did you suggest that Bright was ineffective?"

"It was not necessary to use that word. Bob supplied a much more pointed one. He's going to be a problem, Fred. He used the meeting to insult me."

"Bluntly?"

"We didn't even make it up to blunt," I said. "Do I have another war going?"

"Not necessarily. He has no reason to take any action against you, and we need nothing from him at the moment. It is just his opening position."

"For negotiations. Right. Would he attack if he had a reason?"

"No. He is not offensive."

"I'd say he is."

"No less than he finds you. Hopefully he will continue to find Governor Bright the same." Fred was bemused. "No, he usually is defensive rather than offensive. It is intriguing. It may mean he feels vulnerable."

"He didn't act like it. Who did Melvin use to control the state parties?"

"There are several people. That will be another set of meetings when the time comes."

"Kings have lots of meetings. I think I'd rather march an army into battle, the way kings used to do it."

"They probably had meetings back then, too. Some things are basic to the human soul."

I wandered the streets that evening and contemplated the basics of the human soul. The streets were crowded with Saturday merrymakers. It was a warm evening for October, but of course, I was in the South.

I mingled with them but I was not merry. These were basic human souls. They lived without what I had but they still lived, so it must be possible. Why would they want to? What were they doing here? Even without a billion dollars, they would still have the compromises and conflicts.

But I was not part of them. I was above the crowd, or outside it at least. There wasn't a correct preposition. What was the wall? The money? I was richer than all of them together, yet I was the one on the outside. What would it be like to be one of them?

13

Sunday I toured museums for a while. There are too many things in the world.

My homecoming Sunday night filled my wife with joy. Her weekend had been more fulfilling to her than mine had been to me. She had a house.

"It's empty," she said. "We could move in now."

"Was it anybody's we know?"

"No. A man named Gilchrist. He had some computer company that made him rich, and then he lost it. I didn't ask for details." She had no interest in people who lost their fortunes, or how.

"Is it new?"

"Just a few years old, and it's beautiful. Can you come to see it tomorrow?"

"Sure. About one thirty?"

She asked about my weekend, for show, but her attention was riveted on the new project. I was soon in my office.

I looked around the room, with its view over the back lawn and garden, the dark cherry desk, the bookcases and books. It was a comfortable place, and I'd miss it. But the first question I had to deal with was: Should I tell Katie that it had been broken into?

It was subtle, but I knew. Papers were not as I'd left them, the chair was at a different angle, and the books especially were noticeable. Governor Bright would not benefit from anything I had there; I was sure he was the ultimate culprit. I was glad Melvin's papers were in the bank.

I looked in the back of my desk drawer. I kept a cash envelope there, for convenience, with a few thousand dollars in it. It was out of place but intact.

Surely Melvin's office at the big house had been burgled, also. If Angela found out, she'd panic. Maybe the security there was good enough to keep the governor's minions at bay.

No, there was no need to tell Katie. I looked up the Gilchrist dwelling on the Internet. It was time to get out of our insecure little house.

Sometimes wealth is so wonderful. I used a fair amount Monday morning, and when I picked up Katie and Francine after lunch, I had a surprise for them. We drove thirty minutes away from town, even past a few farms, and then turned in at a discreet gate.

It was a nice place. It had that rough, rustic, honest feel that only a great deal of money can create. There was lots of stone and wood, a cozy, twenty-foot-tall fireplace that had taken a crane to erect, a friendly country kitchen that a Boston restaurant would envy; and just like any other old farmhouse, it had an indoor pool, wine cellar, sauna, greenhouse, and ten bedrooms. To complete the rural theme, it was on seventy acres.

"Stone floors are always cold." Francine had maintained a running commentary of flaws.

"I like cold floors," I said.

"You shouldn't make your wife walk on them."

"I'll teach her how to wear shoes. I think she has some."

"There are only a few rooms with the flagstones," Katie said. "We'll have rugs."

"There aren't enough cabinets in the kitchen, either."

We were standing among the dozens of them. "There are plenty," Katie said. "And there's a whole pantry, too."

"It's not a pantry," I said.

"What?" Katie opened the door. The room was about six by ten with two walls of shelves and two of floor-to-ceiling cabinets, with a plain wood floor and no windows. "Of course it is."

"No it isn't."

"He wouldn't know," Francine said.

"No," I said. "It's the mother-in-law suite." I leaned my elbow on one of the hard shelves. "This is where she sleeps. And why do you think the door locks from the outside? There's even room for more than one."

Katie only rolled her eyes, but Francine couldn't resist snapping back.

"I wouldn't put it past you to have another wife tucked away somewhere. What were you doing over the weekend, anyway?"

I ignored her again. "Are you sure you like it?" I said to Katie.

"I think it's wonderful," she said. There was no doubt she thought so.

"Well . . ." I put just a little doubt in my voice.

"What? Is it too much?" Would the candy be snatched from her hand?

"I told you," Francine said. "He can't afford it."

I ignored her again. Katie had my complete attention. "It's yours, babe. I bought it this morning."

Oh, what a gratifying reaction. Her mouth fell open, and she leaped onto me with a hug as big as the house. Francine smiled, too, but tried to hide it.

All it takes to create happiness is money.

14

Tuesday morning, and even if Katie was no longer occupied with looking for a house, moving would be a much more consuming task. Would we just bag up our few belongings, load them on the mule, and haul them to the new homestead?

"Jason, I don't know if any of this furniture will work in the new house. Mother and I have been discussing it. The living room suite would just be swallowed in that great room. And the table has been all right for a French Provincial dining room, but it would be completely out of place on that flagstone floor."

Completely. She could make do, of course, but I could feel her pain.

"It's okay, Katie. I want the house to be right. Of course you can get new furniture."

"Thank you, Jason." She gave me a sweet hug. Was she starting to take seven-digit checks for granted? Or maybe the task of furnishing all those acres of rooms was weighing heavily on her mind. Fortunately, she was not easily daunted.

Three days passed, and by Friday of my second week I was settling into a routine. There had been no distant thunder from the governor's mansion, Fred and I were back on speaking terms, and

Eric had behaved for a whole week. I'd behaved for a whole week. Was there anything really wrong with this life?

The day of the move had been set, three weeks hence, although we'd really be camping there until the rest of the furniture had been delivered. Much more money was flowing out of the bank account, and I decided it would be necessary to economize. I'd have to not buy another house for at least a month.

"How's Angela?" I asked Katie that night at dinner.

"Life is very hard for her."

"How so?"

"Loneliness. She has nothing to live for."

She was just sitting in that house every day? "What could she be living for?" I asked. Not that I wanted to know. Any reason Angela had to live would probably have the opposite effect on me.

"I've been thinking. Could she do anything for your foundation?"

"Surely." Nathan would be back from Africa on Sunday. What could be done? "I wonder if she would be on the board?"

"Maybe. I'll ask her."

"Should I ask her?"

Katie shook her head. "She's still offended from when you ransacked Melvin's office."

"I didn't ransack it! I took papers that were business related."

"She said you left it a mess."

"Of course I didn't." And then I knew. "I was there Thursday a week ago. When did she actually look in the office?"

"I don't know. We talked about it Tuesday at lunch."

What should I say to Katie? Apparently the governor had sent a messier team to Melvin's office than he had sent to mine.

"I'll apologize to her. I really didn't mean to. I'll call after dinner."

"Maybe you should."

After Angela's maid answered, it was five minutes before she came to the phone, which gave me a long time to think.

"Yes?" came her little purr.

"Angela, this is Jason." Which she knew.

"Yes?" Exactly the same.

"I wanted to ask you to do something for me." That was the best I could come up with in five minutes.

"I'm not sure I'd be able to, Jason."

"I guess it would really be more for Melvin." Take that.

"What would that be?" If a marshmallow could talk, that's what it would sound like.

"I'd like for you to be on the board of the Boyer Foundation."

"Oh." It wasn't the word, just the vowel sound, drawn out, like a marshmallow being stepped on, real slowly. "Oh. I don't know if I could."

"I'm sure you could. You could be his voice on the board. You must understand his vision for the foundation better than anyone."

"Well, I don't know. What does Mr. Kern say?"

"He's still out of the country. But he'll be back tomorrow, and I'm sure he'll agree."

"I really don't think I could."

"You should, Angela. The foundation doesn't have Melvin anymore. It needs you."

"I really don't know."

"Please think about it."

"Maybe I will. Good-bye now." I don't like cats, and this is why. I decided to say nothing about the office.

"Good-bye, Angela."

The phone rang as soon as I had hung up.

"Hello, Pamela," I said.

"Hello, Jason. I'm calling to tell you your office is ready downtown."

"Thank you. Is there any furniture in it?"

"There were some things in storage. Let me know if you want it different."

"When will you move in?" I asked her.

"I'll be there Monday."

I was there Saturday.

Ah, the view was sweet from the corner office on the

forty-second floor. I was higher up than Bob Forrester, and he didn't own the view outside his window. I owned a lot of mine.

On the streets far below, the people wandered through their small existences, and maybe they glanced up at the highest point in the city and wondered who was there. I looked down at them and I didn't question why I was above them. Maybe I was finding the answer.

The room was worthy of its altitude. The desk was aluminum or steel, so modern it wouldn't even be in style for another ten years—but I liked it. I would have liked anything in that room. The carpet was dark blue and the walls a light gray. The two interior walls, that is. On the top floor, the windows were ceiling to floor. Those two walls were all glass.

On the dove colored walls were beautiful framed antique navigation maps of the waters I sailed so often. What a marvel, that Pamela. I leaned back in the desk chair and just comprehended who I was. It took a long time.

And then, onto that cold metal plateau of a desk, I poured Melvin's files.

After three hours I knew it all. Melvin had constructed his "special framework" very carefully. Four executives in my employ were the keystones. They were more crooked than snakes, very highly paid, and none of them had been on Fred's list of people I needed to get to know.

Yet they were straight arrows compared to the kleptocrats masquerading as state procurement officials. The whole racket amounted to highway robbery. Literally, in the case of the Department of Transportation.

None of it surprised me. Seeing it in print nauseated me.

And what was I supposed to do with it all? For how long could I legitimately claim to be surprised? At the moment, I could sink the governor and all his cronies at the cost of putting my own Gang of Four in prison. The longer I sat on it all, the more I became part of it.

Governor Bright knew that. He knew this smoking gun would soon be covered with my fingerprints. I was only safe as long as I could claim to be innocent. If I didn't use it soon, I never could. He didn't believe I would anyway.

And Fred's point was true—that the kingdom was brittle. I might take the governor down, but I'd be cracking my own foundation. Was I really enough of a leader to rebuild twenty or more companies into real, competitive, efficient businesses? Not likely. But was I enough of a leader to hold Melvin's framework together, and did I even want to?

I chose sixty pages that were incriminating enough just by themselves to send the framework up in flames, made copies, and stashed them in my briefcase. The wad of originals I locked in my safe room.

Then I leaned way back in my chair again to survey the world beneath my feet. I closed the door in my brain on the closet full of skeletons. Well, even if I was seated upon a mountain of graft and corruption, the view was very nice, and I wanted someone to show off to. I called Eric.

"Hey, are you doing anything?" he said.

"I'm looking out my window."

"What window?"

"Come and see."

"Where?"

"Take the elevator to Fred Spellman's office, but just keep going all the way up."

"Cool, Jason. I'll be right there."

Why am I here? To have a great time and enjoy my wonderful life. I called Katie and asked her to meet us downtown for an early dinner.

When I let Eric in, the joy of brotherhood flowed between us like Niagara Falls, except with dollar bills instead of water. He sat in my chair and appreciated every ounce of wealth and power represented by that room as much as I had.

He pointed to the fifteen-by-twenty-foot space between the desk and the door. "Right there. You should have a Corvette."

"For show. Right."

"Or a Jaguar. Like some people have a pool table or a bookcase in their office. A Jaguar, on the forty-second floor."

"You could probably spare one for me."

His eyes lit up. "I could! I could get a new one, and you could have the old one."

"A used car in my office?"

He leaned back. "Used by *me*. That's better than new."

There were no other chairs in the room, so I was leaning against the wall looking at him. "What would you do with your life if you weren't rich?"

"I guess we'll never know."

"Sometimes I think I'd like to try it."

"Philosophy makes my head hurt. Money is to spend, not to think about."

My brother had a transcendent ability to indulge himself; it was the only profound thing about him. "Rule Number 87—a little pain is good for you."

Eric shook his head in pity. "Where's supper?"

"Across the street."

We descended Olympus.

Nathan Kern called that evening, freshly back in his native habitat.

"Jason, this is Nathan Kern. I want to get together with you when you have an opportunity."

"Sure. How was your flight? It's a hard trip from Africa."

"I stopped in Switzerland on the way back at the World Health Organization. So today's flight wasn't bad at all. And the time in Africa was excellent. Quite excellent. Very illuminating. This is a whole new type of program for us, and I want to tell you about it."

"I'll look forward to that," I said, only half lying. "And, Nathan, I have a question. I wonder what you would think of putting Angela on the board."

"Angela? On the board of the foundation? Why, Jason, I think that might be an outstanding idea. Have you discussed it with her?"

"She had doubts. If you called her, she could probably be talked into it."

"I will. Certainly."

"And maybe I could come by the foundation Monday. I haven't seen the office."

"I will be there."

15

Life was so good that by Monday I was suffering from conflict deprivation.

I had the old reliable problems I could pull up at any time: all the corruption I owned; the governor, and now the senator, I was trying to own; Melvin's murder, if it had been, and by whom. They were all just different chocolate chips in the same cookie.

But the sun was shining, and the cookie gently crumbled.

I pointed the Mercedes west, around town, to a gentrified semi-suburb, still recognizable as the rural village it had once been. Just past a very upscale neighborhood, I turned through a gate in the stone wall, marked with an immense but tasteful bronze sign mounted on a massive stone pedestal.

Melvin H. Boyer Foundation.

A small parking lot appeared, and the two-story headquarters it earnestly served. The spaces were marked, *Mr. Hyde, Dr. Fitwell-Monoque, Dr. Grambling, Mr. M'fele,* and ultimately, *Mr. Kern.* The second row of spaces, occupied by twenty or more less prestigious cars, was not marked. The staff no doubt.

I set my car in a space marked *Visitor.*

The building itself, of mellowed brick and polished wood, might have been from the same architect as my new house, just with his dial changed from "House" to "Office." The budget knob was not changed from "Obviously Expensive."

The receptionist, whom I had never seen before, stood immediately as I entered.

The executive offices were arranged around the reception lobby and took up the whole first floor. I had only a moment to glance at the displays of good done that filled the room.

"Mr. Boyer. Mr. Kern is expecting you. Please come this way."

I was escorted into the prestigious office of the director.

This sumptuous room provided a second chance to be impressed by displays of the foundation's works, and wasn't the real purpose of the foundation to give a person a second chance? It was an eclectic mix of architectural models of inner city recreation centers, African *objets d'art*, photos of smiling state officials, and Nathan at his desk.

He leaped up at my appearing.

"Jason! What a pleasure." He shook my hand, and the receptionist retreated. "It is so good to see you!"

And it was. There was so much good for me to see. It was not the same as the opera, which was the grandiose height of human culture. This building was founded on a different importance—that of human worth. The budgets of the two were actually nearly the same.

I met Dr. Hugo Grambling, a sociologist, whose groundbreaking insight on the risks to youth of urban culture could hardly be underestimated. Dr. Gloria Fitwell-Monoque directed the foundation's programs in the schools. Mr. Cordele Hyde was at the state capital, lobbying on behalf of the disadvantaged.

I could direct Mr. Hyde to four of my own executives who could advise him on lobbying.

And Mr. Ebenezer M'fele was in New York at a UN conference on aid to developing countries. He had so greatly expanded the scope of the foundation's efforts since he had come on board the previous year. With the new African projects, they were truly thinking globally as well as locally.

We went upstairs to the staff offices. These people were not introduced to me, only pointed out. They were researchers, writers, and accountants—the full-time staff. Others were contracted in as needed.

The overhead alone for this operation, as I knew from George Elias, was four million a year, the majority of it executive salaries and their travel expenses. They spent six times that on programs.

So much good was done, one might wonder how any bad could be left in the world. At least, in this one state. But I knew better, at least concerning this one state.

As we passed the receptionist, she deferentially interrupted our tour.

"Mr. Rosenberg is faxing some papers."

"Very good. Set them on my desk." Nathan returned his full attention to me. "Jacob Rosenberg is our legal advisor. He is newly on the board. Your father was very impressed by him, and I'm sure you will be, also."

The ground floor was not all offices, I found. There was also the board room. Nathan and I settled there after the tour, amid yet more conspicuous exhibits of accomplished charity, and discussed the past and the future.

This had been the salve for Melvin's conscience, where it hadn't been seared senseless. Had he really had enough inner conflict that he'd needed this much of a foundation to ease his guilt? Was I going to have enough guilt that I needed something this big to ease mine? I tried to look at it objectively. Nathan was doing lots of good things. It was reasonable for a person with extra money to use some of it philanthropically. There didn't have to be other motives, and did the motives matter anyway?

"I expect I've been presumptuous," Nathan said, "simply assuming you would take on your father's role with the foundation." He lit a cigarette. We obviously needed a smokescreen for this conversation.

"It would have been a natural assumption," I said.

"Then I would like to ask you, what is your expectation? What do you think of the foundation?"

"I'm very impressed." Melvin probably had been. "And there's no question about the funding. That will continue as it has."

Nathan laughed. "I hadn't really had a chance to consider that it might not. That would have been upsetting!"

Upsetting, right. At least upsetting. I could imagine these experts trying to get real jobs.

"As for my own participation," I said, "I'm not sure. I'm willing to put money in. For now, we'll leave it at that."

"That's quite a lot."

"And I'd like to get together once in a while, Nathan. We started a conversation two weeks ago that I'd like to continue." I considered the man in front of me—sophisticated, sincere, intense, waiting patiently for the next words of this callow youth. "I've been going through Melvin's papers. The picture they're painting isn't nice."

"I understand."

"How do you feel about the money you got from him, knowing where it came from?"

He leaned back with a deep sigh. "I've simply done the best I could with it."

"I've been wondering," I said. I hadn't meant to get into this. "You warned me before, how money corrupts. I knew it was true, but now I've seen more closely how that works. What if . . ."

"Yes?" he said, after my long pause.

"What if I shut it all down? In some way that wouldn't put too many people out of work. But what if I got myself out of it all?"

His stare was piercing, right through me. As debonair as he might be, his eyes were the eyes of a very deep man.

"I think you would have done a very noble thing."

"Even if the foundation lost its funding?"

He took a moment to load, and let me have it with both barrels. "The foundation's good work is small compared to the evil that your family's business practices have wrought. On balance, shutting down the foundation would be a small price to pay to restore integrity to this state."

He said it calmly, which helped me listen the same way. Then I calmly considered whether I should deck him, and then whether I should just fire him.

"Well, I asked for it," I said. "You wouldn't have said that to Melvin."

"He wouldn't have asked. Would you actually consider taking such a step?"

"I don't think it's possible. The tumor is too big and too deep. The patient would die on the operating table."

We stepped back from the precipice. "It is something to think about," he said. "I agree it would be, at least, tumultuous."

Time for a new subject.

"Did you have a chance to call Angela?"

He smiled. "Yes. It was an excellent conversation. She didn't commit, but she had a number of questions. I think she will decide to join the board."

"Good," I said. "That will be to everyone's benefit."

Back toward my office. I decided I needed a second opinion on the meaning of life.

"Mr. Spellman's office," the voice said.

"This is Jason Boyer. Could you please tell him that I'd like to drop in, in about thirty minutes? If he's free."

"Just a moment." I was pulling out of the foundation parking lot. "He would be pleased to see you."

As much as I would be to see him. I got on the highway and crossed the vast space between Nathan Kern and Fred Spellman.

Fred was waiting, as large as life.

"I'm just checking in," I said. "Is anything happening?"

"From Governor Bright? No. I've heard nothing."

"Is that good?"

"Probably not. Although I expect he's still off-balance."

"I've been through Melvin's papers. I guess I know a lot of the details now."

"I would advise you to stay away from the individuals named in those papers."

"My own employees?"

"They're doing what you employ them to do."

"That's an interesting point," I said. "It was Melvin who employed those gentlemen."

"Of course."

"But I'm going to have to claim them as my own, sometime."

"Yes. In what context do you mean that?"

"I can't play ignorant forever."

"No. Are you worried that these people might betray you? Or that they might need encouragement that you continue to approve of their activities? That might be useful, but it should be done very carefully. With this type of person, a financial bonus would be the best way to enhance their cooperation."

Yes, this was certainly an alternative viewpoint on life.

"That had crossed my mind," I admitted. "But that's not what I mean. My threat against Governor Bright is to expose the whole bid-rigging arrangement. It's only a threat while I'm still supposedly innocent. But the threat fades the longer I don't use it."

"I know." He'd been through all those angles. "Which you should have considered earlier."

"What if I still mean to carry through?"

"Then go ahead and do it, and get it over with." Apparently Fred was one person who no longer believed I would. What did that say for Bright or Grainger? "But Governor Bright will quickly decide you're not serious, if he hasn't already. If he ever thought you were. So I suggest you start working on your next step."

"I will think about it," I said. "Would you have any thoughts?"

"I wouldn't."

"Perhaps a financial bonus would enhance your cooperation?"

He scowled, but he did appreciate the humor. "Just remember, you are now the man in the locked room with the gun, and the governor is the desperate one, trying to disarm you. That may be just as dangerous a place to be in."

First opinion, second opinion—I wanted a third opinion. I got back into the elevator and pushed the up button.

There were signs of Pamela, but no Pamela. After the morning of facing other people in their offices, I settled into my own.

What is my opinion?

What am I doing here?

Pamela's gray head popped through the open door. "Jason?

There you are!" She blinked suddenly and dabbed at her eyes. "It's like your father sitting there."

That's what I'm doing here: being Melvin. Except I didn't hold her observation against her the way I did against Fred.

Instead, I jumped up and smiled and gave her a hug. Then I sat her down at her desk and I pulled up a chair and we talked for an hour. It was partly business, and a lot about old times.

It was a strange feeling, remembering my youth with someone who'd watched me go through it, and enjoying the conversation.

But then she had papers I'd asked for from George Elias and my corporate accountants, which easily filled my remaining afternoon hours. I was trying to get some handle on what would happen without Melvin's framework.

I called home at four, and Rosita told me Katie was out at the new house.

I surprised her there. The place was being transformed. Furniture was arriving, the grounds were trimmed—it was all feeling snug and homey and palatial.

Katie was in jeans and a sweatshirt and I was still in my suit.

"Do I have any other clothes here?" I asked.

"No. Everything's still at the old house."

"Are there any stores around here?"

I thought my wife might swoon. I called Rosita and told her to put dinner in the freezer, and Katie and I went shopping. Dressing Eric might have been fun, but he was no substitute for her own husband. The first place we found was a farm supply store, and I soon had a new identity in good, honest work clothes. My pants even had an actual hammer loop.

Autumn was running rampant through the trees. We took a slow back road and explored our new district. There were still farms and open spaces and countryside.

"I hope it stays this way," Katie said.

"I'll just buy it all. Then we can keep it the way we want."

The roads were lined with stone fences and paved with yellow leaves, and stands sold apple cider and Indian corn and fall flowers.

Everything was gold except the sky, and Katie had her head on my shoulder.

We got back to the house and I ordered pizza, just plain peasant food, and when it came thirty minutes later, I tipped the kid a hundred dollars. Katie was giggling like a high-school girl at the fun and adventure of it. We ate our first meal there sitting on the flagstones in the dining room, imagining our lives in that new place, the rulers of the world. That was my third opinion.

I went back out Wednesday to see the progress again. She was spending a huge amount, but no one could do it with better style.

On Thursday I was talking to some division president or other on the phone when Pamela tapped on my door.

"Mrs. Boyer's on the other line."

That was not what she called Katie, so it took me a second to realize who she meant. I threw the man overboard and switched lines.

"Hello? Angela?"

"Jason?"

"Yes, I'm here."

"Jason," the forlorn voice whimpered. "I won't be on that board."

"The foundation? Oh, Angela. Are you sure?"

"I won't."

"All right, Angela. Is something wrong?"

Something was wrong. Even Angela was not this erratic.

"I just won't."

"That's fine. Has something happened?"

"Good-bye, Jason."

It was fine. Completely fine. I slammed the phone down, but only after she'd already hung up. It would spare Nathan a lot of headaches to not have this person to deal with. I called him.

"Yes, Jason? This is Nathan Kern."

"Nathan, have you talked with Angela?"

"Well . . . yes . . . just last night. Did she call you?"

"This moment. She said she would not be on the board."

Long pause. "What else did she say?"

"That was all."

Long pause again. "She didn't say why?"

"No. Did she tell you last night?"

"Well, I talked with her quite a while about the foundation. But she actually seemed quite excited about it. She was very interested."

"In being on the board?"

"Yes. Absolutely."

"That's what she said?"

There was a long pause. "She still hadn't committed, but after the conversation I was certain she would."

"So she changed her mind," I said.

"She gave no reason at all?"

"No. I asked."

He sighed. "Very well. I will be out of town a few days, over the weekend, at a conference in Washington. I'll call her when I get back. How strange."

Exactly.

Not for the first time, Angela had ensured that Katie and I had something to talk about at dinner.

"She didn't say anything about why?" Katie asked.

"No."

"I'll talk to her."

"It's okay, really. I don't want a lunatic on the board."

"I think she just panicked. She felt she was being pushed too hard. She's really very fragile."

I shrugged. "I give up. From now on, I won't go near her. I obviously cause her great pain."

"Give her some time."

"No problem. She can have years if she wants."

I was tired. At that moment, I'd run out of energy for dealing with people. It had been a long three weeks.

Katie found me in my office later.

"I'm having lunch with her tomorrow."

"Good for you," I said. "I think I'm sailing for the weekend."

"Good."

"Yeah. A little recreation." No Fred, no Nathan, no Angela. Even no Katie, just for a weekend.

"You've been working very hard. Isn't it going to rain?"

"That's okay. I need gloom. It's good thinking weather."

"Don't think too hard."

"Not too hard."

"What will you be thinking about?"

"Meaning of life, purpose of existence, what color carpet for the hall upstairs."

She smiled, a little tightly. "I don't trust you with any of those."

"Then you can take care of the carpet."

"I don't think you should worry about the others, either."

"I probably will."

"Jason." That was what she didn't want to happen. "Everything is going very well. Don't try to make it seem wrong."

I nodded. "I'm trying to make it seem right."

16

Friday afternoon, the boat rocking on the waves, and I was alone.

What am I doing here? I ask that question a lot. So was I really serious about answering it?

There was a little haze, and the land twenty miles away was lost in it and the horizon edge of the water was dulled instead of sharp. The sky stretched above it all, blue and endless.

For the first time, at least since college, I had work to do and responsibility. Maybe that would be enough? Do the right thing, get up every morning, go to the office, bring home the paycheck. Works for a lot of people, even if their paycheck doesn't have so many digits.

Doesn't work for me. I put up some sail. I wanted to feel motion.

What was the wind in Fred's sails? Power, pure power; he was addicted. I could try addiction. I had the opportunity, and it wouldn't take long to get completely devoured. A quick and painless way to go. If I was really considering it, I must already be halfway gone. But I wasn't ready to give in yet.

Okay, put it on the shelf, but keep it handy. The wind was slowing, and my forward motion with it.

Self preservation. That one was good for dealing with the governor, but it was pretty limited. Ultimately it was just a method of living, not a reason. It felt good, though, and it was a good name for a lot of what I was doing, a better name than *anger* or *revenge* or whatever, even if those were more accurate.

My brother, the noted philosopher, suggested just maximizing pleasure. That only works if your pleasures are simple. Basically, it was the same as addiction.

I enjoyed Katie. Coming home to the wife, and someday children, was the big thing for most of those stiffs clogging the freeways at rush hour. It wasn't a good reason to sell my soul to Melvin's framework.

What was Katie's purpose in life? Recently, it had been to spend money, which was very addicting. Somehow, all the reasons were sounding the same.

Was there even a right reason? Did there have to be? Maybe it was my own personal problem that I was never satisfied. But I never was, and that was the only conclusion I could come to in the whole long afternoon.

The wind was gone, but I left the sail up. Something was missing from it all and I was stuck trying to figure it out. So . . . just forget it all. That would be the answer.

It was dark and I was lost at sea. There were no lights. I shook my head to wake up; I'd never before fallen asleep out from land alone like this. I flipped on the cabin lights, and they didn't. Nothing. The batteries were dead?

The GPS, the radio, nothing. No power.

At least the flashlight worked. I checked the electrical panel. Both batteries were dead. How long had I been sleeping? Six hours. Long enough for the refrigerator and the lights to drain every little electron.

In the dark, I pulled down the sail so I wouldn't get blown any farther out. If I'd been going in a straight line, home was behind me. I checked the compass to guess where I was. Lost at sea, basically. The Atlantic is big. I was probably out in it, out of the Sound.

The outboard was too big to start by hand. I tried anyway. The correct procedure was to use the batteries to start the motor, and use the motor to charge the batteries every few hours. Or just don't run them down.

Oh well. As long as I didn't get hit by a freighter or a hurricane, I'd make it through the night, and the forecast hadn't included any hurricanes. Just rain. I still had the sail and the wind, and in the morning light I could find my way home.

So much for having a billion dollars.

What a long night.

The earth turned very slowly—the stars stood still and I was dragged beneath them. I didn't feel like trying to sleep, so I listened to the sea and felt the wind. I saw some lights as ships passed, but all very far off. I didn't want to go down into the cabin, so I sat in the chill air. My new windbreaker helped some.

Maybe the cold was penance. What am I doing here, in the night? I couldn't forget the question, and the answer that satisfied in the daylight didn't work in the dark. The blue sky hadn't seemed bothered by my amateur musings; this black infinity mocked them.

But I was stronger. I could overcome dark and cold. I just couldn't make the clock move any faster.

It was a long night. Finally I slept.

Rain woke me, light drops on my face at four in the morning. I retreated below. There was plenty of food in the cooler Rosita had packed, and I ate ham sandwiches and cashews, waiting for the sun.

The rain tapped on the deck above, then drummed. When at last I'd finished the trip across the black side of the planet and came out under the sun again, the day was no less dismal. But it was good enough. With light, I was in charge again of my own fate.

I trimmed the sail and brought the boat around and headed back in something like the way I'd come. I didn't have a good wind, but I was moving.

I knew I must be, at least, but there was no sign of it. If I kept the heading northwest, I'd have to reach something.

The breeze failed, and I had to make do with gusts, from every direction, turning the sail to catch them. I was at the limit of my sailing skills.

The morning passed, I ate lunch, and even the endless afternoon sailed by faster than my boat. I really had no idea how far I was from anything. It was a hard day, and I finally admitted I'd be at sea for another night.

Katie would expect a call, but she knew sometimes it didn't work out. No one would look for me before Sunday evening, twenty-four hours away. Then it would be Monday before they could search, and only if the clouds broke.

Hurricanes and freighters—just avoid those two.

The lead sky faded to black, but at least I was tired. Sail down, secure the boat, eat. What was left in the cooler? Enough, but I ate sparingly. Ten o'clock with the rain still falling.

I was lost in the dark. There was a haven somewhere, a place for the boat to get to and be safe. What about for me? I had no such certainty. I didn't even know where I was to wonder why I was there.

I needed a wind behind me. It was midnight and my drifting was finally to sleep.

I woke disoriented, my bed alive. I fought to stay in it, but then I knew where I was, and I rushed up on deck. Stars swung wildly above. Waves coming over the side soaked me as I pulled up enough sail to bring the bow into them.

The rocking calmed, and it was back-to-front instead of side-to-side. Four o'clock again, black sky but a million stars, and a bunch of them in a long straight line along the horizon due north.

No more sleep. With the seas as high as they were, I needed to keep watch.

Two hours later I saw the end of the night. The water held the dark as long as it could, but the sky rushed into day. Then the sun breached the horizon, the water had its own cataclysm, and the sky was left behind with its cautious brightening. There were no clouds except in the farthest west, and they were the last to feel the day.

The stars and shore lights had disappeared. I couldn't see the shore but I knew where it was, and the wind was steady from the southwest.

The adventure was over.

I'd discovered Long Island. I put in to charge the batteries and call Katie.

"Montauk?" she said. "What are you doing there?"

"Just following the wind. I'll be home by six."

"Was everything okay?"

"Yeah, it was fine," I said. "Anything happening at home?"

"Fred wants you to call."

"I'm sure. I'm on vacation until I walk through the front door."

I was fully in the twenty-first century as I put into the wind, with GPS, radio, and food. Before noon I'd cleared Long Island, and the southwest wind was pushing me fast into the Sound and toward home. The last sixty miles took four hours.

I had the marina in sight at four thirty, back in my safe haven and right at the edge of cell phone range, and my cell phone rang. It was Katie.

"Jason?"

She sounded terrible.

"What's wrong, Katie?" She was sobbing, and I said again, "What's wrong?"

"It's Angela. She's dead."

17

I was holding Katie, telling her it was okay, we were okay, I was right here with her. It was like the last time, but only a little. Last time it was Melvin going over a cliff, but that was his own fault, in one way or another. He wasn't innocent.

Here I was holding Katie again, but it was much worse. It was too terrible to think of cottony Angela writing her little note, holding the gun to her head. How did she even know how to use a gun?

The rain had begun again. Katie had finished crying, and we had been sitting, just silent. Melvin's death had meant change, but Angela's meant only loss. Katie was grieving for Angela's despair that we couldn't help with, her loneliness that we couldn't fill, even the friendship, of some type at least, that was lost.

Eric arrived dripping, wide-eyed and somber. But this time he had experience, he could deal with it. I couldn't hold both of them, so I left them with each other.

Who was supposed to make the arrangements? Had anyone called her sister or brother? They were all estranged, of course. Only a funeral might bring them together. But Melvin's hadn't.

I called Fred. Good old Fred. Yes, all the arrangements had been made long ago by Melvin. Fred was executor—everything would be taken care of.

And by the way, just for my information, this would not cause any complications concerning any Boyer interests. All of Angela's connections with Melvin's estate were strictly for her lifetime only.

Which was now over.

"It also means you now have full rights over the main house and grounds," he said.

"I'll find a demolition company," I said back to him.

"Wait until after the funeral," he said. "You needn't be annoyed. I'm just advising you." He sounded annoyed.

"Then you wait until after the funeral, too."

"Very well. Have the police called you yet?"

"It was suicide."

"Supposedly, but if it isn't . . ."

I pushed the little button that made him go away. He didn't call back.

Nathan Kern called later to express his deepest regret and sympathy. I accepted just as deeply.

It was just four weeks since the last time. That had been on a Sunday, too, that we'd sat together mourning. But they really didn't know when it had happened, this time, Sunday morning or Saturday night. They just found her in her puffy pink parlor after she didn't show up for breakfast, and her bed hadn't been slept in. Three maids and a cook lived in the place. It sure took them a long time to notice she was missing.

They were all unemployed now, as well as the gardeners and other staff. Katie would fix that soon enough. We'd need a real staff for our new mansion. It was actually convenient. Although . . . Melvin and Angela, their two employers, both dead, one month apart. Before we hired these people, we might want to get references.

We had our own quiet dinner, the three of us, long after dark. It helped some, and Eric slept in the guest room. I didn't sleep in my own bed. I just laid there in it, even after Katie finally went to sleep. I'd been looking forward to a real night's rest, but it would have to wait.

We were all better in the morning. Katie wondered if we should go out to the big house, but she couldn't think of any reason why. She just wanted to do something.

"No one else will," she said.

"We'll wait until afterward," I said.

"What will happen to the house?"

"I haven't thought about it."

"Somebody has to live there."

"I'll call Nathan Kern. He probably knows lots of homeless people."

"Jason, be serious." Apparently we were not quite up to sarcasm yet.

So I thought about it seriously, for about fifteen seconds. "I guess I'll sell it."

"It's your father's house!"

"Do you want to live in that place?" I asked.

I never would. I'd sell that place as fast as it was decent. It was one part of Melvin I really could disown. Maybe I actually would find a demolition company.

No, I'd sell it and give the thirty pieces of silver to the foundation.

"Maybe it would be best to sell it," she said. "It would be an end."

Endings are good things. The morning ended and we could eat lunch. Eric's grief had pretty much ended, too, and he was ready to get back to self-indulgence.

"Do I need to say anything at the funeral?" he asked.

"No," I said. "I will."

"What about Aunt Celeste and Uncle Damon?"

"I haven't heard yet." Angela could've just as easily been at peace with her siblings, but they were all more comfortable with distrust. Celeste would get in from Los Angeles that afternoon, and hopefully she'd be over her jet lag soon enough to make it to the funeral. But she might not. Damon would drive up from New York, if he could reschedule his clients' appointments.

Probably the funeral parlor could rent us some mourners.

Eric had one more question. "Uh, Jason, could I borrow your suit again?"

"Yeah, sure." Katie had better start on his formal wardrobe if this was going to become routine. "Rule number 88—no motor-cycles when you're wearing my suit."

Stan Morton called to offer condolences, and I suggested that Angela would have wanted any news coverage to be very low-key.

"I'll try to respect that," he said. "But this whole story is reach-ing critical mass. First Melvin, and now this. And if the police announce it wasn't suicide it'll be front page."

"Just do what you have to," I said. "And you and I should talk soon."

The family had dispensed with the viewing due to lack of inter-est, so Monday night Katie rummaged out photo albums. I pre-tended to remember fondly the events that had pretended to be worth remembering: Christmases, fall days, Eric and I tossing foot-balls after Thanksgiving dinner, family times where we were all together. Graduation from St. Martins School, from Yale. They were beautiful pictures. When I had a chance to rid myself of the house, I would dispose of these albums, as well.

"Poor dear," Katie said over one picture of Angela and Melvin artificially lounging beside the pool. "What would she really have done with the rest of her life?"

With that, we came to the end of our own real mourning. Wasn't it much better for her this way? Might as well believe that. It had been her own decision to end it all—and we might as well believe that, too, as long as we could, and we'd believe that Melvin had died in an accident for good measure.

When we stopped believing it, I'd have some new questions. Two weeks before Angela died, I'd forced the police to drop the investigation into Melvin's death. If I hadn't, would Angela still be alive?

That night I still didn't sleep. I didn't deserve to.

Tuesday morning Eric came over and we all got dressed in our buryin' clothes. The big funeral limousine came to get us, the same one we'd ridden in for Melvin's funeral. I could have sworn I smelled Angela's perfume still in it.

The church was done up as lavishly as before, but, well, the truth is that the second time is just never the same. The flowers tried as hard as they could, and the candles glowed their little hearts out. It just wasn't Melvin. It was just Angela.

And, good golly, the casket was pink. Another funeral and I couldn't take my eyes off the box, but this time because it looked like a giant strawberry Popsicle. Couldn't someone have stopped her? But who knew what she had planned? Now it was too late.

It was too late to help Detective Wilcox find this Murderer of Boyers. Obviously Angela couldn't have decided to pull a trigger—she couldn't even decide what shade of pink lipstick to put on. Helpless Angela had help with this job. This garish casket held a murder victim.

It was too late to stop the cute little gun. Even if I was rich and powerful and wonderful, I couldn't buy her back. I couldn't order my lawyer or my banker or my secretary to fix the problem.

All I'd done was speed her on her way—removed Detective Wilcox, his minions and his mustache, from keeping this person out of Angela's little parlor.

I ran through the rationalizations. It had only been two weeks before that the police had dropped the investigation. Would they have gotten anywhere with it in fourteen days? They weren't really trying, anyway. They were just attacking me. I'd had no choice.

And now it was obvious that Melvin had been murdered. But back then, what had been more likely—that he'd been killed on purpose, or that he'd just had an accident?

We'd all thought it was an accident, which just happened to be on the night he changed his will, driving home to the mansion he erected with all the money he pried from his rivals' hands as he destroyed their businesses, on the road his own company built on extorted public contracts. Who would want to kill that man?

What should I have done? What would have been the right thing to do? Probably not swat down the murder investigation like an annoying fly.

The questions were the annoying flies, and I swatted them down.

What am I doing here?

"Jason?"

What? . . . I was at a funeral. The priest was looking at me. Who? . . . oh, Angela. I was supposed to say something? I stood up. I slid past Katie and I walked up to the pulpit and everyone was looking at me.

"Why am I here?" Wait, that's what I said last time. Which funeral was this, again? Angela. "Just a few weeks ago, and now again."

The monstrosity of a casket, everyone staring at me. Where was he? There, on the back wall, my little friend. His stone hand was still raised. He was just a rock, sure, and not alive, but what difference did that make? Being alive wasn't helping me at the moment. Tell me something to say.

"Both of them—Melvin, now Angela. Why? Is there any reason for this? I want to know. Is there a reason any of us are here?"

If there was, I needed to figure it out quick. Time had an abrupt way of running out.

"Angela had one goal for all the years I knew her—just to be a good wife to the man she loved. She couldn't get over her loss. I'm sorry she didn't find a new purpose. It's terrible to not know your purpose."

Why was I up here, anyway? Trying to find some shred of meaning in her poor life? As if I'd ever been able to do that for anyone. Wasn't this what we were paying the priest for, to say the proper things?

"The rest of us will go on, but it gets harder." Not near as big a crowd as last time, and neither governor nor senator; but everyone who was there was still dressed very nicely.

Anything else to say? The little saint said no. I went back to my pew.

I wasn't sure what anyone would make of all that, but Katie squeezed my hand and whispered, "Very touching, Jason. That was beautiful." I don't think she was being sarcastic.

The candles radiated, the flowers shimmered, the priest emanated somberness and suitable words and earned his money. Everyone did a good job, and we all took a well-deserved break in the cloud-filtered sun before setting out for the second half.

Nathan and Fred hobnobbed; Eric was forlorn. The siblings had come of course. Katie took on Celeste while I sidled up to Damon, mainly because we were both curious. Damon had Angela's face, but without the makeup it looked decent. We exchanged our pleasantries. That was as far as we got, though. His mind was on the hours he was losing from the office, and I expected him to bill the estate for his time and travel expenses. My curiosity evaporated and I left him alone.

Katie had found a much deeper mine. Everything Angela was, Celeste was not—dark instead of pale in her color, straight instead of rounded in her features, sharp instead of vague in her nastiness. She spewed remembrances of her sister like a machine gun. Even I doubted Angela could have been so bad.

Katie and I finally fled toward the limo. The siblings had declined to ride in it.

"Why is she so hostile?" I said when we were safe with the door closed and the cortege forming.

"Couldn't you tell?" Katie said. "She wanted to marry your

father, but Angela snatched him instead. Wouldn't you hate your sister for that?"

"I can't imagine him marrying Celeste."

"I guess Celeste could, though."

Eric stared out the window at the thousand different grays in the sky and the grays here on the ground, which included us. Then he just stood next to me through the whole graveside performance.

I hadn't been here since the last funeral, and I noticed how nice Melvin's grave looked. The sod had rooted and blended with the rest of the grass. It was very peaceful, and the new grave was an interruption. But soon it would blend like the first one had, and they could get on with their eternity together.

"Jason?"

It was Eric's first word since we'd left the church. "What?"

"Where is our mother buried?"

It took me a few seconds to climb out from that ton of bricks.

"You don't know?"

"No."

He'd been two years old. But no one ever told him?

"We'll go up there tomorrow."

"Is it close?"

"No." He had just never thought to ask? Or he'd been afraid to?

Katie sniffed and dabbed with her little handkerchief. She was in gray. It wasn't her best color, but she'd known it was apt for the day.

Damon spun his wheels in the gravel turning onto the main road, and there could have been no more final sound to end the event.

Eric was staring at Melvin's headstone, like an abandoned child. Which he was.

I wondered if he'd been here since the last funeral. The monument had been set, and it was very nice. Big but not gaudy, very solid, with three chiseled lines:

MELVIN HOWARD BOYER
UNITED STATES SENATOR
PHILANTHROPIST

And below them were the dates. I counted syllables—six, seven, four. It was haiku.

Angela's stone would be next to his. I hadn't seen it, but I could guess. Matching design, just smaller.

I checked the obstacles between me and the car. Fred and Nathan were double-teaming; that was going to be a tough one to get through.

Celeste was at my elbow. "Which one is the lawyer?" she said. Of course—she wanted a gander at the will.

"Fred Spellman," I said. "He's there, the large gentleman."

The cannonball flew straight, and the obstacle went down. "Let's go," I said, and Katie and Eric followed me. Fred was hopelessly outgunned, and Nathan was pinned down in the crossfire. I smiled at Nathan, snubbed Fred, and opened the door for my wife and brother.

But on the drive home I relented and called Fred's office. "Tell him I'll see him at eight o'clock tomorrow," I told the secretary. Mourning was over—life would just have to go on somehow.

Wednesday I fulfilled my promise and arrived
in Fred's armchair a full two minutes before
eight. I had other business for the day and I
wanted to get this over.

But Fred still had anger to vent. "You've wasted precious time."

"I've been busy."

"So has the governor. Do you understand what this means?"

"*This* refers to Angela's suicide?"

He snorted. "If you want to call it that."

I tried to make myself comfortable, but I wasn't. "Okay, so it
was no suicide. And we know for sure now that Melvin was murdered, the investigation will be re-opened, and Angela probably
died because I interfered."

"You understand the ammunition that this has given the governor."

"A big pile of it."

"A very big pile. The investigation is open, since Monday, and
late last night the whole story of your interference was leaked to
Channel Five." I'd been playing with fire, and Fred seemed grimly
pleased that I was getting burned. He didn't seem concerned about
Angela herself.

"I didn't interfere in any way they could use against me."

"Bright will do whatever he wants. He owns the state police, and Channel Five enjoys sensational news. He will let you know that he did not like your interference. Anyway, Mr. Wilcox will call on you soon. You had best be ready for that."

"I will be."

"You need to give Stanley Morton something for Channel Six and the newspaper so he's not left behind."

Maybe I had been wasting time. This mass was definitely critical. "We talked briefly. I'll call him again."

"You will not be able to stop the investigation."

"I'm not trying to," I said. "Is this still his way of negotiating?"

"It would be up to you to offer a deal, and it would have to be good. Bright isn't merely threatening. He has his opportunity, and he is going to try to destroy you. If you had only negotiated, this could have been prevented."

"But I didn't. Now I have no choice," I said. "I think it's him or me."

It took him a minute to say the words. "At this point, you are both in the locked room, and you both have guns. Someone will have to fire first. I don't see any other way out."

"Then I'm pulling the trigger."

I gave Fred a few seconds to muse. "The end of an era," he said. "Harry Bright and your father went back a long way." Back to the present. "I don't know what will happen."

"I've got one advantage, Fred. I really am innocent, and he's not."

"That's a very small advantage. I don't suggest you count on it helping you."

"I know. How should I do this? Take my briefcase of papers to the FBI? Publish them in the newspaper? Challenge Bright to a duel? Loaded pistols at ten paces. You can be my second."

"A duel would favor the coolest head, so you would both miss, and I would not want to be nearby. Talk to Stanley first. He may or may not want to be on the front lines."

"And what about you, Fred?" How did this man feel about being on the front line?

He frowned. "What do you mean?"

"Are you in on this?"

"What choice do I have? You're paying me to advise you."

I'd been hoping for something a little deeper. "Would you quit if I'm too big of an idiot?"

"Oh. Not for a while."

I wanted to know how deep the loyalty went. "How long did you work for Melvin?"

"Nearly from the beginning." I did not sense any sentimentality. "I was a staff lawyer for the state assembly, and he asked me to advise him on dealing with the state government."

"That was before he went to Washington."

"Yes, by several years."

"Did you know my mother?"

"Slightly." A little bit of the old Uncle Fred was resurfacing. "She was ill. Eric was an infant, and you were a small child. In those circumstances, she did not socialize."

"When she died . . ." I didn't know what to ask.

"Yes?"

"How did Melvin react?"

"He didn't react to such things, in any public way."

He'd always been that way. "You knew him very well, though."

"Through the years I did get to know him. But not back then."

Change the subject. A little. "Did he take chances? How would he have fought this war with Governor Bright?"

"Ruthlessly. In the earlier days he did take big chances, but after a while he didn't need to anymore. In this situation? He would have easily won. For one thing, he would have been much more feared. Channel Five would have been very reluctant to side with the governor."

"I guess I'm not very fearsome."

"If you come out of this alive, you'll be feared."

I thought about whether I would want that, then, suddenly, about the word Fred had used.

"Is that literal?" I asked.

"What?"

"If I come out alive?"

"I didn't mean it literally. But you should be very careful. You're wealthy; spend some money on security for yourself and your wife."

Up, up, up. In my very own formidably secure office, guarded by Pamela herself, I prepared to call Stan Morton.

One more pause: Was this it? Think it through. If I did what I was planning, Bright would not survive, at least as a politician. That wouldn't stop the murder investigation, but the goal would be changed to finding the killer instead of killing me. That's what I needed.

And Bright was too dangerous. I needed to be rid of him. What was the right thing to do? It was ruthless, brutal, risky, but there was no right or wrong here. This was politics. The world without a corrupt state government under my control would also be risky, but there was right and wrong there. I could do right.

Okay, the pause was over. Governor Bright had assailed me and I would punish him. I would punish Melvin, too. Let loose the dogs of war.

"It's about time you called," Stan said. "Everyone here knows the police are about to call Angela Boyer's suicide note a forgery, and there are funny noises about you and why the investigation got frozen two weeks ago. I'm going to put up a report on the news tonight, so if you want any input into it, give me some words quick."

"I've got lots of words."

"Should we meet?"

I had my other business for the day, and it was already eight thirty. "No, I'll say them here."

"Is this on the record?"

"Not yet."

"Okay."

"Melvin was murdered, and so was Angela."

"That's reality?"

"I have no proof, and no specific suspect," I said. "But I'm sure."

"Everyone knows that. Next?"

"The governor wants to use the investigation to annihilate me. My guess is he'll pick me as the murderer."

"Are you? Wait, you said you have no specific suspect. Do you have an alibi?"

Far out at sea for the whole weekend, no communications. And the night of Melvin's wreck, I was home alone. "Actually, no."

"Interesting, but not news. I'm still waiting."

"So I'm taking Bright down first."

"That's news. What do you mean?"

"I am finding out that his dealings with my companies aren't legitimate, and I'm going public."

"The public reads my newspaper. You want me to break this story?"

"Yes."

There was a thud, a pause, then Stan's voice, breathless. "Sorry, I dropped the phone. Okay, Jason, on the record, tell me stuff. Do you have any clue what this means?"

"I have a clue and I have many documents from Melvin Boyer's estate. They have lots of details about bribes, bid-rigging, kickbacks, and intimidation. There are lots of names of Governor Bright's appointees."

"What about your side?"

"Heads will have to roll."

"Where are these documents?"

"In a safe place."

"I'm coming over there. This is the end of Bright. This is . . . Does Fred Spellman know you're doing this?"

"Yeah, I told him. He's not real happy."

"I bet. Okay . . . um . . . these documents . . . Are you acknowledging that you're giving them to me?"

Good question. An unnamed source? Stan would be snowed under with subpoenas. And it would be better if I gave them to the police voluntarily, before the police came asking for them. "I'm meeting with the FBI tomorrow. Someone on my staff sent you an unauthorized preliminary copy."

"We can work with that."

Almost nine o'clock. I sat down with Pamela
to give her the sixty pages from my file cabinet and instructions.

"Take these papers," I said, "and make
three sets of copies. Put the originals and one set of copies back in
the file room. Mail one copy to Nathan Kern. At exactly nine fifteen, a man will come in here and say the word *Natalie*. Give him
the third copy."

"Yes, sir," she said. "Is there any note to put in Mr. Kern's envelope?"

"I'll call him. Mark it *Personal*."

"Anything else?"

"Make an appointment for me. Have the most important FBI
person in the state here tomorrow at nine." Wait. "No, get someone
from Boston or New York. From outside the state."

"All right."

"Have Fred Spellman there, too. And one more thing." This was
a little hard. "These four people." I gave her the list. "Do you know
them?"

She gave me a sweet, inscrutable, grandmotherly look. "Of
course, Jason." The FBI and these four in the same breath. She
knew what that meant.

"I need to fire them."

"Oh dear."

"How would Melvin do that?"

"That would depend on their positions and his reasons."

I was getting to be in a hurry now. "Take a letter. One of these to each of them, copy to their division presidents, board officers, and personnel files. 'Dear John. After reviewing records of your performance, I find that it is no longer possible to continue your relationship with this company. I am terminating your employment effective immediately. Jason Boyer.' Will that do?"

"Honey, you must know what you're doing."

"Not hardly."

She was typing faster than any human could while she asked, "How do you want them delivered?"

"Have couriers deliver signed originals to the division presidents, and the presidents are to personally hand them to the individuals. But make sure it happens today. This morning."

"I'll make sure. The copies for you are printing."

"And I'll be unavailable the rest of the day."

By nine twenty I had navigated twenty blocks to reach the edge between downtown and the gentrified clump of historic townhouses, restaurants, and clubs that were slowly encroaching on the real working-class neighborhoods farther on. I parked in a garage under a six-story brick building, elevated to the fifth floor, and knocked on the one door in the small lobby.

After not too long of a wait, the door opened. Eric's blurred eyes stared at me a moment. Then he grinned.

"Jason!"

"Let me in," I said.

"Yeah, come on."

The maid did a good job keeping up with him. The living room was neat, and nothing was out of place in the kitchen.

But it was uninspired—no better than his old wardrobe. No theme, no color plan, too many textures. Leather and brass sofa and matching chairs circling an unmatching slate coffee table with heavy wood legs. Thick, deep green carpet. One whole twenty-five-foot wall a single huge entertainment center with five televisions. Not a thing on the walls. Tsk, tsk. He didn't even realize he was living in squalor. Someday Katie would have to turn her attention to this place.

"Do you want anything?" he asked. He didn't get to be host very often. He'd been eating breakfast, a bowl of cereal in front of one television.

"Orange juice," I said. He poured a glass and brought it to me.

"So," he said as I drank it, "did you mean it?"

"That's why I'm here," I said.

"Wow. Okay. So when should we go?"

"When you're ready."

"I'm ready." He took his bowl to the kitchen, emptied it into the sink, rinsed it, and set it on the counter by the dishwasher. His maid had him well trained.

He was well trained in general, always doing what he was told. For today at least he would be in charge. "You drive," I said.

"Cool." He appreciated it. I never rode with him. "How far?"

"New Hampshire."

"That's where she was from, right?"

He wouldn't have dared to ask Melvin, so I was the only other person who could have told him anything.

"Why didn't you ever ask before?" I said. "I just thought you knew."

"Well . . ." He hesitated. "I don't know. I guess I didn't want to know."

I just waited, and he went on.

"When I was little, when we were off at school, I liked to pretend I had a mother back home, like everyone else."

"Sure."

"If I didn't know anything, I could still pretend whatever I wanted to."

"Are you okay with going today?"

He nodded. "I want her to be real now."

"Here's a new rule, um, Number 90. Don't ever be afraid to talk to me about anything."

"Unless you're mad."

"The spaghetti was a special case. I said I was sorry."

"And you skipped Number 89."

"I'm sure we'll get to it soon."

Eric had opened a closet, and he took down a bright green helmet. He held it out to me. "Here you go."

I would maybe wear a helmet when he was driving, but that was not what he meant. This was a motorcycle helmet.

"Uh . . . okay," I said. Bright Kool-Aid green. Couldn't it at least be any other color?

"And here." It was the matching jacket. "It's cold. Do you want the pants?"

I was supposed to be Motorcycle Man? Eric waited for me to not decide.

"You want the pants. And the boots. Why be cold when you can be cool instead? And if I drop you, it won't hurt as much."

Eric In Charge was a new experience for both of us. I submitted to his directions, and there we were, Evel and Knievel, tromping through the garage past my perfectly comfortable car, past all his perfectly comfortable cars, to the Boyercycle Zone.

He selected the largest horse in the stable, a two-seat Honda Goldwing. He put on his helmet, and so did I. All systems go, Houston. Ready for countdown.

Eric stuck his hand under my chin and moved a switch.

"Can you hear me?" he said inside my head. The helmets had speakers.

"Yes."

"Cool. I've never had anybody to talk to before."

Not that we would much, but I wouldn't have to pound on him to get his attention.

"Don't kill me, Eric," I said.

"Is that Rule 89?"

The astronauts climbed into the space shuttle, Commander Eric first, Navigator Jason second. Five, four, three. The engine roared to life. Two, one. A jerk (the motion, not the passenger). Blast off.

We made a wide left sweep toward the exit, then right, faster and tighter, into the road.

"Lean into it, Jason. Don't fight the turns."

The rocket sped down the quaint and historic road. "Have you ever had a rider before?"

"No. It's different." Right turn. I leaned into it. "That's better," he said, then gunned the engine. "Hold on."

I held.

He twisted the handle grip and the motorcycle accelerated hard.

But not too hard. Lots of people drive these things, so they couldn't be too difficult. I could feel his skill, though, and his confidence, and his exultation. He wasn't going to drop me.

Lean right into the entrance ramp. Around the circle, the concrete twelve inches from my shoulder, moving very rapidly. Onto the highway, back to straight ahead, back to vertical, back to fast. Increase to real fast.

"You still there?"

"Right behind you."

He gunned the engine. "Get ready."

I couldn't judge the speed. We passed cars and no cars passed us. But he knew how to do this; he'd never had a ticket.

"How do you like it?"

"It's real sweet, Eric."

He did this about every day. Just following the roads, every paved mile in New England, two wheels or four wheels, whatever he felt like.

We crossed into Massachusetts. "Where are we going?"

"You know where Laconia is?"

"Yeah."

No map. He knew the way. This was his life, or his escape from life.

How were he and I alike? The boat and the bike were both speed and power, but sailing was a contest, me against the sea and wind. He was master of this machine and the road under it, no contest.

This was his world to be in charge of. He'd never been in charge of his life—always shuffled from school to school, told what to do, never certain of what would be permanent. I was his only permanence.

And I was always in charge, of him and everything else. I hated anyone telling me to do anything, so they didn't. Maybe I got along with the wind because I had to respect it. There isn't much else in my life I have to.

This was the same wind we were cutting through. My brother didn't respect it, he reveled in it. He was the wind. He was a Boyer as much as I was.

What a wonderful bright day we were in, and there were mountains around us. I'd missed the New Hampshire border.

What about the Rove side? I just had memories of her, and Eric had nothing. How much of our mother did either of us have?

No clouds, just blue, blue sky. The sky and the bike were the only things not moving. The mountains moved slowly.

"There's a place up here if you want lunch."

"You're driving," I said.

Off the highway, lean way over to the right. Country road.

"Up here" meant "way over there." All the curves they'd taken out of the highway they'd put on this road. Lean left, lean right, slow behind a car, fast around it, up a hill, down a hill, fork right, hard left. This was more of a contest.

Slow down, we were stopped. It was a diner built off a white house with a gravel parking lot, a picket fence, and some flowers. Suddenly it was easy to breathe, and quiet. The ground was solid and unmoving.

I took a few steps and pulled off the helmet. Eric was still sitting, his helmet off, grinning and watching me. "Are you okay?"

"I'm okay. It just takes a minute to get my balance."

He swung himself out of the saddle and unzipped his jacket. I was hot and I took mine off.

We went up the steps and in the door. The inside was the same as the outside, nice, plain, a little worn. The floor was tile. One table had people.

The woman behind the counter had been there a long time, thirty years maybe. She glanced up from the cash register.

"Eric. You brought a friend." She stared at me. "Looks like he's your brother."

Eric smiled real big. "Yeah, he is. I've told you about him? This is Jason."

"I'll be with you in a minute. What do you want to drink?" she asked me.

"Just water."

She was already filling a cup with lemonade. She brought the two drinks to the table.

"Hamburger, mushroom and Swiss," she said, writing, without asking him.

"Two of them," he said. "It's great," he said to me.

"Okay."

"Anything else?"

"Onion rings," I said.

"Me too," little brother said. "Thanks, Hazel."

Hazel was friendly but not talkative, and someone else came in for her to attend to.

"So you come here often."

Eric nodded. "It's one of my places." Hazel's lingering aura left just the right mood.

"So, what do you remember about our mother?" I didn't even really know what to call her.

"Wow. Um, I don't know. All the pictures make me think I remember her. I wouldn't though, would I?"

"You were two," I said. "I don't think so."

"What do you remember?"

"I remember . . ." It's hard to put in words what you experienced before you knew the words. "I remember her in bed, or sitting. She sang lullabies to us. I remember thinking she was different from other people because she didn't move. She just sat in her chair or in her bed." Only to Eric could I say this. "I remember feeling loved. I loved her. I wish you could remember."

We ate the food, which was passable, and we dealt with our tragedy. It was the first time we had.

Melvin was thirty-two and she was twenty-one. His father had died, and he was already rich and getting richer. His mother introduced them at a Christmas party. The Roves were a respectable old New Hampshire family, and she was very pretty. He swept her off her feet. They honeymooned in Paris and Rome and Athens. She was shy but brave, and he was bold, and together they were dashing. They had those two free and golden years together, then three more as happy parents. He had become very busy by then.

Then, partway through her second pregnancy, the doctors found something wrong. The baby was fine, the delivery was easy, but the cancer could not be stopped. There were two more years as she weakened. She had the best care, but he had many other cares, and she understood that he could not be with her as much. Her affection had only her children to be lavished upon. As her life faded, it intensified, and she lived fifty years in only half that many months. When she died she was young and wise, both full and emptied of life, her husband, for once, at her side. I had pieced it together from the fragments I had.

And I think, I think, she learned what she had lived for. Maybe she had always known, or maybe it was in the last years that she came to know. As a child, I put everything I could into my memories of her—impressions and details I didn't understand but I knew were important. And now as an adult I sift through the memories, artifacts left by an ancient world, and I try to decipher what they mean. And . . . I think they mean that she knew, absolutely, why she lived the life she did.

"You were at her funeral, weren't you?" Eric asked.

I was, and again my memory of it was of a five-year-old's impression—of a big church with big pews and the casket far away, and endless sitting, and my first smell of death: flowers and candles. At my funeral I will have neither.

After the service I did not go to the cemetery. I was packed off to someplace that had toys, and a woman with a sharp nose read books to me about rabbits.

"Have you ever been to her grave?"

We were back on the motorcycle, ready to pull out onto the road.

"Twice. Somebody took me a couple years later. I don't know why. Then I came once when I was in college."

We were not far. Eric kept going on the two-lane road, winding, climbing, and falling, and then I told him where to turn. And then it was ahead of us, a simple white wooden country church and its timeless churchyard.

There was nothing to say. We got off the bike, and I doubted the suitability of our appearance. I took my jacket off and left it. I would have even taken off the leather pants, which were over my regular pants, but it would have been awkward; and then I would have had to put them back on, which would have been even more awkward.

So we disturbed the cemetery with our gaudy presence. But that small, quiet place was strong enough; its presence dwarfed ours. When the first graves were dug here, it may have been clear and open. Now huge ancient trees shaded it.

I knew where her grave was, and we walked straight to it. It was proper for the surroundings—calm, modest, and meaningful. We stood beside it, and I was completely lost.

Why am I here? There had to be a betrayal here, somewhere. She died of cancer, not a broken heart, but Melvin still betrayed her. He betrayed her by betraying us, me and Eric. And now I had betrayed Angela, and we'd both done it for the same reason—that money and power had rendered inconvenient what should have been important.

Why was I killing Governor Bright, or at least his career? Because I don't like people telling me what to do? Jason is in charge—nobody bosses me around? Because the money is in charge.

Is this how it's going to be for the rest of my life?

There was a conflagration back home that I'd ignited. I was going to pull down the governor and half his administration. I was going to rock the state—people would go to prison, lives would be ruined. There was a lot at stake. But it had to be done. What other choice did I have?

What would my mother think of me?

"Ready?" I said. It was time to get back.
"Yeah."
We walked back to the church, but then I turned to look in.

This was not where the funeral had been, but it should have been. A real church, hallowed by generations of lives centered around it and what it stood for. I only smelled wood. Was this the church her family had been part of? She had gone to church. She had taken me; I suddenly remembered that.

"Why aren't they buried together?" Eric asked.

"I guess this place wouldn't have done for him." No crashing waves, no drama, no room for an appropriate monument, no room for Angela. And . . . and he wouldn't have been at home here. There was something in this church I didn't understand. What did this place stand for? People found meaning here.

"When I die, you can bury me here," Eric said.

We had the helmets on, and the words came from every direction.

I settled behind him on the motorcycle. "I hope I don't have to bury you," I said.

"I don't mean anytime soon."

We didn't pass Hazel's on the way back. Eric cut across to the closest highway ramp, and we were on our way home.

"Are you ever going to get married?" I asked my helmet.

"I guess," it answered. "Why not?" Eric had obviously thought about this very deeply.

"When?"

"I don't know. When I meet somebody."

The life he was leading didn't make that likely. Eric had decisions to make about his life, too.

"I'll have Katie find you a wife."

"Okay." He was probably not being serious.

"Anything particular you want?"

"Friendly. Like she is."

Katie could be friendly, when she wanted. What was she going to think about the upcoming war? Or about the truth of Angela's demise? She didn't know what was about to happen.

"You should take me to my house," I said. "And you need to stay for dinner. We'll be on television tonight."

"Cool. What about your car?"

"I'll have someone get it."

21

Katie was watching as we rocketed into the driveway, and I suffered her amusement stoically. I even let her take a picture of the Brothers Having Fun. Then I changed into unwrinkled clothes and prepared for our little family meeting.

Our life was going to change. It had when Melvin died, but we were going to start feeling the day-to-day reality of it after the six-o'clock news shoved us and our brawl with the governor into every living room in the state.

But I did not call the meeting to order. It was called to disorder instead by the arrival of a television truck in the driveway and the ringing of the doorbell. We were under assault.

I ordered that the bell be ignored and called the police to clear the invaders from my property. The television station they were from was not the one I owned.

"Jason, what is going on?" Katie asked, but I told her to wait. I left her and Eric spying out the front windows through the closed curtains while I went to my office.

I called Pamela.

"Were those letters delivered?" I asked.

"Yes, Jason. And I have some very urgent requests for meetings with you."

"Schedule them for tomorrow morning, all together, and have Fred in on it. But I don't want to meet with any of the men who were fired."

"I'll set it up just after your first meeting. Mr. Patrick Donovan of the FBI is coming down from Boston at nine o'clock."

"Thank you very much. And I need to call someone at Channel Five news."

She provided me with the correct name and number, and I called Glenda Sweeney, the producer. I was on hold for less than ten seconds between the secretary and Glenda herself. Almost as if she had been awaiting me.

"Mr. Boyer, it's so nice of you to call," she said.

"Ms. Sweeney," I said. "Take your people away from my house." I was not actually throwing a tantrum. I had thought this out.

"I'm sorry for the inconvenience, Mr. Boyer. But we are trying to get some information. You may not be aware—"

"I'm quite aware, and you aren't. You'll need your truck downtown this evening."

"But Mr. Boyer . . ."

She was off-balance, and I pushed her the rest of the way. "You should watch Channel Six to get filled in on the details. And I'll give you access to them, too, if you don't antagonize me."

I gave her three seconds. "I don't want to antagonize you, Mr. Boyer. Could you tell me what will be happening downtown?"

"When that truck is away from here and parked in front of the governor's mansion, you can call me back."

"We have more than one truck."

"You'll need them all in town," I said. "Good-bye."

The men in blue were imposing law and order on the front yard. The truck backed out of the driveway and pulled up to the curb, and its occupants stayed carefully in the road and off private property. One officer came to the door, and I thanked him and sent him back to his post. Then the truck itself drove away.

"What is happening?" Katie said as we sat down for our family meeting.

"A lot of stuff," I said. "I'm firing the governor today."

"You're what?"

"I'm getting rid of him."

"But . . . I thought . . ." Eric said. "I don't think he works for you."

"You might as well hear it on the news," I said. "They'll probably explain it better." The curtains were still drawn in the front room, and I opened them. "It has to do with the police thinking that Melvin was murdered."

"Wasn't he?" Katie said.

"Now they think Angela was, too."

"I thought she . . . Didn't she do it herself?" Eric said.

"What about her note?" Katie asked.

"On the news tonight, they'll say it was forged."

They were approaching overload. Rosita popped in.

"Mr. Jason, you said I should tell you if Miss Glenda Sweeney calls."

"Thank you. I'll take it in here," I said. My audience would benefit from listening in. "And, Rosita—could you bring us some snacks?" I picked up the phone. "This is Jason Boyer."

"Mr. Boyer. I have a truck at the governor's mansion. Now, could you tell me what will be happening?"

"This is off the record?"

She paused. "I'd rather it was on the record."

"All right," I said. "Then this is what I'll tell you. It's been one month since Melvin Boyer died and I took over his businesses. I've looked into his dealings with the state government, and I've decided to go public with what I've found."

"And what have you found?"

"I won't say anything else on the record."

"Mr. Boyer." Her tone said she knew what I'd found. "You aren't really blowing the whistle, are you? I don't believe it. You'd be committing suicide."

No, murder. And the victim was already dead. "It doesn't matter to me what you believe. And I don't know what Governor Bright believes, either. But I think you should be ready to ask him tonight, after Channel Six does its report, and even more after the newspaper comes out tomorrow."

"Mr. Boyer, what about the report that you interfered with the investigation into your father's murder?"

"I only urged the governor's office to not interfere with it."

"May I schedule an interview?"

"No. I'll schedule it."

"Soon?"

"That depends on how well you cover the whole story. I might also talk with some people higher up in your organization first."

"I understand." Which meant she knew how far the field was tilted.

"I'll look forward to talking to you later."

I set the phone down and looked back to my listeners.

"I don't get it," Eric said, finally.

It wasn't fair to him, either of them, to do it this way. Katie had had some warning, and Eric maybe had a clue, but neither of them were ready for what they were about to see.

And the clock was about to strike six.

We watched Channel Six, with Channel Five up in the corner of the screen. Six led with the story and Five gave it the "coming up later in the show" treatment. They wanted to hear Six's report first.

We settled comfortably into our chairs, Rosita's little appetizer snack close by, as the war began.

The opening salvo was massive. The talking head stared us straight in the eye and spoke his words of destruction.

"Good evening, I'm Bill Sandoff. Today we begin with a report on corruption in state government that could reach our highest elected officials, and involves some of the biggest names in the construction industry. Channel Six has obtained key information from knowledgeable sources that details a longstanding system of bribes and kickbacks that has cost the taxpayers millions of dollars and lined the pockets of many senior members of Governor Harry Bright's administration.

"First, Jill Abernathy reports on the businesses involved, and the man behind the system, the late Melvin Boyer. Before we begin, we have to disclose that the Boyer family is a major stockholder in First

Media, the owner of this station. Jill?"

Step by step, they laid it out. Melvin's death and the cleaning of the corporate house by his son Jason (unavailable for comment on this day). The outline of the bid fixing schemes and a list of the larger state projects and the profits reaped from them. Calls late in the day to the specific Boyer businesses to speak with the named executives, and the reply that those individuals were no longer employed.

Then back to the deaths of Melvin and then Angela—the brief details and the bombshell information that the deaths were being investigated as murders.

There were pictures and video, location shots, even a university expert on state politics. The big guns were leveled at the governor's mansion, and every shot was blasting another gaping hole.

"Governor Bright's press secretary has only promised that the governor will make a statement later this evening. Channel Six will bring it to you live," Bill promised us.

"And finally," he said in his *And finally* voice, "even as the governor and his administration are caught in the center of this unfolding scandal, what about the man who opened this Pandora's box?"

And there I was. It was the same three-year-old wedding shot Channel Five had used a month ago. "Jason Boyer, who inherited his father's position as the wealthiest and most powerful industrialist in the state, appears to be making a bold move to transform that position."

And that was it. Bill poured one more bucket of words all over us and he was done. Seventeen minutes of talking, and it was done. The governor was done, Melvin was done—who knows what else. I couldn't tell how I felt. Well done, maybe.

Channel Five's report began five seconds after the other ended. It was a very flat version of the murders, mostly the evidence of the brake line and forged suicide note. The victims were portrayed as community pillars, and the perpetrator as obviously an insider who stood to gain from their deaths. Only at the end was there just a brief sentence about some unfounded allegations concerning

Melvin's business dealings. It would have been interesting to see the original version.

We changed venue and sat down to our dinner of salmon quiche. It was quiet at first. Eric was the first to word a question.

"Did you know all of that?"

I nodded. "Yeah. I gave them most of it. They were doing what I told them to do."

"They said you just found out what he was doing when you looked through his papers."

"The details. But I've always known."

"I didn't know."

What a day he was having—gaining a mother and losing a father. "Fred Spellman was in on it for years. He helped Melvin put it all together."

"Uncle Fred, huh."

"'Uncle Fred' is about as real as Santa Claus. And Stan Morton, who runs the newspaper and Channel Six, has always known. Senator Forrester got elected in a deal with Melvin. Basically everyone in state government has either known what Melvin was doing, or was even on his payroll."

Eric was still struggling. "Why didn't they do anything about it?"

"Why should they? They were all making a lot of money from his deals."

"It was illegal."

"Well," I said, "that's why I'm stopping it all."

I felt good saying that, and it was true. Just not the whole truth.

Eric was still getting all the pieces put together. "So that's why you're doing all this."

"I want it to end. I don't want to be a criminal. This is the best way."

He stared at me, maybe with respect. "Okay. I guess I see."

"It was probably all going to come out anyway, sooner or later. I wanted to control it, instead of letting the governor."

"Yeah, the governor . . ." Eric had the edges of the puzzle together now, and he was starting on the middle. "He must be pretty mad right now. What will he do?"

"I don't know. I think he should resign."

"I guess so. I see what you meant, that you're firing him."

He would have said more but it was Katie's turn.

"Not everything Melvin did was wrong," she said.

"No, not at all," I said. "A lot of his business was straight."

"So what will all this do to us, Jason?"

Katie had never believed in Santa Claus, but she was wondering about the Christmas presents.

"I'm not sure," I said. "It'll be hard getting through it. But you don't need to worry."

"What would they do to us? If it was illegal, would they want the money back?" Katie needed assurance.

"We'll be fine," I said.

She preferred anxiety. "What if the governor tries to fight back?"

"Fred and I have discussed that."

"What will you do?"

Apparently Katie had not completed her training in how to be a billionaire's wife, at least the course on what not to ask about her husband's business affairs.

"It depends on what the governor does. I don't think he can do very much."

"Everything is ready to move to the new house next week." That was the big thing on her mind. She had mastered the How to Spend Money sections of the curriculum.

"It's fine. Nothing will stop us from getting into the new house. It's more important now than ever."

"Everyone's heard of us now," she said, putting her own pieces together. "We're famous." She didn't mind that, but she wanted to be ready first. "I don't think we should wait to move."

"Could we do it tomorrow?" I asked.

She was already thinking, staring into the distance. "Yes. We can. We will. Then we'll have a gate, and we're going to need it." She looked back to me. "You're doing big things, Jason." A new worry came to her. "What will Mother think?"

"Keep us apart," I said. It was not a joke.

We all had too much to think about, and it was an edgy evening. I finally told Eric to take a guest room when he couldn't bring himself to leave. We didn't go to bed, though, and finally Governor Bright made his awaited appearance.

He read his statement at the press-room podium, flanked by aides and officials, stating his shock at the allegations and promising a complete investigation. His tone was stentorian, authoritative, and somber. He also added his regret that "this young Mr. Boyer" couldn't have first brought the evidence to him, the state's highest official and guardian of the public trust, instead of sensationalizing it.

He took questions because he had to. There had been a lot that he hadn't said in his statement, and the reporters had noticed.

Did he still have confidence in his Secretary of Transportation and Secretary of Finance?

"I am sure Mr. Howland and Mr. Gilbert are as anxious as I am to investigate every accusation."

That was the most truthful thing he'd said so far. I almost laughed.

Bill Sandoff went for the big one. "Mr. Governor, did you personally have any knowledge of these alleged criminal practices?"

The look in the governor's eye showed what he thought of Bill. Then his mouth started speaking.

"I will personally oversee the investigation, and I am sure it will find no evidence of anything criminal in my administration."

Surely he hadn't said that. But he had, with a straight face.

"Mr. Governor, shouldn't the investigation be independent?" This was a newspaper reporter. "Would the public trust you to investigate your own administration?"

And then Clinton Grainger's careful spin went out of control.

Harry Bright turned red, which looked very patriotic with his white hair and blue suit. "Trust? The public placed their trust in me at the last election. If you want to find criminals, I'll tell you where to look. Follow these accusations back to their source. Melvin Boyer was poison to this state, but in one month his son has already done worse damage than his father ever did."

The reporters were momentarily stunned by his outburst. "Why do you believe Jason Boyer is making these allegations?" asked one loud voice.

Bright had strayed from his script and couldn't find his way back. "Because he's trying to cover up the murders of his own father and mother. Well, I won't be intimidated by his attack. We'll get to the truth of it all."

Every mouth I could see dropped open. This stunned moment was longer but ended in greater chaos.

"Be quiet," I said to the two mouths that could hear me, and we listened to the reporters shouting and watched the governor realize he may have gone too far. He stood, glaring, while the room quieted and the unanswered questions finally settled in a heap on the floor.

"I will not answer any further questions at this time," he said, still glaring. "I will only promise you that the police will uncover every crime, and that every person responsible will be brought to justice. *Every* person. Any further questions may be directed to my press office. Good night."

With his head high and a steely glint in his eyes, he turned and left the room.

Then we saw a different head staring at us. "This is Bill Sandoff. As you have just seen, Governor Harry Bright has bluntly given his answer to the allegations of corruption brought against his administration. While he did not flatly deny charges against his senior officials, he has made a strong accusation of his own, that those charges are politically motivated, or worse. Obviously, the investigations of fraud *and* of the Boyer deaths are now linked. Could Melvin and Angela Boyer have been murdered in connection with corruption at the highest levels of government? Will the facts take the investigators to the governor's office? And what of Jason Boyer, whose motives for exposing his father's business deals have been called into question? The answers to these, and many other questions, are now of the utmost importance. Bill Sandoff, Channel Six News."

Good questions, especially the last one. What of Jason Boyer? He was turning off the television, that was what.

"Jason." In her expectations of billionaire existence, Katie had not imagined an event quite like this. She didn't even know what to ask.

"It's okay." I didn't know what to answer. "But you can see what its going to be like for the next few weeks."

"Do you know what you're doing?"

"I'm doing my best." I took her hand in mine. "This is just part of the job. I didn't start it."

She nodded. "All right, Jason." She was shaken. This was outside her experience, and she needed some way to deal with it.

Then the confused look drained from her face, replaced by her own steely glint. She knew her part in this war. "Tomorrow night we'll be in our new house."

And finally Eric had regained his voice. "What did he mean, our mother's murder?"

"He meant Angela," I said.

"Oh." He was breathing; I could see shoulders moving. Otherwise, he didn't look very alive.

"Get some sleep, Eric. You've been through too much today."

"Okay."

Maybe some food would have helped, but if they felt like I did, they weren't hungry. I called the police to ask them to keep our street clear.

I was still waiting for a good night's sleep, but again I didn't get it. I couldn't keep my mind clear. Friday afternoon on the boat, I'd thought it would be painless to get addicted to power. Tonight it was very painful.

Thursday morning police barricades stood a
hundred yards on either side of our driveway,
and they were besieged.

The newspaper had made it through. I
only glanced at the governor's picture and name in the headlines,
and tossed it into my office.

"I have to go," I told Katie. "I'll be back by noon."

"I'll be all right. The vans will be here in half an hour."

I could imagine the stir that would cause on the street. "Call me
if you need reinforcements."

"Mother's coming."

"We could ask the police to keep her out."

Katie smiled. "I've asked her to move into the new house with
us." It was hard to tell, but she was teasing.

"Okay, I'm sorry," I said. "I'll be nice to her."

"Thank you, dear."

Eric was munching cereal in the kitchen. Rosita fluttered
around him, drawn to hunger like a moth to a candle.

"Motorcycle Boy," I said, "I need you."

Ten minutes later, at eight o'clock, we were in our leather dis-
guises, pushing the Goldwing through the backyard, through the
gate into our back neighbor's yard, and then zoom zooming out his

driveway. At eight twenty, my chauffeur dropped me off at the lobby and prepared to head back to guard Katie.

"One assignment," I said to him as I handed him the helmet and jacket. I had not worn the leather pants. "If Katie doesn't need you, read everything in the paper. I want to know it all."

"No problem. I think I remember how to read."

My own bodyguard awaited on the top floor. Pamela leaped from her desk when she saw me, gave me an actual hug, and nodded at my office door.

"Fred's in there." I had no idea what he thought of the performance the night before. "And Mr. Donovan will be here at nine."

"If you hear gunshots, call the police," I said, and opened the door.

Fred occupied a large chair that had not been there before. No detail, however small, could escape Pamela, and my lawyer was not small. Just in case the chair was inadequate, there was a matching sofa against the wall.

He watched me round my desk and settle behind it; the tables were turned between us.

"What do you think?" I said.

"You are the two biggest fools I've ever seen." He paused for a breath. "You both deserve everything that is going to happen to you."

"Then tell me what you think is going to happen."

Fred had a lot of steam to vent, but he corked it. "Clinton Grainger may be able to salvage the governor. I don't know why he would try, except that he's put ten years into Harry Bright's career."

"The investigation is going to sink Bright. There's no way he'll come out of this."

"If it were left to the state police, they might whitewash the charges. But I don't believe Grainger can manipulate this Mr. Donovan you're meeting. The evidence is too complete. Besides, the publicity is too immense."

"So Bright is toast. What could happen to me?"

"That is more complex."

He hadn't seen this much action in a long time with Melvin. "I think you're enjoying this," I said.

"Nonsense. Although it is interesting to watch the events unfold."

"Or to unfold them. The only thing that could hurt me is a fixed murder investigation. Anything else they dig up will just hurt the governor."

"I doubt you will profit from it, either. I mean that literally."

"I'll survive."

Fred shrugged—which can actually be measured with very sensitive seismic equipment. "Then the real question concerns Clinton Grainger. It is only a matter of time before he abandons Bright."

"He'll look for a new politician to invest in?" There would be plenty of eager clients.

"Most likely. Therefore, he will need to decide whether you would be an obstacle to building a new power base in someone else. In which case, he would want to disrupt you as much as possible while he still has the governor as a platform."

"How would he do that?"

"Blackmail, most likely. He prefers quiet methods. But he could go public if he needed. The governor's outburst put your name in the headlines, and not favorably. And he may still be able to convict you of some crime."

"I haven't committed any."

"I know, and you know, that it doesn't matter. If not murder, at least something. Harry Bright may be doomed, but now it is you and Clinton Grainger locked in the room with a gun. You said he'd searched your office and your father's."

"There was nothing in mine he could use. I don't know about Melvin's."

"Didn't you take everything?"

"Just the files about Bright and the state contracts. There were a few other things that I hadn't got to." I tried thinking like a billionaire. "Could we buy Clinton?"

"Oh, maybe. He may not be interested. He advises politicians."

"I might be a politician."

My mouth said it, and I guess I wasn't real surprised. Despite the pain, my addiction to power was apparently growing, and politics was part of the family business as much as building roads and sewers. Hadn't Melvin been saving me a Senate seat?

Fred nodded. He might have been assuming that the seeds he'd planted before my trip to Washington had had time to sprout. "I see. Then we should have a meeting with him soon." He even had a protective, fatherly look in his eye. "Let me be part of it, though."

"I will." Seriously, I would be a politician? I tried to remember how I'd felt three weeks ago when I'd bit Fred's head off for suggesting it. I didn't feel that anymore. What am I doing here?

No, change the question. What can I be doing here for the good of my fellow citizens and my state? "If you say Melvin had planned for me to run for the Senate, I will fire you."

"I've already said it, so it needs no repeating. At the moment, it adds interesting possibilities. Harry Bright will leave a vacuum, and someone will need to fill it. He would have won a second term in two years. Now there will be a scramble. You need to pick a suitable . . . you wouldn't run for governor, would you?" He was suddenly alarmed.

"No. That's not a fun job."

Fred was relieved. "Exactly. The Senate is much more appropriate. For the governor's mansion, we need to pick a suitable candidate to back, and events will start moving very quickly. If you and Grainger could cooperate on that, it would be an excellent beginning."

It was disorienting, this new Jason. I was getting to know him, although his interest in politics was still a revelation.

The telephone on my desk buzzed, rescuing Fred and both Jasons from further discussion on the subject. "Mr. Boyer? Mr. Donovan and Mr. Kelly of the FBI are here."

"Thank you, Pamela. Send them right in."

The door opened, and right in they came.

It took thirty minutes to get them back out. I gave them the papers I had and opened the locked room to show them the rest. I assured them of complete cooperation by all my executives and officers. I apologized that somehow everything had leaked the day before, just as I'd finally been ready to call the authorities.

They were from Boston; standard procedure to use out-of-state agents in a government corruption case. They admitted they'd had an eye on Melvin for years but never had any evidence. And they appreciated my coming forward.

"I just want to do what's right." There was nothing else for them to say after that inanity, so they finally left.

But Fred had enjoyed it. "Very interesting. You may pull this off."

"I just want to do what's right," I said again, and we laughed together.

We trudged through the next meeting. There were seven gentlemen, of whom I had met five, all thirty years older than I, competent, hard working, loyal to their liege lord. They'd had their job to do—managing large companies, meeting payrolls, balancing budgets—and they'd done their job with honor and pride. All of them were compromised, and all of them were reluctant criminals, and now they wanted to know if they would be punished for their loyalty to Melvin. These were not the Evil Four whose hands were bloody; these were the Tainted Seven—three presidents, two vice presidents, two financial officers—who'd held their noses and closed their eyes but had not quit.

I apologized that they had been caught off guard, but the matter had been very sensitive, and I'd been forced to move quickly. I told them I'd stand behind them, cover their expenses if there were any, defend them completely. But I insisted I wouldn't play the old game anymore.

They were as relieved as they could be, and said they were glad to leave the old regime behind. The old king was dead, long live the king. They filed out, and I wondered about honor among thieves. Don't worry, faithful subjects. When the bullets fly, I'll be standing right there behind you.

"Tell me the specifics of how this will affect your financial position," Fred asked when the room was clear. Even if he was in front of the desk instead of behind it, he was still feeling very comfortable in his chair.

"I've been figuring that out for the last couple weeks. Like I said,

I'll survive. There's a lot of work already in the pipeline and the payment schedule won't change. The next big contracts up for bid won't even start paying out for at least a year. So if we don't get even a single job more from the state, it'll be a year and a half before we feel it. And Melvin had been investing more in the legitimate businesses for the last three years. They're still a small percentage, but they're growing."

"Assuming that Bright is impeached or resigns and is no longer a threat," Fred said, "you will still be vulnerable politically if there is a perception that your wealth is at risk. If this becomes a substantial financial reversal, your influence will suffer."

"I'll make sure no one perceives that."

Now I was glad there were no mirrors in the room. I'd make sure there never were. It would be too distracting to have to look myself in the eye.

Fred heaved himself up and headed for his own duchy. I strolled out to Pamela. "This will be tricky. I want to meet with Clinton Grainger. Can you try to arrange that?"

She smiled at the challenge. "Of course, dear. I'll see what I can do."

"You can let him pick the location, if that will help. And schedule Fred to be in on it. And one more thing. There's a person named Wilcox with the state police. I want to meet with him. And get me Stan Morton."

"He's called twice. And so have most of his peers."

"Hire a receptionist with a real mean voice."

Then I called my dear wife. "I have one more call to make, and I'll be done."

"It's complete chaos here," she said. She sounded like it, too.

"The cavalry is on the way."

"A troop of horses is all I need."

Maybe she was joking, or maybe she was past joking. I kept it brief with Stan.

"Do you need anything from me?" I asked him.

"An interview would be nice. You're starting to become the reclusive young Jason Boyer. I'm keeping the heat on Bright, but I have to cover the other angles."

"Okay, probably tomorrow. I'm moving to a new house today."

"Haven't you been watching? Everybody in the state knows it."

Poor Katie. "No, and I haven't looked at the paper, either."

"Well, it's gone national. Harry Bright's the front page in the *Times* and the *Globe*."

"Thanks. Do whatever you have to. If you want to be fair, you can say a couple nasty things about me."

"Tell me a couple that no one else knows."

"Talk to you later, Stan."

23

I took a taxi to Eric's building to get my car. On the drive home I listened to the radio and I started to realize how high on the Richter scale our little scandal was registering. The embattled governor would be giving another press conference, and there were reports that state offices were being sealed by investigators to prevent destruction of documents. I called Pamela.

"Find out what's happening at Melvin's estate."

"There are quite a few police officers there." She already knew, of course. "They expect to be there through the day."

I don't care about the news, usually. It's insipid and frivolous, politics and shootings, all crime all the time. Now that Bright-gate had hit the big time, it had all the elements that I found so tiresome—murder, sleazy public officials, and big money. Even melodrama: the mysterious and handsome young billionaire.

I had my own street ahead of me. A policeman signaled me a block from the house, before I even reached the circus.

"Mr. Boyer? Just stay to the left and they'll let you through."

The circus wasn't too big, just two television trucks, a few cars, and a dozen people, half with cameras and half with hairdos. I glided up, then through, just quick enough. All they'd have for the midday news was my back bumper.

In front of the house were three large moving trucks and another dozen people, but these were usefully employed. Furniture and boxes were pouring out of every door.

Katie was in the front hall. I wondered if she'd collapse in my arms or order me to grab the next load. I'll never know; she hesitated just long enough for me to lift her off her feet, my left arm behind her back and my right beneath her legs. I swung her a full circle around.

Just at that moment, a big chair from the bedroom was walking past. "You, set it there," I said and the chair dropped to the floor. I gave Katie a big kiss and plopped her into it.

And now that I had established who was in charge, I put my knee onto the carpet and looked her straight in the eye.

"I'm here."

"I see," she said, then she giggled. "It's a good thing."

"It is." We both took a deep breath. "Is all this going okay?"

"Yes." She stood. "Go ahead," she said, and the chair started moving again. "But it's not easy."

"Have you seen the news?"

"Not yet. Only a little."

"Don't think about it," I said. "What can I do?"

"Well . . . just stand here and yell at everybody. I've got to go upstairs."

"Why?"

"To yell at everybody up there."

That's what she thrived on, but the stress was showing.

"Where's Francine?"

"In the kitchen, yelling at everybody."

"How long until they're done here?"

"We're almost done. We're leaving all the furniture here that we won't use in the new house."

"Then come with me."

We walked through the house. I stopped at the kitchen.

"Francine," I said. "I'm taking Katie out back. You'll have to do her yelling for her."

Francine frowned, of which she makes an art. "What do you mean, you're taking her out back? Hasn't anyone told you that you're moving today? You can't just leave."

"Yell at everybody else," I said. "Not at me."

I led Katie out the back door to a bench in the rose garden. "Now sit."

She sighed in relief. "Thank you."

We sat together, suddenly at peace. The turmoil in the house was left behind. "It's really going fine," she said, and then she remembered I was there. "How was your morning?"

"I think everything's under control. I talked with two men from the FBI."

"What did they say?"

"You don't need to worry about it. They're our friends."

She didn't want to worry about it anyway. "We really are almost ready to pull out. It was all such a hurry."

"If they missed anything, we can get it later. We should go on to the new house."

"Are all those people still out in the street?"

"Yes. I guess it'll be a parade. They'll follow us."

"I wish they would leave us alone." But she was proud of me, and that was worth all the troubles. "You're doing what you have to do. But I hope it won't always be like this."

"I guess there's nothing else happening in the world." I wanted to get Katie away from the chaos, and I didn't want our arrival at our new house to be in the center of a media riot. "Let's get out of here."

"I'll tell Eric. He's in your office."

Eric. I had an idea.

"The timing is important," I said. Katie and I were in her car, in the garage. The garage door was open, but no one could see us from the end of the street.

"Do you think they'll fall for it?" Eric asked. He was standing just outside my window. He was even in the khakis and blue shirt I'd just had on.

"Sure. And if they don't, it's not a big deal."

"How do I pretend I'm you?"

"Act intelligent."

"Then they'll know it's me," he said.

"Then act stupid."

"Okay. I can try."

"Rule Number 91—don't do anything that I won't want to see on the news tonight."

I was having second thoughts, but Eric had already sauntered away. I got out of the car to watch.

He wandered slowly toward the left barricade, and there was an immediate reaction. Car doors opened, cameras stood, all centered on the ersatz Jason, the sheep among the wolves. Now I was really having doubts.

One of the two trucks at the barricade at the other end of the street roared to life and shot away, to come around the block. The other scooted after it. I jumped back into the car.

"Five, four, three," I said. He would have almost reached the mob. "Two, one, go."

I didn't squeal the tires. I just pulled out very quickly, made a speedy turn to the right, toward the weak side of the defensive line, and accelerated. The police knew we were coming and swept the barricade aside for our car.

Then we were clear.

Left at the corner. "Lean with it," I said to Katie.

"Lean with what?"

"The turns!"

Right after that, then left. No one was behind us.

"You did it!" she said.

That made everything, the danger, the risks, all worth it. I was her hero.

"I would do anything for you," I said. We were out on the main road.

"Poor Eric."

"It is a far better thing he does than he has ever done before." I slowed down to a regular speed. "I hope none of those reporters are blondes."

"Well, they all are, of course. At least, the women."

"He might be in their clutches, even as we speak."

"You told him to get away from them as soon as we were gone."

"He's easily distracted. And they know we got away, so he's all they have. It might even become a hostage situation."

"Mother can rescue him. He'll be fine."

We were fine. We were away from the old house, and that would help. I was feeling new, renewed, maybe hopeful. Life would be different.

The city retreated and we advanced. Everything was going to work. Evil was defeated! The governor was history, and I was free from him and from the whole iniquitous business. I was really appreciating Melvin. He took the blame when he died, and left the riches for me. Now I had the wad, and I hadn't had to stoop to his level to get it.

It's nice to have someone else die in your place.

We arrived at the front gate alone and soared through, just the two of us. I pulled up to the front door.

We didn't even speak. I opened the car door for her, led her by the hand up the steps, and unlocked the front door. And then it was natural to lift her and carry her over the threshold.

And I wouldn't put her down until she kissed me.

Then we walked through the halls and galleries, exquisitely furnished, cleaned and shining. It was somewhat spare, but what was still lacking the trucks would soon provide. I banished the doubts and disputes from my mind. I would enjoy this completely.

"If I had never met you," I said, "and I had only seen what you had made of this house, I would still know you were beautiful."

"Thank you," she said. "This is what I've always wanted."

From the second-floor landing we had an expansive view of the front grounds. Soon the procession appeared on the horizon—first, a lone white-and-blue figure on a swift two-wheeled steed; then three yellow-and-orange trucks, imperious gliding swans; and in their wake the bevy of white news trucks and cars herded by two black-and-white police cars.

The nobler vehicles entered the grounds and we descended to greet them.

Eric doffed his helmet and grinned. "We made it."

"Well done," I answered.

"Francine's in the police car."

"We'll post bail if we have to." Katie said it before I could. She was energized from our moment together, and she was ready for the next frenzy. The trucks came to a halt, and quickly, many men were following her commands.

My part was done. Eric and I found a place on the third floor where we could sit.

"This is so cool," he said. We were on a balcony looking down on the fireplace.

"It's just money," I said.

"It said in the paper you have a billion dollars."

"Tell me what else the papers say."

In surprisingly cogent sentences, Eric caught me up on the outside world. Most of the sixty pages I'd given to Stan Morton were out now, with times and places of meetings, details of which contracts were rigged, the amounts of the bribes.

The governor had spoken no more public words, but it was getting vicious inside his cabinet as everyone tried to shift blame. "Sources high in the administration" were leaking like a spaghetti strainer, and the cabinet secretaries sounded like ten hungry dogs in a room with one meatball. My former employees were given their share of ink, but they weren't talking.

"They had an article about Henry Malden, the lieutenant governor, since he might end up as governor. It said he doesn't even show up at the capitol very often."

I'd have to ask Fred who Mr. Malden was owned by. "What do they say about Angela?"

The public version was that someone had come to her estate Saturday evening. Angela must have been expecting the person, because she apparently answered the door herself. None of the servants saw anything; none of them saw her through the rest of the evening, until she was found Sunday morning.

"That doesn't sound like Angela," I said. "She must have wanted to keep her meeting secret."

The note was a problem. The first reports were that it was a forgery, but it wasn't. It was in her own handwriting. The wording was strange, though.

"'I don't want this to go on,'" Eric recited. "'It all has to stop. I'll do anything to make it stop.'"

"That does sound like Angela."

"The police think it was part of a note she had written to someone else. The paper was torn."

The gun was in her right hand, but the shot was through her left temple. The police had other evidence, but they weren't talking about it.

"Anything about Melvin?"

A lot about his life and how he had made his fortune. Some about his accident, and the possible brake failure. The main evidence was drops of brake fluid in Fred's driveway.

"That still doesn't seem right to me," Eric said. "You'd have to look real hard, right away."

"Do they have any clue who killed them?"

No. Sources said the police were clueless.

"And you're mysterious and reclusive," Eric said. "Maybe you're an idealist and you want to clean up the corruption. Or maybe you're ruthless, and you're trying some power play, and it's all politics." If the reporters could figure out which, I'd be glad to know the answer.

The show below was more interesting to me. If we were leaving most of our old furniture behind, why did we still need three trucks? Not that I wanted to know the answer.

And watching the ants carrying their loads below, I wondered how all that stuff could fit in just three trucks? They came and came, and went and went, and I was as clueless about them as the police were about Angela.

Occasionally I caught a glimpse of Katie, and we often heard her voice echoing off the stone walls and floors. Then she appeared behind us.

"There you are. Come and look."

We went with her through the bedrooms, the office, the sitting rooms, the living room, the dining room, the kitchen, and on. I didn't feel like I lived in this house—but it was a wonderful, beautiful place where I'd want to feel at home.

"I'm amazed," I said. "We only moved in today?"

"Is it still today?" Katie said. "It seems like a month since this morning. There's still so much unpacking to do. I told the movers to be back tomorrow."

Eric wandered off in search of a television, to catch up on the latest tidbits, and I led Katie back up to my perch above the fireplace.

"I really am amazed," I said. "It's the most beautiful house I've ever seen."

"It's what I'm good at."

"You're good at so many things."

That bought me one of her most beautiful smiles. "We'll be happy here, Jason."

"Together? I'm still the same person, you know."

"I think you've changed."

No. "You're just seeing a different side."

"It's your good side. You aren't so moody all the time."

"You hardly ever see me."

She was too blissful to disagree. "That's because you have so much to do. You're important now. It makes you feel different." She leaned against my shoulder. "I'm so proud of you. You're doing so many good things, and you're doing them so well. You have purpose."

"That would be nice." I'd let the other comments slide.

She laughed.

I had to laugh, too. Maybe I really had changed. "Okay. But just being rich and important isn't enough."

"Then nothing is."

"There must be something."

"Being together is enough for me."

It was for me, too.

It was just after six. I was looking through drawers and closets in the bedroom when my cell phone rang, and it was Pamela.

"Reporting in," she said. "Detective Wilcox of the state police will see you tomorrow at nine in your office. Nathan Kern called. And tonight, you and Fred should be at the downtown Hilton at eleven to meet Clinton Grainger. There's a bar off the main lobby. If he's not there by midnight, we should try to reschedule for the weekend."

"Thanks, Pamela. If there's anything else, let me know."

"Yes, sir. Have you been watching the news?"

"No."

"The four executives you fired yesterday have been charged with lots of crimes."

"Lots?"

"Lots and lots. They are all in custody for the moment, until they get out on bail."

"Oh well. I'm not surprised."

The Gang of Four. I was hungry for Chinese. After I hung up, I looked for Katie.

"Is Rosita planning dinner tonight?" I asked.

"No. I told her not to."

"Did you even have lunch?"

"Just a sandwich . . . no. I never ate it."

"Tell her to order a mound of cashew chicken and pork lo mein, and anything else she thinks would go with it. And I've got a meeting downtown tonight, late."

I went to my new office. The movers had done a good job; even my books were in the right order on the shelves. I organized and filed for a while, and then I remembered Nathan. I never had called him, and he would have received the file I'd sent him with no explanation. I finally found him at home.

"Jason? This is Nathan."

"Pamela said you called," I said.

"Yes. I realize you're having a very busy day, and I'm sorry to bother you. But I received the envelope you mailed to me. I looked through it briefly, and I thought I should call."

"That's fine. I was going to call you, but I forgot. I didn't need you to do anything with it. I just wanted to have a copy of the papers in a safe place."

"Oh, of course. I understand."

"The FBI has a copy now, and so does the newspaper and everyone else, so you probably don't need to keep it."

"I should destroy it, then?"

"Whatever. That would be okay."

"I will, then. I've been following the news since yesterday. Jason, I'm very impressed that you're doing this."

Quickly, I booted up the platitude server. "I wanted it all to come out."

"I said I thought it would be a noble thing."

"I don't know. It won't really hurt me much, and I'll have a clean conscience. I may not even need the foundation anymore. I won't have any evil deeds that I need good deeds to balance against."

He must have known I was joking, but he still took it seriously.

"Well, that would be your decision of course, Jason."

"I'm not being serious. But I'm looking forward to being rich without being corrupt."

"That's not easy to do."

"I'll give it a try." I was really just trying a little banter, but he was the wrong person for light conversation. I should have just answered his question about the envelope and hung up.

"You might consider it first." It would have helped if the man had a sense of humor. Or maybe he did. Maybe he was joking, too. "Remember, it isn't the source that makes the wealth good or bad. It's often the wealth itself that is the issue."

"Well . . . I will remember that. But this is a fresh start and maybe that will make a difference."

He knew when to yield. "In any case, I'm sure your actions yesterday and today will produce great benefits."

"Thank you."

"And I hope that it can all be settled peacefully. Have you communicated at all with the governor or his staff?"

"I'm meeting with his chief of staff tonight."

"Mr. Grainger? Oh, really!" He paused—apparently another phone had rung. Then he was back. "Have you spoken with him before?"

"Twice, briefly. You know him?"

"I've worked with him on a number of inner-city projects that the governor took a personal interest in. He has the governor's ear, Jason. If anyone can work things out, he'll be able to."

"I'm hoping we can work something out."

I feared that the joy with which I was anticipating dinner might be diminished slightly by that conversation. But it wasn't.

Dinner was very nice. I'd seen no sign of Francine—she didn't drive after dark, so she'd been gone for a while. Eric was still with us.

I complimented Rosita on her excellent dinner as she cleared away the white cardboard and chopsticks, and she said it was an old family recipe. We even looked into the kitchen to see her progress in organizing her new domain.

Two new maids were to report to work tomorrow, and gardeners were already employed. Home, sweet home.

At ten o'clock I gave Katie instructions to get to bed early, and I left for the Hilton. It was a longer drive downtown from this house.

Now I had time to think.

I didn't believe it anymore, what Nathan had said. Wealth and power don't corrupt. It's just that corrupt people often became wealthy and powerful.

I had changed in four weeks. It wasn't for the worse, though. Maybe I'd said I'd never take the money, but I knew better now. I'd done nothing wrong in getting it, and I wouldn't have to do anything wrong to keep it. I was going to keep it. I will be rich, I will be powerful. I accept it. Melvin Boyer knew his son, and he'd made the right decision.

Angela? Five days ago I'd been slapping myself about being at fault for her death, but that wasn't really a reasonable way to look at it. I'd smothered a political attack against myself. I'd had every reason to believe that the suspicion of murder was unfounded. Unfortunately, I'd been wrong. But life goes on. For the rest of us, anyway.

The police were still clueless. They wouldn't have been able to prevent it even if they had kept the investigation open. I'd made the right decision.

Melvin? I'd had nothing to do with his death; that was all on his own head. With as many enemies as he'd made, it was a wonder he'd lasted as long as he did. Melvin Boyer. Now, there was a paradigm of corruption, a man who was ruthless to begin with. He'd made his fortune because he was cruel and smart and lucky. But a person didn't have to be that way to be rich. I wouldn't be. I had him as an example of what to avoid.

Had he always been that way? I didn't know him back in the beginning. He probably was. It was already showing when he was married to Ann.

I'd know it if I was becoming like him. I know that I'm not the kind of person he was. And I'm at the exit now, and I've wasted this whole time. I need to be ready to deal with Clinton Grainger, and Fred will be there, too, and this is no time for stupid arguments. So shut up.

24

I parked on the street. It's not safe downtown at night, but I would have killed anyone who tried to mug me in that dark half block to the hotel. It was still quarter to eleven. I found the bar and a booth in it and sat in the shadow.

Ten minutes later, as inconspicuous as a blimp, Fred joined me. Once he was settled, though, the gloom swallowed him, and he was just a presence in the dimness.

"Three of Bright's cabinet secretaries resigned an hour ago," he murmured. "Transportation, Finance, and Education."

"Education?" I didn't even know who that person was.

"The ship is sinking and there's not enough lifeboats."

"Is it going down that fast?" I asked.

"Eileen McCloskey, the education secretary, is making her move to challenge him. She would make an interesting candidate if she can be controlled. She's certainly trying to sink him now, so we could consider her an ally. And she won't be the last."

What pleasant people. Had power corrupted them, or had they been nasty from birth?

"So, who owns Malden, the lieutenant governor?"

"Forrester. Your father brokered the deal between him and Bright."

"So if . . . I mean, when he becomes governor, Forrester is in control."

"No. Henry Malden is a nonentity. He presides over the state senate and funnels information to Forrester, but he has no political skills. Forrester wanted an informant and Bright wanted a lieutenant who would never be a rival. As governor, Malden will be completely lost."

"Then who will be in charge?"

As if I'd needed to ask Fred Spellman such a question. "Whoever is strongest," he said.

"Anything else?"

"I have been advising several of your executive managers on how they are to respond to subpoenas."

"We're cooperating."

"Yes, yes," Fred said. "But the lines must be kept clear."

"Whatever. We'll tough it out. Do you have any suggestions for this evening?"

"Grainger may have something constructive to suggest concerning the current crisis. But mainly you're both just looking. Remember, you've wrecked his main project. He may be holding a grudge. He's going to abandon ship sometime, but his timing may depend on you."

"I agree with what you said this morning," I said. "I'd like him at least neutral. As long as he stays on the governor's staff, he can use the governor against me."

"Exactly. So convince him his future is better as your friend. Give him a small hint and see how he responds."

Friend. The word grated somewhat, in the context of our conversation and setting. It implied trust, and decency—certainly the wrong word.

"What else might he do to fight back?" I was really just thinking aloud. We'd been through everything.

"I haven't thought of anything else. He may indicate something tonight."

On that note, we waited. Noisy, jumbled minutes were passing outside our booth. A television played over the bar, music, talking, lights splattering the room, but we were no part of it. We were the dark and silence that the life of the room broke through and sank back under.

At almost midnight the black deepened as Grainger slid in next to me. I hadn't seen him come into the room. I shifted around into the back corner.

"Busy day," he said. "I can't stay long."

That bordered on the moronic, but there wasn't any better way to begin. The man's alleged genius certainly wasn't in conversation. I tried to think of something equally obvious to say.

"Bright's career is over," I said. "I had no choice."

"Maybe."

"What should I have done?" I wanted to see how personally he was taking it.

"It doesn't matter. The governor doesn't have many choices, either."

It was hard to tell if that was a statement or a threat. His voice was expressionless, and his face would have been if I could have seen it.

"I made a business decision, to clean house," I said. "There were too many risks the old way, including Bright as a business partner." I leaned toward him. "Slamming me with a murder scandal didn't add to the working relationship."

"You shouldn't react too hastily." He sounded weary and carefully patient.

"Last month you said I took too long to make decisions."

"That was a different situation. You've done a lot of damage, and it could have been avoided." It was the first time I'd heard him speak with any inflection to his words, and it was condescension. "It's going to take a lot of effort to repair." Poor Clinton, having to clean up my mess.

Fred rumbled to life. "Don't use that tone. You are speaking to adults here, not that toddler you baby-sit. The governor is finished, and you know it. The issue here is to manage the endgame."

"I'm not conceding that," Grainger said.

"You should," I said. "I don't want to have to do any more damage."

"What else will you do?" Grainger asked.

"That depends on you," I countered. "What will you do?"

"Your cabinet is self-destructing," Fred added. "The police are just getting started. It would be pointless to prolong this. You know you can't win."

"The governor is paying me to prolong this."

"How much is he paying you?"

That was enough for Clinton Grainger to understand the real reason for the meeting. Even in the dark, I could feel his unblinking eyes on me. "I'm not a mercenary, Mr. Boyer."

"I don't think he'll be paying you much longer," I said. "I'm patient."

"It hasn't seemed that way."

"I do what I have to do." And I'd said what I had to say. "And I appreciate that you were willing to talk with me. We'll see what happens next."

"I'm not interested."

"That's up to you. I really am patient, and I won't have to wait long."

"You keep assuming that." He stood. "You may be surprised."

"You know it's over," I said.

"Not yet. I can cause damage, too."

"Nothing can save Bright."

"Mr. Boyer, be careful about throwing stones. You have more glass in your own house than you think." He paused, but I didn't take his bait. "Don't call me again."

"I won't unless I have to," I said.

With that, he slipped back out from the enemy lines into no-man's-land and was gone. We waited a few minutes to let him get away clear, in case anyone was watching.

Fred and I stood at the curb by Fred's car. "Apparently the governor will launch some attack tomorrow," he said.

"What was he talking about?"

"We'll find out. He acted as if it would be substantial."

"I'll be at home. Call me if anything happens."

I pointed at the car parked ahead of Fred's on the street. "Isn't that Grainger's car? It has a governor's mansion parking sticker."

Fred scowled. "He's meeting someone else."

"He might just be getting food."

"No, he's discussing our meeting. I don't like it. He has more ammunition."

I shrugged. "It can't be that bad. Call me anytime."

25

Fred did call anytime. It was less than five hours later when Rosita knocked on my bedroom door and I groped through the dark in my pajamas, trying to find my office in that huge new house.

"Jason," Fred said, indignant enough for both of us. "Turn on your television. Clinton Grainger is dead."

It hadn't even been five days since the last time someone had said that. Just with a different name.

But Fred didn't dissolve into sobbing. He kept talking. "He was gunned down outside the hotel last night, beside his car."

At least I wouldn't have anything to do with this funeral. I switched through the network morning shows. Katie and I had compromised; there was a television in the breakfast room, but it was small.

At first it was only on the local news breaks, but then the New York anchors picked it up. No one hesitated to lump everything together.

"A third murder in Governor Harry Bright's corruption case last night," one face said to a national audience.

"Possibly the greatest scandal in recent American history," another claimed.

I called Stan Morton. "I'm not doing an interview today."

"Huh?" he said. "I don't even know what day it is. You lose track when you don't sleep. Did you kill Clinton Grainger?"

"Who's saying that?"

"Just say yes or no."

"No."

"Good. But you'd say that anyway."

"This is not why I called."

"The interview. Tomorrow?"

"I'll think about it."

Eric must have spent the night, because he wandered in a while later, wearing the work clothes Katie had bought for me, his hair a mess. He stared at the screen and his blurred eyes got big.

"I've heard of him. They talked about Clinton Grainger in the newspaper yesterday."

I played innocent. "Governor Bright is going to miss him."

Eric nodded. "Yeah. Clinton Grainger is Harry Bright's chief of staff and main political adviser. He's been the mastermind behind his whole career."

I turned from the television to look at my brother.

"What?" he said. "You told me to read the newspapers."

"Is that what the papers said?"

"Well, sort of. You could figure it out. Did you know him?"

"I met him a couple times."

"This might . . . Do you . . . Do you think it could be the same person who killed Angela?"

The whole huge cloud had at least one little silver lining—that Eric had something besides cars to figure out. "Um . . . the thought had crossed my mind."

"Wow. This is big. Do you think it made it into the newspaper?"

"I bet it was too late. And Rule Number 92—don't believe everything you read in the newspaper."

"But you said to read it. You own it anyway."

"That's why Rule 92 is so important."

At seven thirty, the governor appeared to make a statement. He was badly shaken, stumbling over his words, his face ashen and his hands trembling.

"This morning I lost a close adviser and a good friend. Clinton had been with me through thick and thin. I often counted on him for wise counsel, especially these last few days. We will all miss him, and I more than anyone." Even if he'd invited them, none of the reporters would have dared to ask any questions. For the moment he'd score a lot of sympathy points with his voters, but the image of the blank eyes and dead expression would surely haunt him forever.

But many questions—Rhetorical News Anchor Questions— were asked of the viewers. "Will Harry Bright survive this latest blow? Is this murder related to the deaths of Melvin and Angela Boyer? What will the authorities find at the bottom of this affair?" And all the questions were answered with all the standard variations of the Rhetorical News Anchor Answer.

"Only time will tell."

When Katie arrived for breakfast, I told her I'd be busy being rich and important for the day, and to not wait up.

"This is not a good habit," she said. "You need sleep."

"At least I've got a reason to be alive."

"Rosita is planning a nice dinner."

It is important to keep priorities. "Okay. I'll try real hard to be here."

I got to Fred's office at eight forty. He had not come down from his indignancy plateau, but the first thing he said as I faced him across his desk was completely lucid.

"Be very careful. The meeting with Grainger last night could blow up in our faces."

"I thought of that," I said. "Motive and opportunity. But we can't hide it."

"It isn't just that you will be a target for the murder investigation. We will also be vulnerable politically if it becomes public knowledge that we were negotiating with him. Unless . . . we could use that to our advantage." He shook his head. There were too many angles for even Fred to work out. He settled into simple ful-mination. "I've never seen anything like this. Everything is in sham-bles. Anything could happen right now. Who knows what might happen? Anything. Any single thing."

"You're feeling insecure, Fred. You should get therapy."

"I don't have time."

I let him rant for a while. He was a poker shark who'd been dropped in a bridge tournament—it was a new game, he didn't understand the rules, and he didn't like it. Right now he was approaching hysterics, and somebody needed to slap him.

Fred's secretary opened the door. "Mr. Boyer? Pamela called. She wanted to remind you that Detective Wilcox would be by at nine."

That was the slap. "The police detective?" he said.

"I arranged it yesterday. I wanted to act cooperative."

"Of course." He was thinking coherently again. "This will be risky, but I see no other choice. It will be best to get it over with quickly."

"Would you care to join us?"

"I think I had better."

Being in an elevator that was trying to lift Fred Spellman to the top of a forty-two-story building also seemed risky, but I saw no other choice. We entered that little room, its door closed on us, and with a mighty effort it began its labor.

"Do you realize the gravity of the situation?" Fred asked.

That was exactly what I was thinking about, except that Fred meant Wilcox.

"Yes," I said. "This murderer is for real, and so is the investiga-tion. I don't want to lose control."

"No one is in control."

We'd made it halfway. Fred was thinking very hard, and he turned suddenly to face me.

"Do you have an alibi for last night?"

"What?"

"What did you do after we separated?"

"I went home."

"Last Saturday night, when Angela was shot. Where were you then?"

"On my boat."

"With your wife?"

"Alone."

"Don't answer any questions he asks."

We made it to the top, and I'd forgotten my worry about whether we would. "I'll have to answer sometime."

"Then just be very careful. Speak slowly so I can stop you if necessary."

"I didn't kill anyone."

"How many times do I have to tell you that that doesn't matter?" The elevator door opened.

"It does matter," I said. "Not to the police, but it does matter."

"Whatever."

We crossed the lobby and opened the door to Pamela's office.

Detective Wilcox rose to greet us, we all smiled, and I was reminded again how much I detested him. Or maybe just his mustache. He had a hard enough job, chasing criminals through political minefields. Why make it harder on himself, when a razor would slay that thing in two minutes?

"Please come in," I said, and we filed into the throne room.

"Thank you for coming," I said when we were all comfortable. "I guess you're very busy today."

"Yes, Mr. Boyer, I am," he said. "But frankly, this meeting is right at the top of my list." He looked like maybe he'd been sleeping as much as Stan Morton.

"It's pretty high on my list, too." I took a breath and began my official statement. "The last time we met, I was of the opinion that the investigation of Melvin Boyer's death was politically motivated. I still think it was. Now, however, I accept that he was murdered. I want to cooperate with your investigation. I still don't trust you, though. Your top boss is Harry Bright, and he'd like to murder me."

Wilcox took a deep breath. "First, Mr. Boyer, let me assure you that the state police are completely independent."

"And I completely believe you."

"And we are only interested in solving these murders. That is my only purpose."

"Then my purpose is to make sure you solve them correctly, because I think the governor has other purposes."

He gave that up. "Anyway, sir, I would like to ask you some questions."

"I think I'd like to ask questions first," I said. "Are you treating all three of these murders as one case?"

"Uh, well, we don't comment on investigations."

I shook my head. "You'll have to do much better than that, Mr. Wilcox. I said I'd cooperate, but I don't need to do it for free."

"I understand," he said. "We're keeping our options open. Personally, I think it's clear the three cases are related."

"Do you have any suspects?"

"No one specific yet. But we have a list of obvious names."

"Who's on it?"

"Mr. Boyer, I can't tell you that."

"You said they're obvious."

"It's obvious who benefited from the deaths."

I'd done pretty well from them—that was obvious. "Melvin had a lot of enemies."

"Yes, he did," Wilcox said. "But that wouldn't carry over to Angela Boyer, or to Clinton Grainger."

"Detective Wilcox." Fred didn't want us to forget he was there. "Is Jason Boyer your main suspect?"

"We don't have a main suspect."

"Jason Boyer, Katie Boyer, Eric Boyer," Fred listed. "Is there anyone else obvious?"

Wilcox shrugged. "I'll just say those are the three names on the list that are underlined."

"Katie and Eric don't even know who Clinton Grainger is," I said. I'd just throw myself on that grenade. Eric recognized Grainger's name, but that didn't count.

"We're just getting started with Grainger's murder," Wilcox said. "I don't even have forensics from the scene yet."

"Next question," I said. "Who broke into my office?"

Wilcox reacted just enough to convince me he knew. "I haven't seen any report on that. When did it happen?"

"Friday or Saturday, three weeks ago. I didn't file a report. Since the police did it, why waste the time? They got Melvin's office, too."

"I don't know anything about that, Mr. Boyer."

"It sounds like the police department needs to work on internal communications. Never mind. What would you like to ask me?"

"Um, back to our list. Do you have any additional names for it?"

"No."

He paused and looked down at his notebook. "How well did you know Clinton Grainger?" It was time to get personal.

"I met him three times."

"When was the last time?" Wilcox asked, still looking down. Fred shifted in his chair.

"Last night," I said.

This was news to him. Fred sniffed. "What time?" Wilcox asked.

"About eleven forty, for maybe ten minutes."

He scribbled. "Where?"

"At the Hilton, in the bar."

He looked up at me. "Any witnesses?"

"I was there," Fred said. "Mr. Boyer and I left together, several minutes after Mr. Grainger. We parted in front of the hotel."

"What did you talk about?"

"I'll just say it was obvious," I said.

Wilcox looked back at his notebook, then at me. "This is very important information, Mr. Boyer. You were the last people to see him?"

"Except for whoever killed him."

Wilcox ignored that. "Did anyone else know about your meeting?"

"I told my wife and brother I was meeting someone, but not who. Pamela, my secretary, arranged the meeting. I don't know if anyone on his staff knew. They said on the television that he was shot beside his car?"

"Yes. He was."

"Where was his car?" I asked.

"Just in front of the hotel."

It had been his car. "Then he was killed after we left. We gave him time to leave first so he wouldn't be seen with us. I think he met someone else."

"Who?" Wilcox said.

"I don't know."

"Why do you believe he met someone?"

"His car was still in front of the hotel when we left. At least, I guessed it was his."

"I see. Would you say you benefited from Clinton Grainger's death, Mr. Boyer?"

"I don't know. We'll find out."

"What do you mean?"

Surely Wilcox knew his way around this neighborhood. "Grainger was advising the governor against me. But he'd probably keep the governor from doing anything irrational," I said. "Now Bright may do something crazy. I think I would prefer that Clinton Grainger were still advising him."

"I see." Wilcox was not writing this down. He turned to Fred. "Mr. Spellman, you were the last person to see Melvin Boyer alive, and now also Clinton Grainger." Then, in a sudden act of bravery, Detective Wilcox stuck his head into the lion's mouth. "Mr. Spellman, where were you last Saturday night when Angela Boyer was killed?"

"Are you putting my name on your list, Mr. Wilcox?" I'd seen many sides of Fred recently, but he was still big enough to have a few more. I looked closely to see if my ears were right. They were; he was about to laugh, he thought the idea was so funny.

"It's just routine—" Wilcox started, but Fred burst out with a snort. He couldn't help it.

"I'll have to defer," he said, when he could. "If you're serious, you'll need to make an appointment. And I'll need to hire an attorney."

Wilcox tried again. "It's just routine. I'll need to ask you these questions."

"Mr. Boyer has been very patient and generous, but I am not."

Fred had gotten over his fit. "If you send me a list of questions, I will consider answering them."

So that's how it would be. Wilcox gave up. He was probably in a hurry anyway. "I'll be in touch. Thank you, Mr. Boyer. Could you keep us informed if you leave town?"

"No," I said.

"I'll have more questions."

"My secretary can reach me. Wait. I have one more question."

That was usually his line, but he stopped. "Yes?"

"Was there really brake fluid in Mr. Spellman's driveway?"

"That is from the original report."

"I had a meeting with Grainger three weeks ago. Maybe you remember? I think he spoke with you afterward."

"Um, he may have spoken with Police Commissioner De-Angelo."

"We discussed the report, and he didn't know whether it was true. He only said they'd been told to make sure there was evidence."

"Mr. Boyer . . ."

I interrupted. "So is the report true or not?"

That required some chewing on his lip. "It might not be possible to corroborate that physically. All I have is that report."

"You would have the person who wrote the report."

"Um, yes." Either it was fake or he didn't know whether it was or not, and possibly he and the author were not on speaking terms. That left the ice under him pretty thin, and it was time to get off the pond. "Thank you again, Mr. Boyer," he said. I didn't press him to stay.

And so he left us. I'd gotten more out of the interrogation than he had, and I would not have minded a little quiet thinking time, just leaning back and contemplating the world forty-two stories below. Something, however, was blocking my view.

"Forrester," it said.

I still tried to get a glimpse of the sun-swept panorama, but the obstacle was too great.

"It's his turn," I said. "I initiated last time."

"I did."

"But you're on my team. Aren't you?"

"I suppose. As much as you will both dislike it, the two of you need to meet. He knows that. He may even initiate it himself. He understands what you're doing to Bright, and that he may have underestimated you."

"Most people overestimate me."

"Either can be dangerous. And the two of you must come to some agreement on a plan of action for the governor's mansion."

"Putting new furniture in or something?"

"Putting a new occupant in it."

"Fred, I don't like the senator, and I don't just mean personally, although that's included. There were no fireworks last time because there wasn't time. I don't like being looked down on unless I'm doing it, and I'm getting to enjoy putting mutinous politicians in their place."

"Don't underestimate him."

"I won't. But he hates the deal he made with Melvin, and I'm getting kind of tired of it, too."

Fred's glower was not approving. "It took your father many years to build his political structure. The conflict with the governor may, perhaps, have been unavoidable—not that you tried to avoid it. But don't destroy powerful men for recreation."

"It's not for recreation. It's because I like throwing tantrums."

"That's recreation. You might also find Forrester a harder nut to crack. He has a lot of money of his own. As I said, don't under-estimate him."

"I am not underestimating his arrogance and hostility to Boyer control. Estimate this: would he hate Melvin enough to kill him?"

"If so, he would have done it long ago."

"Would he hate Harry Bright enough to kill Clinton Grainger?"

"My answer is the same. And he had no reason to kill Angela."

"Did he know her?" I asked.

"Of course he'd met her."

"For some people, that's all it would take."

Fred stood. I'd finally made him mad enough to leave. "Then suggest to Mr. Wilcox that he add the senator to his list. But before the police clap him in irons, you still need to meet with him to discuss your next steps."

"I will. Next week. I'll invite you to join us."

Forrester wasn't the murderer. It had to be Fred. I watched the door close behind him. Who else?

I went through motives. It couldn't be my wife or my brother. They had no connection with Clinton Grainger, assuming he'd been killed by the same person as Melvin and Angela, and assuming that either Eric or Katie could kill anyone anyway. But I could see Fred pulling a trigger.

Fred and Melvin. Maybe Melvin was going to fire him? Melvin was getting too hard to control? Melvin was going to make some big decision that Fred wanted to prevent—like changing his will?

But could Fred figure out how to drain brake lines? It didn't seem likely.

Fred and Angela. She'd found something incriminating? Or Fred thought she might? No problem for him to drop in on business that Saturday night.

Fred and Clinton Grainger? What had Grainger meant, *You may be surprised, it's not over yet*? Did Fred know? Only time would tell. And, if it was Fred, that was a problem. He was smart enough to keep Wilcox from catching him, and that meant that Wilcox would have to pin it on me instead, which was what he'd been instructed to do anyway.

And there was another problem. If I didn't know what Melvin had done to irk Fred, I might do the same thing, and Fred would kill me, too.

I still couldn't really believe that Fred was the killer. It was absurd, really—as much as Eric or Katie might be the killer. Or Nathan Kern. Or George Elias or Harry Bright or Stan Morton or Pamela or Wilcox or Rosita or Francine or Angela's sister, Celeste, or Harriet the Realtor. Or anybody. But there was a killer.

26

"Jason?" Pamela was so good at reality. My imaginations crumbled before her smiling face. "Honey, you should sit down for this one. I was talking with Bob Forrester's secretary in Washington."

My imaginations recovered. "Is this a joke?" Suspicion jumped up beside imagination. "Did Fred tell you to call her?"

"Jason. Of course not. She called me."

"Because if Fred—"

"Just listen, dear. The senator will be in town this weekend and wishes to meet with you."

"This must be a joke."

"Oh no. His secretary asks if you and your wife could be invited to dinner tomorrow night."

"At his home?!"

"Yes, dear."

"I don't believe it. Fred must be behind this somehow. I'm sorry, Pamela. It's just that five minutes ago, Fred was telling me I had to speak with the senator, and that the senator might even call first."

"Then Fred was right. But I really don't think he was involved. Now, the dinner will be very formal. Did all your fancy schools teach you which fork to use?"

"I failed those classes. Did he ever invite Melvin?"

"If your father ever walked through that door, I didn't know about it."

It had been a long week. Two murders, one funeral, one governor demolished, one motorcycle ride to New Hampshire, one move to a new house, four firings. But this was going to be the worst. "Sure, we're available. But I want Fred to be there."

"That'll be tricky. He's inviting you to his house, which is stooping pretty low. He's only giving one day's notice, which also makes him look eager, and that's even worse. He won't like us to make requests."

"See what you can do."

"I'll try. You must have really gotten his attention."

It was time to go through the rest of Melvin's office. I'd be fourth in line, after Grainger's break-in, then the police, and now the FBI. No, fifth. The murderer had been in there after Grainger's people. But there still might be something.

If Angela had pawed through it all weeks ago, that would make me sixth.

I called Katie while I was driving.

"Heads up," I said. "We might have dinner at Bob Forrester's tomorrow."

"What? Why?"

I didn't feel like explaining at the moment. "Does it matter?"

"Of course it does. I have to plan what to wear. Who else will be there?"

"Just us."

"Jason! Just us? I don't believe it."

"Well, and probably Fred."

"He'll be odd."

I'd never heard her real opinion of him. Then I realized she meant he would be unpaired at the table.

"Pamela's still negotiating. They'll find someone if they have to."

"What is it all about?"

"Power and money, what else?"

"Jason, I don't have the right things to wear for occasions like this."

"I'm sure you will find something."

I was at the gate. A policeman let me in, but he was apparently the only officer of the law on the premises. No one else was home. There was yellow tape across the door to Angela's parlor.

I went directly to the office. It had been more than three weeks since I'd last been in that room, and I could tell others had been there. It wasn't a mess. Angela had probably never seen a mess in her life. Well . . . a physical mess, anyway. Most of her life had been a mess.

I didn't even know what had been in the office originally so I had no idea what had been taken, or by whom. There wasn't much. The main file left was his foundation notes. I leaned back in the old wood desk chair and read them for an hour.

They went back for years, and there were gaps. Apparently he'd only kept the interesting stuff in his desk. There were board meeting minutes and reports on specific projects, and a few of the few had handwritten notes. Those opened no windows into his soul. I read them all.

Add $200K was written next to one line about a grant to a library. *NK to continue review* at the top of a page about a food program somewhere.

NK would be Nathan Kern. I couldn't think of anything else Melvin had written that I had read. There was no need to take any of the papers.

It was getting eerie again reading them. The whole place was eerie—the thick carpet, the dark paneling, the books that had never been read. I had to conquer this place, somehow, before I sold it. The Washington townhouse hadn't been hard, but the ghosts here were more recent. I started wandering.

It was different than the last time I searched the office, when Angela had been in residence. I thought about Angela's last night. She'd invited someone over. They'd sat together in the midst of her pinkness and puffery. Had she found something incriminating? Did she know it was Melvin's killer with her? If it had been his killer, of course. How many murderers were on the loose, anyway?

Maybe she didn't realize what the evidence meant, and she asked the person to come explain it to her. As loopy as she normally was, she was completely off the deep end that last conversation I'd had with her. She must have known something was wrong.

The murderer was someone she knew, obviously. She didn't know too many people. Was it connected to Clinton Grainger? Who in the world would know both Angela and Grainger?

Well, Fred. But would any chair in that room have supported him? That was a crucial piece of evidence—no crushed furniture.

In Melvin's bedroom I had a surprise—his closet and drawers were still filled with his clothes. Of course they would be, but it was strange, and what was I supposed to do with it all? Give it to the poor? I'd call Nathan. Most homeless people don't have a decent business suit.

There was a small table by the bed. I pulled open the drawer. It was nearly empty, just some aspirin, reading glasses, tissues, paper and pen, and a book. What would he have been reading?

It wasn't a book. It was a bulky brown leather picture frame that opened like a book. I opened it, and then I had to sit down.

There were two pictures. One of a man and woman, one of two young children. I'd never seen these photos. Probably no one else had, either, except Melvin, in more than twenty years.

Melvin and Ann, Jason and Eric.

I didn't know what to think. They'd been here by his bed, maybe for that long. Suddenly, new doors into his heart were opening for me. I didn't want to go through them, but I still sat on the bed as minutes went by, staring at the pictures. In the end I didn't know if it was better or worse that I'd seen them.

And they'd been by his bed. All this time.

I took the frame with me.

It wasn't as far a drive to our new residence. The road turned and I saw my own house through the trees. I stopped on the roadside to look at it.

"Pamela?"

"Yes, Jason?"

"Find someone real good to put in a security system for my house. There's one here already, but I want something industrial strength."

"Yes, sir. Do you want it in a hurry?"

"Well, yes. It's a dangerous world."

"I understand. I can call the people who maintained your father's system."

"Maybe you should ask around."

"All right, I will. And there's no word yet from the senator's office."

"Let me know when there is." I put my phone away and sat there awhile before I went in. The picture frame was in my briefcase, and I didn't show it to Katie. When I got to my office, I put it in my desk drawer.

I dialed Nathan Kern's number. It was after five, but that hardworking, dedicated man was still there, burning the midnight dollars.

"Yes, Jason? This is Nathan Kern."

"Hello, Nathan. I was calling to ask you about last week. I want to get this straight. You talked to Angela on Wednesday?"

"Yes, Wednesday evening. We discussed her joining the board. As I told you before, she was very excited."

"And on Thursday, I told you she had changed her mind. That was a surprise?"

"Absolutely. I was quite surprised."

"Did you talk to her at all after that? I'm trying to figure why she got spooked."

"No. I had meant to. You called in the evening on Thursday, and on Friday morning I flew to Washington for a weekend conference. When I returned Sunday afternoon, I heard the news."

"Okay. I just wondered. Something happened sometime Wednesday night or Thursday." One other thought came to me. "Nathan, be careful, okay?"

"What?" He paused. "Oh. I see. Yes, Jason, and you, too. Be careful."

Time to go down to the dining room. I was hungry, and Katie had said supper would be special.

That night we had our first real dinner in the new house. The theme was Traditional New England Farm. The dining room was inundated with wildflowers of the autumn fields and forests, nature blasting right through the walls in its exuberance. Much of the flora had landed on the Rustic Farm Table—dark, polished wood, mottled with more knots and burls than a person could shake a hand-carved walking stick at. Fortunately, there were still several uncovered square yards of the table for our hand-thrown and fired pottery plates and serving bowls, cut crystal water and wine glasses, pewter cutlery, silver candlesticks, and linen napkins in carved wooden napkin rings. Every sparkle of it was brand-new.

And all was secondary to the meal of roast duck, herbed new potatoes, fresh dark bread, and spinach salad, with maple pecan pie for dessert. The wine was French, a rosé I didn't recognize. Our conversation was as comfortable as the food, and afterward we lingered over the pie.

"A person could get used to living this way," I said.

Katie laughed. "I've always wanted to."

"Do you ever question it?"

"No. I know you do."

"All the time." I yawned. Maybe tonight I would finally sleep. "But if I was poor, I'd question that. So there's no way out. I'll always have questions."

"Where we are, Jason . . . it's what everyone wants. Most people never get here, and they just accept that they won't. But there doesn't have to be a reason why some people . . . why it's us. We just are."

We were drinking coffee with the pie. "What if we weren't?" I asked. We'd polished off the wine.

"I don't know. I don't think about it."

I swirled the coffee in my cup, but the wine was swirling in my brain. "Think about it. Say I just gave it all away. What would you do?"

"Why would you give it away?" Her voice was just a little bit sharp.

"I'm being hypothetical. How important is the money compared to me?"

She did not like the question. "Of course you're more important. Now stop talking about it."

"I'm sorry."

Then I saw she was crying.

I'd pushed too hard, even if it wasn't very hard. She was feeling vulnerable. Everything was still too new, and she was being reminded that it could go away, turn back into a pumpkin at midnight. She needed assurance, and as I looked at her eyes blinking back tears, I would have done anything for her. Then she asked for the one thing I couldn't do.

"I want you to just accept that we're here," she said.

"I'll try," I said.

"You always ask those questions, Jason. Why don't you find some answers sometime?"

I didn't know what else to say. I hugged her, and she gave me a little kiss and left the room, and I went up to my office. After a while she stopped by to leave a vase of the wildflowers on my desk.

Eric had apparently gone home, but just before nine he came roaring up to the front door. He'd had a mood swing. The motorcycles had finally bored him, and he was now traveling in a monster Corvette. I heard him from the back of the house, three ballrooms away.

"Channel Six," he commanded. "Press conference at nine o'clock."

We scurried to the television lounge, tastefully decorated with equine accents, and perched on the leather sofa and chairs. Surely I'd seen the room before, but I didn't remember it.

"They arrested Howland and Gilbert today," Eric said. "The first cabinet secretaries in state history to be arrested while they were still in office."

"I thought they had already resigned."

"The governor hadn't accepted the resignations yet. He didn't have time. They're already out on bond."

He snapped on the wall-sized screen and Bill Sandoff's head, four feet tall, joined our cozy little group.

"—will begin in just a moment, when Governor Bright arrives. We have not been informed about what exactly the governor will announce, only that it is major, and that—Governor Bright is arriving—He is proceeding directly to the podium. . . ."

"Good evening." Harry Bright was now filling our room. I resolved to purchase a new small television on which to watch press conferences.

"Ladies and gentlemen, fellow citizens," he continued sternly, gravely, grimly. "I am here this evening to ask for your help in facing together the greatest danger ever to threaten our state."

No one was with the man. No aides or officials had come into the room with him. He was flying solo, and he had no license.

"A monstrous plot has been unleashed on the people and government of this state, and against me personally. One man is attempting to overthrow the popularly elected constitutional government and replace it with his own puppets."

There was only one man that monstrous, and everyone in our little room knew who the four-foot head was referring to. The head itself was breathing deeply and its four-inch eyes were bloodshot and wild.

"He has resorted to every crime in his loathsome scheme. He has personally committed extortion, slander, obstruction, and now, even murder."

The governor was resorting to every adjective in his loathsome speech. And now he was personally committing political suicide. I was hoping he wouldn't crash the plane right into my front door.

"I have been informed by State Police Commissioner DeAngelo that there is no doubt that Jason Boyer faced my aide, and close friend, Clinton Grainger, and gunned him down in the street. This cold-blooded murder—"

The reporters couldn't stand it anymore.

"Mr. Governor! Governor Bright? Is that official? Has Mr. Boyer been arrested? Is there a warrant for his arrest? What about the other murders? Mr. Governor!"

But the hinges had come completely loose. The popularly elected constitutional government glared at us, at me, right through the television camera. His mouth opened and closed and finally one little glimmer of reason broke through the storm and spoke.

"I have no further comment."

But no aides stood aside to let him pass. No one was there. Just the one man at the podium, and even counting him, no one was there. He didn't know how to leave. He was abandoned.

I felt so sorry for him.

The questions rose up again, waves crashing against the crumbling cliff, and he wasn't even hearing them. I told myself that I was not the cause of this man's destruction, and I knew that was true. I couldn't even feel resentment for his attack on me, only pity. Finally he turned and walked slowly to the door, which was still open, and left the room.

Quickly, Bill Sandoff was in charge of our wall. My thoughts were swept away.

"An extraordinary press conference by Governor Harry Bright. Clearly, very upset by the death of his close staff member, Clinton Grainger. The governor's comments raised some very serious questions about—yes, I understand that Police Commissioner Miguel DeAngelo is making a statement by telephone from state police headquarters. Jill Abernathy is at the Channel Six Studio and has that report."

"Thank you, Bill." Jill was not at her best, but she hadn't been expecting to be on, and at four feet tall, a face can't hide anything. "We do have Commissioner DeAngelo on the phone. Commissioner, thank you for speaking with us."

"Certainly, Jill," the voice said. There's something about a phone voice on a news program that seems so authentic. Jill did a great job of professionally listening to it, raptly attentive.

"Commissioner DeAngelo, the governor has just made a very strong statement that you informed him that the police have no doubt that Jason Boyer is the murderer of Clinton Grainger. Is that true?"

"That is not true."

"Have you been speaking with the governor about the case?"

"We have been keeping him informed concerning our progress."

"Is Mr. Boyer being charged with the murder?"

"We are not pressing any charges at this time against anyone in this case."

Jill nodded during the answers, showing us by example how interested the viewers were supposed to be. "Is Mr. Boyer a suspect?"

"We don't comment on investigations."

Jill switched from second to third gear. "Commissioner, the governor has leveled a charge of murder against one of the wealthiest men in the state, who is also apparently his most direct political enemy. 'No comment' really won't do here."

The cop hit his brakes. "Then you ask the governor. Wherever he came up with that, it wasn't from me."

"Thank you, Mr. DeAngelo." She'd dropped into neutral.

"Thank you, Jill."

Jill coasted to a stop. "That was State Commissioner of Police Miguel DeAngelo." My guess was that Harry Bright would be getting no more reports from that commissioner.

And of course, he was Wilcox's boss. DeAngelo was the man from whom Bright ordered office burglaries and trumped-up murder charges. It was pleasant to see that he was now officially a fleeing rat.

"That's enough for me," I said.

"Did you shoot the guy?" Eric asked.

"Don't be ridiculous," Katie said. "Jason was at a meeting last night."

What was that supposed to mean? She only believed I hadn't murdered a man because I had an alibi? What a vote of confidence. "The meeting was with Clinton Grainger," I said.

"You saw him last night?" Eric was excited.

"Fred and I."

"Wow. So you could have gunned him down!"

"Do you think I would do that?" I said.

"He was your most dangerous enemy."

"Who said that?"

"Channel Five."

"Rule Number 93—I don't kill people."

"That's not a rule."

"It is for me."

But Eric was distracted. "Look! It's Henry Malden."

The lieutenant governor was answering questions. He certainly looked the part of nonentity. No, he did not question Governor Bright's ability to continue in office. No, he knew no basis for the accusations the governor had just made. No, he was in no way involved in the kickback scandals. No, he had not discussed any of these things with the governor. No, he saw no reason to ask the legislature to consider an impeachment hearing. No, he had no idea what he was doing here.

The last answer was just my imagination, but he might as well have said it. I waved good-bye and left the room.

Katie followed me.

"I didn't shoot him," I said, so she wouldn't have to figure out how to ask.

"I knew you didn't. Eric is ridiculous."

"Everything's ridiculous right now. So do I call the police commissioner? Or Stan Morton? The FBI person, Donovan?"

I was just thinking aloud, but she took it seriously. "The newspaper or the television news. You need to answer the governor somehow." It was the first time I'd ever asked for her advice about business.

"I was going to give them an interview today, but it wasn't the right time."

"Have them come here. We'll do it together."

"Why?" I wasn't understanding.

"It's time to start introducing yourself to the world, Jason. And if you want to come off well, you're going to need a lot of help."

"What?! I can't act like a nice person by myself?"

"That is way past your acting abilities." Maybe my wife was going to be even more of an asset than I'd realized.

I submitted and called Pamela.

"Call Stan Morton. Tell him that I and my wife will be available tomorrow morning at nine o'clock at my house for a wide-ranging television interview for the purpose of introducing myself to his viewers."

"It's about time. I'll arrange it. Now, sit down. I just talked with Senator Forrester's secretary."

"I'm sitting."

"These are deep waters, Jason. The senator's two grand-daughters are visiting at the Forresters' home this weekend."

"How old are these granddaughters?"

"They have both just finished at Princeton. They are twins, very attractive, and with charming personalities."

"I have a bad feeling about this, Pamela."

"You may bring Fred if you also bring Eric, and I've already accepted the deal. It's time Eric met somebody nice."

"He's too young!" I said. "I'm not ready for him to start dating."

"He has to grow up sometime."

Katie looked at her watch when I told her. "Twelve hours to get ready for television cameras."

"We just moved in," I said. "Nothing's had a chance to get dirty."

"But it's not arranged for television. Where will we sit? What will be behind us?"

"They'll set us up the way they want."

"And then we're going to Bob and Gladys Forrester's for dinner tomorrow night. I did find a dress. I told them I needed it ready for tomorrow afternoon. Who will Fred be paired with?"

"Pamela did her best. When she proposed Fred, the senator met and raised. He put his twin granddaughters into the pot."

"So now they're short one man."

"Not a man. Eric."

"Oh my!"

"It was their request."

She had to absorb this. "We can handle it. But he has nothing appropriate to wear."

"I'm sure you'll fix that," I said.

With a heavy heart I found my little brother, still in his attitude

of devotion before the mighty visage of Bill Sandoff. I turned Sandoff off.

"Eric. I have a job for you."

He switched realities and blinked. "Cool. Is it dangerous?"

"Extremely. Tomorrow evening you are going with Katie and
me, and Fred Spellman, to dinner at Senator Forrester's house. This
is very high society. Can you do it?"

"Remember, they taught us that stuff at St. Martin's? We had
all those classes about how to act and what fork to use."

"Right. That's not the hard part anyway. The senator has two
granddaughters who've just finished Princeton. They'll be there.
Your job is to keep them distracted while Fred and the senator and
I talk business."

I had his complete and wide-eyed attention. "Are you joking?"

"No. I'm as serious as an earthquake."

There was a pause while he recovered his ability to speak. "Are
they good-looking?"

"I've never seen them. They're twins."

"Oh man. Oh man! I'll be there. Wow! Where do they live? I'll
pick them up."

"They are at the senator's house already. You just come here.
We'll go together. And Katie is in charge of getting you ready."

"Okay. That's good. Wow! Thanks, Jason. I'll do it."

"Don't get carried away," I said.

He'd spent lots more time in my television room than I had. He
opened a cabinet I hadn't noticed and was typing on a keyboard
that I didn't even know the television had. If I'd timed him, it
would have been less than fifteen seconds before he'd gone on-line
and was staring at search results.

"Whoa! Check it out!"

"That's them?"

"It must be. It's the Princeton Web site. This is going to be
excellent."

Okay, so they were attractive, in a cute college girl sort of way.
"Their grandfather is a senator."

"My brother is a billionaire."

I was getting exasperated. "You want another plate of spaghetti in your face? I am not joking. Cool your jets, Eric." But it was throwing a bucket of water on a forest fire.

"You just talk your business and I'll handle Genevieve and Madeleine."

"That's their names?"

"I think their mother's French. And their home address is in Paris."

"Oh, right," I said. "Forrester's son is a diplomat." It was now plain that this would be a disaster; Eric would be eaten alive. He'd escaped from the reporters on Thursday, but there would be no escape here.

"I took French."

"So did I, and I remember six words. High-school French will not impress them."

"I remember more than six words." A new thought detonated in his head. "Do I have to ride with you?"

"Yes."

"Then let me drive."

"Eric, neither the senator nor I will allow you to take those young ladies out in your car."

"We'd just go for a drive. I'd take the Jaguar."

"It doesn't have a back seat."

"Three people can fit in the front seat. It'd be fun."

"I'm sure the girls would agree. But it's not going to happen. I would start listing rules but I don't know if you can count high enough."

"Okay. So what am I supposed to do?"

"Just talk. Maybe one of them works on cars."

"Ha, ha. It says that Genevieve majored in international economics and Madeleine was in European history."

"Talk about politics."

"You're not supposed to. Politics or religion."

"All you have to do is keep them busy for a couple hours."

"Yeah, no problem. But it would be way more fun on the road."

"This is work. It's not supposed to be fun."

"It will be. It just won't be as much fun as it could be."

"I will give you one rule. Number 94, right?"

"I'm listening." Not happily.

And what difference did it make, anyway? I wasn't his father. "I don't know. Never mind."

"What?"

"You don't need me to tell you how to act."

The day was over—at least it should have been. It was early for bed but there was nothing else I wanted to do.

At the old house I might have gone running. The grounds here were even big enough that I could have found some circuit to wear myself out on, but it was dark. The swimming pool didn't have water in it yet. I stopped in the kitchen to express my appreciation to Rosita, and I met the new maids there. Then I was wandering again.

I found myself back in the television room. Eric was still glued.

"Did you say we were going to Bob Forrester's house tomorrow night?"

"The senator himself."

"He's going to be on in a minute."

We waited through a highlights reel of the governor's press conference—he did no better than before. Katie found us.

"You're watching television?"

"Eric is forcing me to."

"What's wrong with TV?" he said.

But Bill Sandoff was at the airport. He was having a long day, too.

"Senator Forrester has just arrived from Washington and he should be joining us in just a moment."

A moment was two commercials to sell us cars and hamburgers. Then the senator joined us.

"Thank you for speaking with us, Senator."

It must have been a bad flight. "Of course."

Bill was getting a little ragged himself. "I wonder if you have any comments about Governor Bright?" This was obviously the question that Forrester had instructed Stan Morton to have asked. Bill didn't even try to make it sound unscripted.

"I believe he should resign immediately."

This was a forceful and premeditated attack. Big Bob was no longer watching from the sidelines, and both Bill Sandoff and I were suddenly alert.

"Even before the charges against him are—"

"There is no doubt in my mind." There was a statuesque quality about both the senator and his statements. "This evening it was manifestly clear that he is unfit to hold office. But even more, he has abused the public trust for years and this public exposure is long overdue."

"So you feel that Jason Boyer was justified—"

"Until he gets his own house in order, Mr. Boyer shouldn't be accusing anyone. He certainly shouldn't be attempting to use his wealth to influence government or politics. The Boyer family is even more culpable than the governor in this scandal."

"Do you really mean the whole Boyer family, and not just . . ."

"I would find it hard to believe that Jason Boyer was unaware of his father's dealings."

"Senator Forrester—"

"If you will excuse me, please," the senator said. Poor Bill. He wasn't getting to use his words. They were going to start building up inside, and he would pop.

Forrester had turned away from the camera. Bill turned toward it. "A plague on both houses, says Senator Robert Forrester. This has been a rare look behind the . . ."

This time I interrupted him with the power switch.

"What did that mean?" Katie said.

"Forrester is making his move," I said.

"We're going to his house tomorrow?" Eric asked.

"Yes. And that was his way of telling me what the agenda would be. It's just politics, it's not personal."

"I'm taking it personally," Katie said.

"Go ahead. I might, too."

"Do I have to?" Eric asked. Madeleine and Genevieve were on his mind.

"No," I said. "You just have a nice time. Katie and I will take care of the hand-to-hand combat. And Fred—"

My cell phone rang. I'd rubbed the magic lamp and the genie was squeezing himself out of it.

"Hi, Fred," I said.

"Jason. Did you see—"

"Yes. He's declaring his independence. Except he doesn't think all men are created equal."

"He is strengthening his hand going into our meeting tomorrow evening. I believe we should answer him." Fred was taking it personally.

"I'm having a television interview tomorrow morning," I said.

"Will it be televised in the morning?"

"No, at six thirty tomorrow evening."

"That will do," Fred said. "He'll watch it just before we arrive."

"What should I say? That he's an egotistical, self-important buffoon?"

"That isn't what I would suggest." Fred was regaining his caution. "Be strong but also conciliatory. I would suggest that you say you are surprised at the senator's remarks, and then call for calm and communication. Perhaps you would mention that he has asked you to his house. You need to salvage this relationship, Jason."

"I've already got a mother-in-law. I don't need another relationship like this."

"I'm being serious." He sounded like it, too. "This meeting will be crucial."

"We'll talk tomorrow, Fred."

At eight twenty on Saturday morning, three vans at our front door unloaded lights, cameras, and action. We chose the fireplace room as our backdrop. Katie had thought maybe we would take a tour of the house, but the idea was nixed as being too adorable. The interview was supposed to make me look human, but not too human.

The talent was produced, no less than Bill Sandoff and Jill Abernathy themselves. They tried to put me at my ease, pretending to be normal people and not the famous and important television news celebrities that they, of course, actually were. I managed to be comfortable somehow.

"We'll just interview you about anything we can think of," Bill said. "Then we'll spruce it into a fifteen-minute segment for the six o'clock show. Mr. Morton will personally assess the edit for contexting."

This was a man with serious verb issues. "That sounds fine," I said. "We're ready."

Katie and I were together on the sofa, with Bill in a chair at my side and Jill beside him. Jill had arrived in green but had made an emergency change to blue so as to stand out better against the fireplace stones. Besides, Katie's dress was some sort of dark lavender.

The green would have been completely wrong.

And Katie was enjoying the spotlight. There had been a brief discomfort when the makeup person started plastering us, but Katie had quickly analyzed his methods and they were soon partners in crime.

Then the red light on the camera blinked on. In a jerk, Bill and Jill dropped their masks of pretend ordinariness. Bill suddenly became serious and interested; Jill was softer and professionally friendly.

They went through a variety of lighter and heavier openings to choose from later. Katie and I smiled.

"Mr. Boyer, two months ago very few people had heard of you. You and your wife were well-to-do, but you were living a quiet life, and you didn't expect that to change. Today you are one of the country's wealthiest men, and you are engaged in a very public conflict with Governor Bright that has put you in the national news. But still, very few people know much about you.

"First, I'd like to ask if the stories we've heard are true. You really didn't expect to inherit your father's businesses?"

I didn't, Bill. No. I choked down the false informality so I wouldn't choke on it.

"I didn't," I said. "We had anticipated the estate would go to the Boyer Foundation. It was only after his death that I learned he had recently changed his will."

We ranged through all the topics—of my grief at Melvin's death, of my further grief at learning the truth about him and his crimes, of my even further grief at Angela's death, of the far reaches of my grief at the terrible but necessary exposure of the governor's malfeasance. Even the distant eddies of grief at Clinton Grainger's death. The viewers would consider me so far stretched in my grief I must be in a different time zone.

I'd felt no grief.

Had there been any strong emotions? Rage at Melvin for his idiocy of getting murdered and leaving me his wad, but I'd overcome that.

"Speaking of Mr. Grainger," Bill said. "Were you really the last person to see him alive?"

"I did meet with him late Thursday, at the Hilton. My lawyer was also there. We were trying to find some middle ground, to cool off the attacks."

"Did you make any progress?"

"We did, a little. That's one more reason it was such a tragedy that he died. My last chance of helping the governor died with him." More grief. Grief surrounded and pursued me like a cloud of mosquitoes. How could anyone live with it all?

Katie had her moments. She'd felt that same pesky grief, of course, but she had rallied, with my support. We'd been there for each other, Katie and Jason. Jill Abernathy helped the viewers to see what a strong and caring woman Mrs. Boyer was and how, with great effort, she was effortlessly adapting to her new place in life.

"How did you feel when you learned the truth about your father-in-law?" Jill asked.

"It was a shock," Katie said. "But that wasn't the whole truth about him. He was a complex man, and he shouldn't be judged by just that one part. His foundation has done amazing things, and he was a very good and effective senator. It's been so hard to go through all this. I wish it could have been done more quietly. We tried to keep it quiet. Not hidden, just quiet."

I almost believed her. She was a much better actress than I. She may have even fooled Jill, that expert trained in falsifying sincerity.

Bill asked about our plans. I said we wanted to expand the foundation's work, and I mentioned Nathan Kern by name. Such a gifted man! I expressed hope that the investigations would quickly be concluded, to bring this painful chapter to an end. We would all sleep easier when the killer was brought to justice and Melvin and Angela, and also Clinton Grainger, would rest in peace. And everyone in the state would benefit from a good housecleaning in the statehouse.

Did I have any political plans myself?

Ha, ha, I was quite busy enough at the moment just keeping my head above water.

"He'd make a wonderful congressman or senator," the wife quipped.

I laughed. "You better cut that, Stan," I said to the camera. "We don't want to start any rumors."

"You would, though," Katie said. Meaning, she would love to be a senator's wife. With her expertise in spending other people's money, she'd actually be a great senator herself.

And speaking of senators, how did we feel about Bob's comments of the night before?

"I was surprised," I said. "We've only met a few times, and I've only spoken with him once recently."

"Will you be meeting with Senator Forrester again?" This question had been discussed beforehand.

"Yes, actually. Katie and I will be visiting with him this evening, at his request. I hope we can have some reasoned discussion. The last thing we need just now is more hot tempers and baseless accusations."

Then finally the wrap-up, thank you so much, it's been so interesting. Friendly but not too syrupy—this is an independent news organization of course, not a propaganda machine. How weary I was getting of lies.

The cameras and lights turned off, and so did Bill and Jill. Maybe they were just machines, too. We said good-bye.

"And good riddance," I said. The trucks had left us to go to their next crime scene.

"I thought it was fun," Katie said. "And you could be senator if you wanted."

"We already have two."

"Well, I don't like the one we're meeting with this evening."

In the front hall I met Prince Charming, here to pick up his fairy godmother, to be made ready for the ball.

"How was the interview?" Eric asked.

"You can see it tonight."

"We'll be at dinner."

"You're in charge of recording it," I said. "We'll watch it when we get back."

"Okay." Eric was now officially interested in politics, particularly the personal connections he was about to make. "So what are you going to talk about tonight?"

"I want Big Bob to know who's in charge, and that it's not him."

"It's you?"

"In my opinion, yes."

He smiled. "All right."

I saw big thoughts bouncing around inside his head, possibly knocking other things off shelves or breaking furniture. "I've thought of what Rule 94 was supposed to be. Whenever I actually tell you the truth about something, don't ever tell it to anyone else."

"I know."

"Good."

He left on his mission. So what were we going to talk about tonight? I played the senator's comments through my mind, back and forth, and the more I did, the more riled I got. It wasn't the ends, of trying to gain control over his own destiny, but his means. To sternly advise me to keep out of politics, when it was Boyer power that put him on his pedestal in the first place—that was unnecessary roughness.

My instinct was to pulverize him. Bright had been practice, but not a challenge. This would be the real thing.

And from where had this instinct sprung? It was pure Melvin, although the old man wouldn't have been hasty. But he'd built the edifice stone by stone. I was trying to keep it from falling over, and I couldn't be cautious. I had to maintain my nasty attitude. I called Fred.

"I'm trying to get in the mood for our dinner with the senator," I said. "I was going to get a flyswatter but I can't find any flies."

"Tonight you'll be in a beehive. Be careful what you swat."

"Tell me specifically how Forrester could sting me."

"Just because he has no organization doesn't mean he can't build one. He has money and friends with money. Clinton Grainger is gone but there are other organizers who could put the governor's organization back together for someone else. Forrester couldn't match your machine in just three years, but he could become competitive."

"I don't think he has the personality."

"A good campaign staff can compensate for that, somewhat. And do you have a better personality?"

"Slightly. And I have unions and lots of employees. You don't need personality when you sign paychecks."

"He has his office as senator. He can continue to attack your youth and inexperience, and the media will broadcast his message. Stan Morton can downplay it, but he'll still have to report what a senator is saying. He can't ignore it."

"Okay. But I can get my message out just as well."

"That is true, but this is not the time. Take care of the state government first. It will take all your attention to hold it together."

"I still have to do something tonight."

"Negotiate. Neither of you wants a battle."

Might as well just say it. "Both of us want that Senate seat." There, I'd said it.

"Then this is what you should do. First, blackmail Forrester into resigning. Second, bribe Bright to appoint you to the vacant seat. But do it quickly, before he goes to prison. Third, have a new birth certificate forged to add two years onto your age. As an alternative to the third step, you could have the Constitution amended to lower the minimum age for senators." He was highly exasperated. "Or you could just wait a little while."

"Where do I get the forged birth certificate?" I said.

"When you are in prison for the bribery and blackmail, I'm sure you will make many new friends who can help you with that. Perhaps you can share a cell with the governor, and he can introduce you."

"I'll be patient, Fred."

"Good. That may be the first intelligent thing you've said."

"It took a lot of effort."

"But now you will need to be rational for an entire evening."

"I won't promise, Fred. The senator was a little too pointed yesterday evening. He deserves a jab."

"I agree. By all means, jab him. Aim first, do it prudently, and don't complain when he jabs back. Then get on with business."

"We'll see."

I took the afternoon off from being powerful and was simply rich.

For the first time, I wandered the acres outside to see what I owned. I socialized with the groundskeepers. Two of the gardeners were from Melvin's estate and the third was new. We talked landscaping, and I requested a half-mile path suitable for running.

I sat in the kitchen with Rosita and she fixed me an ice-cream sundae. She was so happy with her new domain. She might go to school somewhere, to learn how to use it all properly. And she didn't mind at all that we had maids now! The maids were also family veterans, so grateful to be with us.

I found my office and locked the door. I'd spent lots of words already today, and I didn't want to run out before tonight. This would be time to think.

I checked the stock market for the first time since Wednesday. The scandals and uncertain future had pushed the share prices down some, but not as much as I'd assumed in my forecast spreadsheets. I'd meet with George Elias on Monday to check cash flow for the next six months, but I knew it would be good through the end of the year at least. Even Katie couldn't spend it all.

The governor was taking care of himself. I couldn't improve on that whole situation, and the television interview would ice the cake. He was no threat at all now, with Clinton Grainger gone, except for his wild screaming. That would hurt him more than it hurt me.

Katie was happy and busy, as long as I supplied cash. She was only doing what she needed to. New house, new . . . everything. It would calm down. It would have to.

I was having lots of quality big brother time with Eric, so he was good for a week or two, as long as Madeleine and Genevieve didn't get predatory tonight.

So, tonight. Senator Forrester was the next item to deal with. According to Fred, Bob was only staking positions, readying for a deal. My agenda was to negotiate. No ultimatums—no tantrums;

just pretend I could act like an adult. That's what I was always telling Eric to do. He was proof that it was not easy.

Anything else? Of course, that irritating murderer. What about that? Commissioner DeAngelo had made it plain he was no longer a lackey of the governor, so the politics of the investigation weren't against me. DeAngelo might even want to get in good with the winning side.

Hopefully they'd catch the miscreant. At the moment, it wasn't my main concern.

I took the picture frame from Melvin's bedroom out of my desk and stared at the pictures for a while. There is such promise, and hope, in pictures of long-ago youth. Promises unkept.

I took a risk. Even though my previous conversations with Nathan had backfired, I still wanted to hear his opinion on the senator.

"I'm sorry to interrupt your Saturday afternoon," I said.

"No, Jason, that's fine. I'm just reviewing some position papers. What can I do for you?"

"I'm talking to Bob Forrester this evening, and I'm not looking forward to it. You know him, don't you?"

"Of course. He's occasionally helped with foundation programs when we needed federal involvement. I suppose you'll have quite a few other things to discuss. He'll have a great interest in the recent political affairs."

"That's the main reason we're meeting." What did Nathan know about Melvin and Big Bob? "I'd like to know your impression of him."

"Well, well. I've known Bob Forrester for quite some time, from school days, in fact. He was years ahead of me, but he took me in hand as a newcomer and was very kind. We've kept up with each other since, at least slightly. He was at the conference I attended last weekend in Washington, though we didn't cross paths. So . . . my impression is that he would be quite above anything improper— and that's more than just an impression. I feel quite certain of it."

"He wasn't part of the family corruption. I know that. But he wasn't above making deals."

"Yes, Jason. I'm afraid that's true. Probably Fred has given you his version of the dealings?"

"Is there another version?"

"Where Fred sees ambition, I might have seen idealism."

Idealist Robert Forrester. Right up there with virtuous Harry Bright. Or frugal Katie Boyer. "I don't know him very well, Nathan, but that's hard to believe."

"I'm speaking of years past. I know he's not a friendly person, and he has an aristocratic bearing that can be unwelcoming. But aristocrats sometimes have a surprising sense of responsibility, of *noblesse oblige*, and Bob once had real plans concerning social justice."

"And now?" I asked.

"I'm not sure he still has those concerns."

He'd gained power. "Idealism is hard to maintain in a place like the Senate."

"Yes, Jason," Nathan said. "I expect you understand that."

"There must be people who survive having power."

"Only if there is something stronger in their life, some higher purpose."

"But what?" I asked, but then there was the roar of many cylinders, and Eric and Katie blew in.

Katie had the goods, a dozen bags at least. She shoved half at Eric, two at me, and kept the rest.

"Now, go," she said. "We will only barely make it."

"This is going to be so cool," Eric said.

Katie's *we* was really an *I*. Within forty minutes I was showered, sitting by the fireplace in my high society suit, with new shirt and tie. Just before six, Eric pranced in to join me.

"Check it out," he said.

He, too, was also wearing new tie, brown leather, and shirt, black linen. Dark brown corduroys, black shoes, a flash of purple socks. No jacket.

There should be a Nobel for whatever it is that Katie does. With our black hair and dark complexion, I never touch brown. Eric could have walked into a Manhattan architecture firm and looked like one of the partners. His spiky hair was a lethal weapon; he had learned to do that to himself somewhere in college.

"I'm charging you for Katie's time. She makes you look so classy, it's worth money."

"It's just the real me coming out."

"Then it's been buried real deep for about twenty-five years."

I was only three years older, but I was going to dinner as an adult, and he still got to be a child.

And then we waited, each of us deep within his own specially constructed aura of style and presence. At six fifteen I thought about peeking in the television room for a slice of our Channel Six interview, but I knew it wouldn't be on until at least six thirty. The recorder would get it and we would enjoy it at our leisure.

At six thirty we stood in awe. Sky blue silk. Glistening pearls and pearl-white shoes. Auburn hair, with more life in it than in most people.

"You're gorgeous," I stammered.

Smile of pearls. "Thank you, Jason. I want to look my best for you."

"I didn't know it got this good."

Sweet smile again. "Then let's go show this senator a thing or two," she said.

Formality would place Eric next to me in the car and Katie in the back seat, but I would have none of it. This lady sat at my side. The dress cost at least two thousand, and once she wore it to the Forresters', she could never be seen in it again. I wanted maximum appreciation.

29

Birds of a feather flock together; we did not
have far to go from our nest to theirs. The sky
was dim. The sun had places to go and things
to do and so did we, so we parted company
with it. It left a few clouds behind, but not many, and some
warmth.

A few trees were getting bare but most were in full glory. In the
twilight they were dull until our headlights kindled them into
flame—red and gold and yellow.

At just five minutes after seven our forces breached the moat
and came to the courtyard of the oldest old money in the state. This
was the mansion that Melvin's grand estate was trying to be.

We dismounted and a young retainer took our steed away. The
drawbridge lowered and we were ushered into the hall.

"Mr. Spellman has just arrived," the squire informed us. "He is
in the library."

We, too, were taken to the library, where we found not only
Friar Tuck but also the Sheriff of Nottingham himself.

I considered my adversary carefully. The senator, tall and
straight as ever, crowned with dignity and silver hair, possessed
every quality that could make him impregnable: office, wealth, reputation, family, height.

"Bob," Fred murmured, "you know Jason, of course. This is Katie, and Eric." It wasn't proper for Fred to introduce my family, but it was less awkward. The senator and I were only acquainted through business, not socially, so I didn't really have standing myself to introduce him to others.

And, of course, we had also now traded public insults and were on the verge of war, not that this would technically affect our proper behavior toward each other. I watched for clues of how the evening was scheduled to unfold.

He stiffly shook my hand and bowed to the lady. Eric's age and *avant-garde* appearance were a problem, whether he qualified for a handshake or a pat on the head. He got the shake—his hair would have impaled the senatorial hand.

And then we were through the first indignity. Everyone had been introduced and we were no longer aliens. The next issue was polite conversation. Certainly the host would have a plan to avoid that. On cue, the library door opened. With maximum drama the granddaughters entered.

And they were all that Eric was hoping for.

The first was a Botticelli, dusky blond, blithe and carefree in a casual yellow sleeveless dress and thin white sweater. Cheerful blue eyes rested immediately on Eric, lighthearted smile shone as the sun.

But directly following came a Raphael, poised and deep, luminous green eyes beneath lustrous brown hair, carefully arrayed in a burgundy pullover and tan slacks. This smile rested on Eric as the silver moon shining on a cloudless night.

Their attention to him centered the attention of us all.

Dark young Boyer was the lone and towering pine, the brooding thundercloud caught in the rays of Sun and Moon. A genial grin slowly lifted the corners of his mouth but his eyes were enigma, unfathomable.

"These are my granddaughters," the senator said. "Genevieve." The blonde international economist. "Madeleine." The brunette European historian. Katie had known perfectly how to dress our young cavalier to match these damsels. "Jason and Katie Boyer"— the introduction was continuing—"And this is Eric Boyer."

This was his moment. Don't say anything stupid, Eric. Please. Or just do it and get it over with.

"Je suis ravi de vous rencontrer," he said.

I do remember more than six words of French, but not as many as he was using. He cocked his head to the side a little and let the smile grow. *"J'espérais avoir ce plaisir."*

"Nous avons beaucoup entendu parlen de vous," Madeleine said, glowing.

"Et maintenant nous commes face à face." Not only was he saying his own words, he was understanding hers.

Genevieve sparkled. *"Rencontrer une personne vaut mieux que d' en entendre parler."* She giggled and said to her sister, *"Je t'avais dit qu'il était mignon."*

Eric blushed. *Mignon* I knew, and it was not helpful to the situation. She'd told Madeleine she thought he was cute.

"Tais-toi!" Madeleine said. *"Tu ne devrais pas dire ça!"*

"Mais je peux dire que vous êtes touts les deux ravissantes," he said. Now he was calling them beautiful, which they were, and things were getting out of hand.

"Now, Eric," said Katie, "don't use all your compliments at once." For a moment her own light had been eclipsed, but only for a moment. Her colors were Monet, but her essence was Rembrandt, stronger in character, and deeper and more powerful in meaning than any Italian master, and worth ten times as much. "We have the whole evening."

"And you'll conduct yourselves properly," Grandpa said, half in humor.

And then, one more entrance. Gladys Forrester was last, shortest, and least concerned. If she didn't care much for us, she still didn't mind showing off a dull scarlet evening dress that was quite becoming with her blue-gray helmet. We had our last round of names.

The tykes had switched to English, and the minimum amount of pre-dinner socializing was accomplished. Now we were even: four gentlemen, four ladies; four Forresters and four Boyers. What Fred lacked in real Boyer blood, he made up for in volume.

We were taken to the dining room. The table was as long as

Katie's, but there was no hint of rusticity here. From the English country garden pictures on the walls to the Wedgwood china settings on the table, we were being told very plainly that the Forresters were better than the Boyers. It was the theme of the evening.

We were seated by rank, the senator at the head, I at his right and Katie opposite me, Genevieve beside me with Fred opposite, Eric beside Genevieve with Madeleine across from him, and the matriarch at the end. It would not have been proper for Katie and I to be so close, but with only eight, the rules were flexible. I did know which fork to use for each of the many courses, from watercress soup and lobster salad to raspberry aspic, with a beef Wellington in between that almost made me wish I were enjoying the meal.

Eight at the table was just enough to keep two conversations going. I couldn't monitor Eric two seats down and attend to Forrester simultaneously, so I had to throw the babe to the wolves.

"The president may yet listen to reason," the senator was saying as the salads were served, this apparently being his designated topic for his dinner lecture. "Otherwise the Senate will rein him in, as usual. I have explained to him more than once that his position is unacceptable."

There was nothing to answer, nor was there meant to be. I didn't even remember what policy issue it was he was talking about. It didn't matter. We were not just being given a clue to the schedule of the evening; we were being subjected to a full volume broadcast that the senator was in command, and the next hour at the table was for him to show off his importance.

There would be time later to wrest control of the evening. I listened and made vague comments. Katie could see Eric, and I watched her for any alarms.

I stole a glance myself. He was surrounded, Genevieve to the left of him, Gladys to the right of him, Madeleine in front of him. His was not to question why, his was to make witty answers and look cute. I heard a few words about his motorcycles. Genevieve was next to me and we should have spoken at least once during each course, but after our first polite two sentences we had tacitly dismissed each other to the assigned tasks.

Fred ate. He shifted his attention to the senatorial end and made even vaguer comments than I, and less frequently. Dinner was fly-over, something to get past between destinations—not that he neglected it. He did not mind that, at the dinner table tonight, only food and not conversation was meant to be substantial. But he surely did know what Bob Forrester was doing.

Because, so far, Bob's plan for the evening had not included any gesture meant to conciliate me. Much more the opposite, in fact, and I had plenty of time to think about it. He had invited me to his house and then insulted me publicly on television after doing so privately in his Washington office weeks ago. Now he was dominating the conversation and stressing his own importance.

I let my thoughts linger on the insult, and a little ember of annoyance broke through my defenses. I lost the senator's thread for a moment but his words continued to blow against me, encouraging the glowing red spark, and it began to spread.

"The subcommittee will decide that, of course," Forrester was saying. "I may require a delay in the hearing if these questions are not answered, but I will not allow the bill to go forward in its present state."

I was getting impatient with this harangue. It was dry tinder for the flame to grow and thrive. Should I stifle the fire or the senator? Katie was keeping an eye on me. She could see the signs. Fred was just eating. He was more aware than he looked, but he didn't look it.

What was I mad about? Of course I was being treated contemptuously. Why should that matter? This was politics.

But it did matter. The flames and heat were mounting.

"One might wonder why the Senate should consider that such issues are important."

Good question, Bob. One might wonder why I was considering his attitude as important. There was no reason to get mad and a dozen reasons not to. I could be patient. There were years to go. Why was any challenge to my own authority so troubling to me? It just was, and the flames kept growing.

"Some might say the consideration is long overdue," Fred commented.

Good point, too, Fred. Because now it was a full bonfire, long past any hope of extinguishing. It was controlling me. What was it? More than just anger. I had to escape.

"But no one is willing to provide leadership," said the senator.

"The politics make it difficult."

Yes, Fred, very difficult. Impossible. There was no escape. Bob's interminable hectoring was driving me mad. Perhaps I was supposed to be honored. Since the president was too unintelligent to receive instruction, I was privileged to receive it instead.

Was this meant to be intimidation? I should be overawed and surrender? Then he'd badly miscalculated. Had he even calculated at all? Did he know he was taking a gamble, hoping that I was too young and insecure to stand up to him, or in his arrogance did he just assume it? Had he considered that I might be driven to a very different reaction?

"I doubt anything will be resolved under the current circumstances," the senator said with finality. We were done with the meal; Gladys had set her folded napkin on her dessert plate. The pompous fool had dragged it out too long, even far too long. The inferno had consumed me, and what was left?

We were back in the library. The senator's speech was over and for the moment we were silent. Eric was on the veranda with the four ladies, just outside the open French doors. I declined a cigar but Fred accepted, so our host was free to smoke one, as well.

Fred started the discussion. "We should get down to business now, I think."

"The whole affair has been a disaster," Forrester said.

It was finally time to draw the long knives.

"I would simply call it unfortunate," Fred said.

"It should have been avoided." Forrester was using the same dictatorial tone. Did he have any other?

He was standing in the center of the room, and I was by the doors. I could see Eric on a bench, the girls on either side, laughing. Were they enjoying his company or just waiting to mock him once he was gone? I would cram him down their throats.

Fred was seated in an armchair that deserved him. He exhaled a vast lungful of smoke. "It became unavoidable."

"It shouldn't have. This has been childish."

Wrong word, Senator. Very bad word to use at this moment. I was not speaking—as much anger as I had, there was still capacity for much more. It wouldn't do to pull the trigger while there was still the risk of one short outburst using it all up.

"It may seem so, Bob." Fred was interpreting my silence as permission for him to manage the negotiations. "But it did become unavoidable, and we took necessary actions. Surely you know the sequence of events. The governor brought it on himself. Certainly you aren't grieved by his departure."

Bob only frowned. "I never meant for Henry Malden to be governor. When I selected him for lieutenant governor, it was only to manage the state senate. Never for this."

"He will be governor on Tuesday. The impeachment bill has been written and will be debated Monday." Fred breathed in, and out. "Would you instruct the state senate to vote it down?"

"Would you?" Forrester sneered at the thought. "Of course not. Even if I had a reason to, Harry Bright is far past rescue. But now there will be anarchy. Malden won't impose order. Someone will need to."

"Jason and I have discussed this, of course."

Yes, Jason. Remember him? He's part of this.

The senator did not turn toward me. "Melvin Boyer might have had influence. His son does not."

I was at least looking at him. Fred waited for me. He was realizing that my silence was not from respect for my elders. It was even causing Forrester a little unease.

"The strengths of the Boyer family have not changed," Fred said. "The assets and organization are still intact. The governor made the mistake of not realizing that."

"Is that a threat?" Four bullets, point blank at Fred's vest.

Fred's cigar smoke deflected them. "Of course not, Bob."

"The governor is a fool. Don't think you've done anything impressive by exposing him. Anyone could have done it; it was no show of strength."

"If that is how you see it . . ." Fred shrugged.

"And a show of strength is necessary, and so I will be meeting with Malden and senate leaders tomorrow morning."

Your strength, Senator? Listening to this was pure jet fuel for the fire.

"We should discus that," Fred said. "I've made a few phone calls already."

"I'm aware of your calls, and there is nothing to discuss. I want you to stay out of this—you and your . . . your client." His voice was rising, so that the galleries and television cameras could catch every word. "Your actions this week have destroyed any credibility the Boyer name might still have had and clearly demonstrated this young man's incompetence and immaturity."

"I really don't think the theatrics are necessary." For Fred, the speech had just been the beginning of negotiations, the senator stating his opening position. Nothing personal, only business. "You know as well as I . . ."

"Excuse me, Fred."

It was time. I turned toward the senator.

"Bob."

He turned to me. A long, thin stream of blue-white smoke spewed from his mouth. Fred's plume was thicker. He had turned to me, also, with a stern warning in his eyes. I turned my back on both of them.

The terrace outside the French doors had a granite rail. It was ornamented with statuary, and I was suddenly pleased to see my little stone friend there! Maybe he had followed me from the church, or maybe it was his twin. His hand was up and he was looking right at me. It was a portent—a sign that fate was with me.

"Eight years ago, Melvin gave you your senate seat." I said it loud enough for him to hear me, with my back to him. Maybe Katie and her hostess could hear me, as well. Eric was not in sight. "If we're discussing incompetence, you were the one who was incapable of winning an election on your own." I turned, and we faced each other. "When you were given the office, there were conditions. And you have not been released from your obligation."

He was furious, his own cold anger finally hot. "Young man, I have already told you—"

"Shut up." We locked eyes. "I expect respect, not condescension." Who would ever have stood up to him like this, against his money and power and pride? Which of us was stronger now?

"You brazen upstart."

"I didn't come this evening for you to reprimand me, or to listen to your conceited tirade. I came to discuss Governor Bright. You thought your show of arrogance would frighten me, and it was quite a show. But you were wrong." We were still eye to eye, and I wasn't sweating. "You made a big mistake, Bob, and it's going to cost you."

"You are making the mistake." He was not backing down, but at least I'd become someone he had to speak to. "Do you think your money can buy you anything you want? You are wrong. I owe you nothing. I am a United States senator, and I have wealth to match yours."

"Bob. Jason." Fred saw the need for an adult to intervene. "You've both had a chance to express your frustrations. Now, let's get past this and move on to the business at hand."

"I think this is our business for this evening," I said. "We are deciding who will be the next senator, and it won't be a cozy deal. It will be whoever is strongest."

"This is ridiculous." Forrester made a quick glance at the ceiling, as if he had just lost patience with the encounter. But he'd blinked and we both knew it.

"I want you to announce that this will be your last term." I looked out the window. The little statue was still smiling at me. I must be doing well.

"I will do no such thing."

I slowly turned back to him. "Are you sure, senator? Do you really want to fight this out? Do you want to see the crowds turning against you? Do you want to read the antagonistic editorials? Face the hostile reporters?"

"Stanley Morton would never treat me like that!"

"How much of his company do you own? And picture the campaign. It won't be like last time. Maybe there will be scandals. This pedestal you've got yourself on will be real easy to knock over. Do you think your precious president or anyone else will care what you think when they see your whole state turning against you? Just imagine what it will feel like when everyone around you is watching you fall and laughing at you behind your back, or maybe to your face. And now you're an old man, too, and you're tired. Do you have the stomach for this fight, senator?" The words were flowing out of me—I didn't even need to think, they just came.

I gave him plenty of time to answer. He didn't, so I did.

"I didn't think so."

Fred was looking straight ahead, not at either of us, just waiting. Forrester had lost focus, too.

"You're as evil as your father," he said.

"I am my father's son."

There was a sound, between a gasp and a sigh. I looked back and saw Katie standing in the open doorway. She was staring at me, her mouth open in shock at the words my mouth had just spoken.

"We're done here," I said to her. "Fetch Eric."

She collected herself. "They just went to see the Rolls Royce. They'll be a few minutes."

"That's fine," I said. "I'll wait outside with you."

I didn't look back into the room. She moved aside to let me pass and followed me out onto the terrace. Gladys was seated on a bench near the doors.

"He can't mean that" came from the library.

Fred's voice rumbled, "He means what he says, Bob."

"This is outrageous. Of course I won't step down." But he knew what the future would be and that he would surrender rather than face that humiliation, and in his voice I could hear the splintering and cracking of his soul. It brought a swift image of Harry Bright, alone at his podium.

Katie was close enough for just me to hear her. "What. . . ?" It was a continuation of her sigh. She was trembling, also, not from the cold, and there was fear in her eyes, of me.

"We'll talk later."

We stood and waited. The earth turned and I was its axis. If I had lifted my hand I could have commanded the stars to blacken or the land to be moved, but I chose not to. It was enough to have extinguished this one star.

Fred approached. "We will discuss this tomorrow," he said. "I would suggest doing it this evening, but your state of mind would make it a waste of time."

"I'll call you," I said.

"You are very effective in tearing down," he said, his own state of mind not very steady. "You should try building up for once."

"I'll do what I want."

He paid his respects to Gladys and left. Katie was stranded beside me—Gladys had heard all and there was no possibility of even a stilted and formal conversation. I doubted they'd been having more than that anyway.

The hostess stood and went. Katie gave her a tight nod and smile, which were not answered.

The chatter and merriment of Eric and his damsels was carnival music on a battlefield. They came down a path through the gardens, one of them on each of his arms. I would have Katie pick one for him. It was time for Eric to settle down and get married. Whichever of the two was the grandfather's favorite.

Eric saw us watching.

"Don't you have anything else to talk about?" he asked, bright as a star himself, and one of the girls giggled.

"No."

"I'll get a ride home later. You don't have to wait."

"We need to go."

"Is Fred still here?"

"He's already left."

He understood. The girls did, too. They disengaged and tittered and grinned, but they understood that there was enmity, and a barrier had been erected. Eric said his good-nights and the three of us walked around the house, not even through it, to our car.

Despite the cool parting, Eric was enthralled. We let him jabber in the back seat.

"Genevieve is leaving for Washington in two weeks. She's going to intern with her grandfather. Madeleine's going back to Paris to graduate school."

So perhaps Genevieve would be the one. Neither Katie nor I felt like talking.

And when we were home, about the last thing I wanted was to watch myself and Bill Idiot Sandoff, four feet high. But Eric was bouncing off the walls, and Katie was curious, so off we trooped for the viewing of the interview.

My thoughts had petrified. That moment of Katie's gasp and the senator's hatred was unmovable, and I couldn't reach any other moment.

Eric diddled with the technology and I had a brief hope that the attempt had failed. But no, the brain that knew little of life knew much of video recording. There was a flash and a frozen image. My stomach turned.

"There you are!" Katie said. For her, this was comforting, this vision of her and my glory, and her tension from the evening dissipated into the humming air.

"I'll find the start," Eric said. As he searched for the beginning, split-second contortions battered the screen, rapid frozen images of my face smiling and shredded. I closed my eyes. This was my outside showing the fragmented reality of my inside, and I couldn't watch.

"There." Now it was Bill who was frozen, mouth gaping. Eric settled back into his chair and pushed the button. "Here we go!"

The mouth moved and words came out, but the static inside my head was too loud. Broken questions and disjointed answers crumbled into heaps of words and there was no place for my ears to put any more.

I tried to concentrate. He was talking about someone. ". . . we found a warm and open man, comfortable with his power and wealth. But there is no mistaking that he recognizes the responsibility that he has inherited along with his riches. He has moved decisively to right what he considers the wrongs of his father. Now he is the silent center of the political hurricane that is sweeping through the highest levels of state government. While investigators are only beginning to unravel millions of dollars of illegal bribes and fixed bids, and three very high profile murders, Channel Six's exclusive interview sheds some light on Jason Boyer."

Not Jason Boyer. Someone else. Someone responsible. Comfortable with power and wealth.

There is nothing silent in my center! I can't do it anymore. I can't play this game.

The Jason in front of me smiled. He was comfortable. He was responsible. It wasn't me. It isn't me! Look at him, at the truth of him. Arrogant, lying—more than any of the rivals he is casting down to set himself up higher. Ruthless. I know him. There is no center at all. Everything in me rose up against being that person.

The four-foot head continued. "Will you be meeting with Senator Forrester again?"

"Yes, actually. Katie and I will be visiting with him this evening, at his request. I hope we can have some reasoned discussion. The last thing we need just now is hot tempers and baseless accusations."

It had ended. Katie squeezed my hand and put a little kiss on my cheek.

"I am so proud to be married to that man," she said.

She hadn't forgotten what she had seen at the Forresters'. The interview had put it in context for her, though, as a use of power rather than a clash of personalities. She was comfortable with that.

Eric said, "You should run against Forrester. You'd kill him. What did you talk about, anyway?"

"We had some differences," I said.

"Who won?"

"Only time will tell," I said. "Good night." I couldn't even imagine when I would ever sleep well again.

30

I was up early Sunday. The house was still dark when I left.

Katie called me an hour later.

"Jason! Are you all right?"

"I'm fine. You saw my note?"

"Yes. But I was worried."

"I want some time to think," I said.

"Because of last night?"

"Yeah."

"Don't worry about him," she said. "They're terrible people. Whatever you have to do, they deserve it."

"I hope not. Someday I might get what I deserve."

"Don't do that! You always turn my words against me."

"No, not against you—against me."

"Last night you said that you were your father's son. That's not bad, Jason. It's why we are where we are."

"Getting born into some family is a pretty random thing."

"But it's what makes you who you are."

"Then why don't I like it?"

"I can't argue with you, Jason."

"It's okay. I can argue with myself just fine. I don't need someone else to help."

"I wish I could help."

How I wish you could. "Just give me time."

"What are you going to do?"

"Decide."

There was a long enough pause after that, that I wondered if the connection was breaking up.

"But I have decided," she said finally. She was breaking up, not the connection. "You're scaring me. You make me feel like everything's built on sand."

"It is. I can't fix it, Katie. I don't know what to do."

"I don't, either," she said.

I told her I'd call later.

My father's son. I leaned back in his old wooden desk chair behind the old wooden desk, among the books that were never read and the globe that was never turned, and the son was the father.

Had he ever asked the questions?

Had he found answers, or had he learned to live without them?

The windows looked out over the gardens and lawn. It was all just starting to fray a little from lack of care. The sky was still clean and tended.

What a beautiful Sunday morning. Five weeks since Katie and Eric and I had sat at our breakfast table in shock at Melvin dying the night before. Now I was the one who had died the night before.

How much longer could I go on like this? I would either accept my fate to be Melvin or kill myself, and they were both the same thing.

But I couldn't go on. I couldn't live with this confusion in my soul—it would be only a matter of time before I would drive myself off a cliff to escape the questions.

It was real, that I would kill myself. All the money and power— that was what it was trying to do, however it could. It would kill. That was its real goal. Melvin, Angela, Grainger—it had killed all of them. Katie, Eric, Fred, Bob Forrester, Harry Bright—they were all mortally wounded. And when I looked at it, I knew the answer.

So it was that I made my decision, life or death, and I chose to live if there was any chance left that I could.

I locked the door of the mansion behind me and then I was standing next to my car. I didn't know what I'd actually decided, only that I had.

Where was I going? I couldn't go to Katie, not yet. I wanted someone who knew what I meant and could help me.

Nathan was only one man I knew who had somehow escaped the sting and poison. I set my course back toward the city.

I called him once I was on the highway. Always polite, yes, he was home, he would be very pleased to see me. Come right over.

In fifty minutes I was in his neighborhood. It was at the other end of town but identical to my own old neighborhood.

He answered the door himself. There was something confusing about seeing him this way, in slacks and a polo shirt, in a domestic setting. Everything was tasteful, balanced. A few things were expensive. It was all comfortable.

We sat in his study. There were lots of shelves, with lots of binders and reports and scholarly books on them. A study where a person would study. Nathan worked very hard, but not to build his own bank account or influence. A person would need a reason to work this hard. What had seemed meaningless before now enticed me with the lure of meaning.

"Sit down, Jason." I got the grand stuffed chair, where so many of those reports had been read. Nathan sat in his desk chair, where many of the reports had been written.

"I need help," I said.

"Whatever I can do," he said, his brow wrinkled.

"I can't do this anymore."

He knew what I meant, immediately. He waited for me to keep going.

"You've been right all along," I said. I was surprised by my own vehemence. "I'm being destroyed. I have to escape."

"Jason." He might even have been wondering if he should call the police, or an ambulance. "I didn't mean it that way. I never meant to imply that you . . ."

"But it's happening anyway. Last night . . . I was just like Melvin."

"I understand. You were at the Forresters' last night?" Yes, he certainly understood.

"It was real nasty. I was. I was everything I hate, Nathan. It was like . . . like it wasn't me. But it was."

"I do understand, Jason."

"It will kill me. I mean that literally. I want to get out."

"What do you mean, 'get out'?"

"I don't know," I said. This was the real decision, and he waited for me. "I want to go back to the way it was, before he died."

That answer crumbled swiftly. "Were you satisfied with your life back then?" He knew I wasn't.

"No. Not really."

"You can't go back anyway. Too much has changed in these last weeks, especially you. Let me ask you a different question." It took him some time to assemble it. "What can you accept of your father's?"

I knew right away. "I . . . no. Nothing. I can't."

"Is there any line you can draw? Could you accept an income, as you had before, and nothing else?"

"I don't know. I don't know where to draw a line. I tried before, but it never worked. There's no right place to draw it." And this was the line in my own mind that I could never get past. "What would you do, Nathan?"

He looked away from me, and he was still and silent. It took him a long time. Even after more than a minute, when he looked back up at me and studied me, he didn't speak.

Then he sighed. "I'm very troubled about saying this, Jason. It's perilous to give counsel to another person when the consequences will be so great."

"I want to know."

"I'm not sure what I would do, because I'm not in your place. I've come to know you, though, and I knew your father, and I've known many people and seen many things. This is what I believe you should do." It was the first time anyone had ever said those words before and I'd wanted to hear them. "Give it up, Jason. Turn away. I don't know what this course of action will do to anyone else affected by it—and that will be many people. I am only speaking to you, about you. Give it all up—everything."

"How?"

"I don't know, but you can work that out once you've decided."

"It would mean the end of the foundation."

"Yes. I suppose it might well mean that." He smiled, a tight, pained smile. "I said before that shutting down the foundation would be a small price to pay to restore integrity to this state. Now my words may come back to haunt me. But the foundation can't stand long if it depends on the torture of a man's soul." He shook his head. "That should not be a consideration to you."

There was an obvious answer.

"Melvin wanted the foundation to have the estate."

"And I was against it." He took another long minute to think it through. "At least, I requested that he change his will. It was his decision." He stood and wandered to his shelves; I guess the binders and books represented to him his real love, and he was looking for comfort. "Even now, I still hope there is some other way. I never wanted such a responsibility. Even in a better world, without vice and moral dilemma, it would be crushing. In this world, the entanglements, the compromises . . . I couldn't, Jason. You more than anyone know how it is."

"Yes. But I don't see another way."

"Break it apart. Sell each business to a different buyer. Please don't put this burden on the foundation. It would destroy it."

"It would take years to divest. You're right; that's what has to be done. The whole structure has to be demolished. But I can't do it. I'm not strong enough. You said it yourself—*I have to give it up*—and you're right about that, too. But you could do it."

"Take the estate for the purpose of divesting it?" He was back at his desk and he sank into the chair. "It might be possible. I wouldn't really know how."

"There are people who do. It's the will to do it that has to be there."

"How would you live?" he said. "You need an income."

"Other people live without inheriting a billion dollars. I can find a way."

Then he asked the question I was dreading most. "What about Katie?"

"I don't know."

What would this do to her? I knew how she would react at first, but then what? I truly didn't know.

"She'll hate it. Money has always been so important to her."

"More important than you? Your marriage?"

"I don't know. It might be."

"I'm sorry. Will you ask Fred Spellman to advise you in any of this?"

"Not likely."

He nodded. "Yes, I agree. If you don't wish to confide in Fred, I can recommend Jacob Rosenberg. He's on the board of the foundation and is our legal adviser. He's an expert in corporate law."

"How is he on divorce?"

"I hope it won't come to that."

"Hope?" I said. "I don't have much."

"But you need hope. Everyone does."

I wasn't going to answer that. I had what I wanted. It was time to get away before Nathan started digging into the next layer of questions. "I'll talk to Rosenberg. Thank you."

"I'll do anything I can. Anything."

"You've done enough."

"You have a long life ahead of you," he said. "This crisis will end—you aren't thinking that far into the future right now, but the future will come. Jason, I've gotten to know you somewhat. You have questions. We can talk about them."

And I almost did. An image came into my mind, of the church-yard with the ancient trees, and the hallowed church. Death and life together. Nathan could answer those questions, as well.

But this was not the time, and there were lots of hard things still to do today. I left with enough hope to face them.

I used most of it up just getting to the forty-second floor, and I was feeling pretty hopeless again. I had a plan, though, and steps I could take. For the moment I was still rich, so I didn't mind calling an expensive lawyer on Sunday afternoon and summoning him to my office.

Jacob Rosenberg was actually not much older than myself, and he was also not in a suit. He wore a trendy little goatee beard and mustache thing, and an air of competence that reminded me of George Elias. He was attentive and not distracted by the view.

"Did you know Melvin?" I asked.

"I met him on the board." He also had an earnestness that reminded me of Nathan.

"And I assume you have an idea of what I've inherited from him."

"Yes, Mr. Boyer. Fairly well."

"Good. You'll need to get very familiar."

This was the point where the decision would start becoming real. I took a deep and lingering look out my magnificent windows. I was distracted by them.

"I won't discuss reasons," I said, "but I want to transfer every-thing to the foundation."

He sat back in the chair. "Everything?"

"All of it."

He was still breathless, but he got to work. "Yes, sir. All right. What is your time frame?"

"How long will it take?"

"I won't know until I see a list of assets."

"Guess."

"If we worked very hard, probably one week for most of it."

That deserved another survey of the panorama. It was getting to be later afternoon. From downtown the highways radiated with light traffic to the neighborhoods beyond. Usually they were lost in the haze but it was the first clear day of October, and I could finally see, farther than I ever had before from that place.

"Make it one week. Start this afternoon."

"Yes, sir."

I opened my desk and found the papers George Elias had given me weeks before. The top one was a little worn—the one with the box at the bottom and the ten-digit number in it.

"Take these. I'll direct George Elias to work with you. His number is in there."

He looked at the list, quickly and professionally, but his eyes still got big as he went through them.

"It's a lot of assets," he said.

"Will there be any problems?"

"I . . . don't see any so far." He looked up. "I believe you've used some of the cash account for your house and expenses?"

"Yes."

"Is there anything else I should exclude, besides your personal assets that predate the inheritance?"

I stared out the windows again, but now I was looking at the stone fireplace, the dining room table, the bedroom suite, the cars. Where had they come from? Even the boat. Was there anything that was mine?

"Don't exclude anything."

He nodded, still with his eyes on me.

"Mr. Boyer, is your wife in agreement with your plans?"

"We haven't discussed them yet."

"I see."

"Everything is in my name," I said.

"Yes, but she has common property rights."

"How will that affect me?"

He was looking through the lists again. "How is the house titled?"

"Through a trust. It's in my name."

"That was to keep your wife off the title?"

"That wasn't the reason. It was better for taxes. And she wasn't involved in the closing."

"I understand." Twice he started a sentence but backed off, trying to find the best words. "How do you think she'll react when you do discuss your plans?"

"She will not be in agreement."

"Will she actively work against you?"

"I don't know."

"Specifically, would she file for divorce?"

"I guess it's possible."

"I see." The sentence was having a hard time getting out. "It can change everything if she does. It would give her standing to obtain a court injunction against any transfer of assets. Short of a divorce, she could only contest the sale of the house. It's her residence. Once she files, everything you own can be contested."

"What if I don't tell her?"

That took more thought. "I don't think it would work. The court could possibly intervene retroactively and invalidate the contracts, especially if the assets were still intact. And, Mr. Boyer, you won't be able to do this secretly. These transactions are going to be public. I think we both know how the news media will react to any news about your family, especially something of this magnitude, and in the middle of all the political scandals going on."

"Go ahead anyway," I said. "If we have to deal with divorce proceedings, we will."

"Yes, sir." We'd been talking for ten minutes or so, and he allowed himself a brief familiarity. "I hope it won't come to that."

"Just be ready for anything."

There was no hope. Now I was speeding
down the highway I'd watched from my high
tower, peeling off the miles between us. I
went through a dozen ways to say it but they
were all the same. We had been such partners, even yesterday, and
now what? Was there any hope?

I pulled up in front of the house. Whose house was it? Melvin's
or Katie's? Not mine. Maybe I should just give it to her.

She was in the kitchen with Rosita. They were side by side at
the table, papers in front of them, planning the week's menu.

"Jason!" I'd startled her. "Where have you been all day?"

"Let's talk," I said.

She excused herself and we walked together upstairs to my
office. She closed the door behind herself. Then we sat awhile quietly, both of us waiting to hear what I would say. The seconds
dragged into a minute and then minutes, and finally the silence said
what I couldn't bring myself to say.

"So, what are you going to do?" she said, struggling, through
tight lips.

"I'm giving it to the foundation," I said.

I couldn't make it any better. The words were hammer strikes
against her. "What will we have left?" The words wavered, barely

making it through the air between us. All I had for her was more blows.

"Nothing, Katie."

"The house?"

"Nothing."

I'd seen two men ruined in just five days, not just their careers but themselves. I'd heard death in their voices and seen it in their eyes. But now, this third time, this voice and these eyes were so precious to me, and the death in them was my death as well as hers. Mine was the fourth life being shattered by my own desperate stupidity.

"No!" The force of her word and the force of her hand against my face were equal.

"Yes." My cheek stung and I thought she would slap me again. I just waited and didn't move.

"You liar." Now the storm broke. "You said I could have this house. You cruel . . . liar!"

"I'm sorry."

"You're sorry! You gave it to me!"

"It wasn't mine to give."

"We could have everything!" She was yelling as loud as she could and still sob at the same time. "Last night we had it all in our hands. There was nothing to stop us. And now, you . . . you fool! I hate you!"

"Don't," I said. Everything she'd said was true. How could I have been more cruel to her? Buy a house, Katie. Buy everything! Anything you want! And now . . . what a fool she was to have trusted me.

The door slammed behind her. Some time later I could move again and I opened it and went downstairs. I told Rosita that Katie wouldn't be down for a while. Then I left. I didn't take anything.

Eric was not home. That was good. The drive to his apartment hadn't been long enough. I let myself in and waited. I focused my thoughts on what I would say here—mainly to pull them off of Katie.

There was a little noise from the street, but it was mostly quiet.

All I could hear was Katie's voice. How could I get her out of my ears?

I tried to concentrate on my brother instead.

What would he be like if he'd had more struggle in his life? There were no roots. A good yank would pull the tree right out of the ground, and he'd be getting a real jerk soon. Me.

My cell phone rang.

"Hello, Fred," I said.

"We need to talk."

"We sure do," I said. "I'll call you this evening sometime. I don't know when. You should come to my office."

"I'm in my office now. There's already been reaction in the state senate leadership. Forrester has been trying a counterattack."

"I'll call you later." That would be another conversation to look forward to.

I waited more. There were no books in the apartment, not even magazines—just all the televisions. The place was swept clean. It was the mirror of his soul, a place to never think. I propped my feet up on the big heavy coffee table. If I stayed long enough, all thought would be sucked out of my own brain. . . .

"Jason?"

I woke with Eric standing in front of me. He was in cool outfit number four—torn jeans, gunmetal sweatshirt. Katie had them listed out on index cards so he'd know what went with what. Or maybe this was outfit number five.

"Hi." I shook out cobwebs. "I guess I fell asleep."

"What's up?"

"Sit down."

He sat facing me. Even he could tell this was serious.

"Is something wrong?"

"Eric . . . I've made some decisions."

"Okay." His face lit up. "You're going to be a senator! Just like—"

"No."

"Then what?"

It was still so hard to say. "I'm giving it up."

"What? Giving up what?"

"Everything."

"I don't get it."

It was too hard to do this! He wasn't opposing me like Katie had, but I was still angry at him for not understanding.

"I'm getting rid of it all! Everything! The money, all of it. I said I would. Back at the beginning, when Fred was reading that stupid will, I said I didn't want it. Why is it so hard to get anyone to understand?"

He was staring at me, his eyes wide. I took a breath.

"I . . . I don't understand, Jason."

Two more breaths. "It's okay."

"Do you really mean everything?"

"I'm giving it to Nathan Kern and the foundation. They'll break it up. They'll sell all the businesses and the stocks, so no one will have it."

"But last night . . ."

"That's what did it. Do you have any idea what . . . how evil I was last night?"

"But you were telling him who was in charge."

"No. You can't know how it really was." I was staring at the floor. "No one could."

"But you don't have to give up. Just get control."

I looked back at him. "I know what I have to do."

Somewhere inside him there was still a deep place, not silted up by hours of highway fumes. "I don't think you're evil, Jason. I think you're better than Melvin. I think you can be better than he was. I think you're smarter than he was. But if you think something is wrong, then you should do something about it. You always do what you have to."

That was as painful to hear as Katie's despair, because it was even more wrong. "Thanks," I said.

He must have heard what I was thinking. "What does Katie think?"

"She's angry and she hates me. I don't know what she'll do."

"Man."

This was much closer than politics and business. This was his parents splitting. Katie was nicer to him than anyone else he knew—he might miss her more than I would. Maybe she should marry him. He'd still have lots of money.

He heard me thinking again. Sweet young Eric—only now did his own welfare occur to him.

"What happens to me?"

"Nothing. Melvin set you up so I couldn't touch anything. It's all separate."

"Oh. What are you going to do?"

"I don't know. I haven't thought about it yet."

"If you need a place, you can crash here."

"Thanks."

So there was some kind of safety net, even if it was sewn together by Melvin's money. I hit the button for the forty-second floor and gathered myself for this next confrontation.

This would be different. Fred deserved no sympathy. Maybe everything I'd done was my own fault and my own decision, but this man was as bad as I was. Partway up I punched the button for thirty. I wanted to have the option of walking out of his office instead of getting a hernia trying to push him out of mine.

I called him and he let me in—he could unlock the doors from his desk. I knew he could get out of his chair, but just looking at him, a person would wonder. I started to look forward to this. I was not real stable at the moment.

"The impeachment bill is moving faster than I thought," he said, as if the whole world hadn't changed in the last twenty-four hours. "It will pass the House first thing tomorrow. I doubt there will be a single vote against it. The FBI has already requested a grand jury, and they should have a criminal indictment by the afternoon." Fred had been building this house of cards for decades, but he was still fascinated by its fall.

There was still the issue of the King of Diamonds. "And Forrester." He allowed himself a scowl. "After your performance last night, we can expect Malden to be a hostile governor." The scowl was worth repeating, and he did. "Do you have any idea the damage you did? I thought we had agreed to overlook his arrogance and work with him. Was that merely a tantrum, or do you have another of your plans?"

"I have a plan, Fred. I came up with it this morning."

"As well thought out as the previous one, no doubt."

For a moment I contemplated the world inside his head and the laws that governed it. He would deserve every ounce of the stroke this would give him. "Even more so. Are you nice and comfortable there?"

"Get on with it."

If I questioned whether I was doing the right thing, at that moment at least it felt good—it just felt a lot more like revenge than virtue. Fred was the serpent in the garden, even if that was not the first image that would come to mind looking at him. There was no regret here. I was going to be free of him.

"I quit."

"Oh, you do?" He studied me and was hardly convinced. "I think not."

This wasn't worth anger. "I've tried the job and I don't like it."

He was already frustrated enough with a long day of wrestling with politicians. "When are you going to grow up? There is work to do. Save your childish antics for some other day. I've been on the phone for eight hours trying to restore some sanity to the statehouse, and now you're losing yours."

"I'm sorry," I said. Actually I wasn't even trying to be, but he did deserve an explanation. "I said at the beginning I didn't want to do this. You almost persuaded me over this last month, but last night undid all that. I'm convinced now that I was right back at the beginning."

"And I am convinced that you are an immature fool. But that can be remedied, possibly."

"No. I'll always be a fool. But I don't have to be evil."

"What?!" No stroke, but close. "Do you mean that petty comment last night vexed you? Of all the absurd ways to have your feelings hurt."

I wasn't angry yet, just annoyed. "You know it wasn't one comment, Fred. It's weeks of rolling in this pigsty. At least I can still see it for what it is, and I've decided I'm getting out."

He had a huge repertoire of sounds of annoyance. "Then how do you propose 'quitting'?"

"Everything's going to the foundation, just like Melvin intended in the first place."

His eyes narrowed; he saw this might be serious. "Nathan Kern is supposed to manage the Boyer assets?"

"He and his fellow do-gooder board members. If you want to cut a deal with Bob Forrester or Henry Malden, you can submit your request to the committee of philanthropists, and they'll get back to you after they've discussed it thoroughly."

"Foolishness. A committee can't manage power. Someone will take control of it from them. They'll be no match for one ruthless board member, or even an outsider who captivates them."

"There won't be anything to take control of. They'll only have authority to divest and disassemble. It'll take a year or two, but the whole cookie is going to end up a pile of crumbs," I said.

"This is madness! Look at what you've done. You've torn down an entire state government. You can't just walk away from it."

"The thing was rotten by itself. Don't make it my responsibility."

"Just days ago you quite proudly took responsibility. I strongly advised you against it. If you hadn't meant to carry through, you should have left it alone. This would be the worst thing you could do."

It was all true, and I'd feel remorse for it when I had a chance. But everything I was saying was true, as well. "Maybe I made a mistake."

"A mistake! Maybe?"

"But probably not. Everyone's better off with Harry Bright exposed."

"There are many others to take his place, and they will be worse."

"If Stan Morton doesn't have his hands tied, he might keep the spotlight on. There doesn't have to be a king."

"Yes, there does. It is the nature of power. It is inescapable."

"Well, I'm escaping."

"Then do it quickly." That was it. The apron string had been machine-gunned. "If you think you can break up your father's holdings, you're wrong. Someone will put them back together. But now it is imperative for you to be removed before you do any more damage."

"Are you threatening me?"

"I don't need to. You are more than enough threat to yourself." He opened a desk drawer and jabbed his hand into it.

And then, for three seconds, I knew with certainty who the murderer was. I knew his motives and I knew who his next victim was going to be. I already had my hand balled and ready when his hand came out of the drawer with a handkerchief.

He applied it to his face, where I had been about to apply my own fist, rubbing off the perspiration of his passion. I was sweating from the adrenaline. I had to get out before either of us committed a crime.

"Good night, Fred."

He already had his own anger controlled and was working through his next move. I left him there, a dinosaur plotting my extinction.

I couldn't bring myself to drive home. Where was home going to be now? I finished my interrupted climb to the top of the building.

I called Rosita to say I would be out for the night, and laid my buffeted body onto the sofa. I'd had my nap at Eric's. Now I was awake.

What would happen after one week, or whenever Jacob Rosenberg finished earning his thirty pieces of silver? I just couldn't picture it. Maybe I wouldn't live that long anyway.

Katie. What should I do now? Even if I could talk her into a life with me instead of money, did I want to? She'd be better off without me. But I had to talk to her—to try one more time, with both of us calm. She needed to be rescued as much as I did, and she was much more worth saving. I had to talk to her.

Just not tonight. I'd had enough.

It was night and the office sofa was as good as a bed, but I wasn't sleeping.

At eleven o'clock I might have been the only person in the building without a vacuum cleaner. Except perhaps Fred. I rode the elevator to the ground, to the empty lobby, and went out into the streets.

Three nights ago I'd been meeting Clinton Grainger in this same dark. I could just get myself shot—if not by an assassin, then just a regular mugger would do. That would end a lot of peoples' problems. I even looked down a couple dark alleys, but no luck.

I drifted. It was like being lost at sea in the dark. I was no more able to get where I wanted to go, because I still didn't know where that was.

There were few cars and no people. The hotels were four blocks away. I came to a corner and I could see the Hilton down the street, even the site of Grainger's last stand.

It made me wonder who had stood there with him and how it was done. Just in the middle of a conversation? Had Grainger even seen the gun? Or maybe they had already parted and Grainger didn't even know he was not alone.

Angela had known what was about to happen to her. What was that moment like, I wondered. It must seem like an eternity. And then, real eternity.

The night was cold enough to shiver in. There was no hope.

32

The sun through my office window woke me up, and I called Pamela and ordered a toothbrush. She arrived forty minutes later, at seven, with that and a razor, comb, bagels, and no questions.

But I had answers.

"Pamela. Sit here." I put her in the Fred chair, facing me on the sofa. "I'm resigning."

She looked at me over the top of her glasses. "That doesn't sound like you're running for the Senate."

"I'm running the other way."

"Tell me all about it, dear."

I talked to myself, and she listened in. I retraced every step from the first funeral to walking the streets in the dark, and each decision I'd made, or whoever or whatever had made. And I repeated the questions that had chased me down the path and had finally caught me Saturday night. She nodded and shook her head at the right times, and when I'd finally run out of gas, she sighed.

"What do you think?" I said.

"I think you have a hard road in front of you."

"Do you ever ask big questions, Pamela?"

"That's why I go to church, dear. Will you be sleeping here for a while?"

"I don't know. I hope not."

"I'll get a few more things so you'll be more comfortable."

"What will you do when I can't afford a secretary?"

She smiled. "My husband and I have saved some over the years."

"Melvin left you some money, too."

"He was very generous. And there are two hundred little children in an orphanage in Honduras who are a lot better off now."

Was that her own mini-foundation? "You knew about Melvin's deals and everything he was doing?"

"Oh, yes."

"But you kept working for him?"

She knew where I was going. "I did. He never asked me to do anything he knew I wouldn't."

"He just asked other people to do it. Didn't it bother you to be part of his organization?"

She paused, and for the first time I was seeing into the secrets behind the secretary. "Every day. I try to live my life the right way, Jason, and it would be very hard sometimes."

Even Pamela was compromised. For the money? "Why did you stay?"

A dear, sweet smile. "I promised your mother I'd look after him."

That was the answer I would never have guessed. She waited for me.

"I don't even know what to say about that," I said. "Uh . . . you were friends with her?"

"Yes. When she married your father, I helped her get settled into her new house. And we stayed close."

"And how were you supposed to look after Melvin?"

"Just be there. We both knew he wasn't the type to take advice, especially from his secretary."

I was taking deep breaths. "Did she say anything about me?"

"She asked me to look after you, too, and Eric."

"Have you been?"

My cell phone started ringing.

"Every day."

I didn't understand, but I couldn't ask. I had to answer the phone. The caller ID said it was Katie.

It was seven thirty. "You found me," I said to my wife.

"What did you do, sleep on a sofa in your office?"

"Yes, actually."

"And you're still wearing the same clothes from yesterday."

"I had a spare suit here in the office."

"You don't need to sleep there. We have beds here."

"Would you want me in the same house?"

"Of course I do, Jason. We're still married."

"Still?"

"We're married, and this is your home. Come home."

"Katie." We were both calm now. "Come with me instead."

"What do you mean?"

"I want you with me. I'm escaping. Will you come?"

"You don't need to escape, Jason."

"I do! You know me. You see what I'm becoming."

"But we can handle it, together," she said. "Don't do this."

"I have to."

"You don't have to! Don't you care about me?"

"I care about you more than anything," I said. "Please come with me."

There was a deep sigh, almost a sob. "Don't leave me."

"I'll be home this evening. We'll figure it out, Katie. We'll be together."

But there was something cold in her voice when she replied. "But you won't change your mind."

"I won't."

Eric called at eight.

"Are you okay?" he said.

"I'm okay. I checked Melvin's will to make sure—you're set for life."

"Oh. That's not why I called."

"I know. I just wanted to tell you."

"Thanks. I was just calling because . . . I think maybe you're making a mistake."

"I'm not changing my mind."

"Come on, Jason." It just didn't sound like him. "If you think you were wrong before, couldn't you be wrong now instead?"

"No!" I wasn't used to him pushing me. "I said I'm not changing my mind."

"I think you should." And there was something cold in his voice, as well.

Fred called at eight twenty.

"Is Jacob Rosenberg working for you?"

"Good morning to you, too. Yes, he is. He's on the board of the foundation."

"I know who he is. He's filed SEC papers concerning the change of ownership of your stocks."

"That's what I told him to do. He works fast."

"And news travels fast. I am not the only one who will hear about this. You *must* reconsider!"

At that moment I felt sorry for him. "I won't. You'll be better off without me."

"Everyone will be better off without you. But your divestment plans are disastrous. They must be stopped."

"Don't hold your breath."

"I won't. I will take more effective measures."

"Stay out of it." Now I felt murderous toward him. "You can go down, too, Fred. In fact, you're a big part of what I'm trying to demolish." A very big part—very, very big. "And by the way, you're fired."

"I won't rant." His voice was very cold. "Just be warned."

"You too."

Nathan called at eight forty.

"I'm worrying about you, Jason."

"That would be justified," I said.

"What should I be doing?"

"Tell me I'm doing the right thing."

There was dead air, then he tried. "I believe you are. But it's your decision."

"Fred disagrees with both of those statements."

"What about Katie?"

"She's not happy."

"I'm sorry. I could talk to her."

She was going to be homeless soon. Maybe she could take advantage of some of his programs. "Maybe later. Right now it wouldn't help."

"If I can help at any time, please tell me."

"I will. Thanks."

At nine, Stan Morton called.

"What are you doing?!"

"I'm sitting in my office, looking out the window," I said.

"Your silence is deafening. I can't get anybody at the state-house to tell me what you've told them to do. So I called Forrester at his house. He'd never pass a chance to cut down Harry Bright. What do I get? A very uncharacteristic 'No comment.' What kind of gag have you tied on to everybody? I've never seen anything like it."

"I'm not telling anybody to do anything. They're on their own."

"Really."

"And Forrester will be his insufferable self soon enough."

"Okay," he said, and I could hear the suspicious look on his face. "So what's the story here?"

"I'd tell you but I'm tired of talking about it."

"If you're tired, I'll send a reporter over with a pillow."

"I'll tell you tomorrow."

"I'm taking that as a promise."

"Whatever. Good-bye, Stan."

Jacob Rosenberg called at nine twenty-five.

"I have a couple papers for you to sign."

"I'm just sitting here," I said.

"Then I'll be right over."

I was ready to make my own calls.

"Get me Senator Forrester's office in Washington."

"I don't think he's there yet," Pamela said. "He was flying back this morning."

"It doesn't matter. I just need to talk to somebody to deliver a message."

I stood by her desk as she levered and forced, and after only a few moments she had a person. I took the call on Pamela's phone.

"What may I do for you, Mr. Boyer?" said the person.

"Please give my regards to the senator," I said. "Tell him that he's free. He can do whatever he wants. I don't care if the blathering idiot rots in Washington, but he better get his own machine to get elected because mine is out of business. And tell him to keep Tweedleleine and Tweedlevieve away from my family or I'll change my mind and tell the newspaper everything about him spying for the Communists."

The person recovered fast. She must have had plenty of practice. "Mr. Boyer—"

"Nyet, comrade. I will say no more."

Pamela couldn't approve of my behavior, as much as she wanted to. "You shouldn't burn all your bridges," she said after I'd hung up.

"I like to watch the flames."

"You might need friends later on."

"Not Forrester. And not Fred. I don't want friends like them."

It was almost ten when Jacob arrived. Lawyers are supposed to be precise with words, but his "couple papers" was not.

"Did you work all night?" I said, looking at his stack.

"Six of us did."

"I'm glad you're taking this seriously."

"Well, Mr. Boyer, time is against us. The faster this gets done, the better, before we start getting resistance."

"The resistance has already started."

He smiled a lawyer smile. "And due to the expenses we're incurring, and the nature of the job, this first paper is to create an escrow account with sufficient funds to cover our bills."

"No problem," I said. That was probably the first thing they teach in lawyer schools, to charge up front if the client is bankrupting himself. I changed the amount from two million dollars to five million.

"The two million was meant to be more than enough," he said. "Anything unused will just go back into the main estate."

"We don't know what might happen these next couple weeks. Let's be very generous, just in case."

"Yes, sir. These papers create a single trust, which all the assets will be assigned to. It's in your name to begin with. These are the papers that will transfer the trust to the foundation. You can sign those when you're ready."

"I won't sign those yet." That would be the crucial moment. "What is the trust called?"

"I've put down *Jason Boyer Asset Trust* as the name."

I found the page where that was written and crossed it out. Above the line I wrote, *Trust for the Termination of Boyer Family Power and Riches.*

"Let's go with that," I said.

"The name is public information, Mr. Boyer."

"I know."

"Yes, sir."

"And these are all the specific assets?"

"Yes, sir," he said. "We got as many as we could. These are transfers designed to avoid sales and capital gains taxes whenever possible. There will be some taxes."

"Which trust includes my house?"

"Let's see." He riffled for just a moment. "This one." It was the trust that also owned the sailboat and the cars and furniture and all my personal assets. "There is a waiver for your wife to sign, if she would."

"I don't think she will."

"That's a sword hanging over the whole thing. She can contest this transfer."

"We'll proceed anyway."

"And as I said before, if she files for divorce, all of this can be delayed or even halted."

"I'm trying," I said. To do his job, he needed to know how it was. But I didn't like discussing it.

"Yes, sir. I just want to make sure you understand that she is the biggest threat to your plans."

"I understand."

He understood that he was not to press the subject. "And this is a power of attorney. It gives our firm the right to conduct transactions on your behalf for the sole purpose of moving assets into the main trust. It's to prevent delays when we need ancillary papers signed."

I was reading the fine print. "No. I want to do my own signing."

"Yes, sir. We'll keep some couriers available if we need to bring papers to you quickly."

We got to work. Pamela only interrupted one time.

"Fred's on the phone," she said.

"Tell him I'm busy signing lots of papers."

"Do you really want me to?"

"No." I picked up my phone. "Yes?"

Fred's voice came out of the receiver like an earthquake. "I want to know if you'll change your mind." That was all he said.

"I won't."

The line went dead.

We trudged on through the papers, and it was after eleven when we finished.

"Am I free to discuss this with Nathan Kern?" Jacob asked.

"Sure. It'll all be his in another week."

"As long as Mrs. Boyer doesn't interfere."

"Whatever. Go ahead and brief him on the whole thing, and keep him updated if anything new happens."

I gave him a five-minute head start, and then I fled my office and returned to the streets, far different now than twelve hours before. The sidewalks were full and the restaurants were crowded. I stopped at a crammed diner. Everyone in the place got a weekly paycheck and lived off it.

"You know who you look like?" a voice said. I looked up. The waitress was waiting for my order.

"Who?"

"Jason Boyer, that millionaire."

I smiled. "People have been saying that all weekend."

After lunch I bought a newspaper. The state senate impeachment posse was in full pursuit of the governor. The editorial was a call for him to step down. There was a picture of me on the front cover. I wandered back toward the office. Two women on the sidewalk stared at me and whispered together.

It was spooking me. I didn't like this feeling of being noticed and recognized. I thought about Fred and his handkerchief and his hand in the drawer. I thought about Clinton Grainger, unarmed.

I found a gun store.

I knew nothing about guns. I told the man I was working late more often and I didn't like walking the streets at night. He told me what I wanted, an automatic pistol that he had in the back.

And there were waiting periods and background checks. I gave him my Jeff Benson driver's license for the transaction. He studied it very carefully and decided he could trust me. He'd let me take the gun now, and he'd take care of the background checks later. He was so helpful.

I said I wanted to try it. He didn't have a place—it took a lot of expense and licenses to run a shooting range, but maybe I could just put a couple bullets into a block of wood he had. The block had a lot of holes already and I added two more. It's not hard to fire a gun.

I didn't want to carry it in my pocket, so he showed me some holsters, the kind worn under a suit jacket. Of course, I'd need a concealed gun permit to use it. I told him I'd get the permit before I used the holster.

It was all easy to do, especially with such an accommodating salesperson. He smiled just like we were old friends as he handed me back the driver's license, less the three hundred-dollar bills that had been clipped onto it. The bulge under my left arm hardly showed.

"I am not here," I said to Pamela. "Completely not here."

"Yes, sir."

I closed my door. I could still back out. I could call Jacob and tell him to shred the papers. I could apologize to Fred. As long as I had the money, he'd be my friend no matter what I did.

As long as I had the money, Katie would be my loving wife.

"Katie, I've changed my mind. I'm sorry. Will you forgive me?"

"Oh, Jason! Of course! I love you, dear! We are keeping the house, aren't we? And all the money?"

No, I couldn't do it.

That brief moment of indecision was very short, about the length of time it would take a person in the lobby downstairs to see me come in from lunch, maybe make a short telephone call, and ride the next elevator up to the top floor. There was a commotion in the outer office.

My door opened. Pamela was trying to warn me on the intercom and also stop the intruder, but he was much bigger than she was.

"Jason Boyer." he said. Shabby black suit stuffed with muscle and fat, greasy cheeks, ragged dark hair—most bouncers were better dressed.

I stood up. "Of course I am."

"I'm serving you papers that your wife, Katherine Boyer, is suing for divorce."

He had laid a large envelope on my desk. It would have been a cheap thrill to hit him, to punch him in the face, but it would have just made it all worse.

"Get out," I said.

But he had more words to say. "By court order you are specifically prohibited from selling or liquidating any property—"

He paused for a split second, looking at my suit jacket. He'd spotted the holster. In his line of work, he had to be aware of things like that.

"I said get out."

"By court order you are also required to surrender to Katherine Boyer the deed to your residence on Old Post Road. By court order you are required to transfer to the bank account listed in these papers an amount of no less than twenty million dollars for Katherine Boyer's expenses while the divorce settlement is negotiated. By court order you are prohibited from any communication with the following people—Jacob Rosenberg, Nathan Kern, Stanley Morton, or any employees or agents of those individuals or organizations they are associated with. By court order—"

"Get out or I will kill you."

He shrugged. There was a limit to his tenacity, and he'd said enough. He turned and walked out.

Pamela was beside herself.

"I'm so sorry, Jason. I couldn't do anything."

"It's okay. It's not your fault."

I didn't have time for the rage. I soothed Pamela and then called Jacob Rosenberg.

"What do the court orders say?" He was incredulous.

I read them again.

"Who's the judge?"

"Walter Willis."

"Okay, no problem," he said. "That's Harry Bright's cousin. It's twelve thirty. . . . I'll have them all struck down by one o'clock— except the first one about selling or liquidating. Your wife has a right to that injunction."

"Find a judge who'll cancel it anyway," I said. "Are any of your cousins judges?"

"Two of my uncles are, actually, but they're both in Boston. They couldn't make it stick anyway. It would get immediately reinstated."

"I was joking."

Some amount of time passed. I only knew that because the sun was at a different angle than it had been. I could only think about Katie, and they were thoughts that couldn't be put into words. Only that we'd each made our decision and we had not chosen each other.

"Jason," Pamela said. "I'm sorry. Stan Morton just offered me five thousand dollars if I could get you to talk to him."

"Take it," I said.

"I didn't mean . . . I just thought I should tell you how desperate he was."

"Then we'll split it. I'll talk to him." I picked up my phone. "Stan."

"Jason. Tell me this is not true. Your wife is filing for divorce?"

"It's true."

"No."

This was how the fox would feel with the hounds everywhere. "I'm not allowed to talk to you anyway."

"The court already overturned that order."

Right. It was one thirty. "I said I'll talk to you tomorrow. It sounds like you know everything anyway."

"The world is going to know by this evening. What is going on?"

"I don't know anymore." And I hung up.

It was the dog's day. Pamela was at the door again. "Jacob Rosenberg is on hold."

"Okay."

I left him on hold while I put my head down in my hands. What had I been expecting anyway? That everyone would just smile and give me a hug? What was I doing here?

"This is Jason Boyer."

"We're stopped. There are five lawsuits against you so far."

"What lawsuits?"

"By stockholders. They claim you're devaluing their stock by your attacks on the governor. We can't do anything with your stock until they're thrown out."

"Then get them thrown out."

"It'll take time, and I've only got so many people here."

"If you need more people, get them."

"Yes, sir. And your wife's injunction against selling or liquidating is still in force. Whoever is advising her knows they have the trump card."

"Do whatever it takes."

I hung up. What had I been reading weeks ago? It had been *Bleak House* by Charles Dickens, where there are so many lawsuits over a dead man's estate that the whole thing is eaten up by the lawyers' fees. The villain in that book was a lawyer.

"I'm still not here," I said to Pamela, "and I will be gone for a few minutes."

Down twelve floors.

I'd missed the first part of the thug's attack on my office, the part where he pushed past the secretary. So at Fred's office, I re-enacted it.

His secretary looked up from her desk as I came through the outer door and she reacted fast, pushing buttons and scrambling out of her chair.

"Mr. Spellman is with clients," she said and planted herself between me and the inner door, so I would have to physically shove her aside to get to it. No problem. I got to it and threw it open.

There they were—what a spectacle.

Katie was in the big chair. I only saw her shoulder and brown hair, which I'd recognize anywhere. She was wearing a dark purple-and-black dress I remembered from the day we'd looked through the new house. No pearls. She didn't turn.

Eric did. He was on the sofa and he started, guilty as Benedict Arnold, his eyes and mouth wide open.

"Jason . . ." he said.

But my attention was on Fred at his desk, the source of all evil.

"Stop it," I said.

"I am stopping you. And you are intruding."

"And you are fat," I said.

"And you are an imbecile. Now get out."

"That's what I said when your man came to my office a few hours ago, but he wouldn't. He just kept talking. 'The court orders you to give her money,'" I mimicked the man's voice, right into her ear. "'The court orders you to give her the house.' I might have given you the house to get it over with, but not now."

"Jenny," Fred said into his intercom, "call the police." To me, "I know better than to ask you to negotiate. You've proven you can't, one of your many flaws."

"And you," I said to Katie. She didn't turn. "Three years we've been married, and one day is all it takes?"

She didn't answer. She couldn't. She was shaking, staring ahead into space.

"Get out," Fred said.

I was back to Fred. "I'm not ready yet. As corrupt and rotten as you are, it's not enough. You have to pull them in and destroy them, too."

"As long as your wife's divorce suit against you stands, you are prevented from doing further damage," Fred said. "Fortunately she understands the importance of that."

"And she understands the importance of money. How much did he promise you, dear?"

"Jason . . ." She turned to me. I could see the torment in her, the same as the torment in me.

"You're divorcing me!" I said. "What am I supposed to think?"

"He said only I could stop you."

I could hardly speak. "Don't stop me. Katie, don't stop me."

It was too much for her. She was starting to break. We stared at each other, except neither of us could see anything through tears.

"But, Jason . . ." It was Eric. I turned to him for just a moment, and when I looked back, Katie had turned away from me. I exploded at him.

"Why are you even here?"

He cringed back. "Fred wanted me."

"They just want to use you. You're no match for him, Eric. Get away from him."

He exploded at me. "Stop telling me what to do!" For two seconds he was defiant and angry; then he buckled. "You're always ordering me around." Now he was whining. "I can take care of myself."

"Then go ahead. I'm sure tired of doing it."

"Now will you leave?" It was Fred. "No one wants you here."

"Please leave, Jason."

Katie said it. The one last wall standing toppled.

"Don't stop me!" I said, or yelled, or screamed. "I will do this. You will not stop me."

"I will stop you!" Fred roared.

"You'll have to kill me," I said. Then his hand was in his drawer again, and I was beyond any caution to wait and see what he was reaching for, and I had my own gun in my hand. There was sound—Katie, panicked and screaming.

And then I was hit hard, Eric throwing himself into my left shoulder. I was close to Katie's chair and I fell against it, still on my feet. He lashed out at my face. My right arm was pinned but I got my left hand on his back and pushed him down. He was still off-balance and he fell.

On the floor, he scrambled back, ready to lunge again. But the fight was over.

"Go. Now." Fred had not moved, but there was a heavy black

revolver in his hand, pointed at me. Katie stopped her fool screaming.

"The police are in the lobby," the secretary's voice said. "They'll
be up as quickly as they can."

I walked out.

I must have taken the elevator, but I only knew that I was back
at my desk and the sky out the window was clouded and Pamela
was staring at me from the doorway, white as a sheet. Standing in
front of me was Nathan Kern.

"Jason?" He'd said it more than once. "What happened, Jason?"

In my ears and eyes, Katie was still screaming and Eric's face
was red and enraged.

"I went to talk to Fred."

"What happened? You look terrible."

Nathan's face was getting clearer, and Eric's was fading.

"Katie and Eric were there. We . . . it didn't go well."

The screaming was fading, too.

"Your lip is bleeding."

I felt it. "It must have been when Eric hit me."

"Oh dear!" Nathan's astonishment was probably comical, but I
still couldn't focus.

"I'm okay," I said to Pamela. She slowly backed out and closed
the door. "We screamed at each other and I pulled out a gun," I said
to Nathan.

As slow as I was thinking, he was slower. He gaped. "Was anyone hurt?"

"No. Not by the gun, at least."

"But why? Why did you have a gun?"

"Just . . . Fred had one. I wasn't going to use it. Then Eric tried
to tackle me."

"Where did you get it?"

The gun was worrying him. "I just bought it. Today."

"Do you still have it?"

It had been in my hand. I looked; it wasn't there. The holster
was empty, too.

"No." What had happened to it? I couldn't remember. "I thought I had it."

"But you don't?"

"I must have dropped it when Eric hit me." I had some impression of setting it down.

"Then it would be in Fred Spellman's office?"

"Yeah." I really didn't remember. "It must be. I'm not going to call and ask him."

"I will." Nathan was more upset than I was, nervous and quivering. He tried to lighten up. "You look frightful, Jason. I'm afraid your lip might become quite swollen. You go clean yourself up, and I'll call Fred."

I headed for the washroom out in the hall. Pamela nabbed me as I passed her desk.

"Let me look at that." She had a damp washcloth and she cleaned off the blood, very carefully and precisely. Nathan was calling Fred. Mommy and Daddy were taking care of me, and I didn't mind. No police had yet appeared. At least Fred hadn't sent them after me.

"That should do," Pamela said. "It isn't bad. I don't think it'll show."

I trusted her expertise on busted lips more than Nathan's. "I have a feeling my picture will be in the papers this week."

"I could put some makeup on it."

"No thanks."

When I got back into my office, the call had apparently been completed. Nathan was sitting on the sofa, smoking a little cigarette, still shaking.

"I'm sorry, Jason. I hope you don't mind." He stubbed it out in an ashtray he apparently carried with him. His fingers jabbed the cigarette into it like a hen pecking corn. "I'm not used to stress like this." He took a breath to clear his smoke. "Fred says he has the gun and will not give it back."

"He can have it," I said. I was thinking at about regular levels now. "What are you doing here?"

"Oh! Ha! Yes. I was quite taken aback by the way you came in. But you must have been surprised to see me, also. Our phone call this morning left me uneasy. I wanted to say again, in person, that I'll do anything I can to help."

"Thank you, Nathan." I was sort of done with being tended to. "I appreciate it."

"I mean it! I know you're having difficulties. Jacob has briefed me on some of them. You shouldn't have to do this alone."

"I can't think of anything you could do."

The next question took lots of effort. "You said you saw Katie?"

"She was there."

"Did you . . . Is she going through with the divorce?"

"Yes." I was listening to her anguished voice. "I think she is. I don't know. Maybe she won't."

"Could someone talk to her?"

"It's the money, Nathan. She wants it too much." I calmed myself. "And Fred's using her. He'll never let go of her."

"But isn't there some other way?"

"I could give in to her. I could offer her twenty million dollars, or fifty million, and she'd take it. But then she'd be gone, and I don't want to lose her. I want to fight for her. Maybe I can convince her."

"You have to try," Nathan said. "Don't give up. You'll need her support after all of this, more than ever."

But she was lost, and his words were pushing me back over the edge. "It doesn't matter!" *After all of this* was only a vague and threatening image in the dark, and there was nothing I wanted of it. "You should go, Nathan."

He tried to answer, but there was no answer. "I'm sorry."

"So am I."

The door closed behind him. What would I do afterward, after it was over? Was there anything to do? I was collapsing just at the thought of it. There was nothing I wanted of life. I'd seen through it, and there was nothing but Fred's evil and Katie's greed and even Eric's mindless drifting.

I changed back into the clothes from Sunday.

"I'm leaving," I said to Pamela. "I won't be back today."

"Please be careful."

"I'll be careful."

"Call me if you need anything."

I drove. Storm clouds piled above the road, and mid afternoon was twilight in their shadow. At three o'clock I was at the marina. I hadn't decided to come here. It was reflex.

The sky was thick and heavy gray and the wind was hard out of the west. I could see whitecaps in the bay beyond the inlet. I put out; the sail caught a gust and went stiff as plywood and yanked the boat out into the turmoil.

I let it run. We fled the land, the boat and I, caught in the wind's vise and with no thought of escaping it. The spray was heavy as rain, stinging my eyes. The open water of the bay was rough and confused against the boat and against my skin.

Clear of the bay were real waves, and I outran them. I would mount one, the deck inclined steep enough to fall from if I didn't hold on, and then the boat passed over the crest and hung and then fell itself into void, slamming the water six feet down.

Black was soaking the clouds just like the salt water was soaking my clothes. I was freezing cold and wet, but I was flying and putting ever more miles between me and everything that was back there. There was no going back against that wind. Behind me was a red flare of sunset flat on the horizon.

Hours passed, and miles. I'd been blown north of Martha's Vineyard and into Nantucket Sound. Before me was pitch black. I would have to choose to not race into it. Despair was driving me harder than the gale, and I'd have to overcome them both to turn away from the night's empty chaos. I had no reason to try.

"What am I doing here?" I screamed it into the screaming wind, and the clouds answered with a downpour. *"Why should I live?"* The Atlantic ahead of me had an answer, a dark answer and an ending. I flew toward it. The storm took me and held me, and my boat became an eagle in the night rain and I was soaring into blackness.

When I did turn, it was almost too late. For a while I thought it was. I was almost out of Nantucket Sound and I thought about just grounding on Monomoy Point, but I cut the corner in time. It was a steep tack. The waves were almost straight on portside, Monomoy Island was leeward, and the boat was bucking like a bull. Then I saw buoy lights bobbing wild, and I got between them. The water flattened, I fought the sails down and started the motor, and threaded the needle into Chatham on Cape Cod.

Then I was walking on firm ground. I had to talk to Katie. There must be some way out.

I rented a car. It was after nine o'clock.

The rain on the windshield was the same rain I'd stood in on the deck, but on the road it was not an element, just an annoyance. Here in the car I could oppose the forces against me. The roads didn't toss and the wind didn't touch me.

The radio had come on when I started the engine. I forced myself to listen to the news.

". . . took the oath of office with just his wife in attendance. Governor Malden has given no sign what actions he will take to restore order to either the statehouse or his own agencies. He begins his administration with only seven of Harry Bright's cabinet members still in office.

"Yet even the momentous events in the capitol today have been nearly overshadowed by the startling news of a split in the powerful Boyer family, itself rocked by scandal and murder. In a widely watched television interview Saturday, Jason Boyer had positioned himself as a rising power in state politics and business. Now, two days after their flawless appearance, Boyer and his wife of three years, Katherine, are headed for divorce amidst a storm of lawsuits.

"Neither was available for comment. Speculation has been wild, however, after sources in police headquarters confirmed that Mrs. Boyer met late this afternoon with investigators assigned to the inquiry into the murders of Melvin and Angela Boyer and Clinton Grainger. While Police Commissioner Miguel DeAngelo had previously denied that Jason Boyer was a suspect, this evening he back-pedaled, stating that Mr. Boyer was, quote, 'obviously a person of great interest to us, including his movements at the times of the murders.'

"Jason Boyer inherited his father Melvin Boyer's estate, including . . ."

These were the forces more difficult to oppose. But I had to.

I was in my driveway before eleven. The front of the house was dark. I let myself in. I was hungry.

Lights were on in the back hall and the kitchen, and I found Rosita unpacking grocery bags.

"Mr. Jason!" She didn't know if I was friend or enemy.

"Is Katie still up?"

"I don't know, Mr. Jason. I have only come back from the grocery store."

"It's late."

"Yes. There is still so much to do in the new kitchen."

I climbed the stairs. The upstairs hall light was also on. I stopped at the closed bedroom door.

What will I say to her? I had to bring some end to this war. Somehow. Was there any way? I could compromise. She could have the house and enough money. It would be better for her to break loose; she'd never understand me.

But the bed was empty, unused. I went back to the kitchen.

"Would she have gone out?" I asked Rosita.

"She was here when I left."

"I'd like to find her."

I went back up the stairs and opened doors. What was the point of sitting in the big, wonderful house all alone? She'd find someone else. A couple years from now she'd be over it. I came to my office door and pushed it open.

I didn't touch her. I couldn't move. She was in my reading chair, slouched sideways, glass eyes fixed on the ceiling. Her mouth was fallen open and blood covered half her face and had dribbled across the black and purple of her dress. But her hair was still loose and untouched.

I don't know how long I was there.

I couldn't move. I couldn't think. Neither of us could.

And then I touched her unmoving hand. It was cool and limp.

Something pressed against my shoe—I looked down. How natural to see a handgun on the floor.

I held it. It was familiar. It was probably mine. I didn't really remember what mine had looked like.

I looked back at her and I couldn't understand what I was seeing. It was just Katie, cold and quiet, terrible. I knew she wouldn't speak to me, or move, but that was all I could comprehend.

Finally, sound! Harsh, abrupt; I'd been holding the gun too tight. Now there was a bullet in the ceiling, too.

The echoes circled and died away, and we were back to silence and not moving. Forever not moving.

Then there was screaming. I turned to the door. Rosita was the one screaming. Her hands were on her cheeks, her mouth open in a circle. I held up the gun to show her what had made the sound, and she left. I heard her running, down the hall, down the stairs, screaming, screaming.

In the jumble and ruin of my thoughts, something stirred. I was still just looking at her face. I would have straightened her up in the chair, but I couldn't bear to touch her again. I heard Rosita's screams from outside the window. She was running down the driveway.

The thought pushed up from under the debris and formed itself. I had to get away.

It was not from rational process. It was instinct, and only that growing primal urgency uprooted my feet from the floor and made them carry me to my desk and open the drawer and reach for the thick envelope in the back.

The first thing that came out in my hand was the picture from Melvin's bedroom. I set it back in the drawer and tried again and found what I was looking for, the cash envelope I kept for whatever reason I might need it. I hadn't known why I might need it.

I dropped it. Twenty- and hundred-dollar bills scattered across the carpet. Suddenly I was moving fast. Fear and survival instinct were pushing me. I collected as much as I could find. I had to reach under her legs, and my hand brushed her ankle. I pulled my hand back and left those bills where they were.

I had to get away. I turned to leave. Should I look at her one more time?

But I couldn't. I sprinted down the hall, took the stairs two at a time. The front door was still open from Rosita. I dashed through it to the drive, where I'd parked. I had to get away.

But my car was gone, and someone else was parked in front. Had someone heard the screams and already come? Or had this car already been there? I couldn't remember if it had.

The gun. It was in my pocket. I'd put it there when I dropped the envelope. If someone else was close by, I'd need it to defend myself.

Then I remembered that this was the rental car. My car was back at the marina. I got myself in and turned the key and the tires screamed as I escaped.

The rain was heavy. Ahead, I saw signs for the Massachusetts Turnpike. It was well after midnight.

The adrenaline had finally drained and I could think. It had been seeing her, and Rosita screaming—I'd panicked and run. Now I knew why: Rosita had heard the shot, she'd seen the gun in my hand. She thought I'd killed . . .

Everyone would think so. The police would. It would be obvious I was the . . . the person who had . . .

Who had killed her. Katie. She was dead.

It must have been a dream, it couldn't be true. How could she not be alive?

Even if I hadn't been there, they'd still be chasing me. It was so obvious I was the one. It had even been my gun.

It couldn't be true. I'd go back. It wouldn't be true.

I kept going. I didn't get on the turnpike; it was watched too closely.

What was I doing? The more I thought, the more I had to get away. Melvin, Angela, Grainger. They'd accuse me of all of the murders. What could I do? Fred and DeAngelo, they'd make sure I was convicted. Being innocent didn't matter. Fred always said that.

Every way I thought of it, it was worse. The first murders had left no trace, but this one used my gun, my house, my . . .

Oh, Katie. I pulled onto the shoulder of the road until the shaking stopped. Katie was dead.

Where was I? My car was at the marina—the boat was on Cape Cod. I'd rented this car with my Jeff Benson driver's license. It was as if I'd planned to make myself hard to trace. Eventually the police would figure it all out, and it would be more proof against me. For now, it would help me get away.

I needed to get far away. The police would have been at the house by now and would be looking for me everywhere. There was a New England map in the glove box. I picked a road to Keene, in New Hampshire. I'd stay off highways.

The rain finally stopped about two. I'd bought gas in Keene, and I was crossing the bottom edge of Vermont. Francine would know by now that her daughter was dead. Eric would know, too. They'd have searched his place and questioned him. He'd tell them about me pulling out the gun in Fred's office. Fred would know, of course. He'd have already talked to DeAngelo, the police commissioner.

The gun! Fred had kept it. How had it gotten to my house? Wasn't it the same gun?

It all made sense. It had to be Fred. He was the only one. The last person to see Melvin; he was in the right place to kill Grainger. He was obviously someone Angela would let into the parlor.

There would have been no problem getting to Katie.

Why? I didn't know. Katie had changed her mind? I could guess a hundred reasons—I'd have to know everything Fred knew to guess which one. It would have to do with money and power, of course. He'd do anything.

One small sign beside the road and I was out of Vermont. It was so quiet. "We're in New York," I said. She must be asleep.

No. She wasn't there.

It was three thirty and pitch black on the two-lane road. A long time since I'd pulled myself off the couch in the office and eaten Pamela's bagels.

Albany was ahead. I pulled into a shopping center so bright I couldn't see. Behind the all-night grocery store I found the employees' cars.

It only took two minutes to unscrew the license plates from a red pickup and another three minutes to put them on my car. My brain was spinning and throwing out thoughts, but my actions were still just reflex.

My old plates I put in my trunk. That was enough adrenaline to get me through Albany wide awake.

Then I had to stop. I parked in a hospital lot filled with cars and leaned the seat back.

It wasn't sleep, just a vehicle for hallucinations. Inside my skull she was alive. She was a rainbow, her dress every color in turn, her pearls a long shoreline of lights in the dark, and I was on the black waves looking for her. I woke in dread of all the nights ahead of me.

It was seven thirty, the sun in my eyes.

I bought a razor and a toothbrush. The clothes I had on were the same I'd sailed in last night, and they stank and were stiff with salt. I used the razor to scrape the rental stickers off the car windows. I didn't use it on myself.

The newspaper headlines were Harry Bright and Boyer divorce. Nothing about Boyer murder. Maybe it hadn't happened.

The New York Times had a picture of Henry Malden taking his oath of office. With his hand up, he looked like the stone statue in the church. I thought about Katie's funeral. First I thought how terrible it would be, looking at her casket. Then I remembered I wouldn't be there. Francine had always known I'd kill her daughter.

I forced myself to turn on the radio. It was loud static; I was far from the station I'd listened to the night before, driving back from Cape Cod. I searched channels.

Classical music, country music, traffic and weather. Maybe nothing had happened. I'd wake up next to her, and Rosita would have breakfast going. I was hungry. I pulled onto the interstate toward Binghamton. Top forty, classic rock. News.

". . . a massive hunt for the billionaire and apparent murderer. Early this morning the Coast Guard was added to the list of law enforcement agencies seeking Boyer after his car was found at his marina and his personal sailboat was missing from its berth.

Authorities now believe Boyer may have been involved in three other murders that have rocked the state, including his father, his stepmother, and a political rival. State Police Commissioner Miguel DeAngelo has personally taken charge of the investigation and search. In a statement earlier, he said that the victim, Katherine Boyer—"

I turned it off. She was Katie. We both disliked *Katherine*.

I was doing ninety. I slowed down and pulled off. There was a big discount store at the exit and I bought some clothes. I counted the money in the envelope—forty-five twenties and seventeen hundreds.

A week ago, twenty-six hundred wouldn't have been enough to dress for dinner.

The clothes were cheap and fit poorly; I'd hate for Katie to see me looking like this. I bought a hat, a baseball cap I could wear down over my face, and sunglasses.

I had breakfast at a truck stop. I sat in a corner in my disguise and watched the news on the monitor across the room. The volume was high enough to hear in the parking lot.

There was no other news anywhere in the world. It was all mine. They did family history about Melvin, and the FBI investigation into his criminal practices. They did Angela the eccentric widow. They did political scandal. They did impeachment and conviction. Harry Bright was doing his part to keep the story alive—he was refusing to leave the governor's mansion. They did shutdown of state government and anarchy in the departments and investigations and arrests.

They did the murders. They did Melvin's faked accident and Angela's faked suicide, and Clinton Grainger's unfaked murder. And over and over they showed it, in grainy news video from the street, the white-covered stretcher carried out the front door of my house and gently set in the ambulance.

They had Commissioner DeAngelo personally directing the investigation from the podium in the press room by answering questions from reporters. He told them the suspect was armed and dangerous and that his brother was under police protection. He also confided that he'd suspected Jason Boyer from the beginning.

Motive and opportunity. It was obvious. Melvin's death? DeAngelo waved the report right there on television. Brake fluid on the driveway. Irrefutable proof.

The whole state was shaken and cracked. Everything that Melvin had touched was on the television screen. What deep and wide roots he'd put down, and how damaging it was to pull them up. So many lives he'd touched, and every one was dead or dying.

In Pennsylvania I changed plates again, taking them from a blue Ford van parked behind an auto repair shop. It was past noon.

I was far away. This was not where they would look for me. Here, I just had to be careful, and I had options, west or south.

But my mind was still back at the house, in my own office.

It had to be Fred. Katie, what did you say to him? How did you threaten him? Did you even know? Or maybe she was just an innocent bystander. Did Fred kill her just to get me out of the way? If so, he'd accomplished it.

There was nothing I could do. All I could do was hide from the police, and from Fred. At least the police wouldn't kill me, probably. Was there any chance the state police would find the real killer? No.

I found a library and spent two hours looking online for every detail they'd reported. My picture was everywhere. I moved to a different computer behind some shelves, less out in the open.

It had been my gun; the bullets matched the ones I'd fired at the gun shop. There was a story about how I'd been rearranging my assets, possibly to transfer funds overseas. It was definite that I had no alibi for Angela's murder or for Melvin's murder, and that I'd met with Grainger Thursday night. There was a lot of information that only Fred would have known.

He would kill me next, unless he got me convicted first, which would be just as good. I was his fifth victim either way.

As the sun set I drove into West Virginia. It was high October, when Katie and I usually took a weekend in a quaint New England inn and appreciated the colors and warm days and cool nights. We'd shop for Christmas presents. We probably had reservations somewhere. Katie had made them last year, maybe even for this coming weekend? We hadn't had a chance to talk about it.

I'd have to sleep in the car again. Behind a big camping store, I found a dark corner. I leaned the seat back and slept in it for the second time.

It was no better. Instead, it was much worse.

The store was cavernous. I spent five hundred dollars on camping equipment—a tent, a stove and pots, sleeping bag, food, more clothes, a map of state parks. I called most of  them from a pay phone before I found an empty campsite. I didn't want to use my cell phone or credit cards, so I couldn't reserve it; I just had to get there first.

It was two hours away, south of Charleston, but they still had openings when I got there. I paid for three nights. They wanted a name and address, and I gave them one of each, not mine. The tent was up in five minutes and then I was horizontal on the sleeping bag.

I slept through the afternoon without dreams, my first sleep in a couple weeks that was worth the effort.

That evening, Wednesday, I was hungry enough to eat the food I'd bought. I was finally still. Katie was dead, I knew it now, even if I kept thinking she'd climb out of the tent, blinking in the sunlight and running her hand through her hair, smiling, wrinkling her nose at the stew.

"Let's get something else to eat," she'd say. *"Do they have Italian here?"*

She'd look at the tent. *"And let's find a bed-and-breakfast. I can't sleep in that thing again."*

"Sorry, dear," I'd say. *"We're stuck here. We have to hide."*

"You have to, Jason, not me. I'll go into town and find someplace more comfortable. I'll be back in the morning."

And she was gone.

I got up with the sun, as much as there was in the clouded sky, and my mind was clouded more. I showered and put on clean clothes and ate a decent breakfast.

I was restless—sitting was no good. I got into the car and drove to Charleston.

There was a big library downtown. There was still no other news in the world, only mine. Harry Bright had finally left his office and was now under medical supervision.

But the news pigs had found two new troughs. The first was the manhunt. They'd found the boat and identified the rented car. The timing showed that it had all happened before the murder. Boyer had driven from Cape Cod to his house in the rental. Obviously part of his plan.

A neighbor of the Boyer townhouse in Washington DC had seen Jason Boyer on the street there yesterday. She'd recognized the picture from the television, but police had found no traces in the house itself. There had been many sightings, in fact—even overseas.

The second trough was going to keep many investigative reporters employed. What would happen to the money? A trustee would be named. Petitions were already filed. The first named Eric, the younger brother and only other member of the family. I could smell Fred a thousand miles away.

And another petition requested that the Boyer Foundation be given the responsibility. I hoped Jacob Rosenberg kept his doors locked at night.

I was back at the campsite before supper. There was really nothing to do now but sit. I had escaped and I was safe enough. What was next? I walked a few miles on a trail, just in case an answer was leaning against a tree close by.

I came to a fork in the trail.

What could I do? I had to prove that Fred was the murderer. The police would not. I'd have to go back.

I didn't know what to look for. If the police caught me, it would all be over. Every power I knew was against me.

Why should I even try? I was sitting on a fallen tree beside the path. There was a mountain view—vast waves of stone and earth, thousands of feet high and unmoving, foaming not white but crimson and umber and gold, and the salt in the breeze was burning wood. It was all just a sea to be lost in.

Why not give in? "Miguel, buddy, here I am! Slam that prison door!" What was the point of fighting? No need for money in prison. Three meals a day, no expenses. Whatever I did, that's how it would end. Or else it would end worse.

At that moment, looking out on the wilderness, I had no fight left. All I'd wanted was to be rid of all the money and politics, and I was.

What was left to fight for? I had to give up. I was too tired, and the fight was too hard.

As I didn't sleep that night, I fought to give up the fight. But there were faces in the dark. Katie first, and Angela, and Harry Bright. Clinton Grainger. Bob Forrester. They were all victims of Melvin's empire, snared by their lust for power or money and then destroyed; or destroyed by someone else's corruption, if theirs hadn't been enough. Fred driven mad and murderous by power had killed four times, and even he was a victim.

The faces cried out for vengeance, and justice, and no one else could hear them.

I pushed them away. Wasn't it just human nature to be captivated by wealth? It wasn't my fault they'd made their decisions. Another face pushed itself back into my mind.

Melvin, looking at me as he never had in life. What was in his eyes? Entreaty? It was only my imagination—it wasn't really him.

He conjured up another face—Eric. The next sacrifice on the insatiable golden altar.

There was nothing I could do! What could I do?

And beneath all the turmoil around me was the havoc within me. If it was all hopeless, if I couldn't stop Fred or save Eric, could I just find out why?

On Friday I went back to Charleston, to the library. With Harry Bright "convalescing in a medical institution," his storyline might have faded; but he kept it alive. He was consumed with revenge against both me and his turncoat police commissioner, and from his supposedly secluded location, he managed to keep firing white hot incitement against the inept investigators.

DeAngelo was having second thoughts about being personally in charge of the chase. Besides the humiliation of not being able to find me, a new blister on the scandal had popped. There had never been any brake fluid on Fred Spellman's driveway.

The revelation might have been leaked on Harry Bright's orders. It apparently came from the state crime lab. DeAngelo's retort had been immediate. He had full confidence in the current director of his crime lab and there was absolutely no doubt that the original report had been true. And if it wasn't true, then it had been faked on the former governor's orders.

So much for ever knowing whether there had been brake fluid.

There was also the first word from Eric, just a short statement. "I am still shocked and overwhelmed by the events of last week. The management of the family holdings is a heavy responsibility, which I hope to stabilize after the confusion of recent events." Was that released in written form or was Fred also a ventriloquist? Eric could sit on Fred's knee and just move his mouth.

But he was not yet being given the chance to stabilize. A judge had ruled that guardianship of the Boyer assets was an urgent concern, but he would not rule anything else until he'd heard arguments from all parties. I wondered whose uncle that judge was.

There wouldn't be enough room on the front page of the newspaper for all the headlines being generated.

And meanwhile, the manhunt continued. I leaned back in the wooden desk chair. The library was an old, ornate building. The computer tables were positioned end-to-end, long rows crowded between metal bookshelves. Half of the computers were in use. I'd picked the emptiest part of the table, at the far side of the room from the checkout desk. One woman was two chairs away and no one else was close.

I read the article about the search, which seemed to still be concentrated back home. Hundreds of calls to the hotline were arriving from all over the country.

The woman had left and I was alone at my end of the row. I glanced up at the librarian stationed at the checkout desk.

Her eyes were fixed on me, and she had a phone in her hand. The woman who had been near me was next to her, talking. I looked away. What were the chances that it was nothing to do with me? It didn't matter.

I couldn't run. I had to leave, just like any customer might, and lose anyone watching me. How much time did I have?

I erased the Internet browser history and quickly paged through Web sites on cholesterol and herbal remedies to fill it with something else. I stood up.

The two ladies about went into hysterics.

I sauntered around the first bookshelf, out of their sight. Evasive maneuvers. Around a corner, through more shelves, up some stairs. Was there any other way out besides the front door?

I followed exit signs down another stairwell. It came out almost where I'd started but closer to the desk.

The ladies were not in their watchtower. They were farther back, walking slowly past the ends of the shelves, stopping at each and nervously peeking around. I walked out the front door.

From my parking spot on the street a block from the library, I did see a police car roll up to the curb and a policeman in no hurry stroll up the steps to the doors. I slipped down the street and away from that library forever.

I hadn't shaved in four days, but it would be weeks before my beard would be any disguise. I couldn't wear the stupid hat and sunglasses everywhere. Far from the library, I found a drugstore and searched the hair colorings. I had no choice and I hated it.

I took the box back to the camp and read the instructions and managed the whole messy, foul-smelling process in the bathhouse.

It was the only place. People came in and out but no one stayed long enough to see the before and after and know what I'd done.

It was a poor, ugly job of bleaching, and it was not me in the mirror. I felt violated. When I was caught, this was the picture that would be in all the papers and news shows.

I went back to my tent, and now the face I'd just seen in the mirror was the one I couldn't get rid of. Who it was, I didn't know.

Friday night. I drove six miles to a fast-food place, ate, and drove back. As hard as I tried, it still took less than an hour. At the counter, though, I'd stood face-to-face without hat or glasses, and no one had called the police.

Now I was back at the old homestead. A storm was coming, up in the mountains—I could see it far off, just like at sea. The clouds cheated the day of its last half hour of light. I crawled into the tent as the first rain fell. The car would have been drier, but I had bad memories of that car and rain.

The sound of the rain on the tent was a muffled drum. I could hear the rain on the leaves and ground outside. Flat on my back, I stared at the brown nylon ceiling. One week ago . . . that had been the night of the roast duck and maple pecan pie. It had been our one dinner in the house. If only I'd known—not the future, just if I'd known to enjoy it as much as it deserved. The future we'd still owned that night was so bittersweet. It had been the promise of years of life together in that fairytale castle.

But it had been built on sand. The fall of the magic kingdom had been so fast and so far.

It was all so irretrievably gone.

Why? Why would I never see Katie again? What was the reason for that?

Every time before I'd reached this point of weariness, of wanting to put an end to it, I'd come out of it somehow. This time was the darkest. I needed a reason to keep fighting.

To even keep breathing! Why? Why had this happened? But I didn't have enough energy to maintain the sudden rage.

"But you need hope. Everyone does."

The voice spoke out of the darkness. Nathan.

Just that thought was enough to get me through the night.

36

Saturday morning I began the journey home.

I woke feeling a strange lightness, and then I remembered my last thought before sleep. Nathan.

Of everyone involved in the Boyer morass, he was the only one standing on firm ground. He wasn't owned by money, he wasn't dominated by power. I was ready to listen to him. If I had no hope of anything besides capture and all that would come after, I at least had hope that there would be an answer to the questions.

And if there was any way to prove Fred's guilt, it was not in West Virginia.

I crossed Pennsylvania, passed north of Philadelphia, and by midafternoon I was in New York traffic. I fought through it.

I reached JFK airport before dark and parked in a massive sea of cars. I left a thousand dollars taped under the passenger seat and had a thousand in my wallet.

From the terminal I took the subway downtown to Grand Central Station and bought a ticket for Boston on a train with stops in between. It was late afternoon now, and I had forty minutes to wait.

After the solitude of the campground I was disoriented by the crowding and noise, but it was enlivening. And in New York City no one gave me a second look. I sat, inert—I was used to sitting.

Of course there was a television, and of course it was spewing news, and of course the news was me. It was important to know if anything was happening, so I watched it. But there was nothing new. The only change was in the growing anger of everyone involved and the ferocity of the war over the money.

Suddenly there was a fragment of video, of a stone church I had seen and a few people I knew, walking slowly to a line of cars.

". . . yesterday afternoon, Katherine Boyer was laid to rest . . ."

I stumbled out of the waiting room desperate to escape that vision.

Then I was on the train. The sun was just setting, and I leaned back in my seat and I tried to sleep. I would have to ask Eric where they buried her.

I woke twenty minutes out from my destination. I was off the platform before the train was on its way to Boston.

It was nine o'clock and dark. I checked the bus schedule. I had an hour to kill before the bus to Nathan's neighborhood. No, to waste—I didn't kill. Someone else was the killer.

I would get to Nathan's house before eleven. I could only hope he was there and not on one of his interminable conferences. I imagined him reading in his study. By candlelight—my imaginings were fanciful. I would sit by him.

"What is the reason, Nathan? What am I doing here?"

"I can tell you that, Jason."

But I couldn't imagine what he would say.

The night was cold.

It was an eight-block walk to my downtown office. As I stood at the door of the train station, I thought about taking a risk. I hadn't yet. It seemed like luck or fate owed me a favor for not tempting either of them for the whole week.

Would there be anything in Fred's office? In fifteen minutes I could be at his door. But that would be as far as I'd get.

Eric's apartment was maybe fifteen blocks. Did he still have his police protection? What would he do if I showed up at his door? I couldn't guess.

A well-dressed couple passed me on the sidewalk, and then a larger group. Something had just ended and the audience was starting to fill the streets around the train station. It was the opera.

If only Felicity could see me now.

Still twenty minutes before my bus arrived, and I was restless. I caught myself in a mirror, beach-blond ugly. I was hungry and I broke a hundred-dollar bill to buy a sandwich. I hadn't eaten since breakfast.

A slow walk around the block would take ten minutes, and then the bus to Nathan's neighborhood would be ready to leave. I stepped back out into the night and turned to my left, and at the corner I turned left again.

The street had been empty behind the train station, but as I turned the corner I saw someone in front of me. I had a sudden, queasy feeling. I turned to go back, but someone else was there in the dark, close. I dropped the sandwich. They were both moving right toward me.

There was no room to get away. I lunged at the closer one.

He was surprised and went down, but I did, too, on top of him. His friend pulled my arm to get me off, and I rolled and broke free. He kicked me in the side, but I caught his foot and he went down.

The first one was up and landed a kick on my back, and then the other put his fist in my face.

The light or the pain, I don't know which woke me. The light was from a window or something above me. The pain was from all over.

Everything else was dark. I didn't try to move. I closed my eyes against the blinding white light. Breathing was too hard. The pain was too much. I couldn't even tell where it was.

Something else was terrible, apart from the throbbing. I took a breath and gagged. It was the smell.

I opened my eyes and the light had moved. I didn't know where I was. The worst pain was my head—my jaw and a place above my ear. I tried to turn over, but the pain in my side and stomach was too sharp.

I was lying on an uneven pile, and my face was against rough metal. I thought as hard as I could and I finally figured it out.

I was in a Dumpster, on a heap of garbage. The top was closed, and just a narrow crack let in sunlight.

There was no use moving. I don't know how long I'd lain there, or how long I had been unconscious. I remembered the train station, and then the fight. What had that been about?

Just a stupid back-alley mugging. I tried to feel for my wallet, but I couldn't move my arm. They'd seen me buying the food, flashing my cash. Stupid.

I was going to Nathan's house. I tried to sit up and almost passed out. Everything hurt, every part of me. How long had they beat me? Why hadn't they just killed me? I wished they had.

I couldn't move. I couldn't do anything. The pain was too much, it was overwhelming. I fainted.

When I was awake again, I could see daylight through the opening, but none was coming in. I had to move. Slowly I turned over, onto my back.

I could tell where the pain was. My jaw, my head, a dozen places. I sat up. The stench was nauseating. I could touch the closed cover, but there was no way I could lift it. Was someone going to open this thing sometime?

It was late afternoon maybe, or evening. I didn't want to be here through the night. Please get me out.

Could I call for help? It would be the end. Billionaire fugitive murderer found in the trash. But I didn't want to be here in the pitch black and the smell.

It would be better to give up. They'd put me in a hospital and the pain would stop. Oh, it hurt.

The garbage truck would come. It would lift the whole Dumpster and everything would tumble out. Just imagining it—falling and crashing—I was sweating. And then into the back of the truck and the crushing. They wouldn't even see me. When would the truck come? I had to get out.

I couldn't give up.

It got dark, then black. There were no streetlights.

I heard voices. There was a clang and the top lifted.

"Why's it closed?"

"I don't know."

The crack was a couple feet wide. A heavy plastic trash bag was shoved in but wouldn't fit through.

"Just put it in the other one."

"It's full. Help me get the top open."

The top lifted farther to the height of its arc, then swung down, slamming harshly against the outside. Then the bags came in on top of me, one after another, and then they left.

It took me twenty minutes to get out—pushing the bags off of me, climbing over them, and then the final drop to the pavement that jolted every bone. But I was standing, outside, leaning against that evil prison. No one saw me. I limped away from it into the shadows.

I didn't know the time. My watch was gone. I felt my pockets. No wallet. All the money was gone. I still had my keys. And something else . . .

It was my gun. Cursed thing, the one time I really should have used it, I hadn't even thought of it.

There was a back door by the Dumpsters where they'd brought out the trash. It was unlocked. Inside the train station was an empty, grimy hall. It was too bright. A clock said it was nine twenty. Sunday night? It must be. There was a men's room close.

What I saw in the mirror was hideous. One eye was bruised and swollen and the lip was split, and the face lacerated and torn—the bleached yellow hair was a scar itself. The shirt was matted with dried blood. It wasn't even human.

I couldn't stay. I stumbled back out into the night. The bus was impossible. I couldn't be seen like this; I didn't have money anyway.

I had to get to Eric.

Fifteen blocks.

I had to keep myself hidden. I had to keep moving. My jaw was the most painful now—I had to hold it with my hand. The jarring of each step made the pain still worse.

I don't know how long it took to go that mile. I was half delirious. People who did see me stayed far away. I didn't stop at the cross streets, and once a car squealed and swerved around me.

His street was mostly empty. I got across it, to his building. It was after eleven, but the fifth-floor lights were on.

The front door was locked. It took a few tries to get the key right, but then I was in. I got in the elevator. I'd forgotten to look for police. I'd just hope they weren't close.

I had to prop myself against the elevator wall and it jerked my jaw when it stopped. I crossed Eric's lobby to his door.

I didn't know whether to knock or just go in. It would be better if he didn't have a chance to call anyone. I put the key in the door and turned.

He was startled. He was watching television, still dressed, in jeans and a clean white pullover. He looked just like he always had.

"Who are you?" He'd stood when he heard the door opening, his reaction surprise and revulsion. He stared at me. His mouth pinched closed and his nose wrinkled. "What do you want?" he said. He really didn't know who I was.

"Eric."

He kept staring, and the reaction slowly changed into simple hate.

"Jason."

I closed the door. "Help me."

He stood aside, shrinking from me. Now he was frightened, too. I staggered into the room and stood for a moment with my back to him, looking at the clean, comfortable furniture, the wall of televisions. He walked around me, keeping his distance. "Jason?" he said again. I nodded. I was about to collapse.

I reached a chair in time, just by the door, and fell into it.

"What happened to you?" And then, "Where have you been?" And then, harder, with anger, "Why?"

"I didn't kill her." It took all my strength to speak.

"I don't believe you."

That hurt worse than anything, or it would have if I could have felt any more pain.

"I need water." I hadn't eaten in almost two days, but even more, I was thirsty. He didn't move. "Please."

He filled a glass and held it out to me; he didn't want to get close. I tried to drink but I couldn't get my jaw to open enough, and most of it poured down my chin.

"Straw," I said.

He found one. It was still difficult but I filled my mouth with the water. Swallowing, I gagged, and lost it again.

He was disgusted. "Drink it slow if it's so hard."

I forced it down my throat. "More."

"Here."

The water helped so much. Now I was desperately hungry but I wouldn't be able to chew.

"I need help," I said again.

"You stink." He backed farther away. "What happened to you? You tried to kill somebody who could fight back?"

"I didn't kill her!" I screamed it at him but it was a hoarse whisper. "I didn't kill her!" I tried to stand up but I couldn't.

"I still don't believe you." He said it quietly. He was in pain, too. I could see what this week had done to him.

"It was Fred."

"No! You're lying." That made it worse. I should have known how he would react. "You hate him!" he shouted.

"It had to be. He had the gun."

"You had the gun."

"No. I dropped it."

"No you didn't! You walked out with it. I saw you."

It was too hard to understand. "What?"

"You walked out of Fred's office with the gun in your hand," Eric said. "We all saw you."

"But Fred—"

"Shut up, Jason!"

I was too confused, and there was too much pain. "But it had to be him."

"No. Everybody knows you killed her, and you killed Angela, and . . ." He couldn't say it.

"I didn't." I had no more strength. "I didn't kill her, Eric." It wasn't Fred? It had to be Fred. "I didn't kill anyone." Then who killed Katie? Now the pain of her loss came back stronger than any of the other pains, and I started crying, and then I leaned back into the chair and I was sobbing, my head in my hands, the world more black and terrible than it had ever been.

"I'm calling the police."

I looked up to him. "No." This was even worse. How could I stop him? "Please."

"I have to." He picked up the telephone.

"If they find me I'll never . . . I'll never . . ." I'd never what? I couldn't remember. He pushed three buttons, 9-1-1. I had to do something.

"I need the police," he said.

"No." It would be over. How could he be such an idiot? I couldn't stop him and I couldn't get away. I thought about what I had in my pocket.

He spoke into the phone, standing by the big coffee table, his eyes on me. "My name is Eric Boyer." Should I even stop him? The police would come and it would finally be over. They'd put me in a hospital and the pain would stop, and the running.

No. I had to make him stop. I put my hand around the handle.

"My brother, Jason Boyer, is in my apartment."

His eyes were locked into mine. My finger was on the trigger. I had to stop him. Why had he always been such an idiot?

"Yes, ma'am," he was saying. "Detective Wilcox told me . . ."

I pulled the trigger.

The gun wasn't as loud as the shattering of the huge television screen. Eric's head jerked toward the glass explosion, his mouth hanging open. For the moment, he was stunned. I had to move fast. With every ounce of energy I had and more, I launched myself out of the chair at him. I didn't know what I was doing besides stopping him.

I slammed right into his chest and he fell backward with me on top of him. There was a crack as his head hit the slate table, and I felt his body jerk and then go limp.

"Hello? Hello? Mr. Boyer? Are you there?" The little voice piped from the phone. "We're sending help. Are you there?"

I was still on him and I could hardly move. Something had hit my jaw, the pain was white-hot. I rolled off and sat next to him. It seemed like he was breathing, but he didn't move.

What could I do? There was nothing I could do. I took hold of a chair and pulled myself up until I was standing. The only sound was the telephone. "Mr. Boyer, the police are coming. They'll be there in two minutes. Mr. Boyer, can you hear me?"

It was the same as before, in my office, with Rosita screaming. I had to get away. I threw the gun as hard as I could through another television.

If there was anything I could have done, I would have stayed. But there was nothing I could do.

"I'm sorry," I said. Again, I fled.

I stumbled out to the elevator and rode it down to the garage. I should have taken his car keys but I didn't think of it. There were all his beautiful automobiles filling a whole wall of the garage—his life.

If he was going to die, I should have carried him down so he could die in one of them.

I got out to the side street. The sirens were coming fast. I crossed the street and found the alley behind the row of businesses. They weren't so antique and picturesque from behind.

Sirens screamed, car doors slammed, lights flared. I heard the locked front glass door shatter and I saw a cruiser cut off the garage entrance. I had only seconds to get moving.

As steadily as I could I walked the length of the alley to the next side street. At the end, I turned toward the blocks behind.

A hundred times in the dark I woke. Some of the times were from pain, some from dreams, some were from voices and the tread of feet above me or sirens in the street outside. And some were from the cold.

My body couldn't sustain consciousness. Each time I'd wake in terror. The nightmare images would all be a jumble: Eric's face, Katie's face, screaming, Fred with a gun, men in dark streets. Then I'd remember what they meant just as I slid back under the waves, too wounded and weak to struggle.

Daylight found me under the front porch of an old derelict house. I was lying in dirt, and the floorboards were twelve inches above my head. It was better than a Dumpster.

My jaw was fighting for my attention against all the other aching muscles and bruises. I knew I could move when I had to and I knew how bad it would hurt.

How badly was Eric hurt? It had to be that he was only hurt. Why was he such an idiot? Surely he would be all right. He was still breathing when I left. I had to find out.

It was time to move. The pain clamped down on me, just like I knew it would, and I crawled out of my rathole into the bright light.

The house was close to the street. I was about ten feet from the sidewalk. The neighborhood had once been better, but it looked like it had gotten mugged and thrown in the trash. I fit right in.

I didn't know which way to go. I got to the first corner. If I went south I'd cross the line into Eric's affluent quarter. It must be close.

Four blocks was all. I came out within sight of his building. I pulled back into the alley.

I found a trash can behind a restaurant, full of garbage. Right on top was a half-eaten chicken sandwich. I tried to take a bite but my jaw couldn't do it. Then a man inside yelled at me and waved an empty bottle like a club. I shuffled away.

What was I supposed to do? I wanted to find out about Eric, but I couldn't think of any way to see the news. Could I really have killed him? How had this happened? Why had it happened? I was only trying to stop him from calling the police. I was trying to get away. I'd always hated that big, heavy table, so out of place in that room.

Now there was only one place to go. I needed to get to Nathan's house. I hardly remembered why, except that it was the only place left. And I hardly knew what direction to go. I just started walking.

I didn't care about the police. It would be ten miles, or fifteen or twenty. I walked right down the main roads that I knew. I couldn't spare the energy to wind through back roads and neighborhoods. I saw plenty of cruisers, but no one stopped. They obviously hadn't gotten a description out of Eric yet. My torn, polluted clothes and my bruised face were a complete disguise.

I didn't know how far I'd gone, and I wasn't sure I'd make it in one day. Every step got slower and harder. I was starting to forget where I was going. I had to keep awake enough to not get lost. Pain had transcended the sense of feel—it had become an element of existence.

Sometime in the afternoon I passed a park with a water fountain, but it didn't work. I had paused, though. Now I couldn't get started again. I just sat on the park bench and let the afternoon go by.

What would happen at Nathan's? Would I kill him, too? What kind of curse was on me?

I stood up on my feet and walked so the pain would drive the thoughts out of my head. I was still not giving up.

At sunset I was away from the city. I couldn't remember how much farther, but somewhere ahead on this road was a village center, and past that was his street.

But I couldn't go. It wasn't a matter of will anymore but of physical impossibility. There was a belt of trees and bushes along the road, and I collapsed into a shadowed ditch.

And there was a miracle there, an old coat, and I slept under it.

The coat had probably been in the ditch for a year or more. In the morning I brushed the dirt and spider webs off of it and put it on. I wasn't thinking at all now, only moving.

It was still early and cold, and walking didn't warm me. But the coat helped a lot and I was thankful for it.

I turned off the main road onto a street with driveways. I found a newspaper still lying in one. Back on the main road I came to a fast food place with tables outside. It wasn't open yet. I sat at a table and opened the paper.

MURDERER STRIKES AGAIN

I just stared at it. I couldn't even think what it meant; just that it was more terrible than anything else that had happened. But then I saw the smaller type.

Doctors Upgrade Eric Boyer's Condition to Guarded.

I wouldn't have let go of that newspaper for a steak dinner. I devoured it for any clue about him.

He was conscious, as of sometime yesterday. He'd had a concussion. There was no major damage.

That gave me energy enough to want to read the rest of what

was happening. Harry Bright had told the reporter that if they wanted to see brain damage, they should look at Commissioner DeAngelo's department. Nothing else could explain how his entire Division of State Police could let the most wanted man in the world get past them to attempt another murder.

DeAngelo had answered that the police protection had been suspended at Eric Boyer's request after his police escort had given him a speeding ticket.

But most of the news was about the hunt. There were now roadblocks around the whole city, watches on all the bus and train and air terminals, at all the ports and marinas. Hotels were reporting anyone vaguely resembling the fugitive.

There were no police left to look for a tramp sleeping in the bushes. I had to agree with Harry Bright: they weren't doing a very good job.

I finished reading. It was time to get on. It had warmed up, and I thought about abandoning my coat, but it was my only friend.

Then there was another miracle. In the trash was an almost full twenty ounce bottle of soda. I savored the liquid and calories and caffeine. It was enough for the moment.

It still took me four more hours to get to his house. It was after noon.

I saw no sign of anyone watching. Nathan would have refused police protection. He had nothing to fear from me.

Surely he knew. He didn't think I was the killer. What if he did? He'd give me a chance to explain. Would he believe that it was Fred? I didn't know if I believed it anymore.

I went around the block, to the house backing against his. There was a way through to his house that was covered by trees and fence. I made my way slowly into his backyard. Now what? His door would be locked. The house would have alarms on all the doors and windows.

I'd wait in the bushes for him to get home.

I sat for an hour, but it got painful. I shifted to bushes against the house. They were smaller, but there was room behind them. I tried a window, but it was locked.

He had to believe me. Nothing would work if he didn't. The reason I was going through all of this was to talk to him. I couldn't see anything past that. Maybe because there was nothing. Maybe I'd fought through the pain and hiding and wretchedness without a reason. I waited.

I'd done so much waiting the last week. It was good practice for prison, or being dead.

The sun descended. When would he get home? Would he eat out? I still didn't even know for sure that he was coming home at all. He might have just left for a month-long conference in Bombay.

A car pulled into the driveway and around to the back of the house. It wasn't him; it was a woman in a gray uniform. She let herself in the back door. I waited two minutes and silently opened the door myself and followed her in.

I didn't know if she was the maid or the cook or what. The kitchen was the first room on the left of the passageway, but it was empty. I needed a place to hide. I opened a closet. It held brooms and mops. I closed the door and kept looking.

In the hall I stood still, listening, and I heard her upstairs. I hurried through the dining room and front hall to Nathan's study.

There was a door on the far side. I opened it. It was a conservatory, with glass windows and plants in pots on the floor and hanging. I had no idea Nathan would have had such a place. It wasn't visible from the front street. I closed the door behind me and wedged myself behind a chair. Most of the pain was from my bruised, pounded muscles, and it was starting to fade. Just my jaw was getting worse.

I waited.

I couldn't hear anything from here, or see her leave. It was about four o'clock when she'd come. I kept waiting.

At six thirty I unrolled myself and let what blood I had left back into my knotted limbs. Nathan might be home already. The maid might still be cleaning or cooking. I opened the door.

The study was dark and empty. I crept through the house. There were lights on in the front hall but no cars in the driveway or garage.

I went upstairs and found a bathroom. What a luxury it was,

after the past days. I cleaned myself as well as I could. I'd take a shower soon, after he got back.

The kitchen was lit, and a casserole dish was warming in the oven. The timer showed forty minutes to go. The smell of it cooking was overpowering, and there were cabinets of food, but I left them. I went back to the study.

I didn't know how to meet him. He'd be startled. I practiced: "Nathan! It's Jason. I'm here!"

The voice sounded strange to me. Had it changed, too, like everything else? I wasn't used to it.

"Nathan. I'm Jason."

It was hard to speak anyway. I sat in the armchair. He would arrive anytime in the next hour.

The room was so organized. The amount of paper he went through must be immense. Just the notes from his years of conferences took shelves.

I opened one binder. The pages were filled with his neat, straight writing. The meeting had been a decade before, but at the bottom of the page a line had been drawn and another paragraph added, dated years later. These were the records of his life, these notes about poverty and crime and hunger. What if this was the answer, Nathan's purpose in life—to do good? That was why Melvin had hired him, to do the good that a rich man didn't have time or interest for.

I heard the garage door opening, a muffled groan like thunder in the distance.

I practiced again. "Nathan. I need help." Would he recognize me? "Nathan. I'm Jason."

The roar of a car engine echoed in the garage and then died. Where should I wait for him? He might not come to the study. If he didn't, I'd go to him in the kitchen.

The garage door closed with the same growl. A door opened, back by the kitchen. Would he have anyone with him? He was in the kitchen now. I'd hear him talking if he wasn't alone, but it was silent. Faintly, I heard the oven door open and close.

Even Nathan Kern would wonder what was for supper.

There were footsteps in the hall. I put the binder back on the shelf.

"Mrs. Hammond?" He was at the foot of the stairs. Somehow he knew someone was in the house. "Are you there? Hello?"

I was standing in the center of the room and he was in the doorway, his eyes wide, his hands half raised.

His mouth dropped open. "Jason? Is it you?"

"I didn't kill her."

39

It was too much for him. His mouth moved and his eyes blinked. I suddenly wondered if he had a weak heart.

He recovered enough to speak. "Where have you been?"

"You have to believe me. I didn't do it."

He nodded. "I believe you."

I could have fainted right then over those words. I almost did, and he moved quickly to catch me. But I stayed upright.

"Are you all right?" he said.

"No."

"Sit down."

I dropped back into the big reading chair, and he pulled another chair up close. For a minute or two we didn't talk. Everything had been just to get here, and now I didn't know what to do. He didn't know what to say, either.

"I found her," I said. "It was my gun, but I didn't do it. I didn't have the gun."

"Of course."

"Remember? Fred still had it. He's the one, Nathan. He killed her."

"Fred Spellman?" He was still stunned just from seeing me. "But . . . surely not . . ."

"He had the gun."

"But that doesn't mean . . ." He stopped and breathed and got his hands to stop trembling. One of them darted into his suit coat and pulled out the cigarette case. It was reflex. He didn't even know he'd lit it until he'd inhaled the smoke and couldn't blow it out with my face inches from his.

He turned and exhaled. "Excuse me. It's all a shock." He gave the nicotine time to do its job. "Someone else could have found the gun," he said.

"From Fred's office?"

"Eric was there, of course." He saw me react. "No, I don't mean he would have used it. But he may have taken it, and then someone else took it from him. Or Katie took it. That would have been quite likely. And then it was there in the house when . . ." He didn't finish.

I was sagging. So much had depended on finding the killer. Now I was back to the beginning, not knowing at all.

"It's too hard," I said. And what had Eric said about the gun? "I don't know if it matters."

"But it does! Of course it does! Jason, everyone is convinced you killed her and your father and the others."

"I don't think I care anymore." I needed him to say something profound.

He did. "When did you last eat?"

"Saturday morning."

"Let's take care of that. Come to the kitchen."

I wrestled down a few bites of the casserole, but my jaw was excruciating. Nathan didn't ask questions. I drank a glass of milk through a straw, and ten minutes at the table slowly undid a little of the damage of the last three days.

"Now," he said. "It seems you're exhausted. I wonder what you've been through! But I think we need to make plans."

The "we" was as energizing as the food. I'd had so many guards up, and it was such a relief to let some of them down.

"I was sure it was Fred," I said.

"Yes, we'll get to that. But no matter who it was, it was still someone." He shook his head. "I can help you, Jason. But I'm afraid I don't know much about these things. I'm not sure what to do. You need medical attention, and you need food and rest. Maybe my own physician could come here."

"No. It's too risky."

He nodded. "Whatever you say. But I'm sure you can stay here safely for a few days. I'll tell Mrs. Hammond not to come for the rest of the week." He set his jaw into a grim smile. "We'll work out what to do. You're safe now. We'll get through this fight."

Now I was beginning to crumple. Again I wondered if it even mattered to me. Maybe it wasn't Fred. I'd used everything I had and far more to get here. "I can't fight anymore."

"You need to rest. After you've eaten and slept, you'll be ready to keep going."

Keep going . . . wasn't just getting to this house all I'd been trying to do? "But why?"

"We need to find this murderer, Jason. That's the important thing."

It was hard to just keep talking. "I've given up on that. There's only one thing left I want. Just tell me why."

"Why you should keep going?" He was confused.

"Why is all of this happening?" Was that the question? "Why shouldn't I give up?" It was so hard to even think. "Why am I here? That's why I came to you."

We were in hard kitchen chairs, not beside the cozy fire I'd imagined. But this was why I'd come. It wasn't about Katie's or Melvin's deaths—it was about my life.

He took time to answer, and I was fading. But in his eyes there was such deep thought, and I stared back and kept myself awake.

"Life is precious," he said. "Look at yourself, Jason. I don't know what you went through to come here, but I can see in you that it has been terrible. If you don't know why you want to keep living, you still know that you do."

"But I have to know why!"

"Of course. Certainly. Everyone needs a purpose, something

they can serve. You need a purpose outside of yourself. You've only had yourself as your life, and through these terrible struggles you've finally seen how unworthy that is, how without value. Now, and only now, you can start to look for something else."

What was he saying? This was what I'd wanted my whole life, to hear this. The answers. From someone who knew. This was so important.

"Eric said I had the gun," I said.

He was bewildered for a moment. "He . . . what?" He didn't know what I was talking about.

"You called Fred, and he told you he still had the gun." Suddenly, inside my head a vortex had opened, spinning, pulling in every thought. "But Eric said I had the gun in my hand when I left Fred's office."

He'd changed to the new subject, but he hadn't caught up with me yet. "Well . . . he must have been mistaken. It must have been very confused at that moment."

"Because that means I'd have brought it up to my office, where you were." Now the whirlwind was throwing the thoughts back out, strange thoughts, in strange patterns. "That afternoon, before I met Clinton Grainger at the hotel. I told you I was meeting him."

The intimate, confessional mood between us was far gone. "Jason . . . what are you saying?"

I didn't know. The words were hardly mine. I was too tired to think. I could only watch the thoughts whirling by too fast to see what they really were.

"Was there something in Melvin's notes about the foundation?" It couldn't be true. Nathan was the only one who had withstood the corrosion of the money and the power. I had to believe it was possible for a man to do that; I had to believe he had answers. "Angela found something in them. Grainger had seen it, too, when he raided Melvin's office. All that I'd left there were those files on the foundation, and Grainger got copies of them. That's what he meant that night, his 'surprise.' He knew something about the foundation, and he was going to use it against me. And he met someone else afterward."

"What are you talking about?" Now there was anger in his eyes. It was mirroring my own.

"You knew Melvin was going to change his will. If he'd had his accident a couple hours sooner . . ."

He forced calm back into his eyes and breathing. "Jason. Do you know what you're saying?"

Could it be? How many times had I already been wrong? "I don't know."

"I was in Washington when Angela was killed."

Of course. I slumped back in the chair. "I'm sorry, Nathan." How could I have accused him?

"Come with me," he said, very gently. "I'll show you my notes. They're in the study. That will be proof."

I could picture them, neat lines filling sheets of white paper. As ordered and right as everything about him. He turned on the study light, and I stood by the wall of binders as he stopped at his desk.

"I'll need my glasses." He was looking through a drawer. "I'm sorry I was angry. You're not yourself."

I'd been so close to hearing his words. How could we get back? I glanced at the shelves, my back to him. I couldn't work out how they were ordered. It must have been by subject because the dates weren't in order. It suddenly bothered me, or something did. I turned abruptly to ask him.

The bullet hit my shoulder—it would have been my back if I hadn't moved.

I dropped. It was reflex, or pain, or the force of the impact. My arm was on fire. I tried to scramble behind a chair, but then I saw his face, set in nervous determination, and the gun at arm's length pointed right at my head.

His hand was only trembling a little.

I was frozen. Panic pressure in my head ripped my thoughts apart. My heart was exploding in my chest. The terror was like iron chains holding me. I heard myself telling Fred, *"If a man has a gun and he's trying to kill you . . ."*

I stared at Nathan, beyond thought, and at the round black hole of the gun. I couldn't move.

"You can either dodge bullets or . . ."

He looked away.

He'd been startled. The gun moved away. It wasn't just blood pounding in my ears; there was some other sound. He looked back to me and straightened his aim, but the sound was louder.

Someone was knocking on the front door and ringing the bell.

I shoved the chair aside to get behind it. He fired again but was distracted. I felt the chair shudder. I was still pushing and clawing to get behind it.

There was a crash and Nathan turned and started toward the door to the hall, the gun still in his hand. At the doorway he stopped, his face white and confused. He pointed once more, wildly, and fired. The wall above my head splintered.

I was close to the door to his conservatory. I lunged toward it. It wasn't latched and I fell through into the pots and branches.

Someone was shouting, and I heard Nathan saying, "In here! He's in here!" I got myself upright and threw my side into the sun-room glass wall. It shattered and I fell through bushes and hit the ground.

There were roots, and once I was up I tripped on them and fell. It was too hard to stand again. I crawled through the stiff branches and out onto the grass.

"Out there!" Nathan's voice followed me. "There he is!"

The yard was dark. I pulled myself upright and ran and limped toward the street. A light-colored car was at the curb, and I got around it and crouched by the driver's door.

The front door of the house flew open. I could see two silhouettes in the light of the hall.

"He's out there. I saw him."

"Was it Boyer?" a deeper voice said.

"Yes, yes! It was! He's somewhere here! You can find him! Catch him!"

I was gawking at the steering wheel inside the car. Keys were hanging down from behind it.

"I'll call for backup," the deep voice said.

I yanked the door open and was inside the car. I turned the key and hit the accelerator and pulled the door closed.

It took two minutes to breathe again, and think. The car was an unmarked police cruiser. I was on the main road back into town, the road I'd walked that morning. The fire in my jaw had spread to my shoulder.

As the panic subsided, the pain swelled. I was tired of it. I kept driving. I was tired of everything.

The road widened and I picked up speed. A highway ramp was ahead and I pulled onto it. From the highway I could see the skyline ahead like a line of teeth. I raced into them.

Traffic was light toward downtown, nothing to slow me. Straight in front was my goal, glowing forty-two stories high.

It probably took less than twenty minutes to reach my exit. I had no time for the red light at the bottom, and the horns and screeching tires amused me. Eight blocks, right turn, three blocks. There were no spaces at the front door so I left the car in the middle of the street.

There was a crowbar in the trunk. Perfect.

I strolled into the empty lobby and looked around—it had become pretty familiar the last few weeks. It would be a good place, this building.

The coffee shop was closed but the television was on, and I stopped a minute to watch through the gate.

". . . again eluding police." It was Bill Sandoff himself. It made me feel so much at home. "The intended victim was Nathan Kern, director of the Melvin Boyer Charitable Foundation, who had been under police surveillance as a possible target. We will continue to update the story as more information comes in. Again, Jason Boyer is still at large, driving a light tan Buick Riviera. He is armed and extremely dangerous." They had a picture up, the same one they'd been using for a week. Everyone must be getting pretty tired of it. "If you believe you see him, call the police immediately. Do not approach him. Commissioner DeAngelo has asked that citizens—"

Good ole Miguel, he'd be squirming right now. I couldn't imagine what the Harry Bright quote would be. It would almost be worth waiting one more day to find out.

There'd be the Nathan Kern story; that would be adorable. *"Kern told reporters how he managed to use his gun in self-defense."* Maybe he could rumple his suit a little.

No, I didn't want to hear it. There'd be an even bigger story soon anyway.

I pushed the elevator button. The doors opened and I was face-to-face with a young lady in a blue suit and two-hundred-dollar hair. I grinned at her and she screamed.

She shoved past me and ran. I think she got blood on her suit. I was covered with it.

Top button. Up and up and up, farther and farther from the ground. Faster, up into the sky, away from all the problems and foolish lives, away from all the people wasting their energy living. They didn't know how useless it all was. I knew better now.

Forty-second floor. Down the hall to the locked door. No fumbling with the key this time. Pamela's desk was empty. She'd finally be free of us Boyers, lucky her.

The second door wouldn't open. The lock had been changed? It was a ruin when I got through it. It hurt my shoulder, all of me, to ram the heavy bar into it again and again, but the pain would be over soon.

There was my view! Breathtaking, and that was going to be literally true very soon. All the lights—lights everywhere. Nathan Kern could have it all. Take it! I was the winner, more than he would ever know. It would all be his or Fred's, the curse of it, and I was glad to let them all kill each other. Gaining that whole world was the worst punishment I could sentence anyone to.

I was seeing his face—the sincere, serious face he'd used to tell me that he'd asked Melvin to change the will. No man would have done that. I knew now, no one could turn down what that will was offering him. Let him have it. It would kill him, too.

Enough of that. How beautiful it was outside! There were blinking lights below, red and blue flashes against the street and buildings. It was a celebration, all for me! I couldn't hear the sirens because the glass was too thick. Not for long!

I lifted the crowbar and swung. Circles spread out from the impact point like ripples as the glass fragmented. Two more swings sent the shards out into space and down into the heap of lights and sirens. The whole panel was gone except for bits around the edges.

There was irony in escaping Nathan's gun just to come here—

but that was panic, and this was truth. Finally I knew the truth! The questions were over! It was all over. I had reached the end and I'd found what was there. And it was nothing. Nathan had shown me the answers just as I was hoping he would.

I had a cool idea: if only I'd had Eric's Corvette in the office. The hole in the glass was big enough to drive it through!

I wanted to see what something would look like falling. I took the big armchair Fred sat in and pushed it to the opening. The wind was blowing in and it reminded me of night air out on the boat. There was even a tinge of salt. I pushed the chair over the edge of the glass and watched it sailing down, riding the wind, disappearing. If only Fred had been in it.

There is sound now in the hall outside the office. They're coming. Time to go.

I stand at the precipice and see what I've looked for, for so long, the real reason a man lives. It is just so that he can die, and there is nothing else. Dying is real life, and living in the kingdoms of earth is real death.

I lean out into the void and feel the gale wind taking me and below are the beautiful lights so far away.

I want it to last forever, but almost before it started, the impact and darkness come.

I didn't feel anything—there was just sound.

Faint sound. Rustling, someone breathing. Some other quiet rhythmic *whirr*.

Footsteps on a hard floor, coming, passing, going.

It was my breathing. My eyes opened, and there was a white ceiling and bright lights. It hurt my eyes, and I closed them.

Something scraped on the floor.

"Tell them he's awake. Get Wilcox."

That meant something. I didn't want to move. I opened my eyes again. It was a hospital room. There was lots of white, and a blue uniform with a policeman in it.

The *whirr* was a pump. A tube from it wandered to my bed and under the cover.

Heavy footsteps, and people came. More police uniforms and another man, a doctor in a white coat. He studied the machines. "Yes," he said to one of the uniforms. "He seems to be conscious." He looked at me. "Good morning."

I didn't talk. People came and went, and I didn't talk to any of them. Time came and went, and I didn't feel like doing anything.

Then I saw a face I knew.

"Mr. Boyer?" I could only stare at him. "Mr. Boyer?"

Something was on one side of my face, wires holding my jaw. I could hardly move my mouth.

"We need to talk with you."

I closed my eyes and opened them, but he was still there.

"Mr. Boyer." He glanced at the doctor beside him. "He's hearing us, isn't he?"

"Yes."

"I need him to talk."

"I can't make him do that."

Detective Wilcox came closer to me. "You've given us a real hard time." He wasn't talking nice. "They say you might not leave here for a week, and I don't want to wait."

"Go." It was real hard to talk, and the words that came out were more like croaks. "Away."

"Don't you wish." He looked away toward the window, thinking and angry. "Where have you been hiding?"

He was going away. Everything was. The sounds stayed longer, but then they stopped, too.

I was awake again. I kept my eyes closed. I didn't want the people to come back. The sounds were still the same.

I felt rotten. There was pain this time. I thought it would have gone away. I remembered the dark and the wind and the lights down and far.

"Anything?" a voice said.

"No, sir. He hasn't moved."

I remembered driving in the dark. It had been raining.

"The doctor been in here?" It was Wilcox.

"Hour ago. He didn't say anything."

I couldn't move. Straps bound me in the bed.

I remembered sitting at a table, eating. Talking.

"DeAngelo wants something for the five-o'clock news."

"What's the problem, anyway? We got him. It's all over."

"They want to know where he's been since he killed her."

I remembered standing in my office at home and someone screaming.

"Nathan . . . Kern . . ." They were both startled and looking at me. "Killed . . . my . . . wife."

Wilcox was in my face. I was staring at his little mustache. "Oh, he did? You told your brother that it was Fred Spellman."

I remembered Eric limp on the floor..

"Kern . . . killed . . . her. All . . . of them."

Everything was coming back. Sailing in the rain and dark. Finding her. Escaping and camping and coming back. The street behind the train station. Walking to Nathan's house. Driving back into town in the police car.

Standing in the broken window, looking out.

"Where have you been?" he said.

I was figuring out that I wasn't dead.

"What . . . happened?"

"They grabbed your legs on the way out and you slammed into the side of the building. Two officers. You almost took them with you." He stepped back from the bed. "They should have let you go out the window."

That was too much to deal with. I closed my eyes. Maybe he would go away this time.

"I'm charging you with four murders, two attempteds."

"Stealing . . . the police car." It really hurt to just talk.

"That I'm charging against Officer Mulcahy, plus being an idiot. He saw you through the window so he knocked on the front door."

I remembered that scene. Nathan and his gun both looking at me.

"Kern," I said. "He . . . killed them."

"Next you'll blame Harry Bright. Look, Boyer, you're dead meat. If you—"

A doctor had arrived, and two nurses. Wilcox backed into a corner while they examined and asked questions. I was still feeling a lot of pain in my shoulder and jaw, and the doctor told the nurse to crank up the morphine. Before they left I was starting to float away.

There was one more thing. "Where is . . . Eric?"

Wilcox's voice floated up to meet me. "He was discharged yesterday, Wednesday."

I was dreaming about bullets. There had been a bullet in me.

"I'll tell DeAngelo he's still too drugged to talk."

Lots of bullets. Bullets in everyone. "Bullets . . ." I heard myself say.

"Yeah, what?" Wilcox had given up on the day.

"Bullets in . . . me. In . . . Grainger."

"What?" He was listening.

"Same . . . gun."

"What do you mean?" I didn't know what I meant. Now I was too far away. He was still talking. "He's crazy. He thinks he shot Clinton Grainger with Kern's gun? That's impossible."

The pain was gone, and everything else.

Another morning came, and I felt much better. As bad off as I was, it was a better place to sleep than I'd had in a while. I figured out it was Friday.

They had rearranged me in the night, propping pillows to put me on my side. After a while a flock of nurses, escorted by three large police persons, removed all the tubes from my body.

I had taken inventory of that body. Rigid wires and not very soft pads held my jaw in a position I didn't like. My right shoulder itched under the stiff wrapping.

With all of this and a police escort attached, I made my premier voyage to the bathroom. When I returned to the bed, the straps were no longer necessary. I was simply handcuffed to the bedrail.

Food was brought, a hospital milkshake. I didn't finish it.

The morning dragged on, and the Mustache did not return. I started to think maybe I had died after all. I refused the lunch milkshake—partly because I was not convinced I wanted to live and partly because it tasted bad.

I'd lost my drugged stupor and I was thinking clearly. There was nothing else to do. I thought about everything I'd done. All the people: Harry Bright, Bob Forrester, Fred, Eric. Nathan Kern. What a mess it all was. Katie.

Oh, Katie.

Morphine wouldn't take that pain away. I couldn't even begin to think about the future.

It was four o'clock and I was staring at the window. There was a sudden disturbance in the hall.

"You can't go in . . ."

"They said I could!" It was Eric's voice. "Haven't you seen the news?"

The guard inside the door stood up. The outside guard was growling. "Nobody told me anything. Hey!"

Eric had dodged them both and was in the room. His eyes locked onto me.

"Jason!"

The police were behind him, but they didn't attempt to lay hands on him.

"Eric."

Now he couldn't say anything; he just stared. He looked fine, undamaged.

Then he came close to the bed, the linebackers staying right with him.

"Do you know?" he said.

I shook my head. He kept staring.

"What?" I said, finally.

"They arrested Nathan Kern."

I felt myself collapse, which was redundant, as I was already flat on my back.

"Are you . . . okay?" I said.

"Me? Yeah! I'm okay. They let me out Wednesday." He pointed to his head. "Nothing."

Too many replies pushed through my own head before I came to the one I meant.

"I'm . . . sorry," I said.

It was beyond him to know how to answer that. But while he was trying, a sorrow welled up in his eyes, of an intricacy I'd never known in him before.

"Sit down," I said. He did and put his head in his hands and wept. I did, too, except I could only lie still in my bed.

At last he looked up. He wiped his eyes and caught his breath. "What happened to your hair?"

"Disguise."

Then he was laughing just as helplessly. "It looks stupid!" I didn't think it was funny, and it would have hurt too much to laugh. When he got his breath again, he pulled his chair up close. "Where have you been? What happened, anyway? They said your jaw is broken, and there was a bullet in your shoulder. And you were all cut up."

"Later."

"All right. Jason, I'm sorry, too."

"It's okay."

"I'm sorry what I thought about you, and that I didn't believe you. And I'm sorry I didn't help you when you needed it."

"It's . . . okay."

"I never really believed it. It was Fred . . . he kept telling me things."

That was something I'd have to deal with. "Later. Turn on . . . news."

We watched for hours. Eric talked as much as the heads on the screen, and I listened. It was hard to keep up with the torrent of words.

The guards did not wait for official instructions. The handcuff was removed. I gave them my own instructions—that no one besides Eric and my hospital staff was to get within a hundred yards of me. I had Eric unplug the phone and we watched Bill Sandoff, CNN, the networks, and everything else the remote could find. It was on every channel.

The police had tested Nathan Kern's gun, and there was no doubt it had killed Clinton Grainger. Nathan's Washington alibi had fallen apart like a cheap lawn chair when they found that his rental car had been turned in with fifteen hundred miles on it for the weekend. Then they'd found the letter from Angela.

Mr. Kern,

I have found papers that dear Melvin had written about you, and I have read some of them. It is too difficult to read them. I think he was very angry at you and I don't understand. I don't want to think about him angry. I believe I hate the foundation now.

I will not call you. I don't want to talk to you. I don't want to think about any of this. I don't want this to go on. It all has to stop. I'll do anything to make it stop.

It was a photocopy they'd found in a hidden drawer in his desk. On the television screen, the lines he'd cut off for the suicide note were highlighted.

And then they'd found the Swiss bank account.

Only Harry Bright was not convinced. "Jason Boyer is at the bottom of this," he was quoted as saying. "I've always known a criminal when I see one."

I fell asleep, and Eric sat by me through the whole night.

41

In the morning, Eric was still there, the first thing I saw when I opened my eyes.

The second thing I saw was a dead cater-pillar. No . . . it was Detective Wilcox's lip.

And he was so sorry for the misunderstanding. Oh, how sorry he was.

The wretched man was treading eggshells on top of eggshells. All the king's horses and all the king's men weren't going to save more than a third of the careers in the Division of State Police, and I, Jason Boyer, was the king.

Would I mind just a few questions? A couple things he hoped to clear up. They had a good idea of how three of the murders had been committed. Nathan Kern was singing like a canary, trying to nurture any mercy in his captors. Wilcox wanted to describe the whole thing, to see if I had any additions or corrections. It had been such a misunderstanding. And had he mentioned how sorry he was?

I sent him out of the room while I freshened up, and when I was ready, I allowed him to begin.

Melvin had told Nathan months ago that he was changing his will. He had not said why. At first Nathan had graciously accepted the decision. As time passed, though, he couldn't. He tried to persuade Melvin to keep the arrangements as they had been. Melvin refused to discuss the matter. Nathan apologized, but he had pushed a little too hard.

Melvin's confidence in his director had been shaken.

I saw how it was, and Wilcox guessed at it, too. Even if Nathan hadn't recognized how deeply the money had him hooked, Melvin saw it right away. The less trusting Melvin became, the more frantic Nathan acted.

He realized his days might be numbered at the foundation, and he couldn't bear the thought of a less elegant lifestyle. So he'd opened a bank account in Zurich and started juggling the budget.

He was not very good at crime, whereas Melvin was an expert. Though he did not think Nathan was dangerous, his notes about the foundation were clear—he was getting very upset with his director. The police had found the whole stack of papers in Nathan's basement.

"This was . . . after . . . Melvin said . . . he was . . . changing . . . his will." The contraption on my jaw was getting real old.

"That's right," Wilcox said. "As far as we can tell from your father's papers and the bank records, none of this was part of the original reason he decided to change his will."

Then Melvin died. Nathan claimed no part of that. He didn't know how to drain a brake line, or even that a car had such a thing.

Nathan hadn't known that Melvin had uncovered the embezzling. After Nathan had talked to Angela about being on the board, she had looked at Melvin's papers. She didn't understand them, except that something was making Melvin angry. She wrote Nathan the letter to say she would have nothing to do with the foundation.

He called her but she was even more determined. She told him she'd call me and tell me to fire him. She'd show me the notes.

"She called . . . me," I said. "She . . . only said . . . she wouldn't . . . be . . . on the board."

"And then you called Kern. That's when he knew she hadn't tattled on him. Could she have been blackmailing him?"

"She didn't . . . like . . . black. Only . . . pink."

"I don't understand."

"You'd . . . have to . . . know her."

"I've talked with other people who knew her," Wilcox said. "She was apparently eccentric, if that's what you mean."

Nathan flew to Washington, but then he drove back to meet with her. He asked to see her privately. But he quickly saw that she was irrational, that his position was threatened, even hopeless. And Angela, helpless fool, had her gun out for protection. How easily he took it and used it. He had the letter she'd sent and saw how it could be made into a suicide note.

It had all been so quick, so natural. It hadn't been planned—it was self-defense. So much was at stake. After he killed her, he took the incriminating files from Melvin's office.

The suicide facade fell through very quickly. He realized it wasn't going to be so easy.

Then Clinton Grainger called. He'd seen copies of the notes, delivered earlier by his agent who had broken into Melvin's office. He could tell they would be worth something against me, and he wanted to see if he could blackmail Nathan onto his side.

I'd called Nathan the afternoon before I met Grainger at the hotel and told him about the meeting. He had hardly a qualm at that point. He bought his own gun that afternoon. He called Clinton and said he wanted a meeting that night, which they arranged for the hotel after our meeting.

And all the while Nathan was working on me, trying to convince me how terrible the money was, how I needed to get rid of it. It was all about to fall into his lap when Katie got in the way.

She was the one who could stop my plan, so she had to be stopped herself. He tried to think how he could stop the divorce or talk her out of her lawsuits and obstruction. But he knew there was only one way.

Then, in my office that afternoon, I'd walked right in with my gun in my hand. I'd set it on the sofa. I'd looked so dazed, he realized I might not even know I had it. He slid a cushion over it. I was clueless.

In those few seconds he'd made his plan to kill Katie—and perhaps get me accused of it by using my gun. It would jeopardize my ability to transfer the money to the foundation, but it would also give the police a suspect. Nathan was getting very worried they would find Melvin's papers in Grainger's office, or that Angela or Grainger had talked to someone else. There were too many loose ends.

So he went to see her that evening.

"What . . . did she . . . say . . . to him?"

"He claims she wasn't open to changing her mind."

"He's . . . lying."

"How do you know?"

"She . . . let him . . . in."

Wilcox considered. "You might be right. It would look a lot worse if he'd killed her even though she was willing to back down on the divorce. It would prove premeditation. And he hadn't expected you to show up just minutes later."

I was tired of talking. And living, too. I closed my eyes. She really hadn't had to die. I wanted to die.

I didn't feel like telling Wilcox where I'd been, which frustrated him. But he was in no position to push. And I'd thought of one other thing.

"Airport. JFK."

"In New York?"

I nodded. "Car. I rented."

"The white Mercury."

"Thousand dollars . . . in it. I don't want it back."

"Right. It's evidence. I'll make sure it doesn't disappear. We'll put it in the widows' and orphans' fund. One more question," he said. "Any idea why your father wanted to change his will in the first place?"

"No."

If only I did.

"Wow." Eric had heard the whole thing. "Everybody is so . . ." He didn't know what word to use.

"Evil." Or whatever. "It's the money."

He was getting it. "That's what you kept saying."

"I . . . hoped . . . Nathan could . . . help me."

"And then you found out he was the killer."

"I hoped . . . he knew . . . something stronger . . . than the money."

"And he didn't. That's why you tried to jump off the building."

"Yes."

He was using brain cells he never had before. "So . . . I guess that means you didn't find anything."

"No."

"What are you going to do when you get out of the hospital?"

"Don't know." This thing would be on my jaw for a month. Another reason to not live that long.

"And . . . Jason . . . what about . . ."

"Melvin."

"Yeah. So, did Nathan Kern kill him? Or else, who did?"

"Don't know."

We reactivated the phone during lunch so I could call Jacob Rosenberg. I was hungry enough to drink the stuff the hospital was providing, but it didn't help my disposition.

Should he resurrect the legal process he'd begun two weeks ago?

"Wait."

Any other instructions?

"No."

Nothing was resolved—nothing was any better. Why am I here? Had anyone ever found an answer to that question?

I was feeling the loss of Nathan. Not the real, evil man, whom I had never liked anyway. I was grieving for the phantom I'd briefly had of a man who knew the answers, the man I could respect. Who could give me what I wanted.

Was there anyone? I would have given everything I had for someone to help me. But the money was worth nothing to me now, the whole billion dollars and empire that went with it. It was all I had and it would also be worthless to whomever I was looking for. Everything I did have that I valued was lost and I'd gotten nothing for it.

I needed a reason to live. I needed someone to help me.

My eyes wanted to close, so I let them. When they opened I was still dreaming.

"Pamela."

No, it wasn't a dream.

"Well, look at you," she said. "I brought some chicken soup."

"I'm glad . . . you're here." For a long time to come every smile would be precious, and she had some real dazzlers. "How . . . did you . . . get in here?"

She smiled again—I was so naïve. "My job is to get things done, dear. Now, Jason, I know you don't want to worry about business or reporters or politicians. I'll take care of everything until you're ready."

"Thank you."

"Is there anything specific you want me to do?"

"Stan Morton," I said. "Come here . . . no cameras . . . and then Fred."

"I'll get them."

"I'm sorry . . . about . . . wrecking . . . the office . . . and the chair."

She sighed. "That's fine. I'm sorry you had to."

I wasn't ready for her to leave. "I don't know . . . what to do . . . now."

"Just get finished with Stan and Fred. Then you'll have time to think."

"I . . . don't want to think . . . anymore."

She just looked at me for a while with her kind grandmother eyes. "You're still here, Jason. I almost lost you."

"You'd be . . . better off."

"You wouldn't, though." She smiled again, just pure sweetness. "I've been praying for you boys every day for twenty-five years. I think you're going to find what you're looking for. Now, what is the doctor saying?"

"I haven't . . . seen one . . . today," I said.

Eric chipped in. "He was in here while you were asleep." He turned to Pamela. "They think they can save his arm. And his mouth will be okay. But . . . well . . ." He trailed off.

"What?" She was concerned. I was, too. I hadn't heard this.

Eric turned to me, eyes worried.

"Your hair. It won't recover. I'm sorry."

"Dope."

Stan Morton managed to take time out from his busy schedule to visit the poor invalid.

"Is that you?" he said from the doorway.

I shook my head. "Elvis."

"That wouldn't be as big a story. *Where* have you been?"

I nodded to Eric.

"Mr. Boyer would like to ask for your help," he said.

"Oh, yeah? What? And can't he talk?"

"He has asked me to speak for him. He would like to have one week to rest. After that, he would like to give an interview. He would appreciate your help in arranging that, and deciding who should participate."

"Do you know . . ." He had to stop and start over. "Do you know who's out there? Everyone! The networks, the magazines, every newspaper in the *world*!" He attempted to calm himself. "There's a reporter from Beijing staying in my guest room. Beijing, China!" The attempt hadn't worked. He tried again. "We're supposed to wait a week? Come on, Jason. Just answer two questions for me, that's all."

"What?" I said.

"Where have you been, and how did you figure out it was Kern?"

I would have smiled, but I couldn't. I pointed to Eric.

"Mr. Boyer is extremely fatigued," Eric said.

"He looks okay to me."

I was going to start laughing, which would really hurt.

"You need to give him another week," Eric said. "He's really banged up."

"There are two hundred reporters in the parking lot. If I don't come out with something, it'll get real ugly. Give me something. I know: today is Saturday. Where were you one week ago? Where did you spend the night?"

Saturday night, a week ago.

"Dumpster."

An hour later, Fred's arrival in the lobby was announced.

"Should I leave?" Eric asked.

"No."

"I'd be glad to." He meant it.

"You're my . . . bodyguard." I'd have been glad to leave, too. But the confrontation would have to happen sometime. And maybe even Fred would be repelled by the devastation he was such a big part of.

Soon we heard the heavy tread. They make hospital doors wide to accommodate wheelchairs and a certain type of lawyer. Sitting was another matter. He stood and stared at me for quite a while, and then he looked for a chair. The hospital issue was one size fits all, but not all at the same time.

"Here," Eric said, jumping up and pushing the two chairs we had together. Fortunately they had strong legs and no arms.

"Thank you." He sat and scowled. "I don't know what we have to say to each other."

"I . . . can think . . . of some . . . things."

"I suppose. I'll ask one question, then. What are you going to do with the Boyer assets?"

At least he didn't waste time faking sympathy for me, or faking any moral sense at all. I tried to think how to say what I wanted in the least painful way. That is, the least painful for my jaw.

"Isn't . . . it obvious?"

"Not to me."

No, not to him. "Look at me," I said.

"You're blaming your calamities on being wealthy?"

"Look at . . . Harry Bright."

"You and he made decisions, and his ruin was the outcome."

"Look . . . at Nathan . . . Kern."

He hesitated. "He was weak." That was the greatest crime Fred knew.

"He . . . killed . . . my wife."

He waited a decent five seconds before answering. "I'm sorry." It was not an apology, just a condolence.

"He killed her . . . to get . . . my money."

"I understand."

"You . . . used her . . . you're guilty . . . as Kern . . . that she died." I hadn't meant for the dialogue to go this way, but his hard heart was infuriating me.

"I did not intend for anything to happen to her!"

"Look . . . at yourself."

He was finally silenced.

He stood and left, and I was left wondering why I'd called him, because it couldn't have gone any other way than it had. It took a long time for the atmosphere to fill the empty space he'd left. The last lingering traces of the triumph over Nathan Kern had finally been blown away.

My war with evil was over. I'd caused damage, but my own losses were much higher, and Fred and all the others like him would just rebuild. The money and evil had won.

I was back at the beginning. The questions were unanswered, if there were any answers. No one was pursuing me, but it was only a matter of time before I would be back at the window, looking out into the black.

And I still had the money that I wanted to be rid of. What was I supposed to do with it?

"Wow." Eric was very relieved that Fred was gone and that his own name had not come up.

Just at that moment, I did not want to deal with Eric.

"I want you . . . to get . . . something," I said.

Man's best friend snapped to attention. He was needed! "What?"

"In my office . . . back home . . . in the desk." I held up my fingers to show the size and thickness of the folding frame from Melvin's bedroom. "A . . . picture frame."

"I'll get it."

Pamela had been praying for me for twenty-five years. That seemed like something very valuable, even if I didn't know what to do with it. I thought of the church where my mother was buried.

Something outside myself. That was what I wanted, even if it had been Nathan who'd said it. I knew one thing that was absolute, that there was nothing on earth that answered any of my questions. Money, power . . . even love, they had all failed.

Pamela thought I'd find what I was looking for. I was looking for a reason to live.

An hour later, Eric was back, and he brought me a reason, one that for a few minutes pushed aside my despair. He brought me a milkshake. A real one, made with real fast-food chemicals. Its purpose was simple and pure—to appeal to my most base instinct and appetites, with no nutritional value at all. I lost myself in it and for a moment again enjoyed living. If they'd left the IV in my arm, I would have sent that wise, brilliant, and golden-hearted young man out for a second one to pump directly into the artery.

I sat up. Transferred myself to a chair.

"I want . . . to walk."

I'd been up a couple times, but now I wanted to walk . . . somewhere. Nurses came scurrying, somehow sensing I had moved. Eric forced them back to a discreet distance. They offered a wheelchair but I refused. I had regained a little dignity.

We rode the elevator to the ground floor, hobbled the length of a hallway, and then I was outside, walking, slowly but in the open air, with no one trying to kill me or injure me or put me in prison.

It was a garden, even. A courtyard, closed off and private. Eric and I were strolling through the end of October.

Dry, swirling leaves hurried past. Everything else was still and stiff, the last chrysanthemums, the empty branches. We had an hour or more until dusk.

Then I felt dizzy—all the muscles suggested that I sit, and I did. I just had my pajamas and robe, and a blanket over my shoulders, and the wind was gusty and chill. I pulled the blanket more tightly around me.

"I have that thing," Eric said. He dug into the pocket of his jacket, a plaid and corduroy autumn coat Katie had picked as a start to his winter wardrobe. That was as far as they'd gotten.

A little fishing and he had the frame, and put it in my hands.

"Did you look at it?" I asked.

"Uh, no."

There was a feeling of a holy relic about it as it rested between my fingers. The civilization that had owned it had fallen and was no more, but this object was clean and untainted and had passed unharmed through the *Götterdämerung*.

My left hand was very limited in its motion by the cast on my shoulder. I held the frame in that hand and opened it with my right. Two pictures—a man and a woman in one, and two little boys in the other.

"Wow," said one of the boys.

"It was . . . in . . . his bedroom," said the other boy. "In the drawer . . . by . . . his bed."

There they were, Melvin and Ann, the two people I most fully did not know. Beneath Ann's sad, tranquil eyes, she knew that she would never know her sons, and they would never know her. She held something that was deeper and greater than just life. It was there in her eyes, obvious to anyone who was looking.

His eyes were unknowable. Did his young wife's coming death harden him and build those walls that shrouded his soul? I'd only known him hard.

Eric had her eyes. That was our biggest difference in appearance, even now. When Eric smiled, he looked so much like this picture of her. I looked at him now, beside me, and then at his own image in the frame. There he was a bright, untroubled toddler, his heart already open and supple as it would be for his whole life. Here in the garden with me he was Ann, but without that sorrow.

I was much more like Melvin, but with greater sorrow. I knew my own face well enough to see the similarities. Heavier brow, eyes deeper set, and empty. In my own picture I was five years old and I had the weight of the world on my shoulders because I knew my mother was dying. I was formed by that sorrow and the sorrow of an unloving father, and it had left me so incomplete.

"Let me see," Eric said. We held it together and absorbed every meaning we could pull from those faces. A cloud had obscured the sun, and I was shivering.

"Is there anything on the backs?"

I shook my head. "Don't know."

He took the frame and slid the glass off from the children's side. It was tight. He had to force it, but he was still so careful. "There are papers behind the picture."

Two folded sheets old enough to have yellowed a little. He teased one of them open.

"Eric," it said at the top in a handwriting I'd only seen a few times before.

"It's from her?" Eric said, his eyes about popping out of his head.

"Read it," I said.

"Eric

Oh my Eric, oh my Eric, your little heart filled with joy,
Time to sleep now, time to sleep now, oh my dear little boy.
Come back home now, come back home now, you've been follow-
ing your star,
Time to rest now, time to rest now, from your wanderings far.
Will you miss me, will you miss me, will you remember this night?
Come now kiss me, time to sleep now, until the first morning light.
Who will hold you, who will love you, when years pass and
you've grown?
I am singing, I am praying, that you'll never be alone."

"She wrote it?" he said.

I nodded—I could hear her voice. "She sang it. . . . It was her . . . lullaby for you."

"I don't remember any of it. And I'm always alone."

"Did she say anything about me?" I'd asked Pamela.

"She asked me to look after you and Eric."

"Have you been?"

"Every day."

"No," I said. "You . . . haven't been. Open . . . that one."

"Jason

Lay your tired head here on my shoulder,
Let me hold you in my arms my precious child,
You are growing, getting taller, getting older,
But I'll still hold you in my arms a little while.

The weight of the whole world is on your shoulders,
In your arms you carry burdens much too hard,
Face a world of troubles, brave young soldier,
But precious Jason, sleep awhile in my arms.

Do questions weigh you down and make you wonder?
The world is hard and never gives you peace,
Lay your weary head here on my shoulder,
God will answer everything you seek."

God knows all my answers. *"I've been praying for you boys every day for twenty-five years,"* Pamela had said. *"I think you're going to find what you're looking for."*

"Other . . . picture," I said. Eric tore his attention from the papers and slid the glass off the other picture. At first I thought there was nothing, but there was. Another folded paper, not yellow, but instead clean white. There was only one person who could have written on it. I took it from Eric and opened it myself.

"Jason—"

I almost couldn't read it. There were just a few sentences, but I was paralyzed. I couldn't even breathe.

I tried again.

"Jason—
 I am at the end. Tonight I will sign my will and I will not return here.
 There is no one else to turn to. You have the strength that I no longer have. When everything is yours, you must destroy it all. You will see what must be done, and no one else will understand. They will fight you, but they will not stop you.
 Now I understand why you are my son, so that there is some-one to right what I have done.

 Eric—
 Stand with your brother, whatever he does. Only you know how.

 My sons—
 You are my only achievement and my only hope."

And then, at the end,

> "*Jason, my son. I trust you and I am proud of you. You will know what is right.*"

It was too much and I was overwhelmed.

There was so much meaning in those words, and more in the words not there. There was no apology for what he knew he was doing to me, hardly even an acknowledgment of his own anguish. That he had left the note where I might never find it spoke much louder of despair than the words themselves.

But now I knew that I had been right. Melvin alone had known without question the truth of power and wealth, and he had answered my questions about them. I would never forget what I had learned.

If I'd found this note the first day, maybe I wouldn't have lost Katie.

Eric was silent, working out his own understanding of these papers. Around us the light faded and the twilight deepened. All we knew was silence.

And in the silence, free of the babble of questions that had always torn at my mind and my thoughts, I knew that God had given me a life and a purpose.

I shivered in the growing dark, the paper in my hand that so perfectly expressed the man, my father, who'd written it—and that told me why I lived and what my purpose was. I couldn't take my eyes off it.

Be the first to know

Want to be the first to know
what's new from
your favorite authors?

Want to know all about
exciting new writers?
